THE BEA[illegible]

WITHIN

CORY BARCLAY

Of Witches and Werewolves
Book III

This is a work of fiction. Names, characters, places, and incidents are either products of the author's imagination or, if real, are used fictitiously.

www.CoryBarclay.com

First edition: March 2018

Cover art by Vaughan Mir (wyldraven.deviantart.com
Cover design by Nick Montemarano (nickmontemarano.com)

ISBN-13: 978-1986335461

ISBN-10: 1986335461

Please consider signing up to my newsletter for new release information and specials at www.CoryBarclay.com

This book is dedicated to my dad, who has helped make my books better than I ever could have alone.

ALSO BY CORY BARCLAY

OF WITCHES AND WEREWOLVES TRILOGY

Devil in the Countryside

In the Company of Wolves

Table of Contents

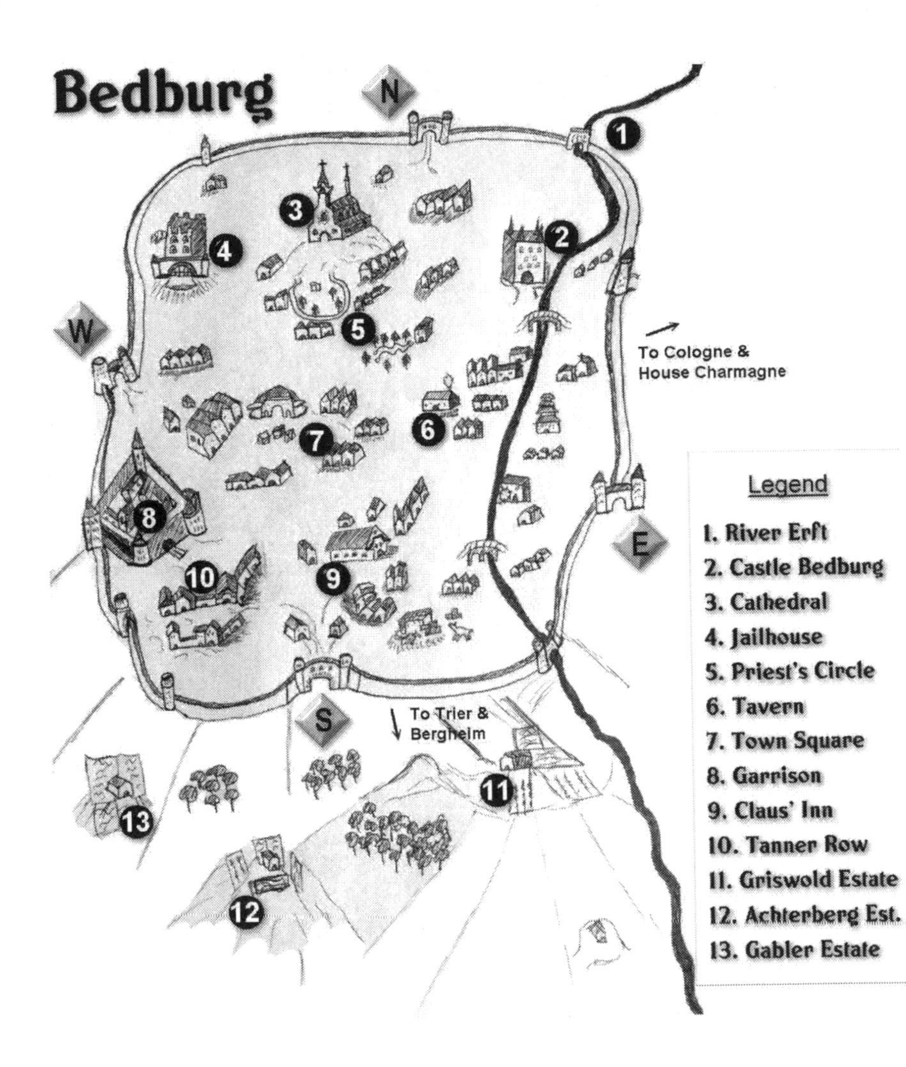
Bedburg
N
W
S
E
To Cologne &
House Charmagne
To Trier &
Bergheim
Legend
1. River Erft
2. Castle Bedburg
3. Cathedral
4. Jailhouse
5. Priest's Circle
6. Tavern
7. Town Square
8. Garrison
9. Claus' Inn
10. Tanner Row
11. Griswold Estate
12. Achterberg Est.
13. Gabler Estate

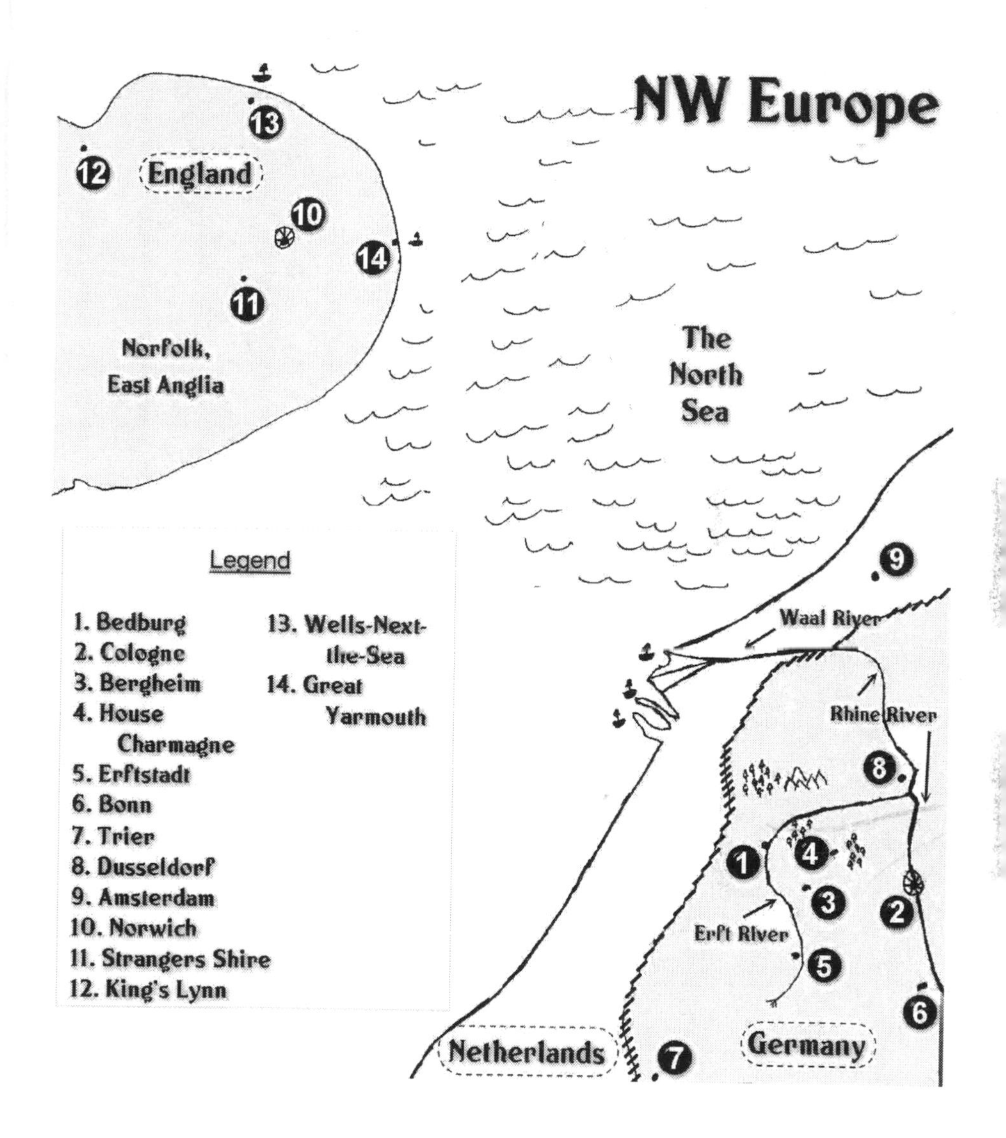
NW Europe
England
Norfolk,
East Anglia
The
North
Sea
Waal River
Rhine River
Erft River
Netherlands
Germany
Legend
1. Bedburg
2. Cologne
3. Bergheim
4. House
Charmagne
5. Erftstadt
6. Bonn
7. Trier
8. Dusseldorf
9. Amsterdam
10. Norwich
11. Strangers Shire
12. King's Lynn
13. Wells-Next-
the-Sea
14. Great
Yarmouth

PART I

Shadows of the Past

CHAPTER ONE

HEINRICH

Submerging his brother's bloody head under the rushing water, he felt no remorse.

He was eight years old, his brother ten.

Earlier that morning he'd woken before sunrise to the sound of cackling roosters, the sky still purple and misty from a rainy night. Hopping out of bed, he'd begun his daily ritual of preparing breakfast for his mother and brother. He'd started a large pot of water on the fire, then loaded up an armful of eggs to transfer into the pot once it began boiling. He'd handled the eggs with care, knowing full well there'd be hell to pay from his mother if he dropped any. She was a strict and mean woman, especially when directing her wrath at him.

As he began gingerly placing the eggs into the bubbling water, he ignored the rapidly approaching footsteps coming down the hall. At the last moment, his brother Oscar ran up behind him and gave him a shove, laughing as half the eggs tumbled to the dirt floor, splattering around his feet, the gooey liquid flowing around his bare toes. Eyes wide, he gazed at the mess in disbelief as Oscar ran off, his laughter echoing through the small house.

At the sound of the crashing eggs, his mother, Edith, came bounding into the room. Wearing a nearly translucent white shift, his eyes momentarily fixed on the outline of her chest and nipples before he forced himself to gaze back down to the floor. Though she was a beautiful woman, with dark curly hair framing a pale face and high cheekbones, his mother's dour expression of anger and disgust masked any hint of that beauty.

"Damnit boy! *Again?*" she screeched, her voice high and piercing. "Can you do nothing right?"

His eyes grew hot, ready to burst into tears. *It was Oscar's fault!* he'd wanted to scream. It was *always* his fault.

But he knew he couldn't say that, because it would do no good. He was the younger child—the "troubled" one.

It was because of him that Father had left them.

And it was no secret that Mother blamed him for that, as she did for just about everything else.

Following the birth of her beloved first-born son, Mother had prayed for a daughter. A pious woman—zealous, even, in her faith and obedience to God—she'd yearned for a daughter to carry on the family legacy when she died. A legacy of godliness, of righteousness, of advocacy for women.

But instead *he'd* been born.

Meanwhile, his older brother could do no wrong. Oscar constantly tormented him, yet was never reprimanded, never blamed for anything.

Oh, how he hated his brother.

And as his mother's verbal barrage over the broken eggs continued, he let her words float off without hearing them, pretending to be shamed by the incident as he stared down at the yellow puddle. Inside though, his body trembled with rage and his thoughts grew dark.

When his mother realized he wasn't listening, she grabbed his chin with one hand and, eyes wide with menace, slapped him hard across the face. His vision went white as she spoke like a woman possessed.

"We can't afford to let eggs go to waste, can we now?"

When he still didn't answer, she stormed off, heading for the front door where Oscar had gone.

He rubbed his cheek, feeling the prickly sensation of pins and needles, while he remained focused on the single image still etched in his mind: his mother's shapely breasts swaying gently beneath her shift.

Alone in the house, he walked down the hall to his mother's room. Quietly, he opened her door and peered inside.

Draped over the small bed lay his mother's blue dress. Resting on the floor next to it was her pair of rope-soled shoes. As he approached the bed, he glanced to his right at the blotchy full-length mirror hanging on the wall, frowning at the image he saw there.

Then he took off his clothes.

Tunic, pants, undergarments.

She wants a daughter, he thought, sliding the blue dress on over his head.

Now she won't yell at me.

The dress of course was much too big, its sleeves puffing out at his shoulders, its hems dragging on the floor. Yet he was still able to fasten it tightly at his waist. Glancing back to the mirror, he stretched his leg back and struck an effeminate pose.

And liked what he saw.

"Oh . . . my . . . GOD!"

Heinrich spun around. His bother stood at the doorway, wide-eyed, pointing a finger at him, his ten-year-old brain barely comprehending what it was seeing. Momentarily speechless, Oscar's young vocabulary had trouble providing appropriate words of ridicule, so he just blurted, "You're a girl! Look!" then broke into uncontrolled laughter. "An ugly, ugly girl," he screamed, barely able to breathe, doubling over and rolling on the ground.

Heinrich's face went blood-red. "N-no," he squealed, tears streaming down his face.

"Wait till Mother hears about this!" Oscar bellowed between breaths.

Beneath the dress fabric, Heinrich clenched his fists. "You can't! You can't tell her, Oscar!"

Stumbling to his feet, still laughing, Oscar charged out of the room and down the hall. Heinrich started after him, then realized he was still wearing the dress. Quickly, he changed clothes, then shot down the hallway after his brother.

But Oscar never got a chance to tell his story. As soon as he got outside, shouting, "Mother, mother! You won't believe it!" he found his mother standing out front, deep in conversation with a man. Before Oscar had a chance to say more, Mother snapped her fingers, instantly silencing him.

As the two adults continued their discussion, the man ran his hand over the stack of wool pelts beside him. "These fleeces are of a good quality," he declared, smiling. "I'll take them."

Just then, Heinrich flew out the front door, his face still bright red. But before he could speak, Edith cut him off as well.

"Get away from here, both of you," she yelled. "Can't you see I'm busy?"

"But what shall we do?" Oscar asked, disappointed that he couldn't relay his new lurid discovery to his mother.

"I don't care," Edith snarled. "Go fishing. Catch us some dinner. I'll be at least another hour."

At the mention of fishing, Oscar's eyes lit up. He loved to fish. Nodding vigorously, he headed off to the shed to grab his fishing gear.

"And take your brother with you!" Edith added, crushing his hopes of fishing alone.

Retrieving his rod, net and knife from the shed, Oscar headed out to the river, a five-minute walk from the farmhouse. A short distance behind, Heinrich followed with his own gear. When they got to the river, Oscar immediately headed for his favorite spot, the curve where the river narrowed, the best place to catch fish, while his younger brother rushed to keep up.

Once there, Oscar watched the clear water for a moment before jumping onto a stone embedded in the river bank. From there, with his arms held out like a T, he balanced, then hopped, from rock to rock, reaching higher and higher ground with each step. Yelling back to his younger brother, he kept up his taunting. "I can't wait to tell Mother what a fop you are!" With his back to Heinrich, he couldn't see his brother's expression change—the grinding teeth, the narrowing eyes.

"I should have guessed it," Oscar continued, oblivious to his brother's darkening mood. "I always knew you were a freak, but I didn't expect you'd be so . . . so . . . foppish!" he added, chuckling.

Heinrich squeezed the handle of his fishing knife so hard his knuckles turned white. He looked down at the glistening blade, then shook his head.

He couldn't.

Instead he pleaded with his brother again. "Please don't tell her, Oscar."

But Oscar, still climbing the rocks with arms extended, just glanced back and sneered. "What will you give me if I keep it a secret?" he asked, climbing up another stone before spinning back around with a glint in his eye.

"What do you want?" Heinrich asked.

"You know what I want."

"No!" Heinrich shouted, so loudly and high-pitched that it startled Oscar, making him wobble then lose his balance and, in an effort to regain it, jump too quickly to the next level of stones. As his feet made contact, his back foot gave way, sliding off the slippery surface. With arms flailing like a windmill, he tried in vain to avoid falling to the rocks below by pushing off toward the water.

But he couldn't. With a final breathless gasp, his body tumbled down the jagged embankment, the side of his head bouncing off a large rock with a sickening crack.

Then everything went quiet, the river's rippling current the only sound.

For an instant Heinrich was immobilized by the shock of it all. Then he called out to his brother but got no response. Quickly, he scurried down the bank on all fours—not nearly as daring or nimble as Oscar—and finally reached his brother's limp body. Immediately he saw the bright red gash above his right ear. Gently, he turned him over. His eyes were open but rolled back. Then he noticed his chest—rising and falling.

Faintly. Slowly. Still breathing.

Unconscious but alive.

The sight of his severely injured brother strained Heinrich's young mind. Unsure what to do, he knew he needed to get help quickly.

Yes, that was it.

But then a soothing darkness swept over him.

And suddenly things became crystal clear.

The memory of what his brother had seen.

Of what his brother had said.

Of what his brother had threatened.

And with a disturbing calmness Heinrich knew exactly what needed to be done.

How all his pain, all his mother's anger and disappointment and disgust, all the punishments he'd endured over his short life could finally, completely, be resolved . . .

And before he was even aware, he was dragging his brother's limp body by his arms down the rocks.

And then he was standing over him near the gurgling river. His brother was on his stomach again, so at least Heinrich couldn't see his face.

He looked back toward the house. Then across the empty fields. No one was watching.

He knelt down and dragged his brother's body to the water's edge until his face hung over the side.

Then he pushed Oscar's head beneath the rushing stream and held tight, a thin smile forming on his face.

Not unlike a baptism, he thought.

A baptism in Hell.

Suddenly the chilly water seemed to revive Oscar's survival instincts and he began to thrash. But he was too dazed and injured to resist his younger brother's determined grip. And soon the thrashing stopped.

When he saw no more bubbles rising to the surface, he counted to fifty to be sure before gently releasing his grip. Then he stood, wiping his icy hands on his pants, and stared down at what he had done, his brother's lifeless head still bobbing in the water like a fishing float.

He felt no remorse. Only calm relief.

How he loved the darkness.

And now it was time to tell Mother of the tragic passing of her favorite son.

He feigned panic and grief as he arrived back at the farmhouse and told his mother of the catastrophe at the riverside. Back at the scene, her face twisted in heartache, the tears flowing freely down her face. He watched with a grim sense of satisfaction as his mother knelt beside her beloved son and wailed like an anguished animal.

"Oh my lord!" she bellowed, again and again.

* * *

"Oh my lord!"

Heinrich awoke with a jolt, his body covered in sticky sweat, his hands clutching the arms of his chair.

A doe-eyed young man, looking scared and bewildered, stood over him, his hand resting loosely on Heinrich's knee.

"What is it?" Heinrich snapped, trying to clear the foggy dream from his senses.

"Are you all right, my lord?" the young man asked. "You were shaking in your sleep."

Heinrich Franz grimaced, his bushy eyebrows scrunching together. "I'm fine, boy. Why have you disturbed me?"

"Er, the archbishop is ready to see you, my lord."

Standing up from the chair, Heinrich felt his joints creak. He'd been waiting to see Archbishop Ernst for some time, and must have dozed off. He hadn't slept during his trip to Cologne to see Ernst—the archbishop had said the meeting was urgent so Heinrich and his entourage had ridden their horses hard.

"Then lead on," he told the boy, waving him forward.

The courier took Heinrich down a hallway, to the familiar double-sided oak doors of Ernst's conference room. He knocked on the door and was admitted by two armored guards holding spears.

Archbishop Ernst looked much the same as he had when Heinrich last saw him, when the archbishop had crowned him the lord of Bedburg in appreciation for his success in Trier. He sat—straight-backed and stiff-lipped—behind his large desk, dressed in an embroidered robe. Another man stood next to him. Both Ernst and the other fellow shared similar facial hair features: long mustaches and closely-cropped hair, though Ernst's companion was much younger, perhaps sixteen.

"Ah, Lord Franz, how nice to see you," Ernst said, greeting Heinrich as entered the room. Quickly, he shooed off the courier and both guards. This clearly was to be a private conversation.

So who's the handsome young pup, then? Heinrich wondered. *Why does he get to stay?*

Once the three were alone, Ernst's entire attitude changed.

Sighing and slumping in his chair, he went from blasé to dejected.

"This is my nephew, Ferdinand," Ernst said, motioning to the young man beside him. "I am grooming him for the future."

"The future, Your Grace?"

"I am getting old, Heinrich," Ernst replied, frowning. Heinrich almost felt sorry for him. This man, who Heinrich had helped get seated on the electoral seat of Cologne many years before, was perhaps the only man Heinrich had ever cared for. They'd shared years of turmoil, war, and masterful schemes together.

"A pleasure to meet you, Lord Franz," young Ferdinand said, his voice calm and polite.

"The pleasure is mine, young master," Heinrich replied, sounding equally polite, despite not feeling that way. If anything, he wanted Ferdinand to leave, to let the "adults" conduct their private conversation.

Ernst pointed to the boy. "In fact, Trier was his idea. He's a brilliant young man who one day will make a fine elector. My brother raised him right."

Heinrich's eyes bulged. *The witch-trials in Trier were his idea? If that is true, then I certainly shouldn't misconstrue his politeness for weakness. The young man is a calculated killer.*

Much like his uncle . . .

"Is that so?" Heinrich muttered.

Ferdinand smirked shyly. "You give me too much credit, Uncle."

Ernst shrugged. "Regardless, I'm having him shadow me while I conduct business. I hope you don't mind."

Even if Heinrich did mind, he wouldn't say so. "Of course not, Your Grace."

Ernst nodded, then his shoulders slumped again.

"What's bothering you, Your Grace? You seem . . . vexed," Heinrich said.

"Sugar, Heinrich. Sugar is bothering me." Ernst sighed. He paused, then thought better of it and waved a hand at Heinrich. "It doesn't concern you, though."

Heinrich crossed his arms over his chest. He had no idea

what the archbishop was referring to. And he didn't like being brushed aside like that, either, especially not since becoming the lord of Bedburg.

He tried again. "Even so, Your Grace, what's on your mind?"

Archbishop Ernst put his elbows on his desk and leaned forward. "Eight years ago, the Duke of Parma, Alexander Farnese, blockaded Antwerp's port in the Netherlands, trying to regain the city for the Spanish Catholics. It was the largest trading hub in Europe at the time."

"I'm aware," Heinrich said, nodding along. "But Duke Farnese is an ally. You seem disappointed that he did such a thing. After all, he regained territory for the Catholics . . ."

"Still, two-thirds of my sugar imports came from Antwerp! Yes, he's an invaluable ally—helping us during our own war in Cologne. He's done great things for the True faith. But still, by taking Antwerp . . . he's caused us some . . . difficulties.

"For one, he chased the Calvinists from the city, forcing them north en masse. Which forced the Catholics living there to flee . . . here, to Cologne."

Heinrich was intrigued. He spun the ends of his mustache. "So he took territory for the Spanish crown, but created more strife outside of Antwerp. That is how things go, is it not, Your Grace? It still seems like a major victory for the Catholics."

Ernst nodded. "It was. It is. But by taking Antwerp, he also inadvertently cut off the sugar trade here, which has impacted our economy greatly, giving more power to Amsterdam! In the past five years, Amsterdam has taken Antwerp's place as Europe's center of commerce. And, as you know, we have a . . . *tenuous* relationship with Amsterdam because of their trade deals with England . . . and their tolerance of Protestants."

Heinrich indeed understood. Ernst had lost a powerful piece on the chessboard when Duke Farnese had taken Antwerp. Even worse, an ally had caused the damage. Nonetheless, Heinrich didn't see it as Farnese's fault. Spain was the culprit.

Interrupting Heinrich's thoughts, Ernst added, "Many of our textile imports came from Antwerp as well, and that trade has been severed since Farnese took the city. So, Lord Franz, you can see why I'm 'vexed,' as you put it, yes?"

Heinrich bowed his head. "Yes, Your Grace. I understand. I'm sorry to hear that and I wish there was something I could do."

"Never mind that," Ernst said. "There are other things I need from you."

Heinrich tilted his head. "Such as?"

"For one, the progress of the conversion efforts in Bedburg. How are they going? You've had several months to settle in as lord there. What is the situation with the Protestants?"

Heinrich cleared his throat. "If I'm being honest, my lord, the Protestants are becoming more ambitious. To counter that—and their growing audacity—I've had to strengthen my grip and resolve against them. When they rebel, when they refuse to convert, I am forced to focus on more 'creative' means of punishment—scaring them into submission, much like we did with the werewolf issue a few years back."

Archbishop Ernst chuckled. "Of course. Yes, the werewolf. It was a masterstroke, Heinrich. Its legend still carries throughout the land."

His ego swelling, Heinrich feigned modesty, nodding simply without smiling.

"So we are becoming more . . . *proactive,*" he told the archbishop, "when dealing with the Protestants."

"Don't coat your words in sugar, Heinrich," Ernst said, then realized his own play-on-words and smiled. "We don't have enough sugar for that!" Taking on a more serious tone, he asked, "What does becoming more 'proactive' entail?"

Heinrich sighed, standing a bit straighter, clasping his hands behind his back. This felt more like a battlefield report to a general—which, he supposed, it was.

"As soon as a Protestant is discovered, sprouting up like a weed to cause the city turmoil, he is punished. If we cannot locate him, we find his family, which always draws out our target."

Archbishop Ernst thought for a moment, running his hands over his chin.

"An excellent strategy, Lord Franz," the young Ferdinand

interjected. "Punish the faithless so they cannot get a foothold in the city. The last thing we need is another rebellion."

"Indeed, young master," Heinrich said, a bit annoyed at being talked to as an equal by a young pup simply born into his high position. *Let the men do the talking, boy,* he wanted to say, but of course couldn't.

"Scare them into submission." The archbishop nodded. "Good, good."

Heinrich shrugged. "It seemed to work before."

Ernst stood from his desk. Walking in front of Ferdinand, he began pacing the room, clearly uneasy about what he had to say next.

"What is it, Your Grace?" Heinrich asked cautiously.

Ernst walked to the stained-glass window on the far side of the room, his shape bathed in the rose-tinted light. "There's one other thing I must ask of you, Heinrich. It's very important for the survival of Cologne and the entire electorate."

"Name it, Your Grace, and it will be done." And Heinrich meant it. Archbishop Ernst was the only man he truly felt honored to please.

Slowly, Ernst turned from the window, fixing on Heinrich's eyes. "I need you to marry a good Catholic woman."

Heinrich was dumbstruck. He couldn't believe what he was hearing. *After all the terrible things this man knows I've done? The horrors I've inflicted on women—for* his *cause? He would have me* marry *one?*

At a loss for words, Heinrich sputtered, "W-why?" Nodding to Ernst's nephew, he added, "Was this *his* idea as well?"

Ernst smirked. "If you take more than a moment, Heinrich, I'm sure you'll see why. And, no, this was my idea." Turning back to look out the window, he explained. "I must solidify my strongholds and territories. Many of my lords, barons, and earls are stalwart Catholics. They would never turn their backs on the True faith, since they know the consequences—"

"Nor would I, Your Grace."

"I know that, Heinrich, but you are an anomaly. People don't *see* you as a proper Catholic. You have a shadowy past. In a sense, you're mysterious. You are not a member of parliament or the royal courts—you could be, of course, but you choose not to. You keep yourself in solitude in that Gothic estate of yours, like a ghost."

Heinrich clenched his jaw. "So . . . I am different," he said. "Why does that matter?"

"Because I can't have conflict amongst my subjects! The diocese must clearly be allied and connected. I need to solidify my power in the principality—no, *God's* power. There must be a clear lineage of your Catholic roots in Bedburg. There can be no doubt as to whom that place belongs."

And by that you mean you.

The archbishop turned around. "I don't know why you're fighting me on this, Heinrich. Wouldn't you like a warm body to sleep next to—even an heir, perhaps? See this as a *good* thing. Maybe you can find someone you can learn to love."

Heinrich stifled a groan. He knew arguing was futile. Whatever Archbishop Ernst wanted, he got. It had been that way ever since the archbishop had fought the Cologne War against Gebhard Truchsess, stolen the archbishopric away from the Protestants, and taken the electoral seat for himself. Above all, Archbishop Ernst was conniving. And, as much as Heinrich wished he were wrong, the truth was Ernst's strategy behind the marriage proposal was sound. It would indeed strengthen his power base. Perhaps the man was preparing a move to an even *higher* position. Maybe *that* explained the grooming of his nephew.

Yes, Heinrich thought, *that makes sense. He wants a unified Catholic front for whenever he appeals to Emperor Rudolf or that new pope, Clement. That's why he's so worried about trade in Cologne. He can't appear weak for when he decides to move forward with his plan. His city must be the most prosperous region of the entire Holy Roman Empire . . .*

"So, Heinrich, what do you say?"

What could he say? After a long pause, he nodded. "I'll do it, Your Grace. For you, I'll do it."

Archbishop Ernst clasped his hands together and smiled broadly, seemingly happy for the first time since Heinrich's arrival.

"Wonderful!" he exclaimed. "And now with that out of the

way, I'd like you to view some portraits. We must find you the right woman. And I have several powerful ones in mind. Fantastic candidates, in fact—ones that could indeed strengthen your own standing. If you'll follow my courier outside the hall, he'll show you to the meeting room and the portraits."

Nodding, Heinrich bowed. "Yes, Your Grace." He paused. "Before I go, my lord, I'd like to add someone to the list of possible brides."

"Oh?" Ernst said, his eyebrows arching. "Very good, Heinrich. I'm glad you're taking this seriously. Yes, as long as I approve your charge before you make any rash decisions, that is quite acceptable." He smiled, adding, "Who might it be?"

Someone Heinrich had kept an eye on for some time, ever since becoming lord of Bedburg. A striking woman—rich, cunning, beautiful. And recently widowed. At first, Heinrich had worried she could become an enemy, but now he realized he could explore an entirely different route . . .

"Her name is Lucille Engel von Bergheim."

The daughter-in-law of Ludwig Koehler, lord of Bergheim, she was also the widowed wife of Gustav Koehler, the contemptuous man Heinrich had killed in Trier.

A fact Lady Lucille never needed to know.

Nor did the archbishop.

CHAPTER TWO

DIETER

1592 – Bedburg, Germany

Dieter Nicolaus winced as Jerome Penderwick, the strange little stuttering surgeon from the *Lion's Pride,* peeled off the bandage around his left elbow. He stared at the end of the stump, where the skin was pulled tight together. It had turned purple from the soldering used to cauterize the wound.

"If you d-don't regularly ch-ch-change this, it'll get infected," Jerome said, his beady eyes darting to Dieter's grimacing face.

In the two months since he'd lost the arm—the result of a nasty knife-wound he'd received outside Claus' inn—Dieter had let his hair grow out. Facial and scalp. His goal was to be unrecognizable and so far it seemed to be working. The brown, curly beard running down his neck, combined with hair that now extended past his shoulders, had changed his appearance considerably.

At first, the surgeon Penderwick had been concerned, worrying that Dieter's changed appearance was thc result of depression over losing his wife. But the former priest had assured him that this wasn't the case. It was solely because Heinrich Franz was now in charge of the region and Dieter knew that being recognized would lead straight to jail. Heinrich wouldn't even need a reason; he'd make one up if necessary. Whatever it took to get Dieter behind bars.

But Dieter now had two things going for him that hopefully would prevent that: one, his new appearance. And two, the fact that Heinrich was rarely in Bedburg—despite being its lord—preferring to spend most nights at his estate at House Charmagne, a half day's ride east.

But Heinrich Franz had many eyes and ears in Bedburg. So Dieter couldn't let his guard down; hence, the beard, the long hair, and this secret hideaway—a farmhouse he now spent most of his time at—on the southern outskirts of town.

There were five of them sharing the house. Besides Dieter, there was his dear son Peter, the surgeon Penderwick, Martin Achterberg, and Martin's lover Ava Hahn. The place was actually Martin's old family house and the floorboards were still stained with the blood of Martin's father, who'd been killed by Martin three years earlier—a dark reminder of those horrific days.

Back then, Dieter had often snuck away to the house to secretly rendezvous with Sybil when they'd first met. But that was three long years ago, when the search for the Werewolf of Bedburg was in full swing and the townsfolk were too tense and terrified to bother them. Things were different now. Calmer. So he had to keep his guard up and hope no one would come looking for him.

But even if things were a bit calmer, there was still tension in the area. And that especially worried Dieter. Whenever he'd slink into town, he'd hear the whispers—people describing what a tyrant Lord Franz had become. His renewed crusades against witches and Protestants had destroyed all hope of due process or fair trials. Fear loomed everywhere.

And of course Dieter was one of those Protestants. Which meant he had to do all in his power, for the sake of his son, to *not* become a prisoner of Lord Franz. Peter's mother—Dieter's wife Sybil—was gone. For this, he blamed himself. And he couldn't fail his son again.

The one saving grace was that Peter had blossomed into a beautiful child. Curious, handsome, the shining star of the household. Also, Martin's lover Ava had taken to him as a mother figure which, although Dieter somewhat resented, was clearly something young Peter needed. So while the thought of his beloved Sybil ever being replaced in his son's life disturbed him deeply, he viewed Ava's new female presence as a necessary evil.

Unraveling a fresh cotton bandage, Jerome began wrapping it around Dieter's ugly stump. Over the past month, most of the pain had stopped, except for the occasional phantom aches Dieter had been warned about. As if his missing arm were still attached. But as Jerome tightened the bandage, he did feel a sudden jolt of pain.

"S-so, what will you d-d-do?" Jerome asked.

Dieter gritted his teeth in discomfort. "Don't worry, Jerome. I'll replace the bandage every week."

Jerome gently patted his patient on the back and smiled, his only three teeth protruding from his nasty gums.

Just then, the door of the house swung open, frightening Dieter and Ava, who was bouncing young Peter in her arms. Dieter spun around and Ava quickly tucked Peter deeper into the folds of her clothes. But it was just Martin, darting in from the cold. The sixteen-year-old had practically doubled in size over the past few months. He now stood nearly as tall as his father had been—with defined muscles and broad shoulders and, even at his young age, a full beard.

Another man bounded in behind Martin. Larger and definitely rounder, with a soft face shaped like an apple, about the same age as Martin, but with a much darker glint in his eyes, as if he'd been robbed of his young innocence.

"I've come across another note," Martin exclaimed, holding up a piece of parchment.

Ignoring Martin for the moment, Dieter stared at the larger figure behind him. He recognized that face. Through the corner of his eye he saw that Ava also recognized him. Wide-eyed, face perspiring, she was frozen.

"K-Kars . . ." she muttered, stepping back a pace.

Gazing at Ava, the large man-boy's mouth fell open. "Ava!" he shouted, smiling awkwardly.

"What are you doing here?" Ava asked, "I thought you were rotting in that jail!"

"They finally let me out," Karstan said. "But I'd rather not talk about it."

His expression turned dark, probably remembering that Ava had played a role in sending him to rot in that jail.

As the tension hung in the air, Dieter turned to Martin. "Martin, what is the meaning of this? We are trying to be *discreet.* I thought you understood that."

"Don't worry, we weren't followed," he replied, unravelling

the parchment. "Karstan has nowhere to go since his release from jail. I found him at the tavern. He approached me just as I discovered this new note under the table."

Dieter looked at Karstan, then Ava. The last thing he needed was turmoil in the household. Ava had betrayed Karstan. They'd been fellow thieves for years before Ava had finally sold him out. Making matters worse, Martin had then won over Ava, something Karstan would now realize and be none too pleased about.

Wars had started over much less.

Trying to divert the subject from Ava and Karstan, Dieter asked, "What does the note say?"

Martin stared at the page, his eyes working line by line.

The notes had started about two weeks ago. The initial one had been found pushed under the front door of the local tavern. Aellin, a wench there, had seen it first and, not knowing what to make of it or whom to show it to, had given it to Martin, knowing he was secretly staying with Dieter.

That note had had two names on it, neither of which Martin or Dieter recognized, though Ava had. She explained that the first name belonged to a tanner and the second, the tanner's wife. But since none of them had relations with any tanners in town, they hadn't paid much attention to it, chalking it up to just some misplaced mistake.

"Take a look," Martin said, handing the new note to Dieter.

Dieter read it aloud: "'Adam Jacobo' and 'Martha Jacobo.' Same signature, too: '*Mord.*'"

Mord. A telling clue. "Who would sign a letter as *Murder*?" Martin asked.

Dieter looked up. "Obviously someone trying to tell us something, anonymously."

"Ever heard of Adam or Martha Jacobo?" Martin asked.

Heads shook around the room.

Dieter was stumped. Who was writing these notes? Where'd they come from? What was their point? And, most intriguing, why give them to Dieter and his group?

Perhaps if I go into town I can learn more. It's dangerous, but this is too perplexing, he thought.

Someone knocked at the door.

Dieter growled. *What in God's name is going on here! This place is getting* far *too much attention!*

Rushing to the door, he creaked it open a few inches. Two people stood outside, a man and woman. Middle-aged and clearly scared. The man was clutching a cap in his hands. "A-are you Dieter Nicolaus?" he asked.

"Who's asking?"

Without answering, the man continued. "An acquaintance says you might be able to protect me and my wife."

"Who is your acquaintance?"

"H-her name is Aellin, my lord."

Aellin, the black-haired beauty, the wench at the tavern, the one who'd found the first note. Somehow, she was right in the middle of this mystery. Yet Dieter was skeptical. There was only one way he knew that this man would be an "acquaintance" to a woman like Aellin. And that didn't make a lot of sense with his frightened wife standing behind him.

"I can't help you," Dieter said.

The man looked ready to weep. And his wife did, bawling suddenly, uncontrollably.

"P-please, sir, you must help us!" the man pleaded.

Dieter opened the door a bit further, showing Jerome, Martin, Karstan, Ava, and little Peter all staring back. "I can't!" he growled. "Don't you see how many people we have packed into this place, man? We have no room."

"Aellin said you'd protect Protestants," the man said. "She said you were a . . . a saintly man." His shoulders and head slumped.

Dieter wanted to yell, *How could you ever trust that whore?* Then realized his anger was misplaced. These people looked innocent and hardworking. He wondered what trouble they could be in. A pang of guilt swept over him. Once he'd been a priest and *would* have helped them. And if he were alone, he'd also help them.

But he wasn't. He had others to protect, especially his son. He couldn't just open his door to strangers. And why would Aellin say this about him? Didn't she realize how dangerous that kind of talk was with a man like Heinrich Franz as lord?

It immediately put Dieter and his whole extended family in jeopardy.

We'll need to leave this place now. No doubt about it. Damnit, woman!

The man at the door just stared at Dieter. Then, defeated, he returned his cap to his head and turned to leave.

"I-I'm sorry," Dieter said in a low, pained voice. "I just can't help you."

The man put his hand on his still-weeping wife's shoulder and walked off into the darkness.

Who were those strangers? And speaking of strangers . . .

Dieter spun around, his brow furrowed. "You, boy," he said, pointing at Karstan. "You can stay just for the night. But we can't help *you*, either. I want no trouble."

Karstan nodded. "That's fine, Father. You won't have any."

Taking little Peter from Ava's arms, Dieter retired to the back room of the house. He had things to think about: *Where will we go now? Why is Aellin making me out to be some sort of Protestant hero? I'm certainly not. I couldn't even save my own wife!*

Dieter closed his eyes as Peter breathed softly next to him. At some point in the night, he heard soft voices seep through the thin walls of his room, recognizing them as Ava's and Karstan's.

"Why are you here, Kars?" he heard Ava say. "*Really*? What's your game?"

"I have no game, Ava. I had nowhere to go . . ."

"And you thought you could stay here by befriending Martin? The person who put you in jail? I don't believe you." When the pirate-woman Rowaine had caught Ava trying to steal from Dieter's wife, it had been Martin who'd blamed the pilfering on Karstan, sending him to jail.

"Well . . . I had a feeling I might find you here," Karstan said, finally spilling his guts.

Ava groaned. "I'm surprised Martin let you join him," she said.

"I hold no grudge against him," Karstan said.

But Dieter didn't believe him. He'd known too many sinners, heard too many confessions, to believe this one.

"He's a good man," Ava said.

And where is this "good man" now? Dieter wondered. *Why does he let Karstan speak with his woman?*

After some moments of silence, Ava whispered, "So . . . I can guess why you're here, Kars. But I won't go with you. I'm staying with Martin. I've put my old life behind me."

"No, that isn't why I've come, actually. I came to ask a question. That's all."

"Oh?"

Karstan paused, finding it hard to find the words. Finally, he said, "Why did you do it, Ava? I thought we . . . were good together."

Ava sighed. "Severin was gone. Hugo was God-only-knows where. It had nothing to do with 'being *good* together,' Kars. It was a fantasy. What? Did you think I loved you?"

Clearly hurt, Karstan mumbled, "I . . . I hoped so."

Ava's voice took a mean tone, probably more than she'd intended. "We were going nowhere, Kars. Our gang was through. It was only a matter of time before we ended up dead in an alley somewhere—or at the end of a noose."

"I wish I'd known you thought that way, Ava. It would have saved me a lot of grief." He paused for a moment. "And so you betrayed me because of that? Because you thought we were going to end up dead? How could I miss that in your eyes? How could I be so fooled?"

"I don't know, Karstan. I suppose I learned to be quick and witty from Hugo. And mean from Severin." Then she softened. "And kind . . . from *you*. But you also taught me how to hide my emotions. The three of you taught me everything. And this is what I've become."

Dieter closed his eyes and the voices grew faint. Then he fell back asleep.

The next morning Karstan was gone.

CHAPTER THREE

HUGO

Hugo Griswold sat in a high-backed chair looking bored, one leg crossed over the other, his head tilted in his palm, as Bishop Balthasar berated him. Seated at the head of the council room, he was surrounded by bearded men twice his age and more, all born into families of high stature.

Which, to Hugo, explained why everyone seemed so displeased with him: *not* being born into high stature. That, and perhaps his age. Few sixteen-year-olds wielded the power he'd been given.

"What could Lord Franz possibly see in this *boy*," one of the councilmen cried, a white-bearded gentleman wearing an embroidered tunic over his fat body. Though directing his ire at Hugo, he spoke to the other noblemen in the room as if Hugo weren't there.

But Hugo didn't mind. In fact, he gave his attacker a smug smile, knowing the man couldn't do anything about it. The truth was, while Hugo wasn't sure exactly what Lord Heinrich Franz saw in him, he certainly didn't dwell on it, gladly accepting the rewards that came with such "royal" support.

Hugo waved the letter in his hand—the one with the red-waxed stamp of approval from Heinrich's own pen. That was all Hugo needed to justify his current position of power at Castle Bedburg.

Heinrich had placed Hugo in charge while away on "urgent business" in Cologne. And as surprising as that might have been to Hugo, it utterly boggled the minds of these nobles and parliamentarians, who couldn't stop yelling and whining and getting red in the face.

Perhaps it's because *I'm so far removed from the goings-on at Bedburg that Heinrich gave me this authority,* Hugo pondered, staring at the indignant face of Bishop Balthasar.

"I'm going to have a talk with Lord Heinrich about this madness, young man," Balthasar said, shaking his head, his multiple chins wobbling. "You can be sure of that."

"Of course you will, Father," Hugo muttered. "That's your prerogative."

Several noblemen groaned.

"*Prerogative!*" the white-bearded man shouted. "He thinks because he uses big words, that gives him power over us!"

Hugo shook his head. "No," he said, again waving the stamped letter. "*This* gives me the power, Lord . . ." he paused, stroking his chin as if trying to recall the man's name. "What was it again?"

Of course he knew he was Lord Alvin, a man with many acres of land and two grain mills along the Erft River. But this was just too much fun. As Alvin's cheeks puffed and his nostrils flared, Hugo worried the old man might drop dead on the spot.

"I'm Lord—"

". . . Alvin," Hugo finished, lifting his head and snapping his fingers. "Right. Now I recall. Well, Herr Alvin, when Lord Heinrich returns you can go to House Charmagne and plead your case."

Which instantly stopped Lord Alvin's yammering. Hugo knew none of them would ever go to Charmagne voluntarily. The place was dark, foreboding, and intimidating. No, these men just liked complaining and Hugo was an easy target.

Besides, Hugo hadn't really *done* anything to complain about since Heinrich's departure. Heinrich's instructions had been clear: "Make sure the town doesn't implode while I'm gone." So Hugo had done precisely as instructed: exactly nothing. Bedburg was doing just fine, so there was virtually nothing to do. It was the nobles who were in jeopardy of imploding.

In fact, Hugo's only real project was to oversee the Town Fair scheduled for the following day.

The large door at the end of the hall swung open. Two guards stepped in momentarily to allow the newest visitor's entry. In the hallway, boots echoed as a scar-faced, giant of a man confidently stomped down the red carpet and into the council room.

An eerie stillness enveloped the room as Ulrich—Bedburg's torturer and executioner—leered at the gathering.

Smiling back, Hugo rose from his chair. "Ulrich! A pleasant surprise," he lied.

It was never pleasant to be in the company of Ulrich. He was gruff, sadistic, and downright evil. Three months earlier, he'd tricked Hugo into joining a group of traveling inquisitors to the city of Trier, in the guise of an escort, only to end up slaughtering the group and stealing their identities so that Heinrich—under an alias—could force guilty verdicts on hapless souls.

It had been a diabolical plot, orchestrated entirely by Ulrich, though probably at the behest of Heinrich. And not only had it reaffirmed Ulrich's immense depravity, it had also convinced Hugo that the man could never be trusted.

Still, at the moment he'd rather look at the torturer's ugly, pock-marked face than spend one more minute with these relentless, noble windbags.

"What are you doing here, boy?" Ulrich asked, his eyebrow raised.

Hugo smiled. "Heinrich's put me in charge while away on business."

"*You?*" Ulrich scoffed. Surveying the gaggle of frightened noblemen, he then shrugged, choosing not to press the issue. "Interesting," was all he said.

"I thought the same," Hugo replied. Pointing to a paper in Ulrich's hand, he asked, "What's that you have there?"

"Something I've been working on . . ." Ulrich held up a note.

"Sounds devious," Hugo said with a smirk. He took it from Ulrich and read it aloud. "Adam and Martha Jacobo. Signed, *Mord.*"

He glanced up at Ulrich. "What does it mean? Who are these people?"

"Protestants."

Hugo's brow jumped. "You're sure?"

Ulrich nodded. "Secret ones. I've been keeping a ledger,

listing possible Lutherans and Calvinists in Bedburg, in case Heinrich wants to take action against them."

"Do you have proof that they're conspiring against the Catholics? Or even that they're really Protestants?"

Ulrich scratched the scar on his cheek. "Well, no . . . that's why my ledger isn't official."

"And what's the significance of these two names? Who was this note intended for?"

"I'm not sure. I'm guessing they were somehow taken from my ledger and someone's trying to save them." He crossed his arms over his chest. "Or at least warn them. But I have no idea who wrote it . . ."

"And how did you come by this note?"

Ulrich stifled a laugh. "You're sounding more and more like Heinrich everyday, boy—"

"Don't call me *boy*. I'm not your *boy*. Just answer the question."

Ulrich's smile disappeared. "I have an operative—"

"Who?"

"That's none of your concern, *my lord*," Ulrich spat. "That's between me and Heinrich."

Looking into Ulrich's face, Hugo suddenly realized that, in his eagerness to appear in charge, he may have overplayed his hand and angered the executioner—the last thing anyone wanted to do. Ulrich was not one to provoke. Phrasing his tone more respectfully, Hugo asked, "And what will you do about these two?"

"Also none of your concern."

Hugo pursed his lips. They were at a standstill. Despite technically being in charge, dealing with Ulrich was always touchy. Hugo had once served as the man's apprentice, so trying to now act superior—to a psychopath nearly twice his size—didn't really work.

"Then why are you showing me this?" Hugo asked.

Ulrich snatched the note back from Hugo. "To be honest, I had no idea you'd be here. I expected to see Heinrich."

Hugo crossed his arms. "Then is that all?"

Fascinated by the ongoing power struggle playing out, the

noblemen listened in rapt silence. For a long moment the two men stared each other down, until Ulrich finally seemed to relent.

"I suppose so," he replied.

Hugo gave a curt nod and Ulrich did the same. Clearly, there would be no bowing. Then Ulrich turned and left.

As Hugo faced the noblemen again, Ulrich paused at the door.

"Hugo?" he called out.

Hugo turned. Ulrich was smiling, the scar on his cheek nearly piercing his upper lip.

"Yes?" Hugo replied.

"I'm glad to see you landed on your feet."

The next morning—the day of Bedburg's Town Fair—was breezy and sunny, a perfect autumn day. This would be the last market before the town's brutal winter set in, when Bedburg's inhabitants would brave their months-long, self-imposed hibernation.

Traders, merchants, farmers, and vintners came from all over to take part in the fair. Whether buyer or seller, it was a day to prepare for the long, bitter winter, drawing people from well beyond the city—Jülich, Elsdorf, Bergheim, Erftstadt, and further south.

Even before dawn broke, Bedburg was bustling as merchants set up stands and tents, loading crates of apples and onions, cartloads of wool and linens, wine from various vineyards, mead and ale from the breweries, freshly baked and ornamented breads, confections, cakes and pies, roasted pigs, chickens, ducks and cattle.

Hugo watched from the steps of Castle Bedburg as Tanner Row was transformed into a vibrant marketplace. Even the stink of the hides and animal flesh had been washed away, giving the area a pristine appearance. It looked nothing like it used to, when Hugo and his gang were begging and running schemes on unsuspecting victims. The entire region—not just Tanner Row but other typically seedy areas such as Priest's Circle—had been cleared of the beggars and miscreants one usually found roaming around.

The epicenter of the fair was the town square. From there, the activity cascaded outward—all the way to the taverns and inns and residential districts bordering the eastern end of town.

Hugo watched from Castle Bedburg as the eastern and southern gates were opened. Because of the festivities, they'd remain unguarded for the rest of the day. As the early morning sun warmed the streets, travelers began trickling in from all around. With no specific duties to attend to, Hugo decided to wander around for a while like just any other fair-goer. Heinrich wasn't scheduled to return until later in the day and, even then, was unlikely to come into town. So Hugo could while away his time as he pleased.

The first thing he noticed were the town guards vigilantly patrolling every block, ready to quash the occasional quarrel or disturbance. Hugo knew that as the day progressed, the number of guards would increase, likely double, as the crowds got drunker and wilder.

He walked past a row of stands bearing different varieties of fruit, marveling at the level of salesmanship the vendors exhibited. Vying for the wandering eyes of passersby, they'd offer free samples, then hawk their wares as potential customers savored their free treats. As he passed a peach vendor, he plucked a small morsel and plopped it into his mouth, drawing the silent ire of the merchant who instantly recognized that he wasn't there to buy anything. Unfazed, Hugo just smiled and walked on.

He probably thinks I'm here for the free food, waiting for nightfall to rob drunk fair-goers, Hugo thought. Once upon a time, that is *exactly* what he'd be doing. Such festive occasions presented the perfect opportunity for the town's petty criminals. Something he'd learned first-hand.

But those days were over.

Proceeding further down the street, Hugo ducked into an alley, re-emerging on the west side of the town square. This was the city's busiest section, with hundreds of vendors crammed row after row, in their individual stalls. While Hugo pondered which direction to go from there, a commotion on the far side of the square caught his eye.

Pushing through the crowd, wondering why the guards hadn't stopped the disturbance, he realized it was the *guards* causing the ruckus. Five of them, led by one who towered over everyone else, were harassing two frightened peasants. When he got closer, he realized the lead guard was Ulrich.

Hugo stayed back in the crowd to watch, his curiosity piqued. By now a large gathering had formed, all eyes intently focused on the spectacle.

"Adam and Martha Jacobo," Ulrich yelled to the couple, "I place you under arrest for conspiring against the lordship of Bedburg."

So these are the two from Ulrich's little note, Hugo thought. *What fools to come here in broad daylight . . . But how did Ulrich find them so quickly in this massive crowd?*

The man under arrest was middle-aged, thin and bony, a cap gripped in his hands. He looked absolutely terrified. Even from a distance Hugo could see his whole body trembling. His wife, a bit wider and also middle-aged, was pulling on her husband's arm, trying to yank him away as if they could escape into the crowd.

But there was nowhere to run. Guards and spectators surrounded them.

"W-what have we done?" the woman cried out, finally stepping forward to speak for her frightened husband. "We've conspired with no one! We're innocent."

Ulrich snapped his fingers, then pointed at the two. Instantly, the guards descended on them. The husband, resigned to his fate, slumped his head. But his wife continued to struggle. "We've done nothing wrong, you animals!" she screeched. "Unhand me!"

Calmly, Ulrich walked off, pushing through the crowd which seemed to melt away as he passed. Twenty paces away, he stepped onto a raised scaffold that the city's carpenters had erected for the big auction scheduled for later in the day. His guards followed, dragging the two peasants along. Ulrich stood at the auctioneer's podium and looked out at the sea of faces. On both sides of the podium two vertical poles stood—wooden stakes pounded into the ground to serve as columns for the scaffolding.

Ulrich again snapped his fingers and a guard handed him two lengths of rope. The torturer's fingers moved swiftly and expertly as he formed a familiar loop with one of the ropes, then tied its end to the top of the pole on his left. He then repeated the process with the second rope, attaching it to the pole on his right.

Gasps could be heard from the crowd.

Without preamble, Ulrich took the husband, tied his hands behind his back with a bit of torn cloth, then looped one of the nooses around his neck as the the man wailed in agony. He then did the same to the wife, who stood stone-faced and petulant.

Hugo's first thought was that this was all for show—a sadistic, yet effective, way to terrify the populace. *Surely he can't do something so rash without even the semblance of a trial? What would Heinrich say if he knew of this?*

The murmuring crowd quieted as Ulrich stepped back to the podium.

"In the name of Lord Heinrich Franz of Bedburg . . ." he began, which told Hugo that Heinrich *had* to know this was happening, ". . . Adam and Martha Jacobo are hereby sentenced to death for their habitual abetting of the Protestant cause."

"Where's the proof!" a brave soul yelled out from the crowd.

"Seize him," Ulrich ordered nonchalantly, pointing to the man who had spoken. Two guards bounded down the stairs, as the man turned and fled through the crowd. When the guards looked back at Ulrich for instructions, he shook his head slightly. There was no sense diverting attention from the matter at hand. Then Ulrich turned to his victims, scanning back and forth from husband to wife. "You know what you've done," he announced. "Do you have anything to say?"

The man shook his head. "There is nothing to be said. We are innocent," he mumbled.

The woman shrieked and sputtered. "I curse you all! God will strike you down with furious vengeance for the wrongs you have committed under the guise of His grace! You will all perish for—"

But she never finished. Ulrich shoved both husband and wife off the scaffolding at the same time, their bodies dropping five feet, an audible snap from the man's neck drifting over the crowd like a dried chicken bone splitting apart. His body swayed gently, his feet dangling an arm's-length from the ground, his pants darkened and soiled. But the woman continued to writhe, froth gurgling from the side of her mouth, forming two gooey strings of yellow bile that eventually dripped to the ground. Then, with one final spasmodic jerk, she also went still—eyes popped wide open, face frozen in a silent scream, her body slowly swaying almost in unison with her dead husband's.

After several more seconds of shocked silence, the angry jeers began. The onlookers were appalled—horrified—not only for what had just happened, but for how quickly it had transpired. Without warning, without process, without fairness or mercy or the slightest hint of humanity.

Hugo peered over the sea of angry, stunned faces, his own eyes equally wide and shocked. As he perused the grim scene, a face in the crowd caught his attention. Though he wore his brown hair long and beard thick, the man's stance and gestures were unmistakable.

Dieter Nicolaus.

His sister's husband.

He wore what looked to be a monk's habit, with his arms tucked into his tunic and his head covered by a brown hood.

The former priest hadn't yet noticed Hugo, his attention fixed in horror at the sight of the hanging peasants.

Meanwhile, Ulrich gazed out defiantly at the sea of angry spectators. Then he casually walked down the stairs of the scaffolding and out through the crowd, his guards close behind, leaving both bodies dangling in the wind.

With the immediate threat gone, the townsfolk's disgust quickly turned to rage.

"This treachery can't stand!" a man shouted.

"What gives Lord Heinrich the right?" another called out. "He isn't even present!"

"Those two deserve justice!"

"They deserved a trial, you fool!"

When Hugo turned his attention back to Dieter, he was gone. Off in the distance he could see the back of the brown hood, growing smaller as the man disappeared among the fair-goers.

"Help take them down!" a man yelled, but Hugo was on the move, pushing his way through the crowd, trying to follow the fading image of Dieter. As he struggled through the horde, he thought, *I should have been consulted about this. These people will rebel over something like this . . . that damned foolish torturer!*

He could already sense a change in the fair's atmosphere as word quickly spread about what had just happened in the town square. This was supposed to be a joyous occasion. Now it was quickly, foolishly, turning riotous.

But Hugo was too pre-occupied at the moment, trying to keep sight of Dieter while remaining unseen. He followed him through alleyways and roads. Dieter knew the city's layout just as well as Hugo. And he was obviously heading for the southern gates.

But why is he in such a hurry? And what in God's name is he doing here in Bedburg? Doesn't he know my sister is far away?

Then Hugo realized that maybe that wasn't the case. In fact, he had no idea where Sybil was.

When they reached the gates and beyond, it became harder for Hugo to hide, but he managed to stay in the shadows, keeping a fair distance back. At one point, he was able to advance closer by hiding behind a passing horse-led cart.

As they came to a hill, he watched Dieter crest it, then begin his descent down the other side. Hugo hid in a bush at the top and watched Dieter walk to a small farmhouse where he knocked on the door, then entered.

Hugo knew the place.

It was the abandoned estate that once belonged to the Achterberg family.

What is Dieter doing here in Bedburg? He and Sybil have a child together! Why is he not out searching for his wife?

Hugo knew that Heinrich Franz had conducted a massive

manhunt for his sister, labeling Sybil the "Daughter of the Beast," but had come up empty. He also knew his sister well enough to be confident that she was still out there somewhere.

Does Dieter live alone? Surely he knows he can't stay there . . . he'll be discovered. Worse still, he's a Protestant sympathizer—no, a Protestant *no less! Surely he knows that, if caught, he will be tortured or worse, just like those two in the town square.*

But the main question haunting Hugo was whether to tell Heinrich about Dieter. Doing so, after all, would bring him immense favor from his lord. He'd be the one who brought in "the husband of the Daughter of the Beast."

As he thought of his lord, Hugo remembered that Heinrich would soon be returning from Cologne. It was time to head back to town.

A short time later Hugo arrived at the stables. From there, he rode his horse to House Charmagne, where he awaited Heinrich's arrival.

CHAPTER FOUR

SYBIL

Norfolk, East Anglia, England

Sybil Nicolaus cradled baby Rose in her arms, bouncing her up and down. The babe whined and Sybil kissed her tiny pink ear. Rose's eyes opened and she groped at Sybil's breast. The child was only a few months old and needed to feed frequently.

Staring into the child's deep blue eyes nearly brought Sybil to tears. The baby reminded her of her own child, Peter, off somewhere in Germany, lost to her. Peter would be almost three now and Sybil missed him terribly, as well as her husband, of course.

Claire Durand, Rose's young mother, saw the look Sybil and Rose exchanged and it tugged at her heart. As a mother, she could feel the heartbreak in Sybil's eyes. Gently, she reached over to take the baby from Sybil. Opening her tunic, she bared a breast as she walked to the corner of the room to feed her.

The men in the room took no mind; everyone was too busy.

In the opposite corner of the room Rowaine sat in a small wooden chair. She was watching Daxton, seated at a table a few paces away, discussing something in hushed tones with her father, Georg Sieghart. Ever since Daxton's elevation from carpenter to captain of the *Lion's Pride,* he'd handled his position with the enthusiastic intelligence of a seasoned leader, though he was far from that. At the moment he was pointing at something on a drawing he'd made as Georg nodded in agreement.

Sybil walked out the front door, taking measure of the morning. It was cold, gray, and misty but the green pastures of the Norfok countryside somehow brightened everything. Despite the early hour, people were already engaged in their morning work activities—men hammering and constructing, women bringing their husbands water and food, ox- and horse-pulled carts carrying tools and building materials, armed guards inspecting the goings-on.

After escaping Trier two months ago, Sybil and her company had traveled across the Dutch border, making their way to the North Sea where they'd been able to hide the *Lion's Pride* from their pursuers. After being branded a witch and fugitive, her group had taken up here, a place she knew well, in the county of Norfok, run by an assembly of Protestant refugees known as the Elizabethan Strangers. They referred to their growing town as Strangers Shire.

And she'd returned to Norfolk just in time. Within days of her arrival, her good friend, Claire Durand, had given birth to a beautiful daughter, Rose. Since then, all Sybil could think about was how one day little Rose and her own son Peter would meet and play together.

Most of Norfolk had greeted Sybil with open arms. But some of the Strangers had been less than gracious. The tension came from what had befallen the residents the last time Sybil had visited the area. Back when Gustav Koehler, a ruthless man posing as a tax collector, had terrorized the community. And then the body of the *actual* tax man, Timothy Davis, had turned up buried in Gustav's garden.

These were simple, non-violent folk who kept to themselves. They'd settled in Norfolk to *escape* the evils of city life. Corruption and murder were the antithesis of what they stood for. When Sybil had arrived that last time, she'd lied about who she was. And then all that evil had come—the wrath of Gustav Koehler, the murder of Timothy Davis, the armed guards subsequently brought in from nearby Norwich to patrol the area. When so much misery disrupts so many peaceful lives, someone must be blamed and, for many, Sybil was the perfect scapegoat. So, yes, there was some tension with Sybil's presence there.

The front door opened and Georg came out, joining Sybil to watch the activities in the fields.

"It's amazing," Sybil commented, looking out at the scenery. "You should have seen this place when I first came here. Farmland and pastures all the way to the horizon. That was it.

And now . . . this."

They both gazed off to where Dieter's former church had been rebuilt. Sybil had been surprised when Reeve Clarence Bailey had decided to rebuild it after Gustav had burnt it to the ground. Of course Sybil knew Bailey's ulterior motive: the church would bring in money—generous tithes. But rebuilding the church had set the quiet shire off in a direction of rapid growth. Once the church was built, other buildings and structures began sprouting up around it. The Strangers' land had now become a church town—with the holy building as the epicenter and lots of new construction expanding outward.

Georg responded with a grunt, leaving Sybil to wonder whether he agreed or disagreed.

A few moments later, Georg spoke in a low voice. "Daxton is going to help build something for Catriona." He often called Rowaine by her birth-name, Catriona. But ever since he'd finally found her, Georg had become more and more despondent. Badly injured, Rowaine still couldn't walk and Georg feared she'd never be able to again.

"Daxton is the right man to do it," Sybil said. "He was the carpenter of the *Pride,* after all. What will he build her?"

"Crutches, to begin. Then he's planning something more ambitious . . . some type of chair with wheels on it. Sounds ridiculous to me."

Sybil nodded, smiling to herself. She only hoped whatever was built brought Rowaine out of her morose disposition. She'd become just as despondent as her father. Once the liveliest person Sybil knew—fiery, passionate, demanding—ever since being shot in the back during their escape from Trier, she barely spoke.

Thinking of that escape reminded Sybil of just how much she missed Dieter and their son. It also brought back memories of her plan to find Heinrich Franz, the man responsible for killing her father. So far that plan hadn't moved forward. She had no idea where Heinrich might be. But now was not the time for that anyway. Georg needed to care for his daughter and Sybil could tell that her presence seemed to help him deal with that.

Georg interrupted her thoughts. "I'd like to build something here."

"Oh?"

He nodded. "Put down roots."

"Have you seen the way people look at you here, Georg?"

Georg scoffed. "Of course. That's another reason why I want to build something—get on the right side of everyone."

"What ever will you build to make people like you . . . or trust you?"

Georg grinned—a goofy sight against his leathery, bearded face. He put his arms out wide and said, "A tavern, Beele. What else?"

Sybil chuckled. "I should have guessed."

"Daxton said he'd help me build it." As Georg began describing his plans for his tavern, his spirits rose, but then just as quickly died back down. "But for now I need to take care of Cat. I'm sure you understand. I know you'd like to find Dieter and your son—"

"It's not that I'd *like* to, Georg. I *must*."

He paused, opening his mouth then closing it with a nod. "Of course. My apologies."

"And wouldn't you like to find Heinrich Franz?"

Georg shrugged. "I'm not as hellbent on the idea as I once was." Clearly, reuniting with his daughter Rowaine had eased his obsession over finding and killing Heinrich.

In the distance through the fog, a carriage made its way down the dirt road, heading toward them. Only one person would be riding a carriage through the country, Sybil thought, groaning.

And she was right. A few minutes later, Reeve Clarence Bailey hopped out and sauntered up the small hill toward them, his hands clasped behind his back. He wore a frilly shirt and an expensive robe, looking more like a baron than a humble reeve.

It seems the church has already started to work in his favor, Sybil thought, inspecting the man's clothes as he approached them.

Bailey lifted his chin to stare at Georg. Teeth clenched, his gaunt cheekbones protruded like a skeleton. He'd gained weight since Sybil had last seen him—money and gluttony obviously agreed with him. But to Sybil he'd always be the same untrusting, skinny reeve.

"Thank you for coming, Reeve Bailey," Georg said. Sybil shot him a look, clearly confused why Georg would call for the company of such a man. Clarence Bailey didn't like *anyone* that Sybil brought to Norfolk. He'd only agreed to take Sybil back after Claire and Leon Durand had pleaded with him.

"This better be good," Clarence said. "Do you know how far I had to ride to get out here?"

Sybil frowned, wanting nothing to do with the man. Still, she was intrigued as to why Georg had arranged this meeting.

"I know you don't like me," Georg began, clearing his throat. "That's why I'd like to do something for the people here. I want to show the Strangers that they can trust me."

The reeve put his hands on his hips. "I'm listening . . ."

Holding his forefinger and thumb of both hands in the shape of twin L's, Georg made an imaginary frame of the picturesque countryside. "I can see it there . . ."

"See what?"

"Something everyone can enjoy. I'd like to build a tavern."

The reeve seemed stunned. "Have you told anyone else of this?"

Georg scratched his cheek. "Uh, no. Just Beele here. I've only recently come up with the idea."

"So you'd like to profit off the hardworking folk here."

"N-no, of course not. That's not my intent at all. I'd hire the workers here to help build the place. It would be taxed, so you'd make money. It would be a place for people to enjoy themselves and unwind after a hard day's work."

"Enjoy, unwind . . . and spend their money."

Georg's face contorted. Sybil knew that look. Frustration. Which for Georg wasn't far away from outright anger. But, to his credit, Georg maintained his composure. "I have to make a living, Herr Bailey. There's nothing wrong with that. I like drinking. Everyone else likes drinking, too. There's nowhere in this entire little town for people to go and relax, or get away from their wives at night."

At that last comment, Reeve Bailey's eyes bulged. "You plan to make it a brothel!"

Georg shook his head furiously. "You mistake my meaning," he said. "I just meant it as a place where . . . men could be . . . men . . . and socialize."

At least Georg has the man thinking about it, Sybil thought. She saw the glint in the reeve's eyes. He knew it was a good idea. He was probably just put off that it was Georg's idea and not his own. But Georg pointing out that Bailey would profit from it had seemed to turn the tide. Bailey had already shifted from "bad idea" to just "no brothel."

"Where *men* can socialize?" Sybil asked, taking a step forward. "So women won't be allowed?"

Georg held his palms forward, waving them around, "No! I mean, yes. Of course they would!" He narrowed his eyes at Sybil, as if to say, *Why are you undermining me? We're supposed to be on the same side!*

"This is a quiet, Protestant refuge, Herr Sieghart," the reeve continued.

"I understand that. I'd make sure the place remained civil."

"The last thing we need is more patrolmen from Norwich interrupting our way of life here."

"Agreed."

"And you'll need a license to build it in the town proper," Bailey finished, crossing his arms over his chest.

"How can I get one?"

"Only thc reeve issues licenses," Bailey answered, smiling as he turned up his nose to make clear *he* was in charge here. Never again would the reeve allow another Gustav-type situation in his peaceful little hamlet.

Georg sighed. "May I have one?" he asked, his frustration creeping back.

Reeve Bailey seemed to think about that for a long while. Sybil thought the man utterly absurd—making things far more difficult than necessary. Then again, that *was* his style.

Finally the reeve's eyes brightened and Sybil knew he'd thought of something to use to his advantage. He turned around, looking back toward his carriage, then turned back to Georg. "There is something I need doing, but I can't do myself. If you will do me a small favor, Herr Sieghart, I will give you your license."

Georg stroked his bushy beard for a moment, apprehensively. "What is it you need done?"

"Do you know the primary export of Strangers Shire, Herr Sieghart?"

A pause.

When Georg stayed quiet, Sybil spoke up. "Textiles," she answered.

"Correct, Frau Nicolaus. The Strangers are some of the country's best textile workers. Don't ask me why—I haven't a clue. But for whatever reason, our shire attracts them. I am trying to . . . *expand* that export business."

Now it was Sybil's turn to be apprehensive. Something dubious was coming.

There was another pause as Reeve Bailey appeared to be deciding how much to tell Sybil and Georg. His mouth moved but no words came.

"Continue, sir," Georg coaxed, exasperation in his voice.

Reeve Bailey nodded. "I would like to extend our business to Germany. But that is proving more difficult than I thought. Lords and ladies in Cologne and Münster will pay heavenly amounts for our work. But . . ." he trailed off.

"You can't legally sell to Germany," Sybil said.

The reeve coughed. "Technically, that is correct—"

"Not technically, Herr Bailey," she replied. "That is the law. Say what you mean, please." She was growing tired of this man's antics.

"Fine," Bailey said. "You are right. We are part of England, after all, and the queen is not on good terms with the Deutschland. But I know a man that will do my selling for me, without connecting our shire in the trades. I just need to bring him the goods."

"Then why don't you?" Georg asked. "Seems simple enough."

"There are guards and watchmen where I'd need to go. No one from this region would be safe—they'd surely be recognized and stopped—possibly even jailed. Nearly all the working men in Strangers Shire have done this task before. *I* would certainly be recognized. So you see, we need fresh blood . . ."

Georg nodded. He finally understood.

"I'll do it," he said quickly.

Sybil made a small sound in her throat. "Georg, are you certain? You don't even know the details. What about your daughter?"

"I need to build something so my daughter can live. She will be safe here . . . isn't that right, Herr Bailey?"

The reeve nodded profusely. "Yes, yes. Absolutely."

"And where would I be taking these goods?" Georg asked.

"My operative is in King's Lynn, about forty miles from here—a three-day journey."

Georg thought for a moment. "Fine." He stuck out his hand. "I take your textiles to your man in King's Lynn, and when I get back you give me my license."

After a short pause, Reeve Bailey took Georg's bear-like hand and shook it, wincing from Georg's grip. "Deal," he said.

Once the reeve had gone, Sybil turned to Georg. "I hope you know what you're getting into."

"How bad could it be? I'll need a horse though. And I have a request for you."

"For me?"

Georg nodded. "I'd like you to take care of Catriona while I'm gone."

Sybil sighed. She'd been stuck in this place for too long. She felt restless and needed the wind in her hair—if only to relieve some of her negative energy at being separated from Dieter and Peter for so long.

"I'm afraid that's impossible," she said.

Georg's mouth fell open. "W-what? Why?"

Sybil put a hand on Georg's shoulder and looked up into his dark eyes.

"Because I'm coming with you. *Someone* needs to make sure you stay out of trouble, Georg Sieghart."

CHAPTER FIVE

HEINRICH

Young Heinrich stared at himself in the mirror. This would be the last time he'd dress in his mother's clothes before giving up the fantasy.

Heinrich was almost ten now, the age his brother was when he'd died. It had been almost two years since Oscar's tragic death along the riverside and being an only child hadn't turned out to be as pleasant as Heinrich had hoped. Not when your mother was such a malicious shrew.

Edith still blamed him for Oscar's death—for not saving him. And even though he secretly knew she was right to blame him—just for the wrong reason—he still despised her. When questioned after the incident, Heinrich's excuse was that he'd frozen in fear and, instead of trying to pull his brother from the water, he'd gone running for help. Edith didn't mince words about what she thought of that—spineless, stupid, worthless.

Appraising himself in the mirror, Heinrich turned slowly so he could see how the red dress curved around his body. On his mother, the fabric stopped just below her knees; on him it bunched onto the floor. Yet still, he liked the way he looked in it.

It made him smile.

Mother had been out all day, doing business with a clothier. Edith was a fleece merchant. She'd taken over her husband's wool trading operation after he'd disappeared. And she'd done pretty well, keeping her family out of poverty, raising the sheep, shearing the wool, readying the pelts, and selling them to spinners, tailors, and other merchants.

Lost in the trance of his reflection in the mirror, Heinrich didn't hear the footsteps down the hallway. A moment later, his mother barged in. Her mouth dropped, as did the coins she'd been holding. As the pennies rolled and scattered, her hand rose to her mouth and she gasped.

Heinrich spun around, his face bright red.

"This . . ." Edith shouted, then could hardly finish, so great was her fury. "This is what you do while I slave away to provide us a living? Y-you . . . little bastard! You foolish, foppish bastard!"

Tears streamed down Heinrich's face. He wanted to scream *It's not what it looks like!* But it was *exactly* what it looked like. He had no answer, his mind blank. He just wanted to disappear. He'd killed Oscar to save this secret from getting out. And now…

Edith raced up to him and grabbed him by the ear. With a yank, she pulled him from the room and down the hall as he cried and sputtered.

Opening the front door, she pushed him out.

"Do you see this?" she shouted in a shrill voice. "This is what I have to put up with!"

A man dressed in luxurious clothes stood outside, startled. He took a step back and ran his eyes up and down Heinrich. "Well, she's a pretty lass. Is it so wrong for her to try out her mother's clothes?"

Heinrich wanted to die.

Why didn't she just walk away from me. Why must she humiliate me so?

"Nothing would be wrong with it, Jacques, if *'she'* were my daughter!" Edith huffed, shaking her head. "Unfortunately, this is my *son!*"

The merchant took a closer look at the boy. He started to speak, than thought better of it and just mumbled, "Well . . . then never mind."

"Get out of here you stupid, stupid boy," Edith screamed. And Heinrich rushed off, around the side of the house to the backyard. Leaning back against the shed where his mother kept her fleeces, he slid down to the ground, burying his head in his hands.

Then he wept uncontrollably.

After a time, a tiny clucking noise drew his attention.

Looking up he saw a rat skittering across a branch of the tree in front of him. He grabbed a rock next to him and leaned forward. The rat stopped, tilting its head to stare at him. "Don't look at me like that!" the boy screamed, launching the rock at the mocking creature.

His aim was dead on. With a squeal the animal careened off the branch and fell to the ground, its hind legs trembling. Crawling to it, Heinrich found a bigger rock, gritted his teeth and smashed it into the dying rat. The rodent exploded, spewing guts and blood everywhere. Again and again Heinrich brought down the rock, until his anger ebbed and nothing was left but a bloody pulp.

Afterward, he felt guilty. Gently, he picked up the rat's remains, holding it by its tail, and opened his mother's fleece shed. He chose a pile of wool pelts between several others and flung the rat on top. Then he folded the top pelt over it, leaving his mother with a stinking rat sandwich to remember him by.

Just one of many he'd left her in the past.

Wiping his bloody hands on his red dress, he closed the shed door as Edith came rushing around the side of the house. Snapping her fingers at him, she pointed to the shed. "Bring me that stack of pelts," she demanded.

Heinrich obliged, handing her the middle stack. Snatching it from him, she stared daggers into his tearful, hopeful eyes.

"You're useless, boy," she seethed.

"Utterly useless."

Heinrich awoke with a start and began coughing. Sitting up, he surveyed his surroundings, unclear where he was. Then he recognized the white curtains and leather bench. He was riding in his own carriage.

Sweating, he poked his head out the window. "What was that, Felix?" he asked his driver up front.

The young man glanced over his shoulder. "Oh, it's nothing, my lord. These horses are just utterly useless. Totally uncooperative today."

Heinrich furrowed his brow, then leaned back inside the coach. Closing his eyes, he let out an exhausted sigh and rested his head against the leather backing.

Another nightmare, he thought, shuddering. *Where are they coming from . . . what do they mean?*

A short while later, as the sun set behind gray clouds, they arrived at House Charmagne.

Two guests were waiting for him at the mansion.

One was Bishop Balthasar, sitting at the head of the large dining table with his walking staff across his knees. The other was young Hugo Griswold, standing in the corner, his legs and arms crossed, shooting a disapproving glare at the back of Balthasar's head. Heinrich sighed, took off his black cloak, and handed it to his butler, Beauregard, who shuffled away.

As the elder and most self-important man in the room, Bishop Balthasar took it upon himself to start the conversation. "How was your trip to Cologne?" he asked. "And the archbishop?"

Balthasar had once been the vicar of Cologne—Archbishop Ernst's right-hand man before taking over as bishop in Bedburg, by overthrowing his predecessor.

"Ernst is fine, bishop. But please, I am weary from my travels. Let's move past the chatter." Heinrich took the seat at the foot of the table, across from the bishop. He steepled his hands in front of him. "What report do you have for me?"

Glancing over his shoulder, the bishop spoke softly. "The information I have is quite . . . delicate. Could we not speak in private?"

Hugo, the target of Balthasar's unease, uncrossed his arms and seemed ready to pounce. But Heinrich held up his palm.

"Anything you say, the boy may hear. He stays."

Balthasar shook his head. "I still don't understand why you've given such a young delinquent such power," he muttered.

Heinrich was quickly losing patience. "Please," he said through gritted teeth, "continue with your report."

The bishop took his cane from his knees, smacked its tip on the ground, and slowly lifted himself to his feet. "Bedburg is in an uproar. Your torturer publicly executed two suspected

Protestants during the Town Fair yesterday! Summarily! In broad daylight! The townspeople aren't having it."

"Bedburg is fine!" Hugo said loudly, pushing himself off the wall and stepping forward. "The townspeople don't know what's—"

"I am speaking, *young man!*" Balthasar bellowed.

Heinrich noticed Hugo ball up his hands into fists, but ignored Balthasar's outburst. "I won't reprimand Ulrich for doing what he thought best," he replied calmly. "In fact, it may be just what the town needs right now. To fully appreciate how serious I am about quashing this Protestant plague."

"This violence will only work for so long, Heinrich—"

"*Lord.*"

"What?"

"It's *Lord* Heinrich."

Balthasar stammered. "R-right, my lord. If you don't want to see another rebellion, I suggest taking a softer approach to your methods of punishment."

"Such as?"

"I believe I could convert these weak-minded folk to the True faith."

"We've tried that, bishop. It has failed before."

"We haven't given it much of a chance," Balthasar said.

"Even so. There will always be fringe groups of Protestants who refuse to see the light. In order for their false ideas to stop spreading, they must be punished."

"But—"

Heinrich held up his palm again. "That is my decision, Your Excellency," he said, adding the bishop's title to soften his rebuke. "Let's move on. Do you have other news?"

The bishop hesitated. After a long silence he said, "Well . . . I took a confession the other day, from a stonemason named William." Balthasar hesitated, clearly conflicted about how much to reveal.

"What did William tell you, bishop?"

Balthasar looked toward the wall, away from Heinrich. "It's blasphemous for me to say. It would be breaking the holy confessional covenant between him and God."

"You wouldn't have brought it up if you didn't wish to speak of it, Balthasar. Pray for forgiveness. I'm sure God will understand."

The bishop's face paled. "William confirmed my belief. He admitted to being a Protestant—his whole family believes in the teachings of John Calvin, in fact. And . . . he confessed to planning an attack."

"An attack?" Heinrich jumped from his seat. "What kind of attack?"

"He wouldn't say. He was simply asking forgiveness *before* the fact."

Heinrich slammed his palms on the table. "What did you tell him?"

"That the penance doesn't work that way . . ."

Heinrich took a small notepad from his tunic. He snapped his fingers for Beauregard, who came a moment later with ink and pen.

"This man's full name?"

Balthasar again hesitated. Then, "William Edmond."

Heinrich scrawled on his notepad. "And his family?"

Balthasar stayed quiet for a moment, his face reddening. Heinrich peeked over his notepad, glaring at him until Balthasar relented. "His wife is Mary. They have a son Wilhelm."

Heinrich finished writing, then stared at his pad, reading aloud: "William Edmond, Mary Edmond, Wilhelm Williamson. Good. Well done, Balthasar."

"I've sinned," the bishop muttered, his shoulders slumping.

"Is there anything else?" Heinrich asked, ignoring the bishop's self-pity.

Bishop Balthasar slowly shook his head.

"Beauregard will show you out, Your Excellency," Heinrich said. "One of my carriages will see you back to Bedburg."

The bishop limped out of the room, his head lowered, his staff slowly clacking the stone floor with each step. When they no longer could hear his footfalls, Heinrich turned to Hugo.

"I suspect you disagree with the bishop's diagnosis of Bedburg."

Hugo nodded, opening his mouth to speak. But before he

could, Heinrich cut him off. "That's quite all right. I have an important mission for you."

Hugo's eyes lit up.

Heinrich smirked. Since taking Hugo under his wing a few months back in Trier, there was no question his "conversion" of the young man was now complete. The boy had become a trustworthy apprentice, totally in tune with Heinrich's mindset, available day or night for any and all requested duties.

In fact, Heinrich hoped that Hugo might one day take his place at Castle Bedburg, overseeing the everyday goings-on of the town, while Heinrich took charge of more important issues at House Charmagne. Ever since Heinrich's beloved Odela had been burned alive in Trier, Heinrich had trouble staying at Castle Bedburg for very long. There were just too many painful memories everywhere he looked.

And now, staring into Hugo's puppy-dog eyes, Heinrich finally had the assistant he needed, someone ready to forsake his own family, possibly even give up his own sister for the "greater good." Heinrich had been working on this, reminding the boy that his sister had abandoned him, labeling her "the Daughter of the Beast" to emphasize his sister's evil bloodline. Soon, he knew Hugo would be primed to betray his sister, should the need arise.

And having the young man perform small assignments for him only advanced Heinrich's plan.

"What is the mission, my lord?" Hugo asked eagerly.

"To go to Bergheim. Do you know where that is, boy?"

Hugo shook his head.

"It's on the southern border, only a day's ride. That petulant baron, Ludwig Koehler, rules the place. You will go there as my emissary and speak with him."

"What will I tell him?"

Heinrich reached into his tunic, pulled out a rolled parchment and handed it to Hugo. Sprinting forward to take the paper, Hugo treated it like a holy relic.

"Read that over before you arrive," Heinrich instructed. "It describes everything you need to know. In so many words, my boy, you will find me a wife."

Hugo's head shot up from the parchment. "*You*? Marry?"

Heinrich chuckled. "You can't see it? Well, neither can I. But yes, your mission is to find my next wife. It is the archbishop's wish that I marry. To solidify the Catholic stronghold in the principality. I'm sure you understand."

"And I'm going alone?" Hugo asked.

"I was considering sending Rolf with you—he knows more about the local politics, but he's also old."

"I heard that," a voice called out from the hallway.

Heinrich smiled as the venerable Rolf Anders entered, his white beard swishing as he walked. The two men embraced, then Heinrich turned back to Hugo. "I have faith in you, boy. I'm sure you'll do fine. I feel you are ready for more responsibilities. Isn't that right, Rolf?"

"Absolutely not," Rolf said, shaking his head sternly. Then the shadow of a smile appeared inside his beard. "I only jest, my boy. You'll do fine in Bergheim."

"So . . . I *am* going alone," Hugo said, looking back and forth between the two men.

"Felix will go with you," Heinrich said. "My driver is strong and young, with an able mind."

"I'd better get to reading then," Hugo replied, shaking the parchment.

"Indeed," Heinrich said with a nod. "You leave in the morning. Run along now."

Hugo hurried from the room.

Heinrich turned to his old friend and housekeeper and frowned, his face looking even gaunter than usual.

Immediately Rolf noticed. "What ails you, lad?" he asked.

"I've . . . been having nightmares . . ."

Rolf breathed loudly through his nose. "And what? You suspect premonitions?"

"Ha!" Heinrich pretended a smile. "Absurd. You know I don't subscribe to such superstitions."

"Then why tell me this?"

"I . . . I'm not sure." Heinrich started to fidget.

Rolf smiled warmly, like father to son. "I know a man who may be able to help."

"Truly?" Heinrich looked up at Rolf. "Cure me?"

"I didn't say that," Rolf said, shaking his head. "I make no promises. But perhaps he can help you sleep easier."

"Very good. Then call your man. I must go to Bedburg to see what's going on there for myself." Returning to his autocratic nature, he added, "I expect this soothsayer to be here when I return tomorrow night—the day after, at the latest."

"I-I will try my best, my lord."

Heinrich clapped the old man's shoulder and stormed out of the room.

As he passed the red-carpeted stairs, he glanced up toward his bedroom. He knew he needed sleep, but was afraid what that might bring.

So he continued on.

CHAPTER SIX

DIETER

Dieter was distraught.

Incessantly biting his lower lip, he paced the living room of the Achterberg estate. Ava, Martin Achterberg, Jerome, even little Peter, all stared at him as he nervously shook his head.

"I'm a damned fool," he muttered. "And a coward."

He'd recognized the people executed in the town square, the same two who had come to the house the day before begging for shelter and protection from Heinrich Franz's oppressive Catholic regime.

And he'd turned them away.

He wondered if God could ever forgive him.

"You aren't a coward," Ava told him. "You had no way of knowing what would happen to them."

"Of course I did!" he cried, rushing past her without making eye contact. "I sent those poor people to their deaths. I could have saved them."

Martin tried to reason with him. "They might have brought unwanted attention here."

Which stopped Dieter in his tracks. *Unwanted attention.* He'd been so distressed over what he'd seen in the square that he hadn't yet told the group the other bad news. "There's *already* unwanted attention. And that too was my fault."

"What are you talking about?" Martin asked. When Dieter didn't answer, Martin prompted him. "What aren't you telling us, Dieter?"

"On the way back from the fair, I was followed."

All eyes fell on him, waiting for more.

"By whom?" Martin finally asked.

"Hugo Griswold."

Dieter scanned the faces around the room.

"Your wife's younger brother . . ." Martin said under his breath. Dieter nodded.

On his way home, right before he'd entered the house, Dieter had stopped to remove a pebble from inside his shoe. Sensing he was being followed, he caught a glimpse of Hugo hiding behind a bush. He was sure it was his brother-in-law. If he hadn't been hiding—if Hugo had just approached him, he would have spoken with him. But the fact that Hugo was concealing himself had troubled Dieter. So he figured it best to pretend he hadn't seen him, and casually continue on inside. Maybe that would at least buy the group time to decide what to do. Plus, at that moment he was just too distraught over the hangings to think straight.

When Ava heard it was Hugo, her face paled and her mouth fell open. She seemed about to faint.

Dieter noticed. "Are you all right, Ava?" She was holding Peter, so Dieter took him from her arms.

Handing the child to Dieter, she nodded. "Y-yes, I'm f-fine." Though she didn't look fine and took an unsteady seat on the bench behind her.

"You d-don't s-s-sound fine," Jerome stuttered. "You s-sound like me."

Ava shook her head. "I have a . . . *history* with Hugo Griswold."

Staring at Ava, Martin sounded edgy. "Hugo Griswold is not a virtuous man. I was his friend growing up, and he was innocent enough then. But now he's an arm of Heinrich Franz, and thoroughly conditioned by that hateful man."

Dieter nodded. "Which is why we must leave. Immediately."

Ava opened her mouth to speak up, then paused. "Are you sure?"

Dieter nodded. "Hugo could tell Heinrich, or Ulrich, where we are. And if they somehow connect us to the poor Jacobos, our fates are sealed."

As the color began to return to Ava's face, she shook her head. "Do you really believe he'd do that? Your own wife's brother?"

Martin had no doubt. "He is capable of much more treachery than just that. Dieter is right. We must leave my house at once." Instinctively, Martin still referred to the house as "his" because he'd grown up there and still believed it rightfully belonged to his family, not to Bishop Balthasar and the church who now claimed it.

"Where can we go?" asked Ava.

"I know a place," Dieter said. "But it, too, can only be temporary." *A place that will hopefully bring back memories too painful for Hugo to consider returning to,* he thought. "It's abandoned but should give us some respite until we find something more permanent."

"Where?" asked Martin.

Instead of answering, Dieter walked to the far wall and stared out the small window—the same window he'd stared out many nights, years earlier, while waiting anxiously for Sybil when they first began their rendezvous. The sun was sinking below the horizon. Darkness was coming—the perfect time to make their escape.

"Where Dieter?" Ava repeated.

Dieter turned to the group.

"The Griswold estate—Sybil and Hugo's childhood home."

The group had meager belongings so it didn't take long for Martin, Ava, and Jerome to ready themselves for their evacuation. Martin wore a large backpack with his, Ava's, and little Peter's clothes in it. Jerome carried his weathered medical supply bag. Ava held Peter in her arms.

Dieter stayed behind, watching solemnly as the foursome dashed into the night, up the hill and east. He'd told them he'd join them soon but first needed to speak with someone in Bedburg. Martin had thought that foolhardy. "Why risk your life again? Now you *are* acting foolish."

But Dieter said it was nighttime and he'd be fine under the cover of darkness. So shortly after watching his friends and son disappear up the hill, he donned his cloak, pulled his hood over his head, and started off for Bedburg.

He kept in the shadows because, even in the darkness, the moon was bright, illuminating the streets in a murky yellow glow. Heading northeast, he made his way through the southern district until he heard loud, boisterous voices coming from a building down the road. Orange light poured out the structure's windows.

For several moments he just stood there watching the place, then sighed, steeled himself for what was to follow, and headed for the entrance.

As he approached the tavern door, his heart beat in his throat.

Who will be here? What if I'm recognized?

In months past he'd been a regular here, while doing research with Rowaine and Sybil on Heinrich's whereabouts. Thinking of those two lovely women now—his wife and their dear pirate-lady friend—brought him a pang of both guilt and grief. But he quickly buried the thought.

Pushing open the door, he stood for a moment to look around. No one stared back. *Good.* The drunks were drinking and story-telling around the tables, the whores were busy beckoning men up the stairs, and the bar counter was lined with happy customers enjoying another raucous evening.

Dieter breathed easier. Standing on his tiptoes to peer over a customer in front of him, he searched for a particular person.

And found her, easily.

The most beautiful harlot in Bedburg and surely one of the most popular. She was standing—animated and engaged—by a table occupied by three men, telling them a story that clearly had their undivided attention. Dieter couldn't help smiling, thinking how it was likely *not* her story drawing the men's attention. Not with those breasts bouncing, hips swaying, and jet-black hair flowing.

As Dieter approached, he could see how frustrated she was becoming that her audience was paying more attention to her "assets" than her story.

"Aellin?" Dieter called out softly.

The woman paused mid-sentence to look over her shoulder, ready to bite the rude intruder's head off. But, immediately recognizing Dieter, her face brightened with a warm smile.

"Priest!" she shouted, dropping her hands from the air, instantly forgetting the drunks at the table. She grabbed Dieter's arm and pulled him aside. One of the men at the table bellowed, "What's he got that we ain't got, girl?"

"A brain," Aellin shot back, drawing laughter from the others. Taking Dieter to a quieter corner, they sat at an empty table. "Haven't seen you in some time, priest. And where's that beautiful, fiery mermaid?" She'd had a fascination with Rowaine.

"Rowaine's gone. I don't know where."

Aellin pouted.

Dieter gazed at Aellin's face for a long moment. She was still as beautiful as ever. High cheekbones, fair complexion, dark eyes matching gorgeous hair, and, yes, an awe-inspiring bosom. Dieter felt a twinge of desire, immediately felt guilty, then, with much difficulty, suppressed it.

But more than just beauty, Aellin was a woman who knew her way around town. Better than probably anyone else. It had been she who'd helped him, Sybil, and Rowaine find the secret underground tunnels that led to Castle Bedburg's kitchens. Which had pointed them to Heinrich Franz's lover, Odela Grendel.

Following Dieter's eyes on her, Aeillin playfully joked, "Focus on my eyes, you lecherous dog."

Shaking the blank look from his face, he turned beet-red. "M-my apologies."

It had been months since he'd been with a woman, not since his wife's disappearance, and it literally pained him to sit next to someone so beautiful. Refocusing his thoughts, his face turned grim. "I have a problem, Aellin, and I believe it's your fault."

Her playful look disappeared. "What on earth are you talking about, priest?"

"Why did you send Adam and Martha Jacobo to my residence—no, to my *hiding place?* Why did you think I could help them?"

Aellin held out her palms. "Hey now, calm down," she said. "Everyone in town knows you're a Protestant convert, priest. It's no secret."

Dieter groaned. "But how did you know where to find me?"

Aellin looked over Dieter's shoulder, at the busy tavern, the tables, the bar, the men huddled around the hearthfire. "I have my ways of finding things out, Dieter."

Dieter narrowed his eyes. "You must stop sending people my way. You put my entire family in danger—"

"Your wife is gone . . ." she interrupted, trailing off. Then she winked and Dieter's face flushed again.

Gritting his teeth, he returned to the subject at hand. "I can't help these people." Then he thought of something else. "What made Adam and Martha Jacobo so important, anyway?"

Aellin shrugged. "Nothing, I suppose. They were simply names on a note. For some reason, someone wants to save these Protestants."

"You still have no idea where these notes are coming from?"

Aellin shrugged again. "They've been slipped under the front door a couple times, before dawn. That's all I know."

Another dead end, he thought.

He stood up, looking around the tavern, then heard something.

Or maybe not . . .

It was a conversation at the next table. Despite the room's loudness, certain words coming from two men had caught his attention. He wandered in closer, pretending to be searching for someone across the room. Aellin stood behind him. He heard one of the men say, "If the archbishop had any idea his rival was so close, he'd turn red with bloodlust." The other responded, "Gebhard has no power now, and Ernst knows that. The archbishop has nothing to fear from that old man."

Aellin whispered over Dieter's shoulder. "What are you doing?" But Dieter held up his hand to quiet her.

The first man continued. "Nonsense! *I* heard that Gebhard recently became bishop of Strasbourg. Sounds like he's trying to regain power."

"In France?" the second man said, gulping down his ale. "Then what in hell is he doing in Bonn?"

The first man shrugged. "No idea, but I can guess. Campaigning for Protestants, I suspect . . . needs more support!"

"Maybe," the second man said, finishing his own mug of ale. "Got a feelin' we ain't seen the last of that wily old man."

An idea started forming in Dieter's head. A good one, but dangerous.

He turned to Aellin and walked her a few paces away.

"What was that all about?" she asked, frowning. "Eavesdropping on my patrons?"

Dieter smiled. "I'd like to hire your services."

Aellin's eyebrows arched and she suppressed a chuckle. "*Men!* You're all the same!"

Dieter shook his head. "No, not that. I don't want your body." He paused, giving her a quick up-and-down look. "Well, at least that's not what I meant. I want your mind."

Aellin looked confused. "I don't take kindly to riddles, priest. Even *I* know my mind ain't exactly my prized possession."

"Nonsense," Dieter said, resting his hand on her shoulder and staring into her beautiful face. "I think you know more than you think you know, Aellin."

And then he told her his dangerous new plan.

Later that night, when he returned to the hill above the Achterberg estate, his premonition proved true. Hiding in the shrubbery, he watched armed guards and patrolmen from Bedburg raiding the premises they'd all vacated just hours earlier. Some searched the grounds, others milled about inside.

And there was no doubt who to blame for this.

Martin had been right. Hugo Griswold was no longer a virtuous young man. He'd obviously been transformed into Heinrich's puppet. At least with Sybil gone, she'd never have to know how her own brother had betrayed them.

As he watched the house being torn apart, and the disgruntled soldiers groaning and complaining for being brought out in the middle of the night for a pointless excursion, a new idea began taking shape in his mind.

Rubbing the stump of his aching left arm, he knew that if he decided to follow through with this new plan, someone would try to talk him out of it.

It was both foolhardy and dangerous.

But his guilt over the fate of poor Adam and Martha Jacobo was just too much for his conscience to bear. *I could have saved them.*

And if he chose this new path, there'd be no turning back.

I will be an enemy of the state.

A fugitive, an outlaw, a criminal.

If Heinrich Franz finds me, I will hang.

I know I will never see my sweet Sybil again. But at least this would honor her memory. Perhaps she'll look down on me proudly . . .

He sighed and headed off to the Griswold estate—the childhood home of his wife.

And the further he walked, the more his new idea came to life.

And by the time he reached the Griswold estate, he was sure.

Only through dumb luck had he overheard those two drunks at the tavern talking about Gebhard Truchsess—the Protestant archbishop of Cologne before the Catholic Ernst took over.

But now he knew it was not by chance. That, and today's other events, had brought him to this moment, to this life-changing decision.

I will help all Protestants and their sympathizers escape the persecution of Bedburg and Heinrich Franz.

I will protect them. I will give them refuge.

And I will bring this ruthless regime to its knees.

CHAPTER SEVEN

HUGO

Hugo and his driver left Bedburg on a cool, gray morning, traveling out Bedburg's southern gate and down a road paralleling the Erft River.

Although they didn't expect trouble traveling the short distance to Bergheim, Hugo still brought two men-at-arms with him from Bedburg's garrison. Not so much for protection as appearance—he wanted to present himself to the gentry of Bergheim as a person of importance, not just a boy and his chaperone.

The truth was, Hugo wasn't sure how he'd be received once they got there. Being sent by Heinrich Franz was tricky. An anomaly to many, Heinrich wasn't a *true* nobleman since he hadn't been born into it. So Hugo worried that, as his representative, he could be met with a certain degree of condescension.

His driver, Felix, proved to be a perfect travel companion. He spoke only when spoken to and, when he did, was easy to talk to. So whenever Hugo had a question about the notes he was reviewing during the trip, Felix was happy to offer his opinions.

From the documents, Hugo learned that Lucille Engel was the daughter of Josef Witten von Erftstadt, a wealthy old baron in control of his family's namesake, the city of Erftstadt. Hugo knew that seven electorates—or territories—basically controlled all of Germany and that a key one of those seven was Cologne, whose territory included the cities of Bedburg, Bergheim and Erftstadt, among others. Hugo understood that having power in Cologne's parliament was very significant.

According to Heinrich's notes, Josef Witten von Erftstadt's

original plan had been to give his daughter away in marriage to the powerful Koehler family, the rulers of Bergheim, specifically to be married to Ludwig Koehler's eldest son, Gustav. In return, Erftstadt would receive a seat from the elder Koehler in Cologne's parliament.

And while a part of that plan was realized and Lucille did marry Gustav, the parliamentary power never passed to the elder Josef because Gustav was killed and his marriage to Josef's daughter annulled.

From this information, it was clear to Hugo that the cities of Bergheim and Erftstadt, separated by a mere fifteen miles, were at odds. And that the tension between them was likely fueled by the two fathers—Ludwig Koehler of Bergheim and Josef Witten of Erftstadt—each one in control of his respective city and both responsible for the failed marriage.

The most important document among Heinrich's notes was of course the one reciting exactly what Heinrich hoped to achieve from his marriage to Lucille—what he would give and what he would get. It was Heinrich's plan to turn tension between the two cities and their rulers into positives. And Hugo was intrigued by the way Heinrich explained in his instructions how Hugo was to accomplish that.

As the carriage drew closer to Bergheim, in an effort to ease his nerves Hugo kept re-reading the papers. He had a heavy responsibility ahead of him and the last thing he needed was to be unprepared. Disappointing Heinrich—knowing his temper and tendency for swift, vicious punishment—was usually not a survivable option.

In Hugo's mind there was just one glaring omission Heinrich had failed to take into account: that Heinrich *himself* might not be the most viable groom in the eyes of *either* father Koehler or father Erftstadt, not to mention Lucille herself. But there wasn't much Hugo could do about that.

By the time the sun had peaked in the sky, Hugo's carriage pulled through the northwestern gate of Bergheim. And immediately, Hugo was overwhelmed.

Nearly three times the size of Bedburg, Bergheim's streets reflected the city's bustling population. Workers, peasants, and travelers buzzed about in all directions. Tall buildings of stone competed for space with wattle-and-daub huts. And nestled in the center, a large natural park occupied a huge patch of hilly, green countryside.

After his experiences in the metropolis of Trier, Hugo was well aware that the size of a town directly correlated with how poorly its inhabitants treated foreigners. The larger the city, the snobbier its citizens. Once the people of Trier had learned that Hugo was not just an outsider, but from a smaller town as well, he had not been treated kindly. The only thing saving his dignity had been the fact that he'd played the role of an inquisitor's assistant.

Which meant Hugo had his work cut out for him in this very large, likely haughty municipality.

As their carriage rumbled down the main thoroughfare, a few beggars surrounded them, shaking their cans and hats. *No matter a town's size, some things remain the same,* he thought. Not wanting to be associated with the poor—which could only exacerbate the snobbery—he ordered Felix to ride around the beggars quickly and head straight for Bergheim Castle.

As the castle came into view, Hugo realized it was not much bigger than the one in Bedburg. They rode through a grand archway with ornate spires on top, stopping in front of the mostly-brick structure where a valet greeted them. While Felix transferred the care of the carriage to the valet, Hugo took in the full measure of the place, craning his neck and squinting his eyes. Accompanied by his two armored men, he then headed to the castle entrance while Felix stayed behind with the carriage.

To Hugo's surprise, the inside of Castle Bergheim wasn't at all flashy. Unlike most castles—which tended to resemble grand cathedrals more than luxury living quarters—this one was quite practical and reasonable. No circular staircases or marbled floors or other expensive extravagances. Just a simple structure intended for one purpose only: to serve as a fortress to ward off invaders, not impress visitors.

At the bottom of the staircase, Baron Ludwig Koehler stood waiting, his arms crossed over his chest. A thin man with a beaked nose and permanent scowl, his clothing preference gravitated to the darker side: a deep purple tunic under a crimson cloak. Though Hugo had seen the baron less than three months earlier in Trier, Ludwig had clearly aged. Lines creased the edges of his temples and puffy purple skin sagged below his eyes.

Of course Hugo knew there were good reasons for Ludwig's ancient appearance. He'd lost both his sons in terrible ways: Johannes, killed by Hugo's brother-in-law, Dieter, after raping Hugo's sister; and Gustav, disappearing from Trier under mysterious circumstances and presumed dead.

"Who in God's name are you?" the sullen old man croaked.

Hugo's eyes widened. "I . . . I'm—"

"I was expecting Heinrich Franz," Ludwig continued, his frown growing more pronounced.

After a short pause Hugo said, "You don't remember me, my lord?"

Ludwig scoffed. "Should I?"

"I aided you in Trier. I was Inquisitor Samuel's assistant." The lie over the aliases he and Tomas had used came easily to Hugo.

Ludwig narrowed his eyes. "Ah, yes," he said at last. "Gregor."

Hugo was impressed that the old man had remembered his alias. He bowed. "Hugo, in fact. Hugo Griswold."

Ludwig shook his head and mumbled to himself. "Can no one speak the truth in this Godforsaken land anymore? All these names . . . you and 'Samuel' and . . . *Grand Inquisitor Adalbert.*" He made a guffawing sound. "Follow me, boy," he said, spinning around.

Hugo followed him up the stairs. Ludwig led him to the first door down the hallway and into a large room. It was an assembly hall of some kind with a rectangular table set in the middle. Two women and an elderly man were seated around it: the first woman was petite, with large spectacles and a heavy book opened in front of her; the man was fat, white-haired, and old, with a disdainful expression on a very wrinkled face; and the other lady was blonde and middle-aged, with the same arrogant sneer on her face as the old man's.

Ludwig ordered Hugo's two men-at-arms to wait at the door beside his own guards. They glanced at Hugo for approval, then obliged once he nodded, clasping their hands in front of their stomachs with pseudo-authority.

Ludwig led Hugo to the table and, with a wave of his hand, said, "This boy comes to speak on the behalf of Lord Heinrich Franz of Bedburg," he announced.

The fat old man immediately grumbled. "Rubbish!" And all eyes shot to him as he rambled on. "That peevish bastard can't even be bothered to speak with us directly? And he expects *favors?* This is nonsense, Ludwig. I'm leaving."

The old man made an effort to rise, but struggled against his massive weight.

"Oh, father," the blonde woman next to him said. "Don't be such a grouch. Sit."

The old man breathed hard through his nose, stared daggers at the woman, then relented, dropping back in his seat.

As Ludwig tried to hide his smirk, he introduced the man and blonde woman to Hugo. "I give you Baron Josef von Erftstadt and Lady Lucille Engel."

Ah. Lady Lucille! Hugo thought. He'd found her with ease. He mentally checked off that box from his list.

Lady Lucille was a handsome woman, almost regal in her fine silk robe. But Hugo was more intrigued by the much younger girl at the far end of the table, the one with the spectacles and giant book. Ludwig saw Hugo's eyes focus on her. "And that's Hedda, my scribe and assistant," he said. She seemed strangely familiar to Hugo, but he couldn't place where he'd seen her.

"Sit," Ludwig ordered, so Hugo did. "We are all busy people here," the baron continued, "so let's get to this. It comes as quite a shock to hear that Heinrich Franz wishes to marry Lady Lucille."

"*Shock* isn't strong enough a word," Baron Josef grumbled.

Shooting the old man a wary glance, Ludwig continued. "What does the new lord of Bedburg wish to achieve with this proposal? And what will he give in return?"

Hugo cleared his throat. *So that's it, then. No subtlety. No lead-*

in. Just get to the quid pro quo.

"My lord wishes to form an alliance with the fine city of Bergheim," Hugo stated.

"Let me stop you right there," Ludwig said, holding up his palm. "We are practical people, young man. Our city is prosperous—much more so than your little hamlet. Why would we need an alliance with tiny Bedburg?"

"Because Archbishop Ernst wishes it."

Which got immediate raised eyebrows from all in attendance.

"So the archbishop is behind this," Josef said. "I should have guessed. That . . . changes things."

"Why?" Lucille asked.

Meanwhile, Hedda was eagerly transcribing the conversation in her book.

"Because, my dear daughter," the old man told her, "while Heinrich may be a lesser noble, Archbishop Ernst is not. And if the former can't deliver what we want, the latter could."

Hugo was dying to ask him what it was they wanted, but Heinrich had ordered him to stay on script and not deviate. All eyes returned to the young emissary.

Calmly folding his hands on the desk, Hugo tried to appear in control despite his heart thumping so loudly he was sure the others could hear it. "My lord wants to solidify relations with Bergheim and Erftstadt," he explained, focusing on old baron Josef.

"You mean Archbishop Ernst wants these lands under strict Catholic rule," Ludwig said.

"Are they not already Catholic territories, my lord?" Hugo queried.

Baron Josef answered for Ludwig. "Technically, yes. But Erftstadt, for instance, has twelve wards—twelve separate villages, each with its own mayor in charge of how to control its ecclesiastical elements. We don't go out of our way to persecute Protestants," he said, adding, "unlike Heinrich Franz."

Ludwig nodded. "Your lord's vicious reputation precedes him."

"Yes," Lucille added, "why should I marry such a man?"

Hugo's head swiveled from speaker to speaker, beads of

sweat dotting his forehead and upper lip. Clearly, he was outmatched here. Heinrich hadn't prepared him for this.

"W-well," he said, clearing his throat again. "Lord Franz is willing to give bountiful endowments to each of you."

"That still doesn't speak to the rumor of his ruthlessness," Lucille reminded him. "How do I know he will make a good husband?"

"Was Gustav a good husband?" Hugo blurted, immediately regretting it.

Ludwig clenched his fists. "Excuse me, *boy?* What are you insinuating?"

"N-nothing, my lord," Hugo backtracked, waving his hands in the air. "I meant nothing by it. Pardon me. I only meant to say that we can all benefit from this agreement, despite any individual qualms." As he tried to will his heart rate to slow, he spoke evenly. "Lord Franz is not an evil man. He's a staunch ally of Archbishop Ernst, and he's been asked to wed. It came as much of a surprise to me as to him. I've never even seen him with a woman—"

"Except when he's burning one at the stake," Ludwig shot back.

Hugo sighed, pausing for a moment. But he knew the longer he stayed silent, the more Ludwig's remark about Heinrich's viciousness would reverberate. He needed to regain control before it was too late.

"Would you like to hear what Lord Heinrich proposes, my lords and lady?" he asked.

The men at the table griped, but Lady Lucille seemed to consider the question. "Yes," she said at last, drawing the eyes of both her father and former father-in-law. "I would like to hear his offer."

Reciting by memory from the parchment Heinrich had given him, Hugo responded. "In return for Lady Lucille's hand in marriage, Heinrich will give control of two villages in the Bedburg territory to either baron, redirecting all taxes and tithes to that baron—"

"Does that mean he's passing over land *title*, or just the right to *usage*?" Baron Josef asked.

Hugo didn't know the answer to that one, so he answered with what he knew Josef wanted to hear. "The title, my lord. The villages would be yours—to till, to police, to tax."

"That may perhaps leave one of us fulfilled, but what about the other? You can't expect us to fight over these villages," Ludwig said.

Hugo shook his head. "Of course not, my lord. For the other of you . . . Lord Heinrich will bestow his second seat on Cologne's parliament."

Both of the baron's eyes twinkled. Hugo could see their greed blossom almost like a physical thing. Until then, he hadn't known it was the *seat* they truly coveted.

Baron Josef asked, "He has two seats?"

Hugo nodded. "Archbishop Ernst granted him a second two months ago, when Heinrich advised him he wouldn't be taking residence in Bedburg. So the archbishop created a new seat for his House Charmagne estate in the countryside. Currently it's vacant, but Heinrich hopes to fill it with one of you, so that you might work together in the future."

Baron Ludwig stroked the bottom of his chin, thinking, while Baron Josef nodded slowly. Neither looked at the other, both obviously considering their sudden competing interests. Hugo, with Heinrich's guidance, had brilliantly managed to deflect these powerful men's need for more power away from him and Heinrich and onto themselves. He was quite proud of himself.

But before the two barons turned on each other, Ludwig leaned forward conspiratorially. "You haven't told us what Heinrich Franz wants in return, boy."

Hugo was now the most relaxed he'd been since arriving. He smiled coolly. "What he is giving is far more valuable than what he seeks in return."

Lady Lucille's shoulders tensed, her eyes ablaze. "What did you just say, you little heathen?"

Hugo's eyes bulged, realizing he'd seriously blundered.

Baron Josef took his daughter's cue, slamming his palm on the table, causing Hugo to jump. "That's my daughter you're talking about, you rogue!" he bellowed.

Hugo's mouth fell open.

Shit. And I'd been doing so well.

So he backpedaled. "No, no," he said, shaking his head and hands furiously, "you mistake my meaning—"

"I understood you just fine, you wretch," Josef said.

Hugo had lost them. Both the old baron and daughter appeared ready to leave the table. But surprisingly, it was Ludwig who came to Hugo's rescue. After all, he couldn't allow a deal like this to vanish over a mere slip of the tongue from an inexperienced messenger.

Ludwig turned to his companions. "I understand your apprehension," he told them, "but let's hear the boy out. He's young and stupid. I'm sure he didn't mean anything by it."

Josef thrust a finger in Hugo's direction. "Let your tongue slip like that again and I'll rip it out."

"My deepest apologies, my lords, my lady." Hugo took a breath, then continued. "All Heinrich wants is Lady Lucille's hand in marriage. And for the cities under your control to remain Catholic, a most reasonable demand—that you merely fight any Protestant uprisings and take a hard line with Calvinists and Lutherans . . . and that you'll come to Bedburg's aid if needed."

The barons looked at each other, not speaking, but Ludwig gave an imperceptible shrug.

Of course Hugo was well aware that, when all was said and done, his demands meant little to these men for three very simple reasons: first, because Heinrich was too far away to *enforce* any laws that might require them to punish Protestants in their cities. Second, because both Bergheim and Erftstadt were *already* Catholic. And third, because the barons could simply refuse to aid Bedburg if the time came, and there'd be nothing Heinrich could do about it.

In reality, Hugo realized, Heinrich wasn't asking for *anything*, really, except Lady Lucille's hand in marriage. The barons were getting a far better deal here, and Hugo could see in their eyes that they too realized this.

Was this Ernst's idea? Hugo wondered. *I've never known Heinrich Franz to do anything without careful strategic clarity . . . and an ulterior motive.*

"Those are reasonable requests," Josef said, trying to make the deal sound more neutral than it was. Turning to Ludwig, he said, "I'm getting too old to travel to Cologne and sit on that damned council. I'm willing to concede the proffered parliamentary seat to you if you'll give me the villages."

Baron Ludwig promptly stuck out his hand and Baron Josef shook it.

"Deal," Ludwig said.

Hugo smiled.

"What are the villages Heinrich is giving me?" Josef asked.

"Kirdorf and Oppendorf, my lord. The first has an abundance of arable land, and the second—"

"I want a third," Josef interrupted.

Hugo again cleared his throat. "Er, a third, my lord?"

"I'm willing to concede the council seat to Ludwig, and I'm giving away my widowed daughter in marriage. So I want a third, to make my ward fifteen villages strong."

Heinrich's parchment had warned Hugo of this, but it still caught him by surprise. Fortunately, Heinrich had included a remedy, stating in the letter, "fight for two villages, but allow a third."

Not knowing how to properly negotiate such a fight, Hugo said simply, "Lord Heinrich has authorized me to give you Millendorf as well." Millendorf was right next to Oppendorf and nearly twice its size. Both sat on the northern edges of Bedburg, while Kirdorf in the south was bigger than the other two combined.

Again, Hugo had trouble understanding Heinrich's reasoning here. He was agreeing to give up ownership of three villages that *surrounded* Bedburg, not the best defensive position to take, militarily speaking.

Baron Josef reached out to shake Hugo's hand on the deal but before he could, Lady Lucille, her head shaking back and forth, grabbed her father's hand and pulled it back.

Taking the cue, Baron Ludwig stood from his chair, straightened his tunic, and said, "You've come with a fair offer, boy, and I misjudged you. Baron Josef and I will have an answer for you shortly. But until then, you may return to your home. Good day."

Hugo's heart raced. He'd been so close.

If only that damned woman didn't have a say in . . . her own future.

CHAPTER EIGHT

SYBIL

Driving a horse-drawn cart provided by Reeve Clarence Bailey, Sybil and Georg made it to King's Lynn in three days. They traveled northwest from Strangers Shire, down a densely populated thoroughfare that provided them with safe passage—from both criminal elements and patrolmen—all the way to the seaport town. As they passed farming villages and hamlets, no one paid them any mind; they looked like two ordinary married farmers, a big brawny fieldworker and his younger wife.

They arrived at the entryway to King's Lynn in the morning. Two lackadaisical guards stopped their cart at the gate, demanding a penny payment if they intended to do trade. It was a common tax Reeve Bailey had warned them about.

Flipping one of the guards the money, the other guard asked Georg what he was bringing in.

"Vegetables, sir," Georg said, gesturing over his shoulder to the covered cart. "Potatoes and yams."

The guard walked to the back of the cart and threw back the blanket. Underneath lay four crates, three with potatoes, one filled with yams.

"Bringing them to the market, or for export?" the guard asked.

"To the docks, sir. Export."

The guard hesitated, then nodded to his mate who allowed them entry.

King's Lynn was a large town, responsible for most of the trade in West Norfolk, and the morning was a busy time for exporters, importers, and merchants alike. As their horses slowly pulled them down the road, Georg had to manuever their cart around groups of men and women pulling their own goods in wheelbarrows, crates, and carriages.

Most exports emanating from King's Lynn were wool, grain, and salt. And even though there was nothing illegal about trading textiles, Sybil and Georg didn't want to chance questions about where their textile stock was headed, so they'd simply hidden their cloth stacks beneath their vegetable crates. No one cared where potatoes went.

They passed the bustling marketplace and made their way north toward the docks. Reaching into his pocket, Georg pulled out a small map Clarence had given him. He scrunched his brow, studied the map, looked up, then down, then back up again. Finally he pointed off in the distance to a nondescript warehouse situated between several buildings.

"That's it, at least according to this map," Georg said. Handing the map to Sybil, he snapped the reins and whistled to his horses, setting course for the warehouse.

When they arrived, a man was stationed on a chair outside the building. He got up and walked toward Georg and Sybil.

"Do you head to land or sea?" he asked sternly.

"The sea, if the bishop permits it," Georg said, reciting the code phrase Clarence Bailey had instructed him to use. According to Clarence, the town was once called Bishop's Lynn, and had been a simple parish with a grammar school, market, and thriving import-export trade. In 1537, King Henry VIII took control of it because of its strategic location along the Great Ouse River, which spilled into the North Sea. He also renamed it King's Lynn for obvious reasons. But old ways die hard and most local folk—including the underground exporters and illicit fences—missed the easygoing days when the town was run by a more lenient bishop.

The man nodded and walked back to the warehouse. Reaching down, he grabbed the bottom edge of the wall and lifted up, giving way to a garage. Georg and Sybil rode their cart inside as the man quickly slid the wall back down behind them.

Rushlights and torches lit up the interior, along with of a few small windows which allowed sunlight in. The structure was quite long, with a multitude of barrels, crates and stacks of random goods and accessories lining the walls.

"I recognize the cart, but not the people riding in it," a man said, skulking out from the shadows, carrying a torch. As he approached, Sybil saw a middle-aged gent with a bald head and thick mustache, reminding her a little of Daxton.

Georg started to explain. "We've come on behalf of Reeve Clarence Bailey of Strangers Shire—"

"Yes, yes," the man interrupted. "If you knew the password, then you're all right by me. Come, get down off that thing and let me take a look at the two of you."

Georg jumped off and held his hand out for Sybil. She took it and gingerly stepped down. The man with the torch was about her height, much shorter than he looked from the cart, at least a head smaller than Georg.

"You two married?" he asked.

Georg and Sybil looked at each other, then shook their heads. It made Sybil realize that they should have prepared their background details much better beforehand.

"Shame," the man said. "Married folk seem to do the best work together."

Sybil wasn't sure what that meant. The man looked hard at both of them, making Sybil uncomfortable. She looked away and the man smirked, then held out his hand for Georg. "They call me Guy."

Georg shook it. "Georg," he replied. He nudged his chin to Sybil. "And this is S—"

"Beele. Please, call me Beele," Sybil said quickly, shooting Georg a look. She certainly didn't want everyone knowing her real name, especially if they were doing something illegal.

"So what do you have for me, Georg?" Guy asked, crossing his hairy arms over his chest.

"The same thing Reeve Bailey always has," Georg said with a shrug. "Textiles."

Guy nodded slowly. "Why didn't he come himself?"

"Worried the town guards might notice him."

"And where is he trying to send these goods? Amsterdam?"

Georg furrowed his brow, glanced at Sybil, then shook his head. "No . . . he's trying to sell them to folks in Cologne."

Guy frowned.

Noticing Guy's changing expression, Sybil wondered what they were missing. *Reeve Bailey led us to believe this was routine.*

"Germany?" Guy asked.

Georg nodded.

"Rubbish," Guy said. "The reeve of your little shire doesn't have the money to send goods to Germany! Do you know how much trouble I'd be in if I got caught? I could hang."

"I thought that's what you do . . ." Georg began, getting frustrated. "You know, send things to places they're not supposed to go."

"To an extent, yes. But Germany's too dangerous. The League would kill me if they found out I was lodging in their territory."

"The League?" Sybil asked, giving Georg a look to calm down.

Guy turned to her. "The Hanseatic League." He tilted his head a bit. "Did the reeve not tell you who you'd be working with?"

They both shook their heads.

"Please explain," Sybil demanded.

The man chuckled. "We go back centuries, my dear. That story would take the whole day. Basically, we're a confederation of guilds, formed to help merchants against the overbearing nobility, protecting them from tyrannical trade laws."

"If you're such a powerful underground organization, why have I never heard of you?" Sybil asked.

Guy's proud smile evaporated. "We aren't as prevalent as we once were. I'm the only Hansa representative here, and this warehouse is one of our last strongholds in England. But if we're caught dwelling in the waters of Germany—where the League *began* and where its roots hold strongest—it would be disrespectful and dangerous. I won't risk my ships."

Georg threw up his hands. "Then how does this work? You're telling me we've come all this way for nothing? Christ, *we* have a ship—we could deliver the damned stuff ourselves if we just knew the way!" He turned and stomped back to the cart, leaning against it.

Sybil could tell that something Georg said had sparked Guy's interest. She looked at Georg. "Is this tavern really worth it?"

Before Georg could answer, Guy said, "You have your own ship?"

"Why?" Georg asked with a shrug.

Sybil saw the wheels spinning in Guy's mind. His nose seemed to twitch, causing his mustache to quiver. After a long pause, Georg grabbed a potato from his cart and began tossing it from hand to hand as Guy stepped forward.

"If you have the means to deliver the goods, I have the instructions," he said in a low voice. "Routes, amicable ports, taxmen, traders to contact . . . all in my ledger."

Sybil had known enough greedy people in her life to know what was coming next. "But you won't give us your ledger, will you?" she asked sarcastically, hands on her hips.

"I will," Guy said, lifting his finger, "if you'll do something for me first."

"What?" Georg asked, pushing himself from the cart, tossing the potato back.

"My ledger is a valuable commodity. People would pay a hefty sum for—"

"Just get to it, man," Georg growled. "I'm growing tired of your jabbering." He stepped forward and Guy backed up. Even at his age, Georg was still an imposing figure, especially when angry.

Fidgeting for a moment, Guy cleared his throat. "A nemesis of mine has stolen goods from me. He's taken them on his ship, the *Silver Sun,* and anchored off the coast of Wells-next-the-Sea—a seaport in North Norfolk. I don't know where he plans to take my goods. Perhaps he doesn't either and is now realzing how hard it is to sell things that aren't his . . ."

"And you want your goods back," Georg stated.

Guy nodded.

"What's this man's name? The thief who stole them."

"Corvin Carradine."

Georg looked at Sybil for approval.

Sybil slowly began shaking her head.

This plan is growing too convoluted. And all so Georg can get a license to get drunk when he pleases?

"We could talk to Daxton . . ." Georg muttered, noticing that he was losing Sybil's support.

"Why would he want to do this?" Sybil asked.

"For Rowaine," he answered. "This is all for Rowaine."

As Sybil started to protest, Guy put up his hand up. "Wait, wait," he said. "You just mentioned Daxton and Rowaine?" His eyes narrowed. "What ship exactly are you . . . part of?"

Sensing a shift in power, Sybil straightened her back. "Judging by your look, I think you know what ship we're talking about, Guy."

Guy's face blanched. He started nodding profusely.

Apparently the Lion's Pride's *reputation precedes us,* she thought.

"If we can convince our colleagues to look for Corvin Carradine and the *Silver Sun,* to get your goods back," Sybil asked, "you promise to give us that ledger?"

"And more," Guy said excitedly. "With the *Lion's Pride* at the front of my fleet . . . no one will trifle with that. I'll personally lead your expedition to Germany, if you'd like."

Georg shook his head. "We won't be flying the *Pride's* colors, you fool. Talk about unwanted attention."

Guy nodded again. "Right, right, of course not." He stuck his hand out for Georg and Sybil. "Do we have a deal?"

"We'll have to talk with our friend," Sybil said.

Guy beamed. "Of course. Captain Daxton *Wallace!*"

Both Sybil and Georg were surprised at the level of respect this man was showering on Daxton. To them, Dax was still the loud-thinking, quick-talking carpenter of the *Pride,* not some feared, important pirate captain.

"We'll either return here in a week with what you want," Georg told him, "or you'll never see us again."

Sybil hopped into the driver's seat of the cart, wheeled the horses around and waited for Georg. Then she heard whispering. Glancing over, she saw Guy speaking quietly into Georg's ear.

And during the whole ride back, no matter how hard she tried, Georg would *not* tell her what the man said.

CHAPTER NINE

HEINRICH

It was nighttime and Heinrich was roused by the relentless sound of shouting and a deep orange glow coming from his small window.

He peeked out. To his shock, a large gang was gathered in front of his house, carrying pitchforks and torches. A moment later, Heinrich's mother, dressed in her robe, burst onto the scene to confront the angry mob. She raised her hands, shouting over the din of the protestors. "What is the meaning of this?"

A man stepped forward. "It's your fault, witch!" He pointed to several people in the crowd, one by one. "Her daughter! His nephew! Her cousin! My son!"

"I don't know what you're talking about!" Edith screamed.

"Of course you do!" a woman yelled back. "You cast a hex on them all, for losing *your* son!"

A rumbling chorus of agreement rose up from the crowd. Heinrich ducked from the window and crept to the front of the house.

"We are here to arrest you for the murder of Jacques, the first to fall ill from your tainted, sorcerous wool!"

Heinrich gasped, holding his breath. He was standing behind his mother now. For once, he felt protected. She seemed so strong and resilient.

"I still have no idea what you mean!" she told the man.

"Every person who has laid hands on your pelts," he shouted, "has fallen ill and died. First, Jacques, the transporter. Then, Mary, the tailor. Last, a spinstress and a maid."

"We thought it was a pox at first," another woman yelled. "Then we found out the sickness was isolated—from a single source!"

"From *you!*" someone else shouted.

"Mother?" Heinrich called out.

Edith turned, pushing Heinrich back toward the front door. "Go inside," she whispered before turning back to the crowd. "Don't hurt my child!"

It was the first time Edith had shown concern for the boy.

But to Heinrich, it was too little too late. It couldn't wipe away all the years of abuse. And now, finally, he saw the way to be rid of her.

And not even of his own making!

The gang of angry peasants took Edith prisoner, waving their sizzling torches as they led her away into the misty night.

The next morning, Heinrich traveled to the city alone to look for her.

A trial had already been set for that day. When a shackled Edith looked out into the crowd and saw her son, she screamed, "Tell them, my son! Tell them I'm innocent—that I would never do something like this!"

But Heinrich just stared.

He could have said something, but he didn't.

As he listened to the testimony at his mother's trial, he realized that it had been *him*.

He'd been the one who'd gotten all those people sick.

By wrapping the carcasses of the dead animals he'd killed into his mother's stacks of pelts in the shed—all the birds, the mice, the rats he'd slaughtered every time his mother had made him angry.

They must have rotted and become infected, poisoning all the people who'd then worn them. His mother was innocent. She had no idea she'd been selling tainted, diseased wool.

And he could have spoken up. He could have saved her.

But he didn't.

He wanted her gone.

And so on a glorious springtime afternoon, Heinrich sat stone-faced as his mother was tied to the cross and the kindling was lit.

And he watched the heat grow in intensity, feeling it sear his face, but wouldn't look away.

And he watched his mother's screams turn to cries, and her

cries turn to incoherent wheezes.

And he watched her skin transform from a molten red-hot crust to a gooey, slippery paste as it slid off her bones.

And he watched to the very end.

When it was over, a beautiful woman came up to him.

"My dear, you're the last one here. Why don't you come with me?"

Gently touching his shoulder, she turned to lead him away.

But he just stood there, silently staring off at nothing. Finally, he said quietly, "That was my mother."

The woman wrapped him tightly in her arms. "You poor, poor thing."

But he didn't cry. Instead, he felt the beautiful woman's breasts push up against him and a strange stirring tingle inside.

Then the woman moved him back to arm's-length and smiled. Her hair was blonde like the sun, her eyes blue like the sky.

"Do you have a father?" she asked.

Heinrich shook his head.

"Well I'll make sure you don't starve," she said softly.

Heinrich thought she was an angel.

"Who are you?" he asked. "Why are you doing this? I don't deserve it. I should join my mother on the fire."

"Nonsense, my sweet," she replied, wrapping her hand around his and leading him away from the carnage. As they left, Heinrich turned back, catching a glimpse of his mother's smoldering ashes.

He squeezed his radiant angel's hand tighter as they walked away.

"My name is Odela, my dear," she told him, "and I'm going to take care of you . . ."

"I'm going to take care of you—damned horse, I swear!"

Heinrich shot up, gasping for breath. His heart raced, sweat lined his face. Quickly, he knocked on the top of the carriage.

"Yes, my lord?" Felix said from the driver's seat, sounding

frustrated.

"Where in God's good graces are we?" Heinrich asked, his voice muddled with confusion.

"Almost to Bedburg, my lord."

Heinrich sunk back in his seat. He knew he must rid himself of these frightful dreams.

Felix guided the carriage to the stables. Once there, Felix stayed with the carriage while Heinrich ventured off into the city. He had work to do.

Walking through the streets, he held his head high, glancing away each time a peasant would pass too closely. For the most part people avoided him like a plague, fearing his wrath. Which was just how he liked it.

In fact, he hated being in Bedburg—its muddy roads filled with excrement, the unpleasant odors of the tanneries and slaughterhouses, the poor pathetic people.

He'd gotten used to a way of life far beyond the means of most everyone in the city. And he loved it that way. At first he hadn't wanted a big mansion in the country. He'd thought that staying near town would help him keep a closer eye on his constituents . . . and his prey.

But Archbishop Ernst had insisted on giving him House Charmagne, as a reward for his deadly work regarding the Werewolf of Bedburg. And then the archbishop had awarded him the lordship of Bedburg, for his even deadlier work in Trier.

So now he rarely stepped foot in Bedburg proper.

He knew other noblemen and women frowned on that. A lord who doesn't stay in his own town must not think much of it. But he didn't care. He had no one to impress.

Except . . . perhaps now, Lucille Engel . . .

He was in town because Hugo had warned him of the possibility of a peasant uprising. So he needed to see first-hand how the situation looked. So far, everything seemed the same as when he'd visited nearly a month ago.

Or maybe it was just that the people were better at hiding themselves and their true feelings.

It's just like those damned Protestants to go hiding in the shadows, planning and scheming. Ever since that troublemaking pastor, Hanns

Richter, first stepped onto his overturned fruit crate in front of the church, the people have taken a sympathetic ear to any rabble-rouser with something to say.

Well, not while Lord Heinrich Franz rules Bedburg!

Making his way to the garrison near the west end of town, he searched for Tomas Reiner. A rigid man-at-arms told him that Tomas wasn't there.

"Where is he?" Heinrich asked.

"At church, my lord. As he is each morning."

Heinrich's scowl grew deeper.

Church! What could that man possibly do at church? He's supposed to be cleaning up my streets!

Heinrich proceeded eastward. Passing through the circle where the homeless congregated to beg, he was pleased to see that even the beggars kept their distance from him.

At the base of the hill leading to the church, he stopped. He hadn't been inside a holy site in some time—only when forced to pray alongside Archbishop Ernst in Cologne—and he wasn't about to change that habit. So he stood there and waited, arms crossed over his thin chest, until Tomas came out almost an hour later.

When Tomas spotted Heinrich, he looked surprised—almost shocked—seeing him there. Tomas seemed to have aged in just the few short months since Heinrich had last seen him. Though his hair was still blond, the man's features seemed more weathered. Or maybe it was just that the man seemed more relaxed, less anxious, almost . . . at *ease.*

"M-my lord," Tomas said, "what brings you here to the church?"

"You," Heinrich replied, his arms still crossed over his chest. "You're my garrison commander, lest you forgot."

Tomas nodded. He'd been granted the coveted position as a reward for his work in Trier, helping Heinrich cook the wretched witches. He was now the highest-ranking military man in Bedburg, doing very nicely with a pretty—and pregnant—new wife he'd brought back from Trier. And while he owed all of his success to Heinrich, the man seemed to still harbor resentment at being, once again, under his master's thumb.

"What did Bishop Balthasar tell you in there?" Heinrich asked.

Tomas raised his eyebrows. "*Tell* me, my lord? You know that's between me and God."

Heinrich snorted. "I don't care about what you and God have to say, Tomas. I mean about the stonemason and his family."

Both men began walking. Looking uncomfortable, Tomas scratched his cheek. "He told me the man was a Calvinist sympathizer, and that you want to get rid of him."

Heinrich nodded. "What else?"

Tomas stopped and turned to Heinrich. With pity in his eyes, he said, "Do we have to kill the whole family, my lord? What could the wife or child possibly do?"

Heinrich smiled. "My young, naïve friend," he answered in his patronizing way. "They must perish so there can be no thoughts of revenge. The last thing we need is for some young pup to grow up with hellfire in his eye, aimed at *me*." He turned from Tomas, looking off in the distance. "The entire family knows my edict on Protestants, so they must all pay the consequence."

"What if they repent?"

Heinrich put his hand on Tomas' shoulder and looked into his friend's sad blue eyes. "People like William Edmond can repent with words, but never their hearts."

Tomas shook his head. "But such action could have the opposite effect. The townspeople are unsettled. Have you seen how they look at you?" He motioned to a passing, hunchbacked man who stole a glance at Heinrich over his shoulder, then quickly turned away when Heinrich stared back.

"They're terrified of you," Tomas said.

Heinrich smiled, watching the hunchback limp away. "I know. Isn't it wonderful?" Then his smile faded. "Just do as I say with the family, Tomas."

"It is Ulrich's jurisdiction to arrest guilty townsfolk, my lord."

Heinrich grunted. "Fine, but don't you dare oppose him."

"I wouldn't dream of it."

Heinrich stared into the man's eyes. "Or *me,*" he said, his tone sending the intended chill down Tomas' spine.

"Of course not, my lord."

After a moment, Heinrich broke his stare, patted Tomas on the back, and resumed walking. For a while the two didn't speak, Heinrich instead taking pleasure in just watching the reactions from people they passed. Finally, Heinrich turned to Tomas.

"What have you heard about the peasant uprising?"

Tomas shook his head. "What are you talking about?"

"Don't play the fool with me, Tomas. Balthasar told me the citizens are not pleased. He expects another Protestant uprising because of what happened at the Town Fair."

"Ah yes, that," said Tomas. "They were quite shaken from witnessing the summary executions of Adam and Martha Jacobo. Frankly, I was too. It was so . . . abrupt. Did you instruct Ulrich to do that?"

Heinrich shrugged. "Not in so many words. But I did give him a long leash to do as he saw fit with people resisting my orders regarding Protestants. They must all leave this city. Those who choose not to will die. Plain and simple."

"But my lord, there are more peasants in Bedburg—and likely more Protestants—than soldiers! That might become a bloody battle."

Heinrich clapped Tomas on the shoulder again. "Tomas, there are *always* more peasants than soldiers. That is why unrelenting force is required, to tame the masses. When their minds are properly terrorized, their will is ours. A single soldier can then easily manage ten-fold his number!" Heinrich smiled. "Also, that's why I have *you* leading my forces, Tomas. I trust you will know what to do if things get out of hand. We know it will get worse before it gets better."

"Yes, that's what I'm afraid of," Tomas said, his tone deflated.

"Just stay on the right side of this battle and you'll be fine, my friend. And report to me whenever you see anything out of the ordinary. I can't have the peasants getting the upper hand." Heinrich smiled again, then turned to leave.

"Where are you going, my lord?"

Heinrich waved over his shoulder. "I have matters to take care of at House Charmagne, Tomas. I've overstayed my welcome here."

As Heinrich walked toward his carriage, Tomas shook his head, watching the thin tyrant's black cloak ruffle in the wind.

"But it's *your* town you're abandoning, you selfish, soulless bastard . . ."

By nightfall Heinrich was back in the safe solitude of House Charmagne. He sighed with contentment as Felix brought the carriage through the front courtyard, past the perfectly aligned rows of trees leading to the mansion's front door.

If anything bad happens at Bedburg, I always have this place. My impenetrable retreat.

His eyes drifted to the palisade and ramparts surrounding the estate. Rolf Anders was waiting at the front gate, his back stooped, his hands clasped in front of him. Somehow, the man's long white beard seemed to have grown a few extra inches in the one day Heinrich had been gone.

Tightening his coat, Heinrich exited the carriage. "Rolf, what are you doing out here? You'll catch cold."

Rolf beamed. "You're right on time, Heinrich. My visitor has only just arrived."

At the news, Heinrich forced himself not to sprint to the door, or appear too excited. Instead, he rubbed his hands together thoughtfully as he walked past Rolf.

He was definitely ready for these mind-boggling, debilitating dreams to stop. To have them erased from his mind.

Rolf's man had better have the cure.

Inside the main foyer, Beauregard closed the front door behind Heinrich, then led the two men down the red carpet to the dining room.

A strange little fellow was waiting in the room. Wearing furs and pelts, he looked more ready for the forest than a castle. His hair was black and wiry, his legs bare beneath a wool skirt that stopped at the knees. Tattooed on his clean-shaven face were strange blue symbols, matching the color of his striking, blue eyes. It was impossible to tell his age.

In short, he was unlike anything Heinrich had ever seen, and Heinrich's expression said as much.

"What the hell are you?" Heinrich asked, his voice tinged with disgust.

The man chuckled, a high-pitched, annoying sound. But as soon as he spoke, Heinrich realized he was not what he seemed. His voice carried a soft, deep resonance, flavored with an edge of wisdom that contrasted sharply from his otherwise outlandish appearance.

"My name is Salvatore, my lord," the man said with a thick accent.

Heinrich tilted his head. "Are you . . . Italian?"

"I am neither of the city nor the sea. I am a nomad, a tree-dweller, a soul of the sky." The man put his palms together and raised them above his head, closing his eyes.

Heinrich frowned, unimpressed. "So you're a madman . . ." he said, trailing off. Turning to Rolf, he demanded, "Why have you brought a lunatic to my abode, Rolf? Is this your idea of a joke?"

Rolf chuckled, shaking his head. "Salvatore is no madman, Heinrich. He just has a . . . strange manner about him."

Salvatore opened his eyes and, smiling at Heinrich, gestured to a chair already pulled out from the table.

Which immediately irritated Heinrich.

This man thinks he can command me in my own home . . .

"Where did you find this lunatic, Rolf?"

When Heinrich did not sit, Rolf sat in the chair Salvatore had offered. Leaning his elbows on the table, Rolf said, "I've known Salvatore for many years. We worked together in . . . politics."

Heinrich was shocked. "He was an assassin, too?"

Before Rolf could answer, Salvatore spoke up. "Yes, I was a purveyor of evil in my youth. I sought to separate the souls and minds of the devil-worshippers from their bodies."

"He was a poisoner," Rolf clarified.

"And now I've been brought to separate your thoughts from your mind, my lord," Salvatore said, smiling, his purple eyes widening. Two rows of jagged, yellow teeth greeted his subject.

Heinrich shook his head. "I don't need any separating. I just need these damn dreams to cease!"

Salvatore nodded. "Yes, of course. In your world, you call them nightmares. In my world, they are but images shaping our lives. Every image means something. If that meaning can be deduced, it can be changed. Like waves of the ocean, some are bigger, some smaller, some devilish, some divine. You must learn to ride the waves of your mind to avoid crashing onto the sands of your soul."

Heinrich stared at the man. "What is this blasphemer getting on about, Rolf?"

Rolf smiled warmly. "He is what they call a *benandanti*, my lord. As you suspected, they hail from Italy. A visionary. Or if you will, literally, 'a good walker.'"

"I am not a blasphemous man!" Salvatore stated. "So please take that back."

Ignoring his demand, Heinrich arched his brow. "A *good walker?*"

Rolf tried to explain. "The *benandanti* claim to travel out of their minds and bodies when they sleep—like phantoms in the night. They fight with evil spirits during their body's slumber."

Heinrich shook his head. "I've always known you to be a practical man, Rolf. But I seriously think you've gone senile."

Rolf grinned. "He may be strange, Heinrich, but I've seen his methods. They work. Just give him a chance."

"What will he do?"

Salvatore looked offended, being talked about like he wasn't in the room. But then Rolf spoke several words to him in a language Heinrich didn't understand and the man's yellow-toothed smile reappeared.

"Yes, yes," Salvatore replied. "I can help you combat your dire images. I can shape your thoughts to your will."

"You can cure my nightmares?"

"If you take back what you said," Salvatore nodded.

Heinrich sighed, eyed Rolf, then finally took a seat at the table beside Rolf.

"I take it back, witch-man. You are not a heretic."

Salvatore clapped his hands suddenly, startling both Heinrich and Rolf. Kneeling down, he enthusiastically reached into a small bag hidden away. Heinrich noted that the bag was made from something very strange-looking, some kind of animal part.

Salvatore held up a vial of dark liquid. "Take this potion, my lord. It will help you fight your demons while you are entranced."

"Entranced?"

"Asleep," Rolf clarified.

Heinrich hesitated. He had no idea what was in the little vial.

At best, he thought, *it will heal me. But at worst . . . this man was a poisoner!*

He glanced at Rolf. *I've always trusted him. Why would Rolf try to kill me? If he wanted that, he'd just have Beauregard put something in my dinner.*

Heinrich snatched the vial. "Where are you staying, madman?"

"I am neither of the city nor the sea. I am a nomad—"

Heinrich put up his hand. "Yes, you already explained that." He turned to Rolf. "Give him a room for the night, Rolf." He stood up and walked behind Rolf. Leaning over the man, he whispered, "If he tries to kill me, I don't want him escaping."

"You have nothing to worry about, my lord," Rolf replied.

Heinrich took a long look at the madman, who was now seated at the table, staring down at his own palm as he traced real or imaginary lines with his finger.

Before dwelling on this bizarre image any longer, Heinrich chugged the liquid, then retired to his bedroom to sleep.

He quickly fell into a dreamless, black slumber.

With no thoughts of his brother, or his mother, or his angelic savior.

No thoughts at all.

Just nothing.

CHAPTER TEN

DIETER

"If you do this, you will never be safe," Ava told Dieter as he paced the room of the Griswold house. "You'll always be looking over your shoulder."

She smiled at little Peter, walking on wobbly legs behind Dieter, imitating him.

"I know that," Dieter said, stopping for a moment and swinging around to surprise Peter. The child bumped into his legs and giggled. Dieter whisked him off the ground and held him in the crook of his arm.

Looking up at Ava and Jerome, he asked, "Isn't this what you all wanted?"

Jerome swiveled his head from side to side. "In some ways, y-y-yes. But it p-puts us all in, in danger. Though it is ad-ad-admirable."

"You can never go back to an easy life, Dieter," Ava added. "Not while you remain in Germany."

"I've never had an easy life, Ava," Dieter said. "Plus, I don't plan to stay long." He sat down on the bench next to him and put Peter down beside him. The child quickly jumped off and began marching in circles, mimicking Dieter's pacing. Despite the tension, everyone laughed.

"Where's Martin?" Dieter asked. Dieter had returned from the Achterberg's estate early that morning, before the sun had risen, and Martin was already gone.

"He said he was going reconnoitering in Bedburg," Ava said.

Dieter scoffed. "He acts like we're at war."

"Aren't w-we?" Jerome asked.

Dieter shook his head. "We're a peaceful group, Jerome. We have no weapons and no ill will toward anyone. All I wish to do is aid the unfortunates who have fallen to Heinrich Franz's whimsy."

"Well, when you s-s-say it like that . . ."

"You remind me of a preacher I once heard," Ava interrupted, "in Bedburg, when I was still a young girl."

Dieter smiled. To him, Ava was *still* young, about sixteen. But he respected her courage. After being orphaned, she'd grown up quickly, living on the rough streets of Bedburg.

"He would shout at the top of his lungs on top of a crate," she continued, "waving his arms around spastically. He was daring—preaching near the church, of all places. At first he drew just a few . . . but before long he had dozens listening."

Dieter nodded. He remembered the man well. "Pastor Hanns Richter," he said fondly. "He was a friend of mine. A brave man." Thoughts of Hanns Richter brought Dieter back to when he was baptized. It was at a spring in the middle of the forest outside town. He remembered his head being submerged in the icy-cold water. At the time, the pastor had warned him of Heinrich Franz's malevolence, but Dieter hadn't believed him. Now, it was no secret.

In fact, it was Pastor Richter who'd helped form Dieter's decision to marry Sybil—reconciling the conflict of being a priest, loving Sybil, and somehow still retaining his faith in God. Yet the good pastor had met a horrible fate. He'd been tormented, imprisoned, persecuted, and ultimately killed outside the city ramparts when Georg Sieghart's archers mowed down his group.

Perhaps I am a bit akin to him . . .

The front door flew open. It was Martin. Ava jumped up, running to embrace him. They kissed briefly, and a pang of jealousy swept through Dieter. He longed for Sybil.

"Where have you been, Martin?" Dieter asked, with a bit more hostility than intended. "You worried us all."

"*You* ran errands last night," Martin replied with equal hostility, "and left without telling us a thing. So I did too." He reached into his tunic and pulled out a small piece of paper. "We've received another note."

He handed it to Dieter, then immediately wrapped his arms

around Ava's waist. "Aellin received it at the tavern during the night," he said, staring into Ava's eyes.

"Three names," Dieter commented somberly, staring at the note. "Likely a family."

Martin looked over at him. "Are we going to do anything this time?"

The horrific image of that poor couple dropping from the scaffold in the middle of the square filled Dieter's head. "Yes, we are." He headed for the door. "Right away."

"That's the spirit," Martin said, smiling wistfully. He and Ava joined Dieter at the door.

Dieter shook his head at Ava. "I'm sorry. Just the men are going. It's too dangerous."

Ava frowned, her eyes darkening. "Have you any idea where these people live?"

"Not really. But I have a rough idea—"

"I know Bedburg better than either of you," she said. "Every nook, cranny, alley, and gutter. Do you forget what I used to do?"

Ignoring her last comment, Martin said, "She could be useful, Dieter."

Dieter hesitated, then nodded.

And with that, the three dashed from the house, leaving Jerome alone to stare blankly out the window while little Peter stopped pacing and stared at Jerome.

They hid behind a tree at the outskirts of the town's southern gate, watching two men patrol the gate. Ava immediately made herself useful.

"I'll distract them," she said. "You two hurry in while you can."

Before Martin could stop her she was already on her way, striding toward the gate, hips sashaying in a way that made both Martin and Dieter blush.

Dieter realized how he'd initially misjudged the brave girl. Even at her young age, she was already quite a woman, reminding him of Sybil in both courage and beauty—yet still distinctly different: when they'd first met, Sybil had been innocent, fair, and kind; whereas Ava was dark, streetwise, and confident.

"Are you coming?" Martin whispered to Dieter.

Dieter nodded, shaking off the thoughts of the women in his life.

Creeping along the shadows, they walked quickly through the gate while both guards, their backs turned, carried on an animated conversation with Ava who smiled, flirted, even touched their arms.

Once they got past the gate, Ava's disposition with the guards changed abruptly. Pretending to be insulted by one of them, she walked off in a huff through the gate.

When she caught up with Dieter and Martin moments later, she had a wide smile on her face. She gave Dieter a smirk.

He chuckled. "You were right. I was wrong."

Nodding triumphantly, she asked, "So where do we go now? I suspect their abode would be in Tanner Row."

"Where?" both men asked in unison.

"Where the tanneries are, boys. Keep up." She sighed and walked off.

Dieter tapped Martin's shoulder. "Stay with her."

"You're running off again?"

"We'll work faster if we split up. Do you know what to say if you find this family?"

Martin shook his head.

"Convince them to come to the Griswold's. Tell them it will only be temporary, but that their lives are in great peril."

"What makes you think they'll believe me?"

Dieter stared into Martin's eyes. He thought of the sermons he used to give. "Speak with conviction, my friend—honestly and truthfully—and they will have no *choice* but to believe you."

His words seemed to give Martin a much-needed boost. The young man nodded firmly, then ran off after Ava.

"No matter what happens," Dieter called to Martin, "meet at the tavern by midday!"

Then Dieter headed for the tavern. There was another way

he might be able to find this family.

Since it was a busy morning in Bedburg, Dieter walked confidently—no need to hide—but still avoided eye contact with passing town guards. Minutes later, he arrived at the tavern. At this early hour it was nearly empty, though the smell of spilled ale and other foul odors lingered in the air. Only one man sat on a stool at the bar, his head stooped down in front of him. Behind the bar, a bartender was wiping the table with a white cloth.

"Where's Aellin?" Dieter called out.

"Gone for the day, priest," the barkeep replied. Dieter wondered why the man had called him "priest." He certainly wasn't dressed like one. Taking a closer look at the man, he realized he knew him. His name was Cristoff. He'd taken over for the last bartender, Lars, who'd been a secret Protestant rebel, killed fighting Heinrich Franz and his men during the hunt for the Werewolf of Bedburg.

But Dieter wasn't sure where this man's allegiances lay. Was he also a Protestant like Lars? Or an upstanding Catholic, advocating the interests of Heinrich Franz?

Dieter chuckled at the thought. *No one* was an advocate of Heinrich Franz.

"What can I help you with?" Cristoff asked. "If you aren't ordering something, I've work to do."

Dieter decided to grease the man a bit. "I'll take an ale," he told him.

As Cristoff delivered the drink, Dieter reached out and grabbed his hand.

"Hey! What are you doing?"

Dieter leaned forward. "I'm begging for your help, Herr Cristoff. Please tell me if you recognize these names." He let go of him and pulled out the note.

Cristoff read it, then sighed and nodded. "Of course I do. I see William Edmond at Mass every Sunday."

"Do you know where they live?"

"Why? Are they in trouble?"

Dieter thought for a moment.

Do I trust him? Will he betray me the minute I walk out that door?

He decided he'd have to take the chance. "I'm afraid they are," he said. "Can you help them?"

"What kind of trouble?"

"It's better you don't know, my friend. You don't want to be involved."

Cristoff thought for a moment. "You're right about that." Then he thrust his thumb over his shoulder. "They live not more than half a mile down the road, near the eastern gate."

Dieter nodded, paid for his ale, then got up to leave.

"You didn't touch your ale!"

Dieter smiled. "Too early for me. But don't let it go to waste."

"My husband is working on a house," the woman said frantically, shocked to hear her husband was in danger. Mary Edmond was plump but sturdy. She also hadn't denied being associated with the Protestants.

"Who would want to harm us?" her son asked. Wilhem was a tall, lean young man with sharp eyes and a flat face, perhaps Martin's age.

Dieter shrugged. "I'm not sure, but it seems your father said the wrong things to the wrong people."

Wilhelm hugged his mother. "I can retrieve him."

"Where is this house he's working on?" Dieter asked.

"West, near one of the slaughterhouses," Wilhelm said, suddenly looking ashamed. "I was supposed to help him. But I find no joy in stonework . . ."

Mary grabbed her son's chin. "There's no time for that, boy. Can't you see? Go fetch your father, with haste!"

"No," Dieter replied. "I have two associates who are in that part of town. They'll find him faster. I know it. It would be best if we all go to the tavern, to wait for them."

After talking quietly to each other for a moment, Mary and Wilhelm grabbed a few personal belongings, then left with Dieter. During the entire walk to the tavern Mary eyed Dieter with suspicion since the poor woman didn't know whom to trust. But apparently sensing Dieter's innate goodness she chose to believe him. As soon as they got to the tavern, Mary saw her husband walking toward them from the opposite direction with Martin and Ava close behind. Immediately erupting with a happy shriek, she raced to him.

Once the six of them had gathered in front of the tavern, Dieter said, "We can discuss the matter more when we reach our hideaway. But until then let us stay silent and alert." William, though understandably nervous, nodded, his arm wrapped tightly around his wife. He was tall and broad, with dusty brown hair and a bristly face.

They exited the area out the west gate—not the one they'd entered from—so as not to draw attention from the guards Ava had distracted earlier.

And before nightfall they'd made it to the Griswold estate.

It was then that Dieter realized there was barely enough room to house all of them. And he'd already vowed to himself not to turn anyone away. So what would they do if more came? He needed another plan.

"There is somewhere I must go," Dieter announced.

Martin looked incredulous. "Again? What are we to do with these people?"

"Make sure they stay safe. I will be back in less than a week."

"A week!" Ava cried. "No one is going to stay cooped up here for a week! I demand you tell us where you're heading!"

Dieter sighed. "You're right. We're running out of room. I'm going to seek help from the only man I know who might be able to aid us."

"Who?" Martin asked.

"His name is Gebhard Truchsess. He used to be the archbishop of Cologne before being deposed by Archbishop Ernst."

Martin and Ava's eyes widened, as did all three of the Edmond's. Everyone knew who Gebhard Truchsess was. He was the single main reason for the Cologne War—which had ravaged the principality for five long years.

"What makes you think a man like that would help us?" Martin asked.

Dieter shrugged. "I've heard he's in Bonn," Dieter said. "And with him that close, I must at least try. He could be our only hope for saving these poor souls."

CHAPTER ELEVEN

HUGO

Hugo returned from Bergheim feeling depressed. His mission with the noblemen had been to propose a wedding between Heinrich Franz and Lucille Engel. And he'd laid it out as best he could.

Yet he'd left with no definitive answer.

Heinrich would surely be disappointed. And angry. Hugo could only hope he'd understand, and wouldn't react as he usually did when things didn't go his way. At best, Heinrich's wrath was painful. At worst, fatal.

So, fearful of having to present his less-than-positive report to Heinrich in House Charmagne, Hugo's plan was to sneak into Bedburg and stay low for a few days. That would at least give him time to hear how the lord's trip to Bedburg had gone. He'd also gauge his mood by speaking to his friend Tomas, and possibly Ulrich.

As the carriage made its way toward the western gate, Hugo suddenly froze, his heart pounding. He slammed his fist into the carriage roof and popped his head out the window.

"Felix!" he yelled. "Stop the carriage!"

It was twilight, the sky pale and pink from the setting sun. He blinked several times to make sure the play of light wasn't affecting his vision. But when he looked again, the vision was still there: a half dozen men and women hurrying out the west gate.

And two of the six he knew well.

Even with a hood covering much of his head he could see the man leading the group was Dieter Nicolaus. And the woman bringing up the rear was Ava Hahn—his first love and member of his old gang. She was holding hands with another man whose face he couldn't see.

The other three in the group, walking between Dieter and Ava—two tall men and a woman—he didn't recognize.

As he thought of Ava Hahn, his ears grew hot. He'd spent many nights thinking of running his hand through her luscious hair. But there she was, holding *another man's* hand! Jealous rage quickly smothered his lust. Gritting his teeth, he jumped out of the carriage.

Felix looked confused. "My lord? The town gate is still a ways off."

Hugo waved him on. "Go ahead, Felix. Take the carriage into Bedburg, to the inn. I will see you there later tonight."

"Are you certain, my lord?" Felix asked.

But Hugo was already walking toward the group, out of earshot. Not to confront them, just to follow. Staying in the shadows, he trailed them first south, then east. They kept to the outskirts of town, away from the view of the watchtowers. After a while, he watched them continue down a well-traveled road, finally disappearing into a small house.

Which dumbfounded him.

Because the house was *his house.* At least the one he and his sister Sybil used to live in.

He shook his head and squinted, making sure he was seeing things accurately. But the moon was now bright and there was no mistaking it.

They'd entered the abandoned Griswold house, his childhood home.

Days earlier, when Hugo had last followed Dieter from Bedburg—after the Town Fair hangings—Dieter had gone to the old Achterberg estate.

And now, the old Griswold house.

The two places had only one thing in common: both were abandoned . . .

His brother-in-law and his first love were both hiding. In his own home. With at least four others.

But what are they scheming? And why did Dieter leave the Achterberg's so quickly? Why is Ava there? Should I stop them?

Too many questions. Hugo realized he needed to talk to

someone. Someone who could help him figure out what was going on and what to do about it. But who? Certainly not Heinrich. If he told him, soldiers would be sent, everyone imprisoned or worse, and the house destroyed. Is that what he wanted?

No.

But if not Heinrich . . .

Hugo left the area and headed into Bedburg, more confused than ever.

Tomas Reiner had just left the garrison, on his way home. As he sauntered down the road, a figure suddenly appeared, a dozen paces away, facing him.

Hugo. A thin smile on his face.

Tomas hadn't seen the young man in a while.

Hugo wondered if Tomas was still angry with him for killing his nephew, Severin, months earlier during their journey to Trier.

"Tomas," Hugo greeted him with a tight nod.

Tomas hid his surprise, replying calmly. "What brings you to the garrison, Hugo? I would think Heinrich Franz would have more important things for a man of your stature to do." Though he likely hoped his sarcastic tone would sting a bit, he got no reaction.

Then he noticed the boy was distraught, his eyes darting about, furtively checking over his shoulder.

"What are you scared of, boy?"

Hugo shook his head. "Nothing," he said defiantly. "I came to hear your report."

"My report?"

"Yes, what's been going on in Bedburg since my absence?"

"Your absence?" Tomas said, as if he hadn't noticed he'd been gone.

Hugo said nothing, just kept staring.

Finally, Tomas sighed. "You're becoming more and more like Heinrich Franz every day."

"That's not true. He's a murderer."

Tomas cocked his head. "As I said . . ." then trailed off, not needing to say more.

Hugo growled. "Just tell me what's happened in Bedburg."

Tomas thought for a moment. "Protestants are everywhere. Heinrich wants them dead. Same old business."

"Does Heinrich have a plan?"

Tomas snorted. "Yes, to use me, to capture and try said Protestants."

"Did you agree?"

"I told him it's not my jurisdiction to arrest people."

"And who are the latest names on his list?"

Tomas raised his eyebrows. "You know about the list?"

Hugo cleared his throat. "I know everything Heinrich tells me. He said there's a list of Protestant sympathizers making the rounds in Bedburg's gossip circles."

"That much is true," said Tomas. "This time it was the Edmond family: William, Mary, and their son Wilhelm. A family of stonemasons. Ulrich was placed in charge of arresting them but someone got to them first."

They must have been the three other people with Dieter and Ava . . .

But Hugo said nothing. He thanked Tomas for the information, gave him a curt nod, then headed down the road to the jailhouse to talk to Ulrich.

He saw the scar-faced torturer standing in front of the jail, speaking with a younger man. Though he had lost some weight, he recognized the man. Karstan Hase, another of Hugo's old thieving friends.

First Ava, now Karstan? People from his past seemed to suddenly be popping up all around him.

Hugo wondered what Karstan could possibly be talking to Ulrich about. But as he approached, he found out.

"I don't know where they've gone," Karstan was saying, then turned and spotted Hugo.

"Hugo!" he called out. "What brings you here?"

"I could ask you the same, Kars."

"We were just discussing Dieter Nicolaus and the Protestant uprising."

Hugo's heart began pounding. *How could they have located them so quickly?*

"We aren't sure where they went," Karstan finished.

Hugo quietly sighed in relief.

"Although we know where they *were*. But someone must have tipped them off and they're gone now. *Poof*—into the wind."

Ulrich eyed Hugo disapprovingly.

Hugo worried Ulrich could somehow tell that he knew where Dieter and the others were.

But how does he and Karstan know Dieter had been staying at the Achterberg's abandoned estate?

Trying to divert attention from the subject, Hugo asked, "Do you think Dieter poses a threat to Bedburg?"

"Likely not," Karstan said, "but we know that a few days ago he was talking about saving Protestants."

"Heinrich wouldn't like that," Ulrich added.

"So you've seen them?" Hugo asked Karstan. "When?"

The man nodded, his chins wobbling. "I stayed at their hideaway for a night, to speak with Ava . . ." With a taunting tone, he added, "Oh yes, Hugo. Ava is alive and staying with the priest!"

Hugo kept his expression blank. "I don't believe you," he said.

Karstan nodded again. "They were staying at the Achterberg's and were in possession of a note with Protestant names on it. The names of the people—"

"The two Ulrich killed at the Town Fair," Hugo finished.

So Karstan spied on Dieter and Ava, then betrayed them to Ulrich, had their hideout raided, and got two people killed the next day. Quite the busy man. Perhaps I've underestimated my old friend.

Hugo had learned enough. He couldn't fake ignorance much longer. They'd see through it.

The problem was, he didn't know if he should laugh or cry. He couldn't interpret his own feelings about what was happening.

All he knew was he had to get away from these people.

So he bid Ulrich and Karstan good night and left.

By the time he returned to Felix and the carriage, and arrived at House Charmagne, it was nearly dawn. He hoped Heinrich was still sleeping. He had much to think about before speaking with him.

When he walked in, Rolf was waiting. The old man smiled. "How did things go in Bergheim?" he asked, as they both proceeded down the hall.

"I'm not sure," Hugo answered. "I think I did all right. But I've gotten no firm answer."

"That's the way of the nobility, my boy. Indecisiveness. They can't seem to butter their own bread without help from a friend." Rolf chuckled, clasping his hands behind his back, adding, "Promise me you won't be like that when you're a lord."

When I'm a lord? The very idea caught Hugo off guard.

Rolf had always been kind to him, calm and respectful, and Hugo had always appreciated that. In fact, as far as Hugo was concerned Rolf was the only honest person around. He hoped to be like Rolf when he got older—wise yet wily, and fatherly and understanding when appropriate. Clearly that was how Rolf had survived as long as he had around so many unscrupulous and vicious characters. More than just a trusted friend, Rolf had become a father figure to Hugo, replacing the father he'd lost. The sudden thought of his own father, Peter, caused Hugo's shoulders to slump.

"What's the matter, boy?" Rolf asked, instantly picking up Hugo's discomfort.

Hugo shook his head. "Nothing."

"I'm sure you handled the nobles just fine," Rolf assured him, misinterpreting his sadness. "After all, you made it back here, didn't you?"

Hugo tilted his head. "Should I not have?"

Rolf smiled and shrugged but said nothing. They came to the master's chamber and Hugo heard coughing on the other side of the door. With a sigh, he knocked.

A raspy, angry voice answered. "What?"

"It's Hugo, my lord."

The tone changed quickly. "Ah! Hugo, my boy. Come in, come in. Rolf, you old dog, why didn't you tell me he'd returned?"

Hugo pushed open the door. His eyes widened as he saw Heinrich in bed, blankets pulled up to his neck, sweating profusely, his skin waxy yellow.

"My God," Hugo said. "What in Christ's name happened to you?"

Heinrich chuckled, then broke into a coughing fit. "I'm a bit sickly. That's all. Come, come. And close the window, will you? I'm freezing."

Hugo nodded to Rolf, who left his side and shuffled back down the hallway to his room. Hugo walked to the window and, before closing it, peered outside to admire the rowed trees in the courtyard.

"Come here, boy. Let me take a look at you," Heinrich said, waving at Hugo with a bony hand.

Hugo walked to the bed.

"How did your trip to Bergheim fare? Were you successful in conveying my request?"

Hugo nodded. "I think it went favorably." He didn't want to disappoint Heinrich in his current state. "They are discussing the proposal as we speak. I believe they'll say—"

Heinrich raised his hand. "Let's discuss this when I feel better, yes?"

Hugo stopped talking and nodded.

"You look . . . sad, boy. Why? Is it because you hate seeing me like this?"

Of course that wasn't it. It was thoughts of Ava and Dieter hiding in his old family home, but Hugo wasn't about to tell that to the most bloodthirsty man in Bedburg.

"Yes," he replied.

Heinrich patted Hugo's hand. Hugo stifled a grimace, pulling his hand away from Heinrich's sweaty, slimy, repulsive hand as casually as he could.

"What's wrong with you?" Hugo asked.

Heinrich blinked a few times. He looked even thinner than usual; clearly he hadn't been eating. And his normally gray eyes were black, the lids red-rimmed.

"Rolf enlisted a man to help me rid myself of the awful dreams I've been having."

He stopped. Hugo waited for more.

Heinrich smiled. "The good news is, I think his potion worked. I haven't dreamt in days. The bad news is . . . I think the man's trying to kill me." His smile turned to a scowl. "Be a dear and check on the man for me? Make sure Rolf is keeping him close at hand . . ."

"Of course, my lord." Hugo hurried off. At the door he asked, "What do you plan to do with this man?"

Heinrich shrugged under his blanket. "I suppose I'll have to kill him, if he doesn't succeed in killing me first. What else is there to do?"

Hugo sighed and left the room, heading downstairs to check on the "houseguest." But at the end of the hall Beauregard, the white-headed butler, was waiting for him—a smile half-hidden inside his mounds of wrinkles. The jovial expression surprised Hugo. He'd never known Beauregard to offer *any* expression, much less a *happy* one.

"What is it, Beauregard?"

Beauregard's gloved hand came out from behind his back, offering Hugo a letter.

"A message for you, young master."

Hugo took it. It was sealed with red wax by a house he didn't recognize.

Tearing open the envelope, he skimmed the lines and his melancholy immediately lifted.

Barons Josef von Erftstadt and Ludwig von Bergheim had formally accepted his proposal. Heinrich Franz and Lucille Engel were getting married.

CHAPTER TWELVE

SYBIL

Sybil tightened her coat. It would be a cold day at sea. The men had tried to convince her to stay in Norfolk, that their journey would be too dangerous, but it had been Rowaine who'd spoken up on her behalf.

Rolling into the living room on the crazy chair that Daxton had fashioned for her from wood, an axle, and carriage wheels, Rowaine had spoken of things the men never thought much about.

"Every woman deserves to have the wind in her hair if she wishes," Rowaine said to Daxton and Georg. "You're just lucky I can't go with you."

Georg strapped his heavy belt around his waist—the belt getting tighter and his waist rounder—and fastened his bow and quiver over his shoulder. "I wish you could, Cat."

Daxton nodded. "You have the courage, Beele, I'll give you that. You've taught me to appreciate what a woman like you is capable of. But things may get violent."

"She can handle it," Rowaine said, speaking of her good friend. She stared at Sybil with her piercing green eyes. "Can't you?"

Indeed, Sybil was ready to stand up for herself. "I'm accustomed to violence," she said. "Do you forget, Georg, that I was there when Dieter slew Johannes von Bergheim? Or that I was there at Claus' inn, Dax, when war broke out with Gustav?"

"Yes, you were," Daxton acknowledged. "But can you kill a man? If you're engaged with a ruffian who thinks nothing of your life, could you put an end to his?"

Rowaine pushed her wheeled chair out of the room, returning a few moments later with a pistol. "Take my gun," she said, handing it to Sybil. "Just in case."

Sybil gulped, then tucked the gun beneath her dress. "I can if I must," she said. "But I'm also going to try preventing you savage men from pushing things that far."

Georg and Daxton both went quiet. Georg placed two pistols in his waistband and strapped a sword to his belt. There was no point in arguing—especially when Rowaine took Sybil's side. She was a hardened captain whose fearlessness had clearly rubbed off on Sybil.

There was a knock on the door, then before it could be answered Claire Durand and her husband, Leon, entered. Claire had agreed to watch Rowaine—much to Rowaine's chagrin—while Leon joined the crew on the *Lion's Pride*. Behind Claire and Leon stood seven more local men—husbands and textile workers and builders—who'd also signed onto the ship. Daxton had figured that eleven crewmen would be enough.

Claire held a large banner of soft wool folded in her arms. Holding it up to Daxton, she smiled and said, "Your new pennant, finished just this morning."

It displayed a replica of the Saint George's Cross: a red cross on a white background, one of the most common flags in England. The *Lion's Pride* would be hiding in plain sight.

Daxton bowed and took the flag. And with that, they were ready.

The large group left Strangers Shire while it was still dark, the sky a vibrant purple in anticipation of sunrise. By the time the sun cleared the horizon, they'd be onboard the *Pride*.

The wind whipped the salty air through Sybil's hair, making her squint as she stood by the helm. By now the sun was halfway to its peak in the sky, but clouds shielded its rays and the North Sea was cold and dreary.

When they'd boarded ship, Daxton had ordered two of his men to replace the *Pride's* flag—a leonine face biting into a gold coin—with the Saint George's Cross Claire had made for them. They'd then rowed out of the little cove they'd stored the ship in and headed west around the coast toward the seaside port of Wells-next-the-Sea.

Once the wind picked up, they released the mast furls and stowed their oars. Maneuvering around other ships, they soon cleared the port traffic, their full sails gliding them along a vast empty ocean for as far as the eye could see.

Daxton ran his hand over the wheel, admiring its wood, while Sybil watched.

He seems so at ease.

She turned to Georg, sitting on the bench, his hands nervously clenched together.

And he doesn't.

Georg saw her staring and, reading her thoughts, said, "I don't much like the sea."

Sybil chuckled. "Then why didn't you stay behind with your daughter?"

"This entire plan is my fault, Beele. I must see it through. Even if I die."

Sybil walked over to the man, resting her hand on his broad shoulder. "You won't die, you fool."

Georg ignored her comment. "And to think," he muttered to himself, "all this so I can just get drunk whenever I wish."

Sybil smiled.

The goal of this journey was to get Guy's ledger from King's Lynn, so they could ship the textiles to Germany, which in turn would earn Georg his building license from Reeve Bailey so he could build his tavern.

All this for that.

But even though they both joked about it, Sybil knew there was more to Georg's plan than just the tavern and getting drunk. "You're doing this for Row, you big oaf. We all know that. So you can support her and she can live reasonably."

Georg nodded. "She tried to stop me from this wild plan. And maybe she was right . . ." he trailed off. Sybil started to tell him that his lack of confidence was unbecoming but before she could Leon called out from the lookout tower.

"A ship on the horizon! Anchored not far from the coast!"

Daxton walked to the gunwale and brought out his spyglass.

With Georg and Sybil standing behind him, he surveyed the situation.

"Well?" Sybil asked.

Daxton smirked. "It's got a big, round, silver circle on its hull."

"The *Silver Sun,"* Georg said.

Sybil smiled. "Let's charge him!"

"Not so fast, my dear," Daxton said. "We don't yet know what we're dealing with.

Putting his spyglass away, he cupped his hands over his mouth and shouted to Leon at the lookout tower, "When I give the command, lower the Saint George and raise the lion!" Then he crossed his arms over his chest, looking every bit the captain he'd become. "Let's see what kind of a scare we can give them."

Daxton aimed his pistol at the chest of the young man. The man, maybe twenty, had scruffy brown hair and a handsome face, and Sybil couldn't take her eyes off him. Her heart even fluttered a bit when his eyes locked onto hers.

Georg and Sybil stood behind Daxton, who had taken command of the situation. The *Silver Sun* was much smaller than the *Pride,* with seven crewmen. Once the crew had seen the *Pride's* English flag lowered and its true lion flag raised, their captain had wisely decided not to engage or try to flee.

When they'd first breached the ship, Daxton had been tense, not having boarded another vessel in some time. It brought back violent memories that he'd just as soon leave behind, so it was no wonder that the knuckles of the hand now aiming his pistol were bright white. Sybil touched his shoulder and he flinched.

"You'll lose feeling in that hand if you clench any harder," she said softly.

Daxton inhaled quickly. Glancing around he realized he was the only one holding a weapon. Slowly he lowered his arm, his face flushed—part embarrassment, part relief.

Meanwhile, near the stern, Georg, Leon, and the rest of the *Pride's* crew were keeping watch of the rest of the men of the

Silver Sun. Though the situation was tense, it was not overly so, which Sybil reckoned was a good thing.

Jittery men made stupid decisions.

Her eyes moved from man to man.

Good thing I'm here. Our men are itching for combat, but it doesn't have to be like that.

Over Daxton's shoulder she called out to the handsome young man. "What's your name?"

"Corvin Carradine, ma'am," he said evenly. Sybil found it interesting that, though he was clearly in charge of the ship, he hadn't included "Captain" in his title. Also, he spoke quite politely.

"Well, Corvin, do you know why we're here?"

The young captain scanned the men around him. "I can guess why *they're* here," he said, his eyes moving to Leon, Georg, and Daxton. "But I haven't the slightest idea why *you're* here, ma'am. Please don't take offense, but you don't look like one of Guy's scoundrels."

Sybil arched her brow. "Scoundrels? You're the one on the run, are you not? Wouldn't that make you the vagrant?"

The young man flashed a wistful smile. "I suppose we're all champions in our own story, no?"

Sybil couldn't hide her smile.

"I will respectfully say, however," the man continued, "that your group is on the wrong side of this."

"Why do you say that?"

"Well, you're here to kill me, are you not?"

With a look of surprise, Sybil shook her head. "No one said anything about killing. We're simply here to gather the stolen goods you have—"

"Actually, we are," a voice from behind said. Everyone turned.

Georg stepped forward, pulling a long knife from his belt. "I hope there's no hard feelings, boy. But let's get on with it, shall we?"

Standing between Georg and the young captain, Sybil held her arms up. "Hold on now, Georg. This wasn't part of the plan."

Georg frowned at her. "It's what Guy whispered in my ear, Sybil."

Upon hearing their names mentioned, Corvin took a step back.

"Sybil? Georg?" he questioned, staring hard at Sybil. "So *you're* the Daughter of the Beast, ma'am? Piracy does not suit you, I'll say. You are much too beautiful for it."

Sybil chose to ignore that, assuming it nothing more than an attempt to buy one's life back. She looked at Georg. "What could we possibly gain from killing this man?"

"Don't get attached, Beele. He's trying to charm you. This is why it's better that women don't participate in these things."

"Oh, rubbish, Georg! Answer my question."

He shrugged. "I don't know why Guy wants him dead. It's none of my business. But if we want that ledger, it must be done."

"Is it really worth it, Georg? All for a builder's license?"

Corvin began chuckling. Sybil eyed him with a perplexed look.

"Is that what Guy told you?" he asked, "That if you kill me, his ledger is yours?"

Georg narrowed his eyes but didn't answer.

"Why do you think he wants me dead?" the man continued. He waited for a response, then sighed. "*I* have that rogue's ledger, my friends."

Sybil turned back to him. "Is that why he wants you dead—you're stealing his business?"

Corvin shook his head and grinned. "Oh, no. *Guy* is the thief, my lady. I am sailing to Amsterdam to show the ledger to the other representatives of the Hanseatic League, to prove that Guy is a thief. He's been undercutting and stealing wares from the League, right under their noses, for years. He wants me dead so that I can't expose him."

A long moment of silence fell over the crowded deck.

Finally Georg muttered, "This is madness," shaking his head, still gripping his knife.

Sybil scratched a spot above her forehead, then pointed to the barrels in the ship's holding tank beneath the main mast. "So you didn't steal these goods from Guy?"

"Well, yes. That I did," Corvin admitted. "But they weren't his to begin with. They're filled with sugar and tobacco, all property of the League."

Daxton joined the conversation. "So you just expect us to let you go and take your word for it?"

Corvin smiled again, dimples forming in his cheeks. "Expect? No. Hope? Absolutely."

Sybil looked at Georg and Daxton. "I can't make sense of this. What do you think?"

Daxton spoke first. "I say we kill him and be done with it. You can explain it to your friend in King's Lynn when you get there with his ship and barrels."

Daxton's burst of savagery surprised Sybil. She turned to Georg, who seemed a bit more thoughtful.

"I don't know if we can trust him," Georg said. The young captain, who'd been holding his breath as his fate was decided, exhaled. His chest deflated and his shoulders slumped.

"But," Georg added, "I say we take him to port and figure out what to do with him then. Either way we get the ledger and our work is done. Now that we've heard this man's story, I'm not comfortable killing him based on hearsay alone."

Sybil nodded. She turned back to Corvin, stroking her chin. After a moment, she nodded. "I agree."

Georg turned to the man. "You are no longer captain here; you are our prisoner."

Surprisingly, Corvin smiled. "Of course, my lord. That's all I can expect. But I think we can help each other."

They glared at him, waiting for more.

"First, I have the ledger," he said. "And I'm guessing you have things you'd like to trade overseas—illegal things, or you wouldn't be speaking with the Hanseatic League. Second, I know the people you need to speak with to make that happen." He surveyed his captors, then put up his hands. "So why even deal with Guy at all?"

"Simple," Sybil answered. "First," she said, mocking the young man, "we don't trust you."

Corvin frowned. "Fair enough. But can you harbor an idea

of mine?"

Sybil sighed. "What is it?"

"I'd like to store my barrels at your port," he said. "I can't let Guy get hold of them."

Sybil turned to her companions.

Georg shrugged. "We're returning to the shire anyway, to send back the rest of our crew. I see no harm in that."

Daxton added, "We can always bring the goods to Guy if it turns out he's their rightful owner."

Sybil wasn't so sure. Something about this charming rogue storing his goods at their shire bothered her.

He'd know where we live. She thought back to Gustav Koehler. How he'd found them, disrupted their peaceful shire, caused utter mayhem and destroyed Dieter's church.

No, I'll never let that happen again. Unless . . . we don't store the goods in town, but just nearby . . .

"Beele?" Georg said, gently shaking her shoulder.

She turned to him with a blank look.

"It's up to you," Daxton added.

She felt the crew staring at her.

I really have taken Rowaine's place.

Though it unnerved her, it also gave her a new sense of power.

Then she thought of something.

She smiled. "I have an idea, what we can do with this young man."

And with that, the two ships headed back to port.

The *Silver Sun* captained by Daxton; Sybil at the helm of the *Lion's Pride.*

They decided to stow the cargo from the *Silver Sun* in the same cove that the *Lion's Pride* usually settled in. Georg would stay onboard, keeping watch over Corvin until Sybil returned in the morning. Once Corvin's crewmen were released from their ship, Corvin would be no threat by himself.

It was Sybil's idea, the only way to keep Corvin from

knowing where their actual home was.

And the young captain had seemed to accept his fate, acting not at all like a scared prisoner. In fact, to Sybil he seemed a bit *too* confident, though she did find him pleasant to be around, which gave her pangs of guilt. It made her realize how desperately she missed Dieter. It had been so long since she'd been with a man.

Once they'd left Georg and the young captain at their hidden port, Sybil, Daxton and the crewmen headed back to Strangers Shire.

As Daxton and Sybil walked together, Daxton—seeming to read Sybil's mind—volunteered, "I miss my wife and daughter." His wife was on the other side of the North Sea, on their farm near Amsterdam. Sybil, with similar longings, indeed empathized with the man.

The rest of the way home was a time of quiet contemplation, everyone with much on their minds.

Back at Leon and Claire's house, Sybil happily described their adventure to Rowaine, watching Rowaine's face streak with envy as she heard of their successful confrontation at sea. Then, when the night grew late, Sybil helped Rowaine from her rolling chair, half-dragging her unceremoniously into a bedroom with Rowaine's arm wrapped tightly around Sybil's shoulder.

Sitting on the edge of the bed, Sybil pulled Rowaine's covers up, then gently stroked her arm as she quickly fell asleep. Watching her sleep, tears came to Sybil's eyes, overwhelmed with both pity for her good friend and thoughts of her beloved Dieter. But with Leon and Claire standing near the bedroom door, she stifled her sobs so she wouldn't be seen as weak. Leaning over Rowaine, she whispered, "I pray that you feel better and that you recover, my dear friend. God has a purpose for you. I know it."

It was something Dieter would have said, though Sybil wasn't totally convinced of its truth quite yet. She stood up and followed Leon and Claire into the living room where Daxton was drinking ale by himself at the table, staring blankly into the unlit hearth. From a different room, Claire's young daughter Rose began crying so the French couple excused themselves for the night.

Once they were gone, Daxton looked up at Sybil. "Big day ahead of us tomorrow," he said, a bit drunk.

Sybil nodded, still thinking about poor Rowaine.

"Today I saw more action than I have in a long time," Daxton continued. Despite his inebriated state, it was clear to Sybil how much he had missed being at sea.

"Go to sleep, Dax," she urged.

Daxton stared at her with glazed eyes. He looked like he wanted to say something—that he *needed* to say something—but instead just nodded dumbly, closing his mouth and resting the side of his head on the table. Within seconds, he was snoring.

Rolling herself up in a blanket, Sybil lay on the bench in the corner and closed her eyes.

A loud thud.

Sybil's eyes shot open. She wasn't sure if the noise was real or a dream. She lay perfectly still and listened.

A moment later she heard it again. Very loud.

Then a groan pierced the quiet night.

She jumped up, sweating, her heart racing. Looking around in the dark, she could make out Daxton still fast asleep on his chair, snoring.

She heard another groan and dashed out of the room toward the sound.

Coming from Rowaine's room.

Racing down the hall, she almost ran into Leon and Claire, both in their robes, anxious looks on their faces. Leon held a lit candle as they all rushed into Rowaine's room.

She was sprawled out on the floor by the bed, on her back, rubbing her head and moaning.

"Row! Are you all right?" Sybil cried, rushing to her friend's aid.

She noticed a spot of blood on the ground where Rowaine's head had apparently hit. Sybil cradled her as Rowaine went into a fetal position and started weeping. Gently stroking Rowaine's fiery red hair, suddenly all of Sybil's pent-up feelings burst forth—pity, sadness, helplessness.

"Shh," she said softly. "It's all right. You must have had a bad dream and rolled off the bed."

Trembling in Sybil's arms, Rowaine's continued sobbing. "I-it's not all right, Beele. I'll never be the same!"

Except for the sobs, several long moments of silence followed.

Suddenly Claire let out a gasp.

"My God," Leon echoed.

Sybil turned to see what they were looking at. Wide-eyed, Claire made the sign of the cross over her heart.

"What?" Sybil demanded.

Claire pointed. "It's her . . . her—"

"Her legs!" Leon cried out. "They've moved!"

It was true. Bent at the knees, Rowaine's legs were now up toward her chest.

Sybil's mouth fell open.

"By God, it's a miracle!" Claire cried happily. "You prayed for it, Sybil, and it happened!"

Their loud voices woke Daxton who came rushing in, a knife in his hand, his eyes in a red-rimmed haze. "What the hell's the commotion?"

"Beele has worked a miracle!" Leon announced, still pointing. "Rowaine's legs are working!"

PART II

Resist the Iron Fist

CHAPTER THIRTEEN

HEINRICH

Still sniveling from the effects of that damned potion, Heinrich spent the entire day alone in bed, giving himself plenty of time to dwell on things troubling him. Like, how he couldn't trust anyone. That madman, Salvatore, was a perfect example. The so-called *benandanti* was still at House Charmagne and wouldn't be allowed to leave until Heinrich figured out what to do with him. Heinrich had no doubt that the man had tried to kill him. Yes, his herbal rubbish had apparently nullified Heinrich's dreams. But at what cost?

Will I die on this bed, surrounded by people who only want to see me in a casket?

So, after a day filled with such negative thoughts, Heinrich was understandably relieved to hear Hugo's good news: that Lucille Engel had agreed to marry him. Well actually, that her father, Josef, and her ward, Ludwig, had come to that agreement.

Of course he hadn't been quite as happy to hear that Hugo had given away so much of his land—*three* villages surrounding Bedburg—mostly because he didn't trust Baron Josef, the man receiving those properties. He also wasn't ecstatic about giving away his empty seat on Cologne's parliament to Baron Ludwig.

But Hugo had assured him these concessions were necessary to secure the marriage agreement.

Ernst had better properly reward me for all this.

After all, it was the archbishop's idea to marry a rich, bountiful Catholic woman. And the benefits flowing from that union would all go straight to the archbishop, not Heinrich, since, try as he might, Heinrich just couldn't figure a way to personally profit from the arrangement.

Heinrich decided he needed to get away from his stuffy

chambers and breathe some different air. He got out of bed slowly and, still in his sleeping robe, headed down stairs to feed his pets. Walking through the hall, he passed an opened doorway. Glancing in, he noticed the *benandanti* sitting off in a corner, conversing with himself. *No,* Heinrich corrected himself. On closer inspection the man was conversing with Rolf, who sat across from him, partially-obscured by the open door. The two were speaking in hushed tones and Heinrich wasn't sure what to make of that.

He continued to the end of the hallway, then down the stone staircase that led to the cellar. The room was cold, damp, and smelled sickly and pungent. He walked to a barrel against the wall to his right and reached in, pulling out several morsels of rotting meat. He took them to the far end of the room where a large cage stood. He rattled it several times until he heard low growling. Six wolves crept out from the darkness, warily circling the cage. As they sniffed and snarled, Heinrich tossed in the meat strips and waited.

But the hounds ignored the food, instead continuing to snarl, their yellow eyes fixed on Heinrich as they continued to pace.

"Eat your food, damn beasts," he yelled, knocking on the cage bars. But the wolves turned away, ignoring both him and the food, and continued their pacing.

Perhaps in my ill state, they don't recognize me.

He watched as they kept circling.

Either that, or something is making them edgy.

He heard the patter of steps descending the stairs behind him. Turning, he saw Rolf and his madman friend. To Heinrich's disgust, they approached the cage and stood beside him.

"Beautiful beasts," Salvatore said in his thick Italian accent. "The minds of men trapped in the bodies of savage animals."

Rolf chuckled at Salvatore's strange comment, then said to Heinrich, "You shouldn't be down here, my lord. You'll get sicker."

In no mood for Rolf's wise words, Heinrich snapped, "Don't tell me where I should be in my own house, old man." Suddenly he wanted to be back in bed. His head ached and he wanted to be rid of these two. He eyed Rolf and Salvatore from the corner of his eye.

Perhaps they're plotting together. Could Rolf be a Protestant sympathizer? He's the only person who really knows my plans—to punish the Protestants and use my marriage to Lucille Engel to unify the Catholics.

He stroked his chin, his thoughts growing darker.

Yes . . . perhaps the old man believes I've overstayed my welcome and he thinks it's time for fresh blood. After all, this crazed witch-man could not have acted alone in trying to kill me.

At that moment, Heinrich wished he were armed. Then with a quick move he could slash Rolf's soft neck beneath his jolly white beard and be done with him. And before his madman friend had a chance to react, he could plunge the same blade into his crazed skull, perhaps pry it open to see what his madness really looked like.

Salvatore interrupted Heinrich's thoughts. "They're not eating," he commented, quickly moving his hands around in a crazy, waving motion.

"What are you doing?" Heinrich asked, wanting to kill the man even more. Salvatore muttered a few more words under his breath, this time in a language Heinrich didn't understand, then made a strange whistling noise.

The wolves stopped dead in their tracks, their growling and pacing ceasing immediately. Then, amazingly, the animals stood on their haunches, their tongues lolling out their mouths, their eyes fixed on Salvatore in subordinate stares.

Alarmed, Heinrich asked, "W-what have you done to my hounds?"

Salvatore continued his strange, high-pitched whistle, tapping the top of the cage and snapping his fingers. He pointed to the meat near the center of the cage. Immediately, the wolves got off their haunches, walked slowly to the pile of food, each choosing a different piece without conflict. Then each of them withdrew to a different spot and calmly began eating.

The wolves *always* fought over food, which Heinrich enjoyed watching. Survival of the fittest and all that. So seeing this totally unnatural behavior shook Heinrich to his core. Something was not right with this madman and his sorcerous ways.

Seeing Heinrich's reaction, Rolf tried to explain, "Some *benandanti* are well-known wolf charmers, my lord." He smiled. "I believe Salvatore clearly has the touch."

Salvatore rapidly nodded. "The touch of the ancients. Yes, yes. The pull of the spirits."

Heinrich scoffed. He'd had enough. Pulling his robe more tightly around his waist, as if to ward off some unknown force, he stormed away. As he climbed the stairs he could hear the wolves calmly tearing off and chewing their food.

No snarling, no growls, no fighting.

Which only made him suspect Rolf even more.

That man is clearly trying to get rid of me. But would he really try replacing me with such a lunatic as Salvatore? I must learn more about this witch-man.

Once up in his room again, Heinrich donned proper clothes, then set out with Felix in the carriage for a trip to Bedburg.

It was time to pay a visit to his favorite torturer.

"You've gone soft on me, Ulrich," Heinrich told him in a low voice.

Scratching his nose, Ulrich shrugged. "I just don't think there's anything I could learn of this man. But if you wish to bring him to me, I will certainly interrogate him for you," adding almost as an afterthought, ". . . my lord."

"You've never heard of this . . . *benandanti*?"

Ulrich shook his head. "I am not a learned man."

Heinrich groaned, then another thought struck him.

Could it be Ulrich plotting against me? Maybe they're all working together.

His eyes moved past Ulrich to the little room behind him, not much larger than a jail cell. In the middle stood a table with a small book on it, a book that Heinrich knew was Ulrich's personal ledger. Heinrich's eyes narrowed.

Ulrich has had that ledger for as long as I can remember. He writes every death and execution in it, as well as the names of all suspected Protestants. As I've instructed him to do. If anyone were to get a hold of that book . . .

"And what has happened to the stonemason family I was warned about?" Heinrich asked Ulrich. "What were their names again?" though he remembered them quite well and was just testing the man's memory.

Ulrich responded quickly, without checking his ledger. "William and Mary Edmond, and their son Wilhelm, my lord."

Heinrich nodded slowly. "And?"

Ulrich looked away, touching the scar on his face. "They've managed to escape my reach, my lord. I don't know how. Someone must have alerted them."

Heinrich's stomach twisted into a knot. This is exactly what he feared. Someone *had* gotten to Ulrich's ledger.

Or perhaps Ulrich himself had allowed *someone to see it. That is a reasonable explanation. Who else could warn these damned Protestants if not Ulrich?*

But Heinrich knew he couldn't let his suspicions be known. So he said nothing, instead just breathing in deeply.

"I apologize, my lord," Ulrich said. "I've sent patrols from Tomas to look for them. They will be found."

"Tomas said it wasn't his jurisdiction to arrest people," Heinrich replied, trying to mask his growing anger.

"That may be the case," Ulrich answered. "But once they became fugitives, any lawman has jurisdiction. Tomas, as garrison commander, has the power of the law on his side, and I told him so. I don't have the manpower for a search party, but Tomas does."

Heinrich frowned. "I want that family found, Ulrich. We need to set an example, as you did at the Town Fair, before the people forget."

"It will be done, my lord." Ulrich bowed, hoping Heinrich was done.

But he wasn't. "And even more than that family, I want the man responsible for warning them we were coming! Do you understand?"

"Of course, my lord," Ulrich said. "He will be found."

Yes, Ulrich could easily be the traitor. He has the means—the ledger, and he knows the people—especially the criminals—better than anyone!

But what is his motive?

Heinrich nodded to Ulrich, then left the jailhouse. The sun was setting. This trip to Bedburg had taken much longer than he'd intended, and, as sick as he felt, he was ready to return home. But as he sneezed, an idea popped into his head. Instead of heading for his carriage, he turned down the road leading to the garrison.

He'd speak with Tomas, find out how the search for the family was progressing. He'd also confirm if what Ulrich had told him was true—about Tomas sending out a search party to look for the fugitives. Because if Ulrich had lied about that, he would surely be capable of much worse.

Passing the base of the hill leading up to the church, his eyes instinctively glanced up in that direction. As he began to look away, he did a double-take.

There was Tomas, standing in front of the church, arms crossed, talking to a robed man.

Tomas seems to spend more time at that church than at the garrison.

Even worse, the man Tomas was talking to was none other than Bishop Balthasar.

Heinrich squinted up at the two. They continued talking, not noticing him.

Balthasar had already made his animosity toward Hugo clear the last time he visited House Charmagne. He'd been furious that Heinrich had chosen Hugo to oversee things during Heinrich's trip to Cologne.

Perhaps the bishop not only hates Hugo, but me as well.

Heinrich thought back to that first time he'd led Balthasar—a Jesuit priest and vicar of Cologne at the time—to Bedburg. How he and Balthsasar had so strongly debated the existence of God.

Balthasar surely thinks he's better than other men, as most priests do. Perhaps his entitlement encompasses the entirety of Bedburg. Maybe he would like to see me deposed so he could elect a more Godly man as lord of Bedburg. Perhaps even himself . . .

Heinrich's eyes moved to Tomas.

And with the commander of the militia at his side, Balthasar would surely have the potential to accomplish such a thing. If these two are friends, what's stopping them from arming the citizenry and creating a rebellion for their own cause? By nightfall, they could be at my doorstep, with soldiers and guns and swords.

And perhaps they'd use Ulrich to hang me.

Heinrich had seen enough. He moved away before Tomas or Balthasar could see him, and headed back to the stable where Felix waited with the carriage.

And soon he'd be back within the safety of House Charmagne.

But how safe am I really?

And for how long?

He couldn't sleep. Not because of nightmares. But rather because of how those nightmares now filled his waking world as well.

Covered in blankets, he sat in his straight-backed chair in his conference room, slowly tapping his fingers on the chair's arms. Thinking, scheming, his mind racing.

He had called for the only man he still truly trusted. He needed his opinion. He smirked thinking how this man he trusted was barely a man at all.

And as he waited, he thought of all the men he *wouldn't* call. Because he could no longer trust them.

Rolf, from my own household, jovial and endearing. The man who, as a former assassin, had taught me everything about killing and politics. Yet he could be plotting with Baron Ludwig, whom I've never trusted. Or perhaps with the witch-man, Salvatore, as his agent of chaos.

And Ulrich, my own torturer. A man I've trusted with my life, a man who's always followed orders. Yet he has that ledger, the ultimate means of outing my secrets. He could be angry at his station in life, angry that he hasn't seen more promotions. And seeking to destroy me.

And Tomas and Balthasar. One—the military man, my former bodyguard, my right-hand man in Trier. The other—a man of God, with a hunger for all things spiritual. Separated, they are not threats; Tomas is not cunning enough, Balthasar doesn't have the support. But together . . . they could be my most fearsome foes. Tomas with his influence over the military; Balthasar who may wish to see Tomas in charge . . . a stray voice whispering treacherous thoughts in my former bodyguard's ear . . .

Hugo entered the room. "Are you all right, my lord? You don't look well."

Heinrich could only imagine how he must look. He certainly knew how he felt—heart beating irregularly, face soaked in perspiration, anxiety over all these potential traitors eating away at him.

"I'm fine," he lied, waving for Hugo to come closer.

Hugo stepped forward, his hands clasped behind his back, which gave Heinrich a sense of pride over the young man's progress.

After a long moment of silence, Hugo finally said, "You called, my lord?"

Heinrich nodded. "I wish you to send a message to Bergheim—by way of Felix, so that you may stay here close by my side."

"Of course, my lord. What should the message say?"

"Tell the barons Ludwig and Josef, and Lady Lucille Engel, that they are cordially invited to House Charmagne for a dinner feast, in celebration of our marriage agreement. Tell them that I wish to have the marriage settled as soon as possible with the ceremony here."

Perhaps new alliances will shore up my strength.

Hugo smiled brightly. "Very good, my lord. Is there anything else?"

Heinrich nodded. "I'd like you to extend invitations to Ulrich, Tomas Reiner, dear Rolf Anders, and Bishop Balthasar Schreib. Ask the bishop if he will administer the service."

He stroked his chin and leaned forward. "And now, my boy, tell me what you think of that crazed *benandanti,* Salvatore, will you?"

CHAPTER FOURTEEN

DIETER

Like many German cities, Bonn was settled by the Romans. One of the oldest cities in Germany, it was nestled between the Cologne lowlands and the thick-wooded, mountainous region of Eifel. Traveling southeast from the Griswold house in Bedburg, it took Dieter nearly two days to reach it.

The trip had been arranged by Jerome, the surgeon. Being less-recognizable in Bedburg than Dieter, he'd rented a small palfrey at the stables for Dieter's journey.

It was Dieter's first trip alone from Bedburg. In the past, Sybil had always accompanied him, whether from Bedburg to Amsterdam—to flee persecution—or from England across the North Sea—after being captured by Gustav Koehler and rescued by Rowaine Donnelly.

Dieter arrived in Bonn on his docile steed in the early morning hours of a cold autumn morning. As he passed through the city's medieval wall, his first impression was how subdued things were. Along the roadways people kept to themselves, their heads bent low.

The reason Dieter had come to Bonn was of course to seek the help of Gebhard Truchsess. With Dieter's ever-growing clan of associates and Protestant sympathizers back in Bedburg, he just couldn't continue his plan without some outside support. Gebhard had been the former archbishop of Cologne until he'd converted to Protestantism and the Cologne War had erupted. So there was no love lost between him and the current Catholic leader in Cologne, Archbishop Ernst.

But now came the most important part of Dieter's trip—finding Gebhard Truchsess, who he did not personally know, and asking for his help.

Dieter had no idea Bonn had such a stronghold of Protestants. Yet there was no other explanation for why Gebhard would be here if not to raise support or seek out like-minded Protestant leaders. Dieter would have thought that, being so close to Cologne, Bonn would have been one of the first cities Ernst would have taken over to force it back to Catholicism. In fact, were Ernst to find out Gebhard was a mere twenty miles from Cologne, Dieter had no doubt that Gebhard would be quickly imprisoned on some trumped-up charges and never heard from again.

So the fact that this town of Bonn was so hushed, where the residents didn't seem to worry about other people's business, was—at least to Dieter—a very good thing for Gebhard's continued well-being. It meant that, assuming he was here, it was unlikely Ernst would discover him.

Dieter asked for directions to Bonn Minster. It was the premiere church in Bonn, built some four hundred years earlier, making it one of Germany's oldest holy places. When Dieter arrived, the immense cathedral was an awesome site to behold. The massive gray structure was an homage to Saint Martin, with a huge, blue-roofed spire that rose to the heavens.

Dieter hesitated for a moment before going inside, recognizing full well the symbolism in play here—that he was a Protestant sympathizer stepping foot in an iconic Catholic church. Also, that he wasn't here to pray, but rather to seek information.

Stepping through the massive doors, the interior was busy with activity—parishioners giving prayer in the nave, paying respects to the sacred ground, kneeling before altars and statues. Dieter sat down in a pew surrounded by worshippers speaking in low tones. He hoped that, although unlikely, maybe he'd overhear a conversation about Gebhard's whereabouts.

He soon realized he'd have no such luck. Not only could he barely hear others' conversations, he felt guilty even trying. So he stood up from the pew, walked to the aisle and crossed himself in front of Saint Martin, then left.

Leading his palfrey by the reins, he made his way to the central marketplace. As he passed a group of merchants setting up their wares for the morning, his eyes caught something highly irregular. Near a small, nondescript building off in the corner, about ten horses were huddled together, big and imposing, many in armored barding and dressage with red crosses and suns displayed on their hindquarters.

Warhorses.

Dieter walked over to them. Two men-at-arms stood stoically nearby, guarding the entrance to the building, their hands on spears.

"Excuse me, my lord," Dieter said meekly. He asked, "What is this building?" while pointing to the structure behind them.

Staring straight ahead without the slightest glance toward Dieter, the guard curtly replied, "None of your business, priest. Be on your way."

Dieter wasn't dressed in priest's robes and he certainly didn't otherwise look like one. "You must mistake me for someone else, my lord," he replied. "I am a friend of Martin Luther."

The guard frowned, tilting the spear toward Dieter. "I said be away with you!"

Dieter stepped back. Though not easily deterred, he also wasn't foolhardy. He walked back toward the marketplace.

After milling around in the shadows for almost an hour, keeping a watchful eye on the guards by the building, he noticed a merchant carry a pan of freshly baked bread to the house. The merchant spoke briefly with the guards, who then allowed him to proceed into the house.

Despite hunger pangs now actively distracting him, Dieter was afraid he'd miss something should he take the time to buy food from one of the merchants, so he continued to keep watch from the shadows for the better part of another hour until the guards by the structure finally changed shifts.

Both guards retreated into the house and the spear-wielding one who had reprimanded him was replaced by a younger guard. When Dieter noticed more servants bringing food and gifts up to the house, he got an idea. He walked over to a wine-seller in a nearby booth and, with the precious little money he'd brought, bought a clay flask of wine. Then, donning his hood, he walked back to the new guards, joining the line of people bringing their wares to the house. When his turn came, he said to the guard, "I bring wine from my vineyards near Bedburg, my lord. I hope His Grace will take favor in it."

The guard narrowed his eyes, but didn't deny the presence of a holy man in the house. "Take a sip of your wine," he demanded.

"Pardon?"

The guard rolled his wrist at Dieter. "Go on. Show me that you don't bring poison."

Dieter uncapped the flask and drank a small sip, sloshing it around his mouth for a time before swallowing. For several minutes the guard stood there patiently watching Dieter. When he was convinced there was no sign of Dieter's impending death, he motioned him through.

Dieter smiled as he stepped into the doorway, still wondering what the small house was. He followed a line of other peasants and merchants into a wide room where four men were seated at a table. At the head sat a tall, gangly gentleman with short-cropped hair and a small mustache, dressed not like a holy man but more like a nobleman or baron. As the man accepted each person's offering, he nonchalantly blessed him or her with the sign of the cross as the train of offerors cycled through the room.

When it was Dieter's turn, he placed the wine-flask on the table. "From Bedburg, Your Grace," Dieter told him, "where we are in desperate need of your aid."

The tall man paid him no mind, blankly blessing him while chatting absently with the others at the table.

No response. No recognition.

This journey has been pointless.

As the next man in line pushed and shoved, Dieter was forced to walk off, allowing the next man to present his offering. Then the tall man at the table suddenly quieted the crowd, holding up his hand and demanding silence. He pointed to Dieter. "You there."

Dieter, now close to the door, turned around, realizing the man was addressing him.

"You're from Bedburg, you say?"

Dieter nodded vigorously.

"I remember the fighting at Bedburg, three years back, when Ferdinand of Bavaria came and routed my forces commanded by Count Adolf. I was ashamed I could not make it to the battlegrounds. Were you there?"

Dieter nodded again. "It was a bloody battle, Your Grace. Many great men were lost that day."

The man asked, "What is your name, my son?"

Dieter walked back closer to the table, his heart beating faster. "Dieter Nicolaus, Your Grace. I am a friend to Martin Luther and a friend to Hanns Richter."

A glint shone in the nobleman's eye. He stood and held out his hand for Dieter. Rather than shake it, Dieter knelt then kissed the man's knuckle.

"Do you know who I am?" the man asked.

"I believe you're Gebhard Truchsess von Waldburg, Your Grace. Former archbishop of Cologne, now bishop of Strasbourg, France."

The man smiled fondly. "Then you'll know that Hanns Richter was a great friend and ally of mine, too."

Dieter tilted his head. "Was he?"

Gebhard chuckled. "I sent him to Bedburg to disrupt the corrupt teachings going on there."

Dieter smiled. "Well, he succeeded. He nearly brought the city to its knees. He also baptized me in the cleansing waters."

Gebhard nodded, his face taking on a serious tone. "Why are you here, my brother?"

Dieter wanted to ask the bishop the same question. "Bedburg is again brought to its knees, Your Grace. Only this time it is from a tyrannical secular ruler, rather than from a lost brother."

"I wish I could help, my friend. But alas, my forces are spread thin."

Dieter bowed his head. He didn't know what else to say. Then he realized this was possibly his only chance to ask the man directly: "Why are you here, Your Grace, if you don't mind my asking? Surely Archbishop Ernst would—"

Gebhard held up his palm. "Yes, I've heard that from my

advisors. Please, Herr Nicolaus, not from you as well." He cleared his throat. "I am here on campaign, to raise a new army. I have just been elected bishop in Strasbourg. Rather than retire, as I had originally planned, my new position has reinvigorated me to fight for the Lord. I am speaking with my peers and allies"—he motioned to the other three men at the table—"and making sure I still have some."

"You have many in Bedburg, Your Grace," Dieter said, "but they are oppressed and hunted like beasts. Just the other day two Protestant sympathizers were hanged without trial in the town square. Lord Heinrich Franz shows no mercy for our ilk."

Gebhard frowned, lines forming down his cheeks. "I only wish I had the support in Bedburg that I do here in Bonn. But I'm afraid that city is already lost to me. I cannot help you."

The air seemed to escape Dieter's lungs. So that was it, then. Other than meeting a wise and holy man, this journey had been in vain. Dejected, he lowered his head.

Gebhard gently placed his hand on Dieter's shoulder. "I can see your distress, Dieter Nicolaus. And your disappointment. Clearly, you love your people."

Dieter nodded.

"And what is it you're doing for your oppressed brothers and sisters?"

"Trying to smuggle them out of the city, Your Grace, before they're all caught and murdered."

Gebhard sighed. "A noble cause, brother. And one I wish I could help with. Perhaps once my army is raised, and I can properly battle the Pretender Ernst, I could come to Bedburg's rescue. But until then, I can only offer you a name."

Dieter's ears perked. He looked into Gebhard's solemn eyes. "A name, Your Grace?"

The man nodded. "I have two men in Bedburg, working covertly. I cannot give you the name of one, he is too entrenched. But the other has always been a great help to my cause, having served me well for years, in secret of course."

Dieter waited.

Gebhard continued. "During my lost war against Ernst, this man provided much pertinent information. If you like, I can send you to him."

Dieter's eyes sparkled. "Yes! That would be most advantageous, Your Grace! Who is he?"

"His name is Patric Clauson. May God bless your endeavor to find him, and may He also bless your most worthy cause."

CHAPTER FIFTEEN

HUGO

Hugo could see the changes in Heinrich—his hyper-edginess, the wild look in his eyes, his growing paranoia.

He suspected it was his master's illness causing these symptoms. Heinrich had been feverish for days now and Hugo wondered if the man was going mad.

He only hoped that Heinrich's paranoia wouldn't extend to *him*. Hugo had always been completely loyal to Heinrich and certainly didn't deserve suspicion. But more importantly, Hugo was well aware of the extreme measures Heinrich was capable of for those he no longer trusted.

When Heinrich had asked Hugo what he thought of their newest "houseguest"—who'd basically become a prisoner in House Charmagne—Hugo had said, truthfully, that he thought Salvatore was strange but not malevolent. Hugo honestly believed the man was sincere in his desire to help Heinrich with his nightmares. He just thought his potion was ill-conceived—and likely responsible for Heinrich's physical and mental deterioration.

Heinrich, however, had dismissed Hugo's opinion of Salvatore, implying that Hugo's belief that the "witch-man"—as Heinrich often referred to him—wasn't intentionally trying to harm him was simply naïve. Hugo had silently fumed about that. To Hugo, such a casual dismissal of his opinion was like an insolent parent patting his child on the head before telling him to "run along and play."

The morning after Heinrich had spoken to him about Salvatore, Hugo prepared for his trip to Bedburg. His instructions were to personally invite Tomas, Ulrich, and Bishop Balthasar to join the wedding feast Heinrich had planned.

Before leaving, he and Rolf had breakfast at the dining table.

For several minutes the two ate in silence. Then Rolf said, "Heinrich asked you about Salvatore, I presume?"

Hugo nodded, stabbing at his eggs and watching the yolks leak out.

"What did he want to know, specifically, my boy?"

Hugo narrowed his eyes at the old man.

Why does he care? Is everyone becoming paranoid in this house?

"He thinks Salvatore tried to kill him with that potion," Hugo answered.

Rolf chuckled. "He told me the same. What do you think?"

Hugo took several more bites of food, then looked up. "About what?"

"Do you think Salvatore tried to kill Heinrich?"

Hugo put down his fork. "Well . . . my lord seems to be getting better now. Somewhat. If Salvatore were really the evil witch-doctor Heinrich claims him to be, I'm sure he'd have a better poison to use."

Rolf smiled. "You are wise beyond your years, my boy."

"I think Lord Heinrich is just being paranoid."

"And why do you think that is?"

Hugo thought for a moment. "I'm not sure." He began eating again, then stopped. "I suppose one can be *justifiably* paranoid, no?"

"Meaning what?" asked Rolf.

"Meaning he might have good reason to be suspicious."

Rolf shrugged. "Perhaps he believes his lordship is in jeopardy. He's done so much to please Archbishop Ernst—punishing the Protestants, this marriage to Lucille Engel—that he hasn't thought much about his own people. Perhaps the citizens of Bedburg are getting angry with him about that."

"It's not the first time people would be angry with Heinrich Franz," Hugo added.

"True, my boy." Then Rolf's smile disappeared. Leaning forward on the table, he put his hands together. "He's done many unforgivable deeds . . ." His words trailed off, his eyes turned sad. Hugo could tell the old man was fond of Heinrich—yet conflicted. He'd been helping Heinrich since Heinrich wasn't much older than Hugo was now.

"Heinrich turned into something I didn't expect," Rolf said in a soft voice.

When he didn't continue, Hugo prompted him. "Into what?"

Rolf thought for a while, pulling on his white beard. Looking deeply into Hugo's eyes, he said, "A fearmonger."

Hugo's nostrils flared. He leaned back in his chair.

"I suppose he learned that from me," Rolf confessed. "He plays on the consternation of others to get what he wants. He molds people's terror to suit his own needs. He's a master manipulator—as I was once. So I suppose I shouldn't be terribly surprised. No doubt, it's taken him to great heights. He knows how to play the chessboard well."

Rolf's words reminded Hugo of his own past. He'd started out an innocent boy, wide-eyed and believing. Then his father died and his sister left him. He'd grown up quickly after that, placing his trust in the wrong people: Severin, Karstan, Ava, Ulrich, Tomas. He'd watched the massacre in the mountains near Trier, where his new, dear friend Klemens had been slaughtered before his eyes. Which had forged a rage inside him he hadn't known was possible, ultimately leading him to his own murderous ways—first killing Severin, a long-time acquaintance he'd never trusted; then progressing on to help Tomas and Heinrich kill many others in Trier under the guise of a witch-hunt and inquisition. Looking back, he realized that that first killing of Severin, instead of evoking remorse, had only served to reinforce his confidence, giving him a twisted sense of satisfaction knowing he was capable of such violence.

But all that death and darkness had begun to take a toll on him. He no longer felt right about himself, and didn't like what he'd become. When he'd finally seen his sister Sybil again, years later in that jail cell, instead of feeling anger over her abandoning him, or joy over just seeing her alive again, he'd felt . . . nothing.

And on the rare occasion he did feel something, it was always a confusing, conflicted tangle of both empowerment and fear. Empowered by what he was capable of, and fearful for what he was capable of. He was turning into a younger version of Heinrich, and that both excited and petrified him.

Rolf interrupted his thoughts. "There are two ways to lead your people, my young friend. The first is through fear, as Heinrich does. But as you can see, that can lead to troublesome times." He held up a finger. "He is untrusting and paranoid." He held up a second finger. "People are angry with him." He held up a third finger. "And that means he must always be *fighting back*." Rolf took a sip from his glass of water before setting it back down and continuing. "He is never in a position of comfort—should he try to get comfortable, another thing comes along to destroy his peace. You see?"

Hugo nodded.

"And the second way to lead is through love. Trust. Loyalty. Friendship. I believe if Heinrich could see that, things might be better for him. But it's much too late for that."

"Are you loyal to Heinrich?" Hugo posed out of the blue.

The question clearly took Rolf by surprise. His mouth opened a bit, showing tiny yellow teeth. "Of course I am. I've known him since he was a young pup."

That doesn't speak to whether you're loyal to him now.

Rolf waved his hand at Hugo. "All I'm saying, my boy, is that when it's your time to lead, I implore you to lead by example. Lead with your heart, not your sword."

My time to lead? When did that *become part of the deal?*

Rolf gazed into Hugo's dark eyes. "Can you do that, Hugo? For me? And if not for me, then for the people?"

Hugo stared back at the old man, then slowly nodded.

"I think I can do that, Rolf."

After breakfast, Hugo left the dining room and finished readying himself for his trip to Bedburg. He strapped on his hiking boots and shrugged into his winter coat.

But something was nagging him, in the back of his mind. Also, Rolf's words kept rolling through his head.

Was that Rolf's intent? To distract me? No . . . he just thinks he's helping. Senile old fool. Doesn't he know how busy I am?

He went down to the library, where Salvatore had been

forced to stay. The library was one of the largest rooms in the mansion, with shelves built into each wall up to the ceiling, every one packed with old books and manuscripts. A rolling ladder allowed for easy access to the upper-most shelves. Salvatore was on the ladder, leafing through a section of books near the top.

"Hello, Salvatore," Hugo announced.

With his back to Hugo, Salvatore reached out and grabbed a book, then started down the ladder. "Salutations, young master," he replied, stepping off.

"What's that you have there?" Hugo asked, nodding at the book in his hands.

"A treatise on necromancy," Salvatore said with a gap-toothed smile. It was a thick volume and he cradled it like a baby. "The art of communicating with the deceased."

Hugo's face darkened. He didn't like these superstitious things, especially when they involved a crazed warlock like Salvatore. "You wish to speak with the dead?" Hugo asked.

Salvatore shook his head. "I can already do that in my trances. I wish to control the voices speaking with me. Perhaps this book can help."

"Why don't you let the dead rest? Haven't they already been through enough . . . in life?"

Salvatore shrugged. "Yes, young master, they have. But there is much to learn from the dead. You see, though the dead are dead, they're also alive. They form our opinions and ideals—their deaths make us who *we* are." He waved his arms out to his side, as if that explained his theory. "I see them in my mind. Their spirits wander the seas and the trees and the plains. I wish to cultivate their knowledge so I can incorporate their learnings into my own spiritual adventures."

Hugo scratched his head. This was not the conversation he wanted; he'd come to Salvatore with a purpose, not to discuss dead people and their spirits.

So he changed the subject. "How do you like staying here, Salvatore?" he asked.

The witch-man shrugged. "Though my body is a prison, my mind is free. Therefore, I can be anywhere and be content in this world, you see? There is no trapping Salvatore."

"Great . . . I guess," Hugo said. "And how do you like Heinrich—my master?"

"He is as troubled as the next man. Though he cannot be blamed for that. I do think, however, that his dreams no longer ail him."

"He thinks you tried to kill him."

"I know he does." Salvatore stopped smiling. "And I know I didn't."

"Then why do you stay?" Hugo asked.

Again Salvatore shrugged. "Curiosity. I want to see what happens. And I don't suppose he's too keen on seeing me leave."

"You want to see what happens?"

Salvatore nodded. "I've seen a great feast in my dreams—a premonition, I suspect."

"Well, he is planning a celebratory feast for his wedding party," Hugo said.

Salvatore raised a finger in the sky. "Then my suspicions are confirmed!"

Hugo sighed. "I don't think it's wise for you to stay here any longer. I don't think you should be here for the feast." Hugo was trying to give this crazy man a hint, but it just wouldn't take.

"Was I not invited?" He frowned, looking a bit confused. "In my dreams I was. How strange."

"You are invited, Salvatore, but I don't think you should attend." Hugo spoke his words slowly, hoping the man would understand.

Salvatore moved to a chair by the desk and sat, opening his book. Licking his finger before placing it against the edge of the first page, he began reading, apparently done with the conversation.

When Hugo continued standing there staring, Salvatore finally looked up. "You're probably correct, young master," he said. "Perhaps I will go then."

"When?"

The madman smiled his gap-toothed smile again. "When you least expect it, of course."

* * *

A messenger advised Hugo that the wedding party would arrive by nightfall. He'd spent too much time talking to Rolf and Salvatore, and was running out of time. It was almost midday and he needed to be on the road if he intended to invite the guests whose presence Heinrich had requested and return to House Charmagne in time.

He called for his carriage. On his way out, Rolf tried to speak to him again but Hugo brushed him off, telling him he was too busy. Rushing out to the carriage, by the time he was seated inside, Felix already had the carriage moving, on its way to Bedburg.

Hugo carried three letters with him, tucked in his tunic, one for each guest he was tasked with inviting to the wedding festivities. He was expected to deliver them and return by nightfall to greet the wedding party and make them comfortable at House Charmagne. He mentally calculated that, as long as there were no further delays, they'd make it in time.

Once they reached Bedburg's eastern gate Hugo implored Felix to go faster. They barreled down the road toward their first location, pushing aside merchants and peasants. When they arrived at the garrison, Tomas was outside training with his men. Hugo noted that, just as when he'd trained with Tomas, the men didn't use wooden swords. Tomas insisted that training always emulate actual combat, so the harsh sounds of steel blades clashing, while a bit jarring, was no surprise to Hugo.

As Hugo stepped out, Tomas looked neither pleased nor displeased to see him—his face a blank canvas. Walking up to him, Hugo handed Tomas the letter, saying, "A message from Lord Heinrich Franz," then turned and abruptly left.

Quickly, Felix wheeled the carriage around, traveling back the way they'd come, and headed for the church. At the base of the hill Hugo told him to stop, got out of the carriage, then raced up the incline alone. Barging through the front doors, he was met by Sister Salome and a nearly empty church. Salome told him Bishop Balthasar was not present.

"Where is he," Hugo asked, "if not in his own church?"

"At the castle to speak with Lord Alvin," Salome replied, blushing. Unable to lie, she'd shared what Hugo knew was information Balthasar would rather keep private. Lord Alvin had been the inhospitable, old landowner who'd loudly disapproved of Hugo's role under Heinrich's regime. Not a likeable character at all.

Remember to tell Heinrich about this—Balthasar speaking with Lord Alvin.

Hugo bolted from the church, in too much a hurry to bless himself on his way out.

The next closest destination was the jailhouse. When they arrived, Hugo jumped out, entered through the front door, then rushed down the damp, cold steps to Ulrich's room, where Ulrich sat half-asleep. Hugo handed him the letter. "A message from Lord Heinrich Franz," he repeated, then turned and left before Ulrich could respond.

When they reached the castle, their last stop, where Sister Salome had said Bathasar was, Hugo considered handing his third letter to a guard, but decided the task was too important to leave to subordinates. Since he was well known here, no one stopped him when he entered the castle, quickly finding Bishop Balthasar Schreib in a small room seated across from Lord Alvin.

"What's this?" Balthasar asked when Hugo handed him the letter.

Hugo eyed the bishop and the lord suspiciously, from one to the other.

"A message from Lord Heinrich Franz. He wishes you to officiate the wedding ceremony between himself and Lady Lucille Engel von Bergheim. And he wants you at the wedding feast afterward. Do you accept?"

Bishop Balthasar frowned. Clearly this was a major inconvenience. Hugo almost smirked. Finally, the bishop sighed. "Yes, tell Lord Franz I accept."

Hugo bowed. "He expects you to witness the trade agreements and proposals as well," he added.

"Fine, fine," he said. "When does the wedding party arrive?"

"Tonight." Hugo peeked out the window. The sun was ready

to set. "The wedding is in two days' time."

The bishop nodded. Hugo bid him and Lord Alvin a curt farewell, then left the castle.

They rode out the eastern gate back to House Charmagne. As the carriage picked up speed, a sudden impulse overtook Hugo. He ordered Felix to turn at the next road.

When they'd ascended, then descended, a hill, Felix asked, "Where are we going, my lord?"

"Don't ask questions, Felix, just steer."

They came to another hill, in a wooded area, overlooking an old house.

Hugo's old house.

Though nearly a hundred yards away, Hugo clearly recognized the young man out front, axing firewood, the sky blazing orange and pink behind him.

Martin Achterberg.

Looking much older than last time Hugo had seen him. Now with a beard, he was taller and broader, his muscles glistening with sweat from his work. Only two years Hugo's senior, he looked much older.

"Come on," Hugo whispered to himself, tapping his feet impatiently on the carriage floor.

"My lord, the sun is setting," Felix said through the window. "We should be go—"

"Quiet, Felix," Hugo said, raising his palm.

He just wanted a glimpse. He'd been dreaming of her ever since that day, seeing her at the Achterberg estate, opening the door for Dieter as he returned from the Town Fair.

He only wanted one lasting image, something to satiate his mind.

And then the door opened and she appeared. Beautiful as ever.

Ava Hahn stepped through the doorway and handed Martin a clay mug of water.

Hugo's throat went dry, his voice caught in his chest. He heard a low groan come from deep within. And he felt himself getting aroused, his pants tightening in a certain area.

Then Martin grabbed her by the waist and pulled her close.

They embraced. Then kissed.

Hugo's mouth fell open. He was dumbstruck. His fists clenched. He blinked rapidly, unbelieving.

It was not Ava Hahn and Dieter Nicolaus together, as he'd originally assumed.

Of course not. Dieter still loved Sybil.

It was Ava and Martin Achterberg!

Which made even less sense.

Doesn't Ava know that Martin is a murderer? That he killed his own father?

Doesn't she know he was a former prisoner and fugitive of Bedburg, that he'd escaped his justified arrest and execution? That his mother had burned as a witch in the public square? That he'd been an altar boy for the former bishop of Bedburg, and had probably taken part in grave, disgusting habits with the old man? Does she not know any of that?

How could Ava love such a man?

No. She must not know any of it. She wouldn't love him if she did.

Then a strange thought occurred to Hugo.

Would she love me if she knew my *past?*

It didn't matter.

Hugo looked away, staring out the opposite window of the carriage. Suddenly he caught a glimpse of someone else.

A hooded figure on a horse, flying down the road away from them, heading back toward Bedburg.

Hugo had been followed. Ava and Martin's presence were now known.

But he didn't care.

Let them be caught!

Heinrich Franz had his enemies.

And now Hugo Griswold had his.

CHAPTER SIXTEEN

SYBIL

The "Rowaine Miracle" swept through Strangers Shire like a firestorm. With Sybil Griswold featured in the starring role as the *miracle-maker*—a part she neither deserved nor wanted.

And certainly not the best way to keep a low profile.

When Sybil woke the next morning and shuffled groggy-eyed into the living room in her night shift, stretching and yawning, she was met by Leon and Claire. They were both just standing there, eyes bulging, staring at her as if she'd just arrived from another plane of existence.

"What?" she asked, looking back and forth between them. Before they could answer, there was a knock at the door. Claire opened it. An elderly woman stood outside, her hands clasped before her, begging to speak.

But before she could, Claire cut the old woman off. "Not now, Lady Marie. She's just now waking. Please give her space!"

Lady Marie frowned, wrinkles framing her mouth. Three others stood out in the cold behind the woman. The old woman's eyes moved past Claire to Sybil, who looked stupefied.

"There she is!" the woman cried, pointing a skeletal finger at Sybil. "The Pale Diviner has risen!"

A chorus of murmurs rose from behind as more people squeezed in. Then the growing crowd moved toward the doorway to peer over Claire's shoulder for a glimpse at the newly-christened diviner.

Claire slammed the door in their faces.

The commotion was enough to wake Daxton, who'd been sleeping on a table on the other side of the room. He rubbed his eyes and looked around, trying to get his bearings as the buzzing of exuberant peasants and farmers outside still echoed through the door.

"What is this insanity?" Sybil exclaimed.

"It's our fault, really," Claire said with a sigh. "I'm sorry, Beele. After the miracle last night, I just couldn't keep my mouth shut. Shame on me."

Sybil eyed her accusingly. "What did you do, Claire?"

With a guilty look, Claire explained. "I told anyone who would listen about the miracle you performed. I'm afraid you are . . . famous."

Sybil blinked rapidly. "Me? But I had nothing to do with Rowaine's recovery."

Daxton, still unsteady but starting to join the land of the living, announced, "I'm sure if Jerome were here he could explain what happened last night. Though it *is* quite amazing, Sybil. What you achieved. You don't give yourself enough credit."

"It was God's doing," Leon explained.

Claire nodded. "But Beele was the conduit of His touch."

There was more banging at the door, then a baby's cry could be heard from the back room.

"Damn, they've woken Rose!" Claire cried, storming off. "Get those people away from our door, Leon!" she called out as she went for the baby.

Scared of his wife, as any wise man would be, Leon gulped then swung open the door. "Get away from here, people, before you draw even more attention to her!"

Behind him, Sybil crossed her arms over her chest.

"We just want to see her!" a woman cried out.

"Just a peek!" said another.

"We have much suffering! She's needed!"

Leon slammed the door again and sighed.

Claire returned, cradling Rose in her arms. As she rocked her back and forth to stop her crying, she told Sybil, "As you've already heard, Beele, it didn't take long for them to come up with a new title for you."

"The Pale Diviner," Leon repeated, smiling like he'd thought it up himself.

Sybil shook her head. "First, I'm the 'Daughter of the Beast.'

Now, I'm the 'Pale Diviner.' No wonder they call these people Strangers." She looked at Leon and narrowed her eyes. "And why . . . *pale*?"

Daxton, who was now at the stove boiling eggs, laughed at that. "I suspect it has something to do with your skin, lass. Bony and white. Would you rather they call you the White Witch?"

Sybil sat down at the small table. "I'd rather they not call me anything. I don't like, nor need, the attention."

Daxton brought over a bowl of cooked eggs and set them on the table. "I reckon you don't have a say in it, Beele. You are now the celebrated miracle-worker." He thought about that for a moment, then declared, "*Oracle. Seeress…*" His eyes widened as he reached for an egg, "Ooh, how about *Enchantress*?"

Sybil shook her head, then picked out her own egg and peeled it. After she took a bite, she said, "I have greater things to worry about than fake epithets. We need to leave here as soon as possible, Dax."

Daxton took another egg from the bowl, his face turning serious. "Of course, Beele. You're right." Then he grinned again. "But when we come back, this will be your future! Everyday, you'll get to fight off these poor wretches with a broom. Maybe I'll get you a magic wand!"

When they got to the ship and gave Georg the news about his daughter, he was understandably jubilant—though disappointed that he hadn't been there to witness the miracle himself.

"It really wasn't as big a thing as everyone's saying," Sybil told him.

"Nonsense," joked Daxton. "I saw her hand turn orange when she ran it across Row's arm. Saw it myself! Her fingertips sparkled!"

Georg's mouth fell open. He looked at Sybil. "Is that true?"

"Of course not." Sybil glared at Daxton, elbowing him. "He's just being silly."

A voice came from behind. "Your legend will likely grow as the days pass—especially if you don't show your face to the townsfolk."

They turned to face Corvin Carradine, their prisoner, seated at the bench by the gunwale, leaning back against the rail. The *Silver Sun* was slowly meandering up Norfolk's coastline. With just four of them controlling the boat, it had taken longer than expected to row it out of the cove. But now they were gliding smoothly along the North Sea, their sails billowing in the wind.

"That's how these things work, you know," Corvin continued, resting one leg on his knee, completely calm and content despite being a prisoner on his own ship. "First you're just an oddity—something rare. Then word spreads of your deed and before long your story becomes legend, then myth, then explodes into something far grander than anything close to reality."

"How do you know what it was, or wasn't?" Sybil spat out. "You weren't even there," she said, arguing just for argument's sake, not really knowing why, other than to *not* give this charming man any comfort.

Corvin flashed her his dimpled smile. "Fair enough, my lady." He shrugged. "That's just been my experience."

Daxton scoffed, waving him off.

Georg stayed silent. He wore the same smile on his face that had been plastered there since hearing the wonderful news about his daughter's recovery. It was the first time Sybil had seen him happy since he'd rescued her months earlier from her imprisonment and near-execution in Trier. Soon after that, Rowaine had been shot and injured, her legs paralyzed.

Georg saw Sybil eyeing him. "It's a father's greatest fear," he explained, "that his little girl will never walk again."

Sybil rested her hand on the big man's shoulder. "Regardless, you found her, Georg. You spent ten long years thinking she was dead, remember?"

Georg covered Sybil's hand with his. "You're right, Beele. I cannot take that blessing for granted. But still, I thought I'd crippled my *own* child."

Sybil leaned over, resting the top of her head in the crook of his neck. It was cozy there. She felt protected. She gazed out at the clear blue waters and smiled. The sun sat high in the sky, showering them with uncommon warmth for autumn, its radiant rays glistening off the water's surface.

He may be a drunk and a brute, but he's the best drunk and brute I've ever known.

"Thank you, Beele," Georg said in Sybil's ear, in a voice so low only she could hear. She sensed him brushing off tears.

But rather than deny what she'd done, or continue making light of the miracle people thought she'd performed, Sybil said simply, "You're welcome, Georg."

As they glided on toward King's Lynn, she snuggled in closer, watching the sparkling reflections of light spin off the waves.

By nightfall the *Silver Sun* had drifted past the delta of the Great River Ouse and was closing in on King's Lynn harbor. When it reached the dock, Daxton remained at the helm while Georg and Sybil disembarked and Corvin stayed hidden below deck.

The plan that Georg and Sybil had devised took into account the untrustworthiness of both their prisoner, Corvin Carradine, and Guy, who'd sent them on this retrieval expedition.

The first part of their plan was to convince Guy to join them at the harbor, to witness for himself that the *Silver Sun* was indeed empty. They wanted to see the look on Guy's face when he discovered that fact—if the ship was even his in the first place.

Georg and Sybil walked off the dock and headed for the Hanseatic League's warehouse—not a far walk. Eventually they came upon the same sullen man sitting by the warehouse garage, eyeing passersby suspiciously. Giving him the same pass-phrase, the man allowed them entry.

Once inside, Sybil surveyed the dark surroundings carefully. Were there fewer torches lit this time than before? It seemed so. And where were Reeve Bailey's barrels of textiles and linens? Last time, they'd been stored here in plain sight. Sybil's suspicions grew. Maybe this was a bad idea, placing the goods in Guy's trust while they embarked on their reckless rescue mission.

As Sybil scanned the rest of the area, her eyes met the man himself, standing across the way, his arms crossed, a blank look on his face. They walked up to him and stopped. Guy, beneath the light of a torch, continued to watch them for a long moment before speaking. It was quite unnerving for Sybil, who was glad to have Georg by her side.

Finally Guy spoke. "Is it done?" he asked, looking directly at Georg as if Sybil weren't there. Under the circumstances, she didn't mind. The cold, dark warehouse was bleak and made her skin crawl. She kept glancing over her shoulder, expecting the man who'd let them in to appear, but he didn't.

"It is," Georg replied

"And my goods?"

"Where are ours?" Georg asked, peeking skeptically around at the few barrels in sight.

Guy smiled. "Safely lodged in the back, awaiting your arrival. I had to make room for other goods being shipped here."

Georg said nothing.

"Now," Guy said, "where are *my* barrels? My sugar and tobacco?"

"First, I want to see the ledger," said Georg.

Guy clicked his tongue and shook his head, raising one finger and wiggling it. "It doesn't work that way."

Sybil heard rustling behind her. She closed her eyes to focus better, then heard another sound, someone stepping on a piece of wood.

They weren't alone.

"Georg," she muttered.

"I know," he said in a hushed tone.

Three men appeared from the shadows into the torch light, surrounding them. It was Sybil's worst fear. She felt the hairs on the back of her neck rise.

"Bah!" Guy cried, throwing his arms in the air. "Not yet, you fools! I was just starting to have fun!"

His smile turned menacing.

"What is this?" Georg asked. "We had a deal."

"Deals are made to be broken, you fool." Speaking to the

three men around them, Guy pointed to Sybil and Georg. "These are the two pirates I told you about. Thieves and killers from the dreaded *Lion's Pride.* Now . . . where do I collect my reward?"

Georg calmly shook his head. "I don't know what you're raving about, man."

Sybil glanced at the men surrounding them, suddenly realizing they weren't Guy's thugs at all. They were dressed in the liveries and armor of English patrolmen. They were town guards. With spears in hand and guns in their belts. Trained and dangerous.

Fortunately, mention of the *Lion's Pride* didn't seem to fluster them. Sybil knew that anxious men did stupid things—like accidentally pulling a rifle trigger.

"We'll see about that," Guy said to Georg, flapping his hands at the guards. "Take them to the docks—these thieves stole my goods! Let's see what they've got on their ship."

So Corvin Carradine was telling the truth.

Sybil raised her arms to show she was unarmed, then the guards led her and Georg from the warehouse to the harbor.

This despicable man. Having us return his stolen goods only to blame us to avoid our reward.

As they approached the docks, other traders and sailors gave the town guards wide berth as they walked their prisoners to the *Silver Sun.* Georg seemed unusually calm, though Sybil's heart was pounding.

When Guy finally caught sight of the ship, he grinned, then rubbed his hands together. "Let's see here," he said, jumping onboard. He walked to the first hold, underneath the main mast, and looked in. His grin disappeared.

The hold was empty.

He crossed to the back mast and tossed aside the blanket covering the second hold.

Nothing in there either.

"What's the matter?" Georg yelled sarcastically from the dock. "Can't find what you're looking for?"

Guy growled and clenched his fists, then thrust a finger at Georg. "Where in God's name is my merchandise, rogue?"

Georg shrugged, giving him a blank look. "I have no idea what you're talking about, sir."

Guy pursed his lips and sucked in his breath. Turning his fury toward Sybil, he screamed, "Where are the barrels, bitch?"

Sybil tilted her head, looking confused. Her heart was pounding in her chest so hard she thought it had to be visible to everyone. But keeping her composure, she said simply, "I'm just as surprised as my friend, sir. There must be some mistake."

The three guards shifted their feet awkwardly, one of them saying, "Come now, Guy, what's this all about? Did you drag us out here for nothing, *again?*"

"W-wait, wait," Guy stuttered, waving his hands in front of his face. "They're still murderers! They killed the captain of this ship—one Corvin Carradine. You must arrest them for *that!*" he yelled, his wicked smile returning.

The guards moved toward Georg and Sybil, their leather armor creaking. One of them muttered to the other, "Can we arrest them without a body?" To which that guard whispered, "Just do it—if you want to get paid. Let him produce evidence later."

At which point another voice bellowed out from somewhere below deck.

"You can't arrest them for something they didn't do, gentlemen."

And out walked Corvin Carradine, climbing up the stairs from the lower deck. He smiled, the moonlight shining off his handsome, confident face—making Sybil's heart flutter, more from fright than attraction.

"You can't arrest them for murdering me," Corvin announced, "since, obviously, they didn't." He turned to Guy. "You dim, sad man," giving him the most pitiful look Sybil had ever seen. Still nervous, she had to stifle a laugh.

Guy's mouth fell open. He tried to think of something to say, his head swiveling from Corvin to the guards, then back again. With spittle flying from his lips, he screamed at the young captain.

"You bastard!"

The guards started to walk away.

Then Guy did something no one anticipated. His face red and the veins on his neck taut, he pulled a small dagger from his sleeve and charged at Corvin.

Sybil gasped, her hand flying to her mouth. With his dagger swinging wildly, Guy lunged as Corvin backpedaled. Then, at the last moment, Corvin sidestepped, and as Guy flew past, Corvin spun around and kicked him in the rump.

Guy cried out as the ship's railing caught his momentum, but only partially, bending him at the knees the wrong way before flinging him over the side.

His flailing body hit the water with a loud splat. Several sailors and tradesmen watching from the docks let out a chuckle, some even clapping.

From atop the deck, Corvin hopped onto a barrel, his ego fueled by the crowd's cheers. He bowed his head low, rolling out his arms like a royal jester. When he looked up, his piercing eyes aimed straight for Sybil.

She blushed.

"Do you believe me now, my lady?" Corvin yelled out to her. "That I'm not the bad guy here?"

Sybil nodded, then looked at Georg who was rolling his eyes.

To satiate the crowd, Corvin pointed to the man bobbing in the water. "*That,* ladies and gentlemen, is a bad, bad . . . *Guy!*"

The crowd clapped and cheered more, as the guards left the docks.

Georg stepped onto the boat as Corvin held out his hand to help Sybil on deck. When he flashed his smile again, her face turned a deeper red.

"Quite the performance, Herr Carradine," Georg said to him once they were headed back down the river. A short while later, he asked, "So you'll still help us with the ledger and the trade routes, then?"

Corvin, who'd never stopped staring at Sybil, nodded. Dramatically gesturing toward her, he said, "How could I ever say no to such a beautiful creature?"

CHAPTER SEVENTEEN

HEINRICH

Still recovering from the final stages of his illness, Heinrich Franz did not look forward to what Rolf had suggested he do. Sitting on his horse—who was trying to walk in circles, eager to be gone from House Charmagne—all Heinrich wanted to do was stay home and plan his wedding.

But he'd reluctantly agreed to Rolf's suggestion.

"It would be a decent gesture to show both your future wife and the noblemen," Rolf had told him. "Tour them around Bedburg."

Initially Heinrich had been skeptical. "So they can spy on my defenses and military capability? I think not, old man." He still firmly believed that Ludwig von Bergheim wanted him dead.

"No, no," Rolf had explained. "You mistake my meaning. Don't show them around Bedburg *proper*. Show them the *villages*. The ones you are granting to Baron Josef."

Heinrich still didn't like the idea. "I don't enjoy watching that fat old buffoon openly gloat about his victory while I chaperone him around my territory."

"You are receiving his beautiful daughter's hand in marriage, Heinrich. You are a victor in this agreement as well."

Heinrich had scoffed. "Beauty is a relative term, Rolf. I don't find icy-veined, middle-aged women particularly beautiful."

"Then perhaps *prosperous* is the correct term, my lord. She can bring great riches to Bedburg and greatly enhance your status in the eyes of Archbishop Ernst. After all, she's the Catholic unifier he's looking for."

Rolf was no fool. He knew how to downplay what Heinrich saw as the negatives of the marriage by refocusing him on the positives. And by reminding Heinrich of "great riches" and the positive way he'd be viewed by Archbishop Ernst, he'd finally persuaded the man to agree to this "tour."

So here Heinrich now sat, on this cold early morning, on his too-eager horse, still aching and sniffling from that madman's nasty dream-stopping potion, waiting for his guests to arrive for their daylong journey.

By the time they arrived, Heinrich had managed to calm his horse down—so much so that he'd almost fallen asleep in the saddle while waiting. But when his steed heard the approaching hooves of other horses, it neighed and snorted, bringing Heinrich back to his senses.

"I told you to be here an hour ago," Heinrich grumbled to the riders. Baron Ludwig Koehler sat stiff-backed on a brown mare that was nearly as lean as he was. Baron Josef Witten's mount was an old black stallion. And his daughter, Lucille, rode an energetic colt. All three wore riding gear of the highest quality.

Anticipating correctly that they'd be overdressed for the occasion, and thus make excellent targets for roving criminals, Heinrich had ordered three soldiers from Bedburg to accompany them. The last thing he wanted was for his guests to be robbed by highwaymen in the very region they'd soon control.

Or maybe that wouldn't be so bad, after all.

As the sun rose higher, brightening the sky from pale gray to soft pink, the four riders and their escorts left House Charmagne. Heinrich rode in front, directing the entourage onto the wide dirt road, then dug his heels into his horse's hindquarters, bent his head forward, and broke into a gallop. At first the noblemen bickered, complaining that this was supposed to be a leisurely experience, but ultimately they followed suit, picking up speed to keep up with Heinrich.

They rode away from the sun, heading west toward Castle Bedburg. And when one of the castle's spires eventually came into view, Heinrich turned the party southward.

"Our first stop will be Kirdorf, on the southern tip of Bedburg," Heinrich announced, reining in his horse and slowing the group to a trot.

"Your young emissary told us there is much arable land

around Kirdorf," Baron Ludwig called out, pulling alongside Heinrich. As he did, Heinrich glanced at the man's cramping hands, stifling a smile at his visible discomfort.

"Hugo is correct," Heinrich said.

"What is the primary crop grown there?" Baron Josef asked.

"The plains and uplands around Kirdorf are usually good for rye and potatoes," Heinrich said, though he had no idea what they really grew there. He'd have to ask Rolf.

Baron Josef shook his head. "That won't do. My villages already have plenty of rye fields. I think I'll change them out for oats, possibly beets."

Heinrich frowned. Josef's sanctimonious tone made Heinrich's blood boil. "Do with it what you wish, Herr Josef," he answered evenly.

The sun was just beginning to burn off the morning mist when they reached Kirdorf. The village was fair-sized, with a central thoroughfare wide enough to run their horses abreast. Riding to Heinrich's immediate left was Lucille Engel, giving Heinrich his first chance to get a good look at her.

She *was* pretty. Blonde with barely any facial wrinkles, which he assumed was the result of never having worked a day in her life. She did, however, look extremely uncomfortable, likely because her corset was too tight for an afternoon ride. But more than that, she seemed uninterested, unimpressed. Which Heinrich understood. After living a lavish lifestyle in a beautiful townhouse with maids and butlers, it made perfect sense that a poor village like Kirdorf wouldn't resonate with such a woman. Her father Josef, on the other hand, was showing a keen interest in the place, his eyes darting around in all directions. Heinrich could almost see the golden coins spinning inside his head.

"There seems to be a good amount of acreage here, Heinrich," Josef commented. "I am pleased with this place. Where now are the other two villages?"

Heinrich nudged his head forward. "To the north, on the other side of Bedburg. They're neighboring villages, each smaller than this one. But together, with their good soil and potential for hefty tithes, all three should produce you great wealth."

Heinrich knew that the soil quality in this part of Germany

was actually *not* that robust. Which was why oats, barley, rye, and potatoes were the premiere crops of the land. All were simple crops requiring only mediocre conditions at best. He presumed that Josef, being a successful estate mogul, knew this too but the baron said nothing.

They rode on from Kirdorf, skirting around the western border of Bedburg. Along the way, Baron Ludwig spoke up. "If it's all the same to you, I'd like to see Bedburg."

Heinrich narrowed his eyes and thrust his thumb in the town's direction. "It's right over there," trying only slightly to hide his sarcasm.

Ludwig frowned. "I mean *inside* the city, Heinrich."

Heinrich sighed. This was what he'd worried about—a rival lord spying on his land and people. "We can make greater speed here in the open countryside, Ludwig."

Ludwig grumbled, probably taking offense at not being addressed by his proper title. "Are we in such a rush?" he asked.

Having no answer for that, Heinrich steered his horse toward the city. As he did, Ludwig added insult to injury. "I've heard you've had quite a Protestant problem here lately. I'd like to see it firsthand."

They entered Bedburg through the western gate. The two guards at the gate saluted, stiffening a bit at the sight of so many lords. Passing by the guards, Heinrich gritted his teeth to mask his concern. He didn't want Baron Ludwig to exploit his town by discovering its weaknesses. Hopefully Tomas had been successful in maintaining control over the Protestants and their sympathizers and all would be calm and quiet. No matter how much he disliked his riding guests, he certainly didn't want to ride them into some sort of religious riot. Not only would that be embarrassing, it would also get back to Archbishop Ernst.

Heinrich's incompetence.

Perhaps that is Ludwig's plan. Using any perceived weakness in my city against me. No need to wage war on Bedburg if he can just get Archbishop Ernst to do it for him.

Such could cost me my lordship.

He grew angrier by the minute just thinking about Ludwig's likely plan.

Fortunately for Heinrich, Bedburg seemed relatively serene. Apart from the usual beggars ambling up to the group, they saw no preachers espousing the words of Martin Luther or John Calvin, or rebels screaming out "tyrant" or "warmonger."

Then Heinrich realized why. As he watched peasants duck away as they passed, and merchants quickly wheel their goods in the opposite direction, it hit him: they feared him. In fact, his presence truly terrified them.

Which made Heinrich smile.

Since becoming lord of Bedburg, he'd worked hard to achieve this goal. He understood well that the most efficient way to rule was through terror: forcing the masses into psychological submission. And now, riding through Bedburg for the first time in a long time, the success of his efforts overjoyed him. As the group rode through town, not a single man, woman, or child made eye contact with him.

Just to make sure, he slowed his horse, but the result was the same: no one returned his look. And anyone who accidentally did so immediately averted his or her eyes.

Heinrich inhaled deeply, breathing in the pungent scent of mud and horseshit. At any other time the smell would make him gag. But at this moment, watching his town yield unconditionally to his presence, the stink took on the sweet smell of success.

With an uncharacteristic smile, Heinrich turned to his guests. "Shall we now venture into the next village, my lords and lady?"

Ludwig mumbled something under his breath and, for the first time all day, Lucille spoke.

"The people here seem miserable."

Josef just scoffed. "Yes, fine, let's get going," he answered Heinrich. "I've seen enough here."

Rounding a bend in the road, they came to the poor district of town, near Bedburg's church. A small gang was huddled together in the roadway. Heinrich figured them to be just more beggars waiting to harass the rich noblemen. But as Heinrich's group drew closer, the beggars didn't disperse. As Heinrich opened his mouth to shout them away, a voice from behind yelled "There he is!" and Heinrich's blood ran cold.

They all turned to locate the source of the outcry but

couldn't. All they saw were several people milling about the buildings, but none appeared to be the speaker.

Then they heard another voice.

"It's the bastard who killed the Jacobos!"

Heinrich's eyes shot upward, to the vaulted roof of a nearby building. A man stood on the roof, shadowed by the slanted tiling. A makeshift bridge of wooden planks and crates connected one building to the next, and the next to the next, creating a ragged rooftop city.

"He dares show his face here!" the first voice yelled back. Now they could see someone appear from the top of a different roof with an object in his hand.

"This is *my* city, you devilish dog!" Heinrich shouted up to him. He felt his ears grow hot as he balled one hand into a fist and pointed the other at the man on the roof. "Get down from there this instant and show yourself!"

But Heinrich's anger quickly turned to fear when he sensed something rushing toward him. Instinctively raising his arm, he felt a sharp pain jolt his shoulder.

A hand-sized rock fell to the ground beside Heinrich's steed, causing the horse to neigh, buck once, then stop dead in its tracks. At the same moment, another man, on another rooftop, hurled a second stone at one of Heinrich's guards. But at the last minute the guard knocked the projectile out of the air with his iron wristguard.

"Cowardly heathens!" Heinrich screamed, his injured arm now numb. Thrusting a finger up toward the roof, he yelled, "Get those men and bring them to me!"

Heinrich's three guards jumped from their steeds and rushed down an alley, looking for a way up the building. Bursting into a house where an old woman began shrieking, they knocked her out of the way and found the stairs. Watching the scene unfold below him, one of the men on the roof scurried across a rickety platform, jumped to another roof, then vanished behind a tapestry of hanging clothes.

Heinrich seethed, clenching his horse's mane with his good hand. Turning to the gang of beggars still in front of them, he yelled, "Move out of the damn way, fools!"

But instead of dispersing, the beggars began slowly walking toward Heinrich and his party, looking more like a single, ghostly apparition flowing their way. Hoods hid their faces as they menacingly approached the noblemen's horses.

Heinrich's steed, already anxious, whinnied and began backing up, its hooves clomping the ground as the other horses followed. While they retreated, Baran Josef whispered in a frightened tone, "What's going on here, Lord Franz?" Tightening his grip on the reins, he scooted closer to Lady Lucille.

Heinrich's mind raced. He'd been so confident in his superior position that he hadn't considered an escape route. As their horses continued to retreat, nearing several buildings that would block their escape, Heinrich brought out his pistol, pointing it at the group.

"This is ridiculous, Heinrich!" Ludwig shouted, his voice mixed with rage and fear. "Control your people!"

The gun quivered in Heinrich's hand. Closing one eye, he aimed at the approaching group—not at a particular target but at the shadowy heart of the mass of dark figures threatening him.

Then yelling came from above.

All eyes turned toward the rooftops where a guard was now chasing one of the men who'd thrown a rock. The two stumbled over planks and platforms, then Heinrich saw both of them bound over a rickety bridge connecting two buildings. Meanwhile, the hooded gang continued toward Heinrich's group. Then another shout came from above.

Heinrich didn't know where to look.

Glancing up at the rooftop, he saw a figure trip and lose its balance. It was the man the guard had been chasing. For a moment the man's foot caught in a roof tile giving the guard enough time to close in. The man put his arms up to fight, but the guard simply reached out and shoved the man forcefully. The heel of the man's foot briefly hit something before the man tumbled backwards off the edge. Screaming in midair, he crashed to the ground directly in front of Heinrich, the top of his head hitting first before folding into his chest as his neck snapped loudly.

The crumbled body lay between the approaching group and Heinrich's noblemen, momentarily freezing everyone in place. Which gave Heinrich time to knock back his matchlock and fire into the crowd, a cloud of smoke wafting up from the gun's barrel. One of the hooded figures spun around, clutching his shoulder before falling to the ground.

Heinrich dug his heels into his horse and screamed, "Now!" his tone instantly triggering the animal's flight instinct. The steed reared on its hind legs, lunged over the fallen body and barreled directly into and through the crowd. The rest of Heinrich's party followed, trampling the man Heinrich had shot as the other hooded pursuers scattered to avoid being thrashed by the frenzied horses.

Once well past the carnage, Heinrich's horses slowed to a canter, then a trot.

Huffing and puffing, Baron Josef sputtered, "In all my years, I've never *seen* such rebellion!" Beads of sweat rolled down his fat face while he tried to regain control of his reins.

Heinrich didn't speak. His mind was still reeling at the thought of these haughty noblemen describing to Archbishop Ernst what they had just seen:

Heinrich has no control over his people!

He's more scared of them than they of him!

Bedburg runs wild with cutthroats and insurgents!

When he finally turned to scan his entourage, he was stunned to see Ludwig peering back at him with a wicked smirk on his face. The man wasn't even trying to hide his satisfaction at seeing Heinrich's loss of control.

One man was dead—probably two—and Heinrich still had no idea who his attackers were. But that didn't bother him. They were probably just Protestants anyway.

What *did* bother him was that look on Ludwig's face.

Through gritted teeth Heinrich said, "I think we've seen enough for today. Let's head back to House Charmagne."

Baron Josef and his daughter nodded in agreement.

But Ludwig just smiled. "Nonsense, Heinrich. We still have two more villages to inspect. Lead the way, will you?"

CHAPTER EIGHTEEN

DIETER

The Erft River flowed north through the heart of Bedburg, then just past Castle Bedburg it meandered east, away from the city and into the nearby woods. It furnished water for the city's wells and fish for its food supply. At its densest point, houses and commercial buildings lined both its banks.

Dieter was walking along the eastern shore of the river, in the same woods where Pastor Hanns Richter had baptized him years before. He finally came upon what he'd been looking for—an old, decrepit canoe, which obviously hadn't seen use in a long time. When the Protestant forces led by Count Adolf had attacked Bedburg three years earlier, Dieter had remembered seeing many such small vessels floating down the river. It was the best way for messengers to reach other regiments and deliver their orders to Adolf's army.

Though many other similar boats dotted the banks of the Erft, he only needed one, and this one—partially hidden beneath low-hanging branches of a large tree—suited his purposes just fine.

For a moment he thought of just getting into the boat and rowing away—leaving Bedburg behind so he could search for his wife. But he tossed that cowardly thought aside. He'd made commitments: he had a son who needed him, and he'd agreed to rescue the stonemason and his family.

It took the better part of an hour for Dieter to find, and then whittle down, two large branches into usable oars. Satisfied with his efforts, he set the oars inside the vessel, then dragged it to the water, pushing it down to test for leaks. He smiled when he saw no water bubble up from the bottom.

He pulled the boat back out of the water and positioned it

on a grassy patch just up the shoreline. After camouflaging it with uprooted shrubs and tree branches, he rode his horse back through the woods to Bedburg's eastern gate.

By the time he arrived in Bedburg, it was dark. And typical for the time of year, cold and breezy. After the strenuous work with the boat and oars, the muscles in his hands hurt, almost spasming as he clutched the reins of his horse.

Dismounting near the gate, he huddled in among a group of farmers returning to town to gain entrance without the guards noticing him. Just another weary peasant returning from a hard day of labor, heading for the brothels and taverns.

Which was exactly where he was headed. On his way to Cristoff's tavern, he passed the stonemason family's empty house and thought about them and the others—Martin, Ava, Peter, and Jerome—and wondered how they had all faired in his absence. His journey to speak with former archbishop Gebhard Truchsess in Bonn had taken five days and he hoped all was well back at the Griswold residence.

When he got to the tavern he paused out front to look around, more out of habit than suspicion. Everything appeared normal; no one seemed to be following him. Turning back around, he entered the establishment and was immediately hit with the familiar stench of stale sweat, sour ale, and overpowering humidity.

He gazed around. Cristoff was in his usual position behind the bar, tending to a few patrons, while the bar wenches hovered around tables crowded with the standard variety of rowdy travelers and workers. The night was just getting underway but, judging from the size of the crowd, Dieter figured it would be a profitable night for both Cristoff and his staff.

Rather than order a drink, he marched directly toward Aellin, whom he saw leaning over a table of men in the corner. With her dark hair flowing, and her bosom squeezed together to offer the men a tantalizing view, she was quite a sight. Dieter approached her from behind, resting his hand lightly on her shoulder. She immediately swatted it away, turning to glare at whomever had the nerve to touch her without permission.

"Get your hands off me," she blurted before realizing it was Dieter. He stepped back, raising his hands in surrender.

Her scowl immediately disappeared as she grabbed Dieter and hugged him in a tight embrace. Standing on her tiptoes, she planted a long kiss on his cheek. His face turned almost as red as her lips.

"You're the only one I'll allow to interrupt me without getting my boot up your arse, priest," she whispered in his ear. Then she turned to the men at the table. "These bastards would probably fancy that, in fact," she added, grabbing Dieter by the hand and playfully pulling him away, sashaying toward an empty table in the opposite corner.

"Hey!" shouted one of the men she'd just left. "Where're you going, beautiful?"

Aellin smirked over her shoulder and stuck out her tongue. "Give me a moment, big boy." Then she leaned into Dieter. "You can't be showing up here unannounced like this, priest."

Dieter didn't understand. "Excuse me?"

"There's talk of you rescuing and harboring Protestant fugitives. Is it true?"

Dieter scratched his chin through his beard. "Does it matter?"

Aellin smiled. "I suppose not—the rumors alone are enough to get you in trouble. And *me* in trouble, too, don't forget!"

Dieter nodded. "I apologize, Aellin. But I have urgent business."

Either not hearing him or ignoring him, she stared off in the distance and said, "Even though that bastard did get a good scare today, I reckon." She looked back at Dieter with a wicked smile.

"Today? What happened?"

"From what I heard, Heinrich was chaperoning some of his lordling cronies around town." She leaned in closer. "Actually, I helped set up a roadblock of sorts . . ." Suddenly her face contorted, her eyes glistening. "It got violent. We lost two good men."

"I'm so sorry."

Aellin waved her hand in front of her face, to make sure no one saw her emotional moment. "What was it you need to talk about?"

"I need a name. To find a man."

Aellin waited. "Well?"

"Patric Clauson."

Aellin paused for a moment, then broke into laughter. Leaning in, this time she kissed Dieter full on the mouth. Dieter's throat went dry and his skin turned hot.

"W-what was that—"

"You are a handsome fool, Dieter Nicolaus. I'll say that much truthfully—a fool of the best kind."

The inn was near the tavern. Standing in front, Dieter shook his head. When he'd first heard that name, he should have guessed. That's why Aellin had laughed. The place was just as he remembered it. He went inside. The old innkeeper stood behind the counter, at his usual spot, watching the hearthfire across the room as it flickered and roared.

Nearly a year ago, Dieter and Sybil had entrusted this man with their young son so they could sneak underneath the tunnels for what he now wished they'd never uncovered.

When he and Sybil eventually returned for their child, Gustav Koehler and his brutes had been waiting for them. A horrible confrontation ensued, outside the very doors of this inn, with many men and women—including Mia, Rowaine's lover—ending up dead.

It had also been the last night Dieter ever saw his wife.

And standing here now, it seemed like an eternity ago.

Without looking away from the fire, the old man blankly greeted his guest. "Can I help you?"

"Claus," Dieter muttered under his breath.

Still not catching the familiar voice, the old man chuckled. "Ah, I'm caught. Do your worst, knave," he joked, finally turning around. The muscles on Claus' neck tightened, his body went rigid. "It's you," he said, his voice barely audible.

"You, Claus . . . are Patric Clauson," Dieter declared.

The old man ignored the remark. "I haven't seen you in some time, boy," he said, "though I figure it's for the best. I'm truly sorry about your child."

"Don't worry over that, Claus. Peter is fine."

Claus smiled, sharp lines forming down his cheeks. "Good. Would you like some tea?"

Dieter shook his head. "No tea tonight."

"Where did you hear that name?" Claus finally asked.

"That's not important, my friend. Though it *is* yours, is it not?"

Claus hesitated, then slowly he nodded. "When I was fighting for the Spanish. My God-given name, though I've long since thrown it away. No one calls me that."

Dieter could guess why. Patric Clauson, as he was once known, had been in the Spanish army. Georg Sieghart had spoken of him. He'd been Georg's superior. Dieter figured he must have deserted the army and turned sides, now secretly working with the Protestants.

Why else would Gebhard Truchsess had given me his name?

"It may not be important to you, Herr Nicolaus, but I'd like to know who sent you. Otherwise we have no business speaking to each other, I'm afraid," the old man said.

Dieter nodded. It was a reasonable request, given the circumstances.

"Gebhard Truchsess gave me your name."

Claus frowned. "It sounds like the rumors are true. You're getting far too involved in this whole thing, young man."

"So I've been told." Dieter sighed. "Can you help me, then?"

"With what?"

Dieter shrugged. "Gebhard is in Bonn. He gave me your name as one of his operatives in Bedburg. He said he couldn't send help here, but that you would lend me your aid."

Claus creased his brow, staring hard at Dieter. Dieter recalled watching the old man, back during that terrible confrontation in front of the inn the year before, swinging his firepoker, fighting men half his age. At this moment, Claus's expression was just as dark and serious as it had been that night.

"How many people are you holding?" he asked Dieter, his voice low.

"Three. A stonemason, his wife, and their son."

Claus nodded. Scratching at his white stubble, he said, "Follow me, Herr Nicolaus."

Dieter followed him behind the counter into a small room sparsely furnished with a bed, a nightstand, a rug, and three candles. Dieter guessed this was Claus' sleeping quarters. The old man moved the nightstand off the rug, bent down and, holding the corner of the rug, folded it back to reveal a small latch in the floorboards.

"A secret passage?"

Claus nodded.

"To where?"

Claus' knees creaked as he stood back up. "Everywhere in the city, my boy. The underground tunnels of Bedburg. Plenty of room to hide folks, if you know where you're going."

Dieter was shocked. He remembered the underground passage beneath the jailhouse, but it had dead-ended under Castle Bedburg where they'd found Odela. Now thinking back, he recalled other smaller pathways snaking out from that main one.

"It covers the full breadth of the city?" Dieter asked.

"Nearly," Claus said. "If you're looking for somewhere to store people, until you figure out where to put them permanently, you may use this passage."

"But . . . what about you? If anyone sees us using this trapdoor, they'll know you were part of the conspiracy. You could be tried for treason."

Claus shrugged. "It doesn't worry me. I've lived this long without dying. I can hopefully make it a few more years." He smiled. "Are you sure you wouldn't like some tea?"

Dieter felt like hugging and kissing the kind old man. "Thank you, Claus. You don't know what this means to me."

Claus nodded. "I think I do. I was your age once, trying to do good in the world. Not much has changed, eh?"

Dieter put a hand on Claus' bony shoulder. "The tyrants still rule the world and wish to bend us to their will. But perhaps this will help our cause." He smiled. "They can't destroy us if they can't find us."

"I should hope you are right," Claus said. He rummaged through a drawer in the nightstand, then handed Dieter a folded map. "Here. You won't get far down there without this. Take it and be on your way."

Just to be safe, Dieter decided to leave the city through the south gate this time, rather than the eastern one he'd used earlier. And figuring that walking would draw less attention at this time of night than riding out, he led his horse by its reins, hurrying quietly through the dark streets of Bedburg, keeping to the shadows, his hood over his head.

When he got to the poor district of town, he saw a small group huddled around something, sobbing and hugging one another. Then he noticed the two bodies laying inside their circle, covered in white sheets, and realized the group was praying. With a pang of guilt, Dieter was glad he wasn't wearing his priest's garb, so the mourners wouldn't stop him for a prayer. That was the easiest way for him to be discovered. He thought back to his former days, back when he would have stopped whether the people asked him to or not, and whether wearing priest garb or not. Back then, his mission had been to offer aid of a different kind to the people of Bedburg. Now, however, he had to pick his battles. And the one he'd picked at the moment—protecting his son, his friends, and the stonemason and his family—had to be his priority.

So when he passed the mourners, he simply crossed himself and continued on.

A few streets further, he heard a flurry of hoofbeats in the distance, which was odd at this hour of the night. Quickly, he veered off the road and hid in an alley, turning away as the horsemen neared. Once they'd passed, he looked up and caught a glimpse of them in profile as they turned the corner, their faces briefly illuminated by the moonlight.

And he gasped.

He recognized one of them, the one leading the pack.

It was Ulrich, the infamous torturer of Bedburg.

And they were riding toward the southern gate, the place he'd been heading.

And while that gate opened into the general countryside, from which they could go literally anywhere, something in Dieter's gut told him he knew their destination.

His heart began to race. He quickly mounted his horse. It no longer mattered whether he was recognized; all that mattered now was getting there before they did.

He galloped back to the eastern gate, then blazed straight through it.

Other than some shouts from the guards, no one tried to stop him. Once in the countryside, he dug his heels deep into his horse, gritted his teeth, and raced for a shortcut he knew to the Griswold estate. When he reached the top of the hill overlooking the house, he stopped and scanned the area.

And saw his worst fear.

Clouds of dirt billowed in the air from hooves approaching from the distance. Ulrich's group was definitely heading straight for the Griswold estate from the other direction. Dieter tightened his grip on the reins, whistled to his horse, and flew down the hill. When he reached the house, Jerome Penderwick was standing at the door, his beady little face alert and alarmed.

"Rally the group!" Dieter shouted, jumping from his steed. He waved his hand in the air, "We have pursuers! Hurry!"

Jerome yelped as he ran back into the house. Within seconds the quiet estate was bustling with activity: Martin roused the stonemason and his family. Ava grabbed Peter in her arms. There was no time for packing. Within minutes they were out the backdoor, fleeing toward Bedburg—Martin and Ava with Peter on one horse; Jerome, William, Wilhem, and Mary on foot; Dieter on his horse guarding the rear.

"Head for the woods!" Dieter shouted to them all.

William Edmond called back to him. "What's going on, priest?"

"Bedburg's jailer and his men are coming. We only have a

few minutes' advantage. If we can make it to the woods, we might be safe."

William growled, "Make sure my family is safe, priest. All I wish is for Wilhelm and Mary to be safe."

Dieter nodded, his mind grasping for a plan. "Our best chance will be to split up," he said.

When they'd reached the edge of the woods, he looked back over his shoulder and saw Ulrich's group arriving at the house in a cloud of dust. It would take only a few moments for their pursuers to realize they'd escaped. And the woods would be the first place they'd look.

He sighed and dismounted. It was time to take action. Everything up to this moment, since he'd decided to help the Protestants, had led him to this.

Dieter held out his reins. "Take my horse," Dieter told him.

"What are you doing?" William asked, his voice in a panic. Hesitantly he took the halter. "And my wife and son?"

"I will personally lead them to safety, I promise you." He eyed the rest of his group. "Take Jerome with you," he told William. "Just follow Ava and Martin's horse to Bedburg. Then split up and go in through different entrances."

He reached into his tunic and produced the map Claus had given him. Handing it to Martin, he asked, "Do you know Claus' inn?"

"Of course," Martin replied, wheeling his horse around and snatching the map.

"Go there and tell him I sent you. There are tunnels beneath Bedburg and that is a map for them. Claus will help you."

Dieter turned to Ava. "Give me Peter," he said gently.

Ava hugged the child tightly, tears trickling down her cheeks.

"I promise I will protect him. He is my son. Just do as I say. You both must ride without distraction. There is no time to argue!"

Ava sniffled. "Dieter . . ." she trailed off, hesitating before handing young Peter to him.

Cradling the boy softly against his chest, Dieter looked to William and Jerome standing by his horse, and Ava and Martin mounted on the other. "When you get to the tunnels, if you haven't split up already, do so then. Go different directions."

Turning to William and Jerome, he added, "There's a ladder beneath the jailhouse that lets out near the back of the building. Do you understand? Find the jailhouse on the map, follow the tunnels to it, then exit there."

William nodded. "Yes, sir."

Turning to Martin and Ava, he said, "And you two must exit the tunnel beneath Castle Bedburg. No one will think to look there for you, under their noses. Then the three of you will meet up at William's abandoned house near Cristoff's inn. All right, everyone?"

Everyone nodded.

"You all know your parts?" he repeated, his heart pounding.

"What will you do with my son and wife?" William asked.

"I will lead them away from here, to safety. It's what you want, yes? When I find you, I'll let you know where they are."

William pecked Mary on the lips, then grabbed his son's strong shoulder, his face a mask of conflict—fear, sadness, anger. He turned to Dieter. "Thank you," was all he could whisper, then he mounted the horse and helped Jerome up behind him.

Immediately Dieter herded Wilhelm and Mary toward the woods, while Martin and Ava trotted off toward Bedburg, followed by William and Jerome a few horse lengths behind.

It took Dieter a long while to find the boat. They were now deep in the woods. Not knowing his way, especially in the darkness, he'd finally recognized the peculiar curve in the river, then the large tree under which he'd hidden the canoe.

He could no longer hear the hoofbeats from the rest of his group—William and Jerome on Dieter's horse, Martin and Ava on the other. The only sounds now were some far-off crickets and the occasional rustling of a small animal or rodent. Dieter only hoped that such relative quiet meant that he and Wilhelm and Mary were out of danger.

"Come with us," Mary said, while her son helped her get into the boat.

Dieter shook his head. He looked down at his son's beautiful face. "I have my boy to take care of. But I promise I will not abandon your husband or my friends."

"Where will we go?" Wilhelm asked, pushing the boat into the water while his mother held onto the sides for balance.

Dieter had been planning that for a long while—even before he'd readied the canoe by the river.

"You're going to row north then east. The Erft eventually collides with the Rhine near Düsseldorf. You should be able to find safe passage from a larger boat there. Then you must travel the Rhine to the Waal River. That will take you to Amsterdam."

Mary looked frightened, but her son, though just sixteen, looked determined. "How long will that take us?"

Dieter shrugged. "All the way to Amsterdam? You have few supplies, so you'll need to stop frequently. But you shouldn't have to fear being chased, not along the river. I would guess several weeks, Wilhelm. Can you do that?"

Wilhelm nodded assuredly, smiling at his mother. "Absolutely."

"There's somewhere beyond Amsterdam that I'd like to send you—somewhere you'll be safe," Dieter said. "Acquire passage to Norfolk, in the East Anglia region of England. When you get there, ask the people at the docks where Reeve Clarence Bailey's shire is. You'll find refuge there and can start your lives anew. That's where I will send your husband."

"What's in Norfolk?" Wilhelm asked.

Dieter clenched his jaw. "It was my wife's dream to take root there—to start a new life. Her name was Sybil Nicolaus."

"I didn't know you'd been married . . ." Mary started to say.

A rustling in the bushes startled them. Definitely not a rodent. Dieter spun around, gripping Peter tightly. Wilhelm grabbed one of the oars and took a position in front of his mother in the canoe.

"Who's there?" Dieter called out.

A man emerged from the bushes, his hands held high in surrender.

Dieter furrowed his brow. This was the strangest-dressed

man he'd ever seen, with fur pelts for a tunic reaching to his knees, and fuzzy boots. His arms were sleeveless, covered in blue circular tattoos, as was his face. He looked like a druid, or perhaps a wild Welshman.

Dieter eyed the man.

"Who in God's name are you?" Dieter demanded.

The man smiled, showing yellow teeth. "Not in God's name, my friend, but in the name of the spirits. That is how I've found you, after all."

Dieter cocked his head. "What?"

"I must have found you in my dreams."

Perplexed, Dieter said, "There's no time for this. What is it you want?" The man was clearly mad.

"My lord wishes to kill me and, needless to say, I wish to escape that fate. I came upon this forest to hide, waiting for the changing of the guards at Bedburg's gate so I could sneak in, remove a horse, and flee. But so far I have not seen the chance. So I have waited. Then I came upon this canoe. Did you know there are canoes scattered all across this place? Strange."

"Please hurry with your answer, we have no time for this," Dieter said, glancing over at Mary and Wilhelm.

"Of course. Well, when I happened on this lovely boat, with its newly-whittled oars and freshly-cut brush trying to hide it, I deduced that someone would likely return soon for it. And, well, waterways are even safer than land roads, in my estimation, but going it alone seemed a bit frivolous. So I chanced to wait. At least through the night, to see who might claim it. And . . . lo and behold!"

Dieter was shaking his head at this fanciful story. "And your name?"

"Salvatore."

"Well it's not going to happen, Salvatore."

"And why is that? I am unarmed, I come in peace, and there's plenty of room on the boat."

"I don't trust you," Dieter replied, looking again at Wilhelm and Mary, who seemed as bewildered as he, though no longer in fear.

"You say you're unarmed?" Wilhelm yelled to him.

Salvatore smiled. "Unarmed, yes, my lord. But don't be fooled—these arms are strong! They'll be a welcome addition to your rowing crew!"

Dieter hadn't thought of that. Mary likely couldn't row for much more than occasional spurts. This lunatic could at least shorten the time it would take them to reach their destination. He raised his brow at Mary and Wilhelm. "It's up to you, my friends."

Salvatore clasped his hands together and went to his knees to beg.

"Get off your knees, man," Wilhelm scoffed. Turning to Dieter, he said, "You've wasted enough time here already. We'll take the poor savage. If he tries anything, I'll kill him."

And Dieter didn't doubt that. He was a strong young man, like his father, and absolutely determined.

"In the meantime, go find my father and send him to us, priest," Wilhelm said, speaking with authority beyond his years. Dieter had every expectation that the young man would become a fine member of society, with a bright future. He just needed a chance to get away from the chaos of Bedburg.

Dieter nodded. "I will do just that, my friend. Good luck. And I promise to reunite you with your father"—then looking at Mary—"and husband."

Wilhelm stepped into the canoe, swaying back and forth to gain his balance. He sat in front of his mother and waved the strange fellow over. The man climbed in behind Mary.

Dieter pushed the boat to give it a start. As he watched it float slowly away, Wilhelm turned back to him. "Thank you for everything, Dieter Nicolaus," he called out.

"We won't forget you."

CHAPTER NINETEEN

HUGO

The following morning Hugo was in Bedburg before the sun rose. Ordered by Heinrich to oversee what was happening in the city, he didn't much like what he saw.

The townsfolk were on edge. Near the church, a group of citizens—most holding candles—marched alongside a horse-drawn cart carrying the bodies of two men wrapped in white sheets. As the procession made its way down the street, the man leading the procession shouted, "Two more innocents killed by our tyrannical lord!"

Others lined the street to watch the solemn parade, celebrating the lives of their lost comrades while simultaneously displaying their unabashed hatred for Lord Heinrich Franz.

Watching the spectacle, Hugo knew that someone needed to stop it. It was a direct affront to Heinrich's rule, which, if allowed to go on, would soon poison the entire city.

This was how rebellions were born and rulers deposed.

He stopped to ask a grief-stricken woman how the men had died. She described Heinrich Franz riding through town with his noblemen and picking off innocent townspeople for sport, ruthless savage that he was.

Hugo knew Heinrich was not a good man. But he couldn't believe he'd been so cavalier, so *obvious*, as the woman described. Even Heinrich had more nuance than that.

He also knew that the whole reason for that tour with the noblemen had been so Heinrich could simply show them the city, and specifically the villages being exchanged for the marriage.

At the far end of the street Commander Tomas Reiner stood with his hands crossed over his chest. He looked both bitter and sad. Ten soldiers were positioned behind him, stiff and unmoving. When the procession got within yards of him, he stepped forward.

"This march must end now," Tomas told the leader. "You've had your say—and you're lucky I don't arrest you all. I hesitate doing so only because you are grieving."

Members of the procession began shouting for the leader to proceed. Then, realizing the futility of that, they turned the cart around and headed for the church to consecrate the burials.

At the top of the hill, Bishop Balthasar was already waiting in front of the church, watching the procession come his way. When it got about halfway there, the bishop spoke out.

"You can't bring that cart any further."

The man leading the group yelled back up to him, "And why is that, Your Grace?"

"Because the cemetery you plan to bury your friends in is a holy site. For Christians, of the True faith. It is not a site for heretical vagabonds."

The man in front blew out his candle and turned around to his following. "Did you hear that? The bishop says our brothers here are not good enough to be buried in his *holy* graveyard!"

"Blasphemy!" another man cried out.

"An outrage of the highest order!" a woman shouted.

The leader turned back toward the bishop. "What would God say to you for what you're doing? You're supporting a despot and maniac!"

"I'm doing no such thing," Balthasar said calmly. "But I won't have this sacred land sullied by the arrival of common vagrants and bandits. You must take your fallen elsewhere."

"Where will we go?" asked the man.

"There's a graveyard just past the north gate, outside Bedburg."

Which brought an even larger rumbling from the crowd.

"He won't even let us bury our brothers in the *city!*"

"I can't believe it!"

By this time, Tomas and his soldiers had closed in behind the procession.

"Believe it," Tomas shouted. "This fiasco is over, dammit!

Disperse from the church or I'll be forced to take drastic measures." To emphasize his point, he flicked his wrist and his soldiers instantly loaded their rifles with a flurry.

"They're going to shoot us if we don't comply!" the man screamed, trying to rile the crowd. And it was working.

In an instant, Tomas was in the man's face with his pistol drawn. Speaking in a low, menacing voice, he said, "This is your last warning, Herr Anthony. I won't ask again." He cocked the gun. Suddenly the man was not so brave. He gulped, then nodded before leading the procession back down the hill.

As they headed away, Tomas turned to the onlookers still milling about, ordering them to disperse and go about their day. But Hugo could sense that the tense situation, though temporarily disrupted, was far from over. The place was still rife with seething anger, like a dark storm cloud ready to burst.

As Hugo headed for the jailhouse, he could feel trouble in the air.

These people have not given up. In fact, quite the opposite.

Watching from a distance, Hugo observed two men in chains being dragged by five soldiers. The chained prisoners were filthy, as if they'd been rolling around in a sewer. One was a big and broad-shouldered; the other small and jittery with bulging, terrified eyes.

Last among the soldiers was Ulrich.

Hugo approached him as the group proceeded toward the jail. "What's going on here?"

"We've been looking for these two all night," replied Ulrich, still walking. "Found them in the tunnels underneath the jail."

"Who are they?"

"The stonemason Heinrich's been blithering about. And some other strange, beady-eyed little fellow."

"They were underground you say? Below the jail?"

Ulrich, clearly tired and impatient, stopped to face Hugo. "That's what I said, Hugo. It seems they had some help—aiming to get to the tunnel entrance at the back of the jailhouse. Little did they know, I patched that up months ago." With a smirk, he continued walking, catching up to the rest of the group.

"What will you do to them?" Hugo asked, hurrying behind him.

The jailer shrugged. "What I do best, Hugo. If you'd like to review what I taught you those months ago, feel free to join me and watch."

Hugo's shoulders slumped. He hated what Ulrich did but realized it was likely the only way to get information in this Godforsaken city. So, reluctantly, he followed Ulrich inside the dark prison.

Jerome Penderwick shrieked in agony, turning away as the thumbscrew tore through the nail of his big toe, blood flowing freely and pooling under his right foot.

Hugo turned away. Standing outside the cell, he'd been watching through the bars. Ulrich chuckled.

"What's so funny?" Hugo asked.

"He doesn't stutter when he screams. Odd, but amusing."

Hugo shook his head and closed his eyes.

Pointing at the thumbnail, Ulrich glanced up at Hugo. "You remember how this thing works, don't you? Care to give it a try?"

Hugo's eyes caught a glimpse of the bloody floor and he felt like he might be sick. Turning away again, he muttered, "I'm fine, Ulrich, just . . . get on with it, will you?"

Ulrich grinned, causing the evil-looking scar on his face to wiggle. "This is something we don't want to rush into, son," the torturer replied, the smile on his face widening. Then he turned back to his prisoner and the smile vanished. "Let's try this again, Mister P-P-Penderwick," he said, mimicking the surgeon.

"G-g-go to hell, you animal," the poor man groaned.

Ulrich slapped him across the face hard, drawing a wince and sharp cry.

"You've said that already," Ulrich told him. "I'm going to need fresh words from you if you want to get out of here alive."

He reached down for the thumbnail, then dramatically paused, asking casually, "When did you come to Bedburg, and whom did you come with? Are you a Protestant spy?"

The interrogation had been going on for nearly an hour, while William Edmond sat in the adjacent cell, waiting his turn. Hugo knew that positioning the other man so close had been intentional. Unnerving him—"vicarious torture"—was how Hugo saw it. Soften the bigger man up a bit before the torturer's attention turned to him.

Jerome defiantly shook his head. The left side of his face, red and puffy, had already started to form heavy bruising, his left eye swollen almost shut.

"I'm not a Pr-Pro-Protestant," the man cried out. "I don't know their p-p-plans, so s-s-stop asking."

Ulrich turned back to Hugo. "Perhaps I should remove the rest of his teeth. He's only got about four left anyway." Ulrich snickered. "Maybe that would stop the stuttering. What do you think?"

Hugo's stomach knotted. "I think you're a devil, Ulrich," he said softly.

Ulrich's mouth fell open, feigning surprise. "You wound me deeply, Hugo." Turning back to Jerome, he said, "Answer the first part of the question. When did you come here, and with whom?"

Jerome stayed quiet for a long moment. When Ulrich reached back down toward the thumbscrew, Jerome cleared his throat. "I came here m-m-months ago, aboard the *L-L-Lion's Pride*. I came with Rowaine Donnelly, Daxton W-Wallace, and S-Sybil Nicolaus."

Hearing his sister's name, Hugo's heart fluttered. "What did you want with Sybil Nicolaus?" he asked. "Why was she part of that crew?"

"S-she was to be our g-g-guide in Bedburg. R-Rowaine sought to f-f-find her father and her m-mother's killer."

Leaving the thumbscrew in place, Ulrich reached instead for his rusty pliers, then tapped them on his chin. "I know Dieter Nicolaus was part of that group as well. Last year, when that skirmish broke out at the inn with Gustav Koehler and his men?

I saw Dieter Nicolaus there with the rest of your group. I know the whole lot of you has been operating in secret. Where is he?"

Jerome shrugged. "H-he wouldn't tell me. He left with t-the s-s-stonemason's family."

Hugo heard footsteps coming down the stairs from the jail's lobby. A moment later Karstan Hase appeared from around the corner. Hugo clenched his jaw and tightened his fists, staring daggers at Karstan. "What are you doing here?" Hugo demanded.

Hugo knew Karstan was responsible for that first raid on Dieter's group at the Achterberg estate. Karstan had never been loyal to Dieter, but the boy *had* been loyal to Hugo at a point in time, in fact they'd been best friends. Until Karstan stole Ava away.

He narrowed his eyes on his ex-best friend.

Perhaps he's jealous that Ava was stolen from him, *too. And why he wants to catch her so badly. Revenge.*

Karstan pushed past Hugo. "Move, Hue." He joined Ulrich in the cell. "I see my intelligence was correct," he said to Ulrich. "You have your men."

Has Ulrich replaced me as his apprentice with Karstan?

Ulrich frowned at the boy. "Not all of them. You almost have your freedom—but not until you help me round up the rest."

Karstan sighed, his head drooping.

Now Hugo understood.

Karstan doesn't want to be here any more than I. He's helping Ulrich to somehow gain his freedom. But from what?

"Were you the one following my carriage on horseback, Karstan?" Hugo asked.

Karstan turned. "When you were spying on Ava at your childhood estate? Yes, that was me."

"Why are you helping Ulrich?" Hugo asked, as the jailer looked up and smiled.

"Your sister and her husband got me arrested," Karstan said. "They separated me from Ava. She tried to pilfer one of their purses and was caught by the red-headed bitch. But it was the pretty boy that accused me of the thievery—Martin. And the guards went along with it. Ava didn't help me. So once I've helped uncover those traitors, Ulrich will let me leave in peace."

Hugo had no idea what Karstan was talking about. "So you don't love Ava, then?"

Karstan scoffed. "That cold bitch? Are you insane? Look at the grief she's caused all of us. No, I don't love her, Hugo. She's more trouble than she's worth, and there are plenty of prettier girls out there."

Jerome let out a blood-curdling scream as Ulrich cleanly tore off the man's right thumbnail with the pliers, quickly forcing Hugo and Karstan back to the matter at hand. While the man blubbered, Ulrich slapped him lightly, bending down to examine his face. He shook his head. "This one's gone," he said, letting go of the man's chin as he passed out. Setting the pliers back in his toolbox, Ulrich stood, then walked past Karstan.

"Let's see what the other one has to say."

William Edmond was strapped to a chair in the adjoining cell. Hugo was shocked at how calm and collected he appeared to be. No perspiration, no shaking, no trying to escape his bindings. The man clearly knew something, something that somehow kept him sane and in control. And Ulrich saw that too.

"What are you hiding from us, mason?" he asked.

William shrugged. "I have nothing to hide or offer you, punisher. This is all a mistake. I am not a Protestant."

"But you planned to fight on their behalf and that's why you're here, Herr Edmond. Balthasar Schreib said as much. Your confession to the bishop put you here. How does that make you feel?"

William flexed the muscle of his jaw. He hadn't known the bishop had betrayed his confession, putting him and his family in such danger. But he quickly collected himself. "I'm indifferent to the entire situation. I would expect nothing less from a Jesuit. But I'm not fighting on behalf of the Protestants. That's where you're mistaken."

Ulrich cocked his head. "Then who are you fighting for?"

"I'm not fighting for anyone. Just against oppression and cruelty, like any decent man would. You can break me, but you cannot destroy my spirit. It lives on with my family."

Ulrich twitched, suddenly realizing something. He muttered under his breath, "And every minute we keep you here, the further your family gets from Bedburg . . ."

William stared ahead, unmoved.

Karstan chimed in. "Should I arrange a search party? I'm sure we could find them."

Ulrich waved off the young man. "I'm sure that's exactly what Herr Edmond wants from us—to send troops on a wild chase through the countryside. No, Karstan, they're far from here by now, and only getting farther."

"You're not as stupid as you look," William shot back.

Hugo bit his lip, expecting an outburst from Ulrich. Instead, the torturer just smirked. "I appreciate that," he chuckled.

Hugo didn't know why Ulrich was being so . . . *respectful* of this prisoner. Nothing like his behavior with the other one. It still amazed Hugo how Ulrich could turn his sadism on and off like a switch—one minute inflicting incredible pain, the next thanking the man for his insult.

"What are you waiting for?" Karstan asked Ulrich. "Should I bring you your tools?"

The torturer shrugged. "I don't think we'll learn anything from this one that we won't learn easier from the one next door."

"Are you sure?" Karstan asked.

Ulrich turned to William. "Do you know where Dieter Nicolaus is?"

William shook his head.

"Even though he took your family?"

"I forced him to take my family," William said, shifting in his seat. "And told him not to tell me where they were."

He's lying, Hugo thought, noticing the big man's changed demeanor, how his body tensed. *How could Ulrich not see that?*

But he saw no reason to give up the man.

Though Karstan did. "I don't believe you," he said. "You're saying you were prepared to never see your family again? That's not . . ." he turned to Ulrich. "How can that be?"

William answered for the torturer. "You wouldn't understand, boy. Do you have a family? A man will do the unimaginable to ensure his family's safety. We had fair warning from Dieter Nicolaus that you were on your way. It was simply a matter of survival. Save me or my family? The choice is . . . no choice at all."

Ulrich nodded. "Well said, Herr Edmond."

But Karstan shook his head. "Do something to him, Ulrich. I don't believe this nonsense." He jabbed his finger into the man's thick chest. "This man knew where he was going. The priest must have planned where they'd meet—don't you see that? He didn't go underground to get caught . . . he went there to escape!"

William stared at Karstan's finger. "Despite these straps, boy, point that finger in my chest again and I'll bite it off."

Ulrich chuckled. "Quiet, Karstan. Even if you're correct, I can't see myself breaking a determined family man like this. And don't try to tell me what to do. Remember who holds your freedom . . ."

Karstan grunted and Hugo couldn't help but smile.

"Besides," Ulrich added, "like I said, we can find out where they were going through Jerome Penderwick over there." He nodded at William. "Thank you for your time, Herr Edmond. I'm sorry it had to be this way."

William nodded. "You're just doing your job."

As Ulrich passed Hugo on his way back to Jerome's cell, Hugo touched his arm and leaned in. "Why were you so . . . *kind* to him?"

Ulrich sighed. "William Edmond built the walls around Bedburg, son. When the Protestants first attacked years ago, who do you think manned the city's defense by erecting a makeshift palisade? That man helped defend the city more than any soldier. He also built my house. Do you understand?"

Hugo's cheeks grew hot. He looked away, then nodded. He understood. And now he felt even worse about himself. Humiliating a hero of the city.

What kind of man have I become?

Looking around at the chipped walls of the jailhouse, the grimy, blood-spattered stones and walls, the swollen misshapen face of Jerome Penderwick, it suddenly hit Hugo.

We *are the villains here.*

It was the first time he'd seen himself that way. When he'd been running through the streets of Bedburg thieving, he hadn't seen that as evil, just desperate. When he'd traveled to Trier and Tomas had ordered the deaths of all those people, he'd excused himself as not knowing about it in advance, that he would have tried preventing it if he'd known. Even when he killed Severin, shoving him off the cliff, there'd been good reason: the man had murdered his friend Klemens. And even with that rationalization, he'd still begun feeling tormented about killing him as the months went by. An evil person would never feel that.

But now . . . now he had no excuses. He worked for Heinrich Franz, as his *emissary* and *regent.* A man who just today had killed two people for no reason, without remorse.

And here he now stood, watching the torture of two more men, not caring about them in the least, wanting just answers.

I've become Ulrich.

Worst still, I've become Heinrich.

He wandered from the cell in a foggy haze, his mind reeling over his epiphany. "Where are you going?" he heard someone say.

"I-I don't . . ." shaking his head, he began climbing the stairs to the lobby, then remembered something.

"I'm going to House Charmagne," he said, turning back down toward the cells. "I nearly forgot. The wedding is tonight."

"The wedding?" Karstan asked. "Between whom?"

Hugo ignored him, looking over at Ulrich. "Remember to be there tonight, Ulrich. Heinrich wants you to bring five men with you."

Ulrich waved him away, now busy working on Jerome, who'd just woken up.

As Hugo stepped outside the stinking jailhouse, the last thing he heard were the horrific, spine-chilling howls of evil crushing innocence.

CHAPTER TWENTY

SYBIL

Sybil sat outside Claire and Leon Durand's house, hands folded on her lap. It was midday and a relatively warm afternoon in the shire. Claire sat in a chair on the other side of the patio, cradling Rose. Sybil turned and gave her a tired smile.

Daxton Wallace walked up to the porch dressed in his best leathers, like he was going out pirating. When he reached Sybil, he stepped out of the way to reveal two figures behind him, a middle-aged woman and a toddler.

"This is Kaitlin Baker and her daughter, Maybelle," he told Sybil.

Kaitlin was frail looking, with sunken cheeks and a large forehead. Her daughter looked much like her, but with squinty blue eyes that had a hard time focusing on Sybil. Hiding behind her mother, she had her arms wrapped around the woman's thighs.

Kaitlin put her hand on her daughter's head. "Thank you for seeing us, Madam Diviner," she began, bowing her head.

"It's my pleasure, Frau Baker," Sybil said warmly, smiling. "What ails you?"

"It is my daughter, May," Kaitlin said, running her hand through Maybelle's light-blonde hair. "She may not look it, but she's sick. She's had a cough and leaky eyes for days and complains her eyesight is getting worse. Things she once saw like a hawk she describes now as blurry." The woman's eyes grew wet as she spoke.

Sybil leaned forward in her chair and gazed at the little girl, motioning for her to come forward. With a little coaxing, the girl released her grip from her mother's thighs and nervously stepped forward. Her big eyes stared at Sybil like pools of water, unblinking, a deep frown set on her face.

"Am I blurry to you now, Miss May?" Sybil asked gently.

The little girl slowly nodded. "Yes, Sacred One."

"Please, you can call me Beele," Sybil said.

That brought a tentative, gap-toothed grin from the girl.

Sybil returned the smile, then looked up at Kaitlin. "Her eyes don't appear particularly wet, madam."

"It comes and goes."

"Is it typically worse at any certain time of the day?"

Kaitlin nodded. "During night, ma'am."

Sybil nodded, stroking her chin. She turned to Daxton. "Go inside and get me a handful of bilberries, please."

"Right away, *ma'am,*" he sighed, his tone less than enthusiastic. A moment later, he returned, handing Sybil a small pouch.

Sybil asked the little girl, "Have you ever had bilberries, May?"

The girl shook her head.

"They're a fruit—not too tart, but not too sweet, either. You should like them."

The girl's mother looked puzzled. "How will eating berries help my girl's sight, madam?"

Sybil weighed the pouch in her hand. "They are very good at fighting infections and restoring humors. They can cure bowel problems and poor circulation. I'm hoping that with better circulation young May's eyesight will improve." Sybil had learned this from the local herbalist. Although she was just repeating what the medicine-maker had told her, Sybil's words seemed to carry considerably more "spiritual" weight lately, given her new public image as the Pale Diviner. She handed the pouch to Kaitlin. As the little girl took it, Sybil told her mother, "Take just three or four a day, so she isn't over-sugared. And if they don't seem to help in a week, come back and we can try something a bit more bold."

Kaitlin smiled and curtsied to Sybil, then Daxton. "Thank you very much, my lady and lord," she said, walking off holding her daughter's hand.

Over the next hour, a half dozen more people—all patiently

waiting just down the hill—were brought up one by one by Daxton for Sybil to tend to. After a while, Rowaine appeared at the doorway. "Is that the last of them?" she asked, walking onto to the porch with a slight limp. She cursed when she saw even more people congregating down the hill where a new line was forming. "God be damned, this is never-ending."

Sybil sighed. "How are our supplies doing, Dax?"

"We're running rather thin on your pine bark tinctures and berries. We'll have to fetch more from the market soon. I could go about it in the morning. But you should have enough to last a few more visitors, depending on what ails them."

"Right," Sybil said, waving her hand. "Send up the next one, please."

Ever since the "Rowaine Miracle," word had spread quickly of Sybil's magic touch. By the time she'd returned from King's Lynn with Georg and Daxton—after securing Reeve Bailey's shipment via Corvin Carradine—townsfolk had begun camping near Claire's house, waiting for the miracle-worker to cast her magic. At first Sybil had been baffled, not sure how she could possibly help all these sickly folk. But she soon grew accustomed to—even enjoying—her new duties.

This was now how she started her days: sitting on Claire's porch helping those in need. It gave her purpose, though sometimes she did feel a bit of a fraud. The truth was she had no idea whether any of her recommendations really worked. She knew she wasn't a healer, though the countryfolk obviously thought otherwise, treating her like a saint.

It was all so totally foreign to Sybil—being admired and idolized. And she knew she couldn't let it go to her head. In fact, she'd already instructed Rowaine to stop her at the first sign of either sounding ridiculous or taking herself too seriously.

But for now, she'd accepted her new role as the shire's Pale Diviner.

And she was fortunate to have the rest of her group there supporting her. Rowaine bought the goods from the marketplace and, though she knew little about the items she purchased, she had at least spent time traveling with the surgeon, Jerome Penderwick, so had some knowledge of medicine and remedies.

But not much.

And Daxton was her presenter and peace-keeper, directing each person to her in an organized fashion while keeping any disruption around the house to a minimum.

Georg was the only one *not* much involved, spending most of his time away from the house working on his tavern. Since Reeve Bailey had given him the go-ahead to build, granting him his license, he'd gotten started straight away. He'd made Claire's husband, Leon, his chief architect—the same role he'd played when Dieter's church was built—and on most days five to ten other farmers would come around to help.

Daxton was once again walking up to the porch, but this time with a different look on his face. "Look who I found," he said in a low voice, stepping aside to show the person behind him.

Sybil's cheeks flushed and her heart fluttered.

The dashingly handsome young captain of the *Silver Sun,* Corvin Carradine, smiled back at her.

"Guy Ericsson was found dead yesterday," Corvin began, his face solemn. They were in Claire's living room—Corvin, Sybil, Daxton, Georg, and Rowaine—the women seated, the men standing by the door. "In King's Lynn, under . . . suspicious circumstances. Floating near the docks. At first, they suspected suicide, until they recovered the body and found his boots filled with rocks."

Daxton let out an awkward chuckle. "Someone wanted to make it look like suicide, but failed to puncture his lungs, so he floated up despite his weighted feet." He turned to Rowaine, surprised to see the color had left her face. "Are you okay, Row?"

She closed her eyes. "I'm fine. Just makes me think of Dominic, is all."

Dominic had been Rowaine's shipmate, a sweet boy who—after a savage sexual assault—had jumped ship, killing himself. Rowaine had dispatched the boy's attacker, the captain of the ship at the time, with a commensurate level of her own savagery.

"Don't do that to yourself," Daxton told her.

Georg returned to the subject at hand, asking Corvin, "Do you have any idea who killed him?"

Corvin nodded. "Mysterious death, body in the water . . . I have an inkling. Actually, there were a great many people who likely wanted him dead, but none more than the Hanseatic League. He betrayed them and they do not take that lightly."

"So it was proved he was stealing from the League?" Sybil asked.

Corvin sucked in his breath. "*Proved* is a strong word, my lady. 'Highly suggested' might be a better way of putting it."

"And might you have been the one to 'highly suggest' such a thing?" Georg asked, crossing his arms over his chest.

"I told you that was my plan, didn't I?"

Georg nodded. "And why have you come here to tell us?"

"Well . . . Guy's death brings up some pertinent issues facing the League's work in King's Lynn." He angled his head. "Specifically, that we currently have no replacement."

"Why should we care about that?" Sybil asked. "That man tried to have us arrested and killed. Traitor or not, he was still an arm of the Hanseatic League."

"Do you mind what happens to Reeve Bailey's textile exports, my lady?" Corvin asked Sybil.

"Of course," Georg interjected from the doorway. "Without those goods arriving in Germany, Bailey could revoke my building license and cancel my tavern."

"Then you'll want the merchandise to arrive where it's supposed to. And without a shipping man in King's Lynn"—Corvin shrugged nonchalantly—"who knows where the goods may end up."

"Again," Sybil said, her voice rising, "why are you telling *us* in particular? To scare us? To blackmail?"

Georg stepped forward. "Yes. What's your game here?"

Corvin threw his hands out wide. "No, no, nothing like that, my friends. I assure you, I come as an ally."

"Then out with it, man," Daxton said, nudging his chin toward Georg. "Before we set this big fellow here on you."

"I am here to offer my services—"

Everyone in the room groaned, then began grumbling.

Corvin waved the group quiet. "It's nothing shifty, my friends!" He pointed to Georg. "I am here to offer this man a position in King's Lynn. Under the express permission of the Hanseatic League . . . as their formal representative. We wish for Georg Sieghart to be our new shipping representative there."

Georg raised his eyebrows, pointing to himself. "Me?"

"How do they even know who he is?" Sybil asked.

"He has no experience doing anything like that," Daxton added. "And what about his tavern?"

Joining with the others, Georg asked, "You're asking me to be a smuggler?"

"We are a reputable organization, Herr Sieghart," Corvin replied. "I wouldn't call you a petty *smuggler.*"

"I didn't call myself petty . . ." Georg mumbled.

"You would be in charge of overseeing all goods imported and exported to our warehouse. In return, you'll have every trade route and secret associate of the League at your disposal. It's a lucrative position, my friend. One you should not take lightly."

Sybil stood from her chair. "But why *Georg?* What has he done to gain the League's favor?"

Corvin smiled. "I personally spoke with the higher authorities, my lady, on his behalf." He offered her a little bow.

"You trust me enough to give me such responsibility?" Georg scoffed. "You're either stupid or mad."

Clearly, the conversation was not going the way Corvin had hoped. Nervous now, he said to Georg, "I trust you, yes, and in turn the League trusts you. It's as simple as that. And because they hold me responsible for Guy's death, I must be the one to find a suitable replacement."

"And if I say no?"

Corvin's eyes stared deeply into Georg's. "Don't say no, Georg."

Georg looked at the man for a moment, then asked, "Why not?"

Corvin sighed, scratching his cheek. He opened his mouth to speak, then hesitated. After a pause, his words just spewed out in one long breath. "Because the League knows I'm down here proposing my nomination to you, and if you decline they'll know I've told you too much, and people aren't supposed to know too much about our affairs." He inhaled slowly, then exhaled, adding, "Now do you see?"

Sybil stepped toward Corvin. "Are you saying our lives are in danger if Georg says no?"

"I'm saying . . . yes, that is a possibility." Another long pause followed, no one wanting to speak first. So Corvin continued, turning back to Georg. "Look, you were the one who voted against having me killed when you, and she, and your carpenter friend here, first boarded the *Silver Sun*."

"*Captain*, not 'carpenter friend,'" Daxton corrected him.

"My apologies," Corvin said, glancing over at Daxton before continuing with Georg. "I respect a man who does something like that, especially when the alternative is so much easier. You chose to trust me, or at least you chose to see how far my trust would take you. And I admire that. It's the kind of resolve we wish to see in our associates."

Georg pressed on. "What makes you think I won't steal from you?"

"I don't see it in your character," Corvin said with a smirk. "And besides, you've just learned Guy's fate . . ."

"Georg," Sybil said, "you're not actually considering this, are you?"

"Father," Rowaine added, "I think it's a bad idea."

Georg held his hands up to both women. "It could benefit us all," he pointed out, "and the whole shire. This may be exactly how to gain the people's trust!"

"If all goes smoothly, you'll be a wealthy man," Corvin said, trying to sweeten the offer.

"But imagine the people you'll be dealing with," Sybil said. "Thieves, highwaymen, bandits."

"I've dealt with worse," Georg reminded her. "You forget, I fought for the Spanish."

Corvin nodded. "My job will be to make sure you interact with the least number of undesirables as possible. I will also be captaining the *Silver Sun*, of course."

"What about the tavern?" Rowaine asked. "I thought that was your dream."

Georg snorted. "It's a means to an end, Cat." He smiled. "I can do just as much drinking in King's Lynn as I can here."

"And you can make a lot more money while doing it," said Corvin.

With the seed now planted and watered, it was clear which way Georg was leaning.

But Sybil wasn't finished. "So you're just going to give up on the alehouse? After all we've been through to get that damned license?"

"Of course not, Beele. I'll promote Leon from chief architect to master builder. Claire will love that. It can be my way of thanking them for allowing us to live here, like heathens, for so long."

Everyone thought about it for a while, until Georg finally spoke.

"I accept your offer, Herr Carradine. When do they want me?"

Corvin smiled. "Immediately, my good man. Your first task is to join me in King's Lynn to oversee the shipping of Reeve Bailey's textiles. Along with some other merchandise."

Once Georg was gone, activity at Claire and Leon's estate slowed considerably, though there was still much to be done. Sybil continued with her divine consultations, Daxton took on the head carpenter position for the ongoing tavern construction, Leon Durand managed the project, and Rowaine slowly began re-training her legs, though her back remained quite sore. Sybil's theory was that when Rowaine was initially injured, the bullet had pinched something in her back or spine, paralyzing her, and the fall from her bed had unstrained the pinched nerve and fixed her legs. But she still needed to exercise her legs after not using them for so long.

A few days later, Georg returned to Strangers Shire looking much different. Gone were his rugged beard and long hair.

Except for some pockmarks and facial scars—which he'd vaguely attributed to his "rough-and-tumble" time in the Spanish army—his face was now smooth and his scalp close-cropped. The only thing still bearing witness to the "old" Georg were his clothes—grimy and ragged, more the attire of a beggar or wild man than that of the new shipping representative of King's Lynn.

And he'd returned with a large advance of money—enough to complete his tavern.

"Unfortunately," Georg told his comrades, "I won't be here to see it finished. And neither will you, Daxton."

"What are you raving about?" Daxon asked. "Has that city deranged you so quickly?"

Georg shook his head. "I'm going to need another boat to ship the goods to Germany—through Amsterdam and down the Rhine. I'd like to use the *Lion's Pride*."

Rowaine stepped forward. "It's not yours to use."

Georg frowned at his daughter. "I know that, Cat . . ."

Daxton put his arm around Rowaine. "Come now, Row, don't take your anger out on your poor old father." He smiled. "I was getting bored of building that damn tavern anyway."

"Then I'm coming with you," Rowaine answered, gazing around at the faces in the room. "I've been cooped up here for far too long. I miss the sea."

Daxton nodded, then thought of something. "Does that mean you'll want to be captain again?"

Rowaine smiled, shaking her head. "I'll never be captain of the *Pride* again, Dax. That is *your* job now."

Sybil joined in. "I'd like to go with you too, then."

Which stopped the conversation cold.

After a moment, Georg, Daxton, and Rowaine all shook their heads in unison. Sybil's mouth fell open. "And why not?" she asked.

"We need someone here to look after our enterprises, Beele," Georg said. "Don't you see?" He motioned out to the countryside beyond.

Sybil eyed the group suspiciously. "Did you all plan this?" she asked.

Georg shook his head. Raising three fingers, he ticked off the reasons: "We could count on you to oversee the building of the tavern. Second, you'd be close to Claire so we'd have a place to stay when we return." And with a small grin, he said the third. "And of course you get to continue spiritually uplifting your followers in the shire."

"Grow the legend," Daxton added with wider grin.

"Your job will be more important than any of our's, Beele," Rowaine added.

But it certainly didn't feel that way to Sybil. She turned away, disappointment in her eyes. Yet in the end, she had to agree with Georg' assessment.

She'd do much more good staying than going.

CHAPTER TWENTY-ONE

HEINRICH

It would be a misty, gloomy night at House Charmagne. The winter winds blew bits of grass across the courtyard, while leaves swirled outside Heinrich Franz's window. Standing in his room by the windowsill, watching the fog seep through the last remnants of daylight, Heinrich tapped his feet as he waited for his guests to arrive.

The first carriage pulled in just as the sky darkened. He couldn't make out who was inside from up high in his room. All he could see was the orange glow of the lanterns atop the carriage, growing brighter as it drew closer to his mansion's front door.

Heinrich turned toward his mirror. He straightened his cuffs and smoothed out the wrinkles of his black jacket. Clearing his throat, he took a deep breath, then headed downstairs to his guests.

Hugo and Rolf were standing at the foot of the stairs, their hands clasped behind their backs. Both were dressed in dapper attire. When they saw him appear at the top of the stairs, they both smiled up at him. He didn't return the smile. He had too much on his mind—chaos, swirling inside him like the leaves outside.

"Where's the madman?" Heinrich asked as he descended the stairs.

Rolf frowned. "Don't worry about Salvatore, my lord. This is your day."

"Yes," Heinrich agreed, "and I want to make sure it isn't disrupted by an insane man's schemes. Where is he?"

"Gone."

Heinrich narrowed his eyes at the bearded old man. Rolf

seemed a bit more hunched than usual, more slow-moving of late. Age had definitely caught up with him, physically at least, since his brain still seemed sharp.

"What do you mean?" he asked. "Where did he go?"

"Escaped—dashed out in the night, last evening it appears."

Hugo nodded. "Didn't want to be part of your illustrious wedding, apparently." He smiled, trying to lighten the mood.

"Who let that happen?" Heinrich growled.

Just then, three loud knocks cracked against the oak doors in the foyer. Beauregard, the butler, dressed in his most splendid celebratory garb, opened the door, bowing to the new arrivals—Baron Ludwig von Bergheim and his assistant, Hedda, the first to arrive.

Heinrich had not planned a large ceremony. The wedding would take place behind closed doors—literally—as per his wish. Lady Lucille Engel had had no objection to that.

He wanted to get the wedding over with so he could go about his business of terrorizing Protestants and punishing the rebels.

Beauregard led Ludwig and Hedda down the red-carpeted hallway to the dining room. From the shadows of the walkway, Heinrich watched. As usual, Hedda held a large book under her arm, though the rest of her appearance had decidedly changed. With her curly hair hanging loosely over her bare shoulders, she wore a gown so lavish it looked more like *she* was the one getting married. Heinrich felt a slight animal tingle pulse through his body as he eyed the young woman.

"Shall we present you to your guests?" Rolf asked from behind Heinrich, startling him.

Heinrich shook his head. "Not until the rest of them arrive." He wanted to judge their dispositions from afar, when they were unaware of being watched.

A few minutes later, more guests arrived. This time, Tomas Reiner and Bishop Balthasar Schreib.

Balthasar was dressed for tradition, ceremony, and significance. He wore his finest black cassock, with a purple sash denoting his position in the diocese, a fuschia skullcap, and a pectoral hanging from his neck. Shivering when he entered the house, he rubbed his hands together as his eyes darted around the room. He didn't notice Heinrich watching him from the shadows.

Tomas Reiner wore a uniform of stiff leather and dark boots, with armbands and lapel pins denoting his military position. With his blond hair oiled back and trimmed, he looked like a regal nobleman. He surveyed the interior of the house with an eye of suspicion, as if the walls were cursed. As Beauregard led them into the dining room, Heinrich made a mental note to pay particular attention to Tomas and his generally suspicious nature.

Next to arrive were the crown jewels of the occasion, lord and lady from Erftstadt. Baron Josef Witten von Erftstadt wore a too-tight lavender tunic with a cloak that swept the ground. His white beard was braided. His daughter, Lady Lucille, looked stiff and uncomfortable in a puffy white dress that clung tightly against her body and accentuated her abundant curves. She wore no veil, but one wasn't required because no formal ceremony was scheduled. Clearly trying to alleviate her discomfort, her father held his hand to the small of her back as he gently led her down the hallway.

The last to arrive was Ulrich, the most underdressed participant of the bunch. Not owning a decent suit, he wore a plain tunic, waistcoat, and out-of-style jacket. At least he'd left his blood-soaked apron at home. He was surrounded by an entourage of five armored soldiers, their weapons visible but sheathed.

In all, it took slightly over an hour for the short list of guests to arrive. At the sight of Ulrich and his men entering, Heinrich emerged from his shadowy alcove and approached them.

To Ulrich, he said in a low voice, "Keep your guards outside of the dining room, but close at hand."

Ulrich eyed him curiously. "Will they be needed, my lord?"

Heinrich shook his head. "I shan't think so. Just a precaution."

Ulrich bowed. "Of course."

Beauregard escorted the jailer and his soldiers down the hallway, their armor clanking and creaking while Heinrich discreetly followed ten paces back. Once everyone but Heinrich was in the dining area, Rolf did the honors—announcing his host's arrival as Heinrich stepped through the entranceway.

"May I present to you the lord of Bedburg, Heinrich Franz, a true friend to the diocese of Cologne," Rolf declared, dramatically sweeping his hand around to complete the unnecessary introduction.

Heinrich made his grand entrance, stepping in with open arms, warmly smiling in his most regal way, while his guests—all seated around the long, formal dining table—pretended to be happy to see him. Flipping the hem of his coat away, Heinrich then took his seat at the head of the table, slowly eyeing each guest with a tight smile and nod of the head.

To his left sat Baron Ludwig, with Hedda next to him, followed by Commander Tomas. To his right sat Baron Josef, followed by Lady Lucille across from Hedda, and Ulrich across from Tomas. And seated at the foot of the table was Bishop Balthasar, with two chairs left empty on both side of him.

The plan was to conduct business before pleasure. Specifically, they'd proceed first with the necessary paperwork, followed by a large feast, and ending with dance and drinks. Then Heinrich and Lucille would disappear for their private consummation ceremony.

"Thank you all for coming," Heinrich began. Wiggling his white-gloved fingers, he said, "I know you're all busy people, so shall we begin?"

Some nodded, some didn't.

As the first order of business, Bishop Balthasar pulled out several pages from his cassock and stood. He laid them out on the table, pushing them forward for all to see.

"This first agreement," he announced, touching the page closest to him, "will be signed by both the groom and the bride's guardian, Baron Josef Witten von Erftstadt. It agrees that, in exchange for his daughter's hand in marriage, the barony of Erftstadt will receive the land titles of three hamlets from Bedburg: Kirdorf, Oppendorf, and Millendorf.

"The ownership of all three villages—and all estates and properties in said villages—will thus be transferred upon the legal union of the bride and groom. Conversely, the agreement is null and void if said matrimony does not take place." He looked around the table. "Is that understood?"

Baron Josef nodded, as did Heinrich. The page was then sent down the table, person by person, until it reached Heinrich. At the same time, Beauregard appeared at the dining room door with a jar of ink and fountain pen, which he set down next to Heinrich. Heinrich pretended to quickly read the document—which wasn't necessary since he'd personally prepared it—then with a flourish signed it at the bottom. After blowing his signature dry, he handed the document and pen to Baron Josef, who likewise skimmed through it, then signed it. Setting the pen down, he turned to his daughter and, with a kind smile, gently squeezed her shoulder. But she did not reciprocate her father's smile. Instead, she pursed her lips with a display of icy indifference.

Clearing his throat, Balthasar continued. "The second agreement . . . will be signed by both the groom and the bride's warden, Baron Ludwig Koehler von Bergheim. It states that, upon the groom's marriage to the warden's charge, Lucille Engel von Erftstadt, a single seat on the parliament of the Free Imperial City of Cologne, currently belonging to the city of Bedburg, will be forfeited to the barony of Bergheim. Thusly, upon the transfer of ownership of the parliamentary seat, the baron of Bergheim may do whatever he wishes with said seat—whether filling it himself or with a delegate. Is that understood?"

After both Baron Ludwig and Heinrich nodded, Balthasar repeated the process of sliding the page down the table for everyone to witness. While it made its way down the line, Hedda continued furiously scrawling in her book, apparently transcribing the bishop's every word, including his description of the contents of the papers.

Once Heinrich signed it, he handed it to Baron Ludwig on his left who, with lips moving, appeared to read each word to himself before signing it. Then he looked up at Heinrich with a wicked smile.

As soon as Baron Ludwig laid down his pen, Balthasar cleared his throat again. "Having witnessed the signatures of both agreements, under God, there is one final agreement that must now be executed in order to validate the two agreements just signed. This final document—to be signed by both groom and bride—outlines the legal rights of both parties, under God, and finalizes their union of matrimony." With a fatherly smile, he passed the remaining page down the line.

By the time it got to the head of the table, something had clouded Heinrich's eyes. Momentarily lost in thought, he stared down at the paper as if not sure what it was, then glanced up at everyone before quickly regaining his senses. With an odd smile, he looked back down at the document, then signed it and passed it to Baron Josef who handed it to his daughter.

An awkward silence followed as Lady Lucille, leaving the paper on the table in front of her, gazed at it for what seemed like an eternity. For a full minute the only audible sounds were the whirling wind outside brushing tiny tree limbs against the windowpanes. Finally, Lucille picked up the pen and, bending over to sign, allowed a tear to slide down her cheek onto the page, before brushing it aside and signing the agreement.

Almost immediately the crowd broke into subdued applause. Then all eyes returned to Balthasar.

"As God's witness," he pronounced to all, holding his hands together, "I declare the both of you—Heinrich Franz and Lucille Engel—husband and wife."

Muted cheers erupted from the audience, then quickly died down as Heinrich smiled and held up his arms.

"Now then . . . let's begin the feast, shall we?"

And what a feast it was, a truly lavish affair. Beauregard began it with platters piled high with meat pies filled with duck and lamb set in front of each guest. Then came the garlic potatoes, and snails from France, and oysters, and other fine delicacies—some from the continent, some from the far reaches of the world. Bowls overflowed with exotic fruit in rainbow colors along with dishes of tantalizing pastries and glossy cakes, plus barrels of ale and casks of wine imported from the finest sources throughout Europe.

Everyone ate to their heart's content, with the exception of one: Lady Lucille Engel. The new bride ate like a dainty child, poking at her food, glancing distractedly off in the distance, ignoring the whispered encouragements of her father.

She was simply unable to fake delight. And was clearly depressed by the whole affair—the feast, the loud conversation, but most of all, her marriage to Lord Heinrich Franz of Bedburg.

As everyone but she enjoyed the food and festivities, Heinrich eyed his new bride severely. Truthfully, he wasn't at all upset witnessing her obvious misery. In fact, since he basically felt the same as she did about the marriage, seeing her distress seemed to somewhat alleviate his own gloom. He felt no personal animosity toward the woman. It was just that he hated *all* nobles and people of high birth. But for the time being he would play the role of the happy groom for his audience, conversing exuberantly and feigning giddy satisfaction.

When most of the food and drink and desserts had been consumed, the festivities and energy level began to wane. Conversations got quieter as the guests began leaning back in their chairs, their eyes glazed, their bellies full.

When the time was right, Heinrich, with his white gloves still spotless, slowly stood from his chair and spread out his arms. "I thank you all for joining me on this joyous occasion," he announced, drawing sleepy smiles from his guests, except of course from Lady Lucille, who still refused to look his way.

Heinrich leaned over the table, resting his gloved hands on it for balance. "I have great plans for Bedburg," he told the group. "With this holy union I'm hoping we can accomplish much for our respective territories, as well as for the electorate of Cologne." He reached over and grabbed a half-filled glass, then raised it to the air.

"I'd like to present a toast," he said, waiting for everyone to grudgingly refill glasses and mugs. He closed his eyes and pursed his lips, as if deep in thought, then opened them suddenly, completing his toast. "To new alliances formed, abundant wealth for us all, and new journeys beyond the pale."

The guests mumbled back, then raised their glasses and

downed their drinks in unison.

Heinrich didn't sit. Instead, he slowly ambled over toward Baron Ludwig, stubbing his foot against the table leg as he walked, as if drunk, and cursing about it under his breath. Then he quickly looked up and smiled.

Not really knowing what to make of it all, everyone politely chuckled back.

He then stood directly behind Ludwig and placed his left hand on the baron's shoulder, squeezing gently in a friendly manner, chuckling along with everyone else. Awkwardly, Ludwig turned to see Heinrich behind him, then politely smiled up at him as Heinrich's hand disappeared behind his back.

"Unfortunately," Heinrich announced, his smile disappearing and his voice suddenly dripping with darkness, "*you* are not invited on my new journey." In one swift, fluid motion he plunged a dagger into the flesh between Baron Ludwig's neck and right shoulder. As the baron shrieked, Heinrich slid the blade cleanly through cartilage and bone as blood shot up like a geyser, showering the baron's face and turning Heinrich's white gloves red. As Ludwig's shriek turned into a blood-curdling scream, Heinrich quickly silenced him by angling the blade in a strong lateral motion across the man's throat, nearly decapitating him.

The entire maneuver occurred so quickly, so unexpectedly, that everyone at the table seemed frozen. As the baron's eyes and mouth gaped open, his body began thrashing involuntarily before slumping forward as the skin-flap of his neck hung open and slapped down with a moist squishing sound onto the food-laden tablecloth.

Blood began pulsing out in rivulets, pooling around the remaining plates of meat and fruit. Heinrich casually withdrew his dagger and gazed lethally across the table at Baron Josef, just as the frozen faces around the table suddenly roared back to life in a blur. Baron Josef was the first to react, jumping to his feet and knocking over his chair as Heinrich, with a smooth but powerful flick of his wrist, flung his knife across the table at him.

With a sickening thud, like the hollow sound of a punctured watermelon, the dagger's blade thumped into the old man's round belly, stopping only when the handle edges blocked its path from full penetration. More surprised than in pain yet, the old man wobbled for a moment, then futilely grabbed at his stomach for the dagger handle. His daughter howled, both hands reaching for the sides of her face while the remaining guests leapt from their seats.

As the lethal shock to his system began taking hold, Josef managed to pull the blade out, which only exacerbated the bloodflow. He then fumbled across the table in a clumsy attempt to reach Heinrich. By this time, however, Heinrich had the pistol he'd hidden in the back of his waistband aimed squarely at the old man's face.

"You aren't invited, either," Heinrich whispered to him before pulling the trigger. The point-blank shot made a small, clean hole directly through Baron Josef's left eye, but the exit wound was neither small nor clean, exploding away most of the rear half of his head and showering Lady Lucille with bits of her father's skull and gray matter.

As Josef's body collapsed to the table—scattering dishes, food, and drinks, Heinrich reached down and took the dagger from the man's lifeless hand.

At which point Lucille fainted, sliding off her chair and onto the floor.

Tomas was the closest to Heinrich, but with no weapon seemed as surprised at the turn of events as were the two dead men on the table. Heinrich swung around to face him, gun in one hand, knife in the other. Stepping back, he gave Tomas no choice. "Don't even think about it, Tomas!" he ordered, as Tomas wisely raised his hands to the sky.

Heinrich then looked down the table to Ulrich, yelling, "Now, Ulrich!" The jailer, also wild-eyed over what was happening, hesitated for an instant before obeying his lord by emitting an ear-splitting whistle. The dining room doors burst open and Ulrich's five guards rushed in with weapons drawn. But even Ulrich's professional soldiers were taken aback by the scene before them. One of them, upon seeing the nearly-severed head of Baron Ludwig resting across from the half-missing skull of Baron Josef, turned and vomited on the floor.

Focusing back on Tomas, Heinrich said, "Step back, Tomas!" Tomas, seeing the rage and bloodlust in Heinrich's eyes, did as he was told, giving Heinrich time to turn his attention, and pistol, to Bishop Balthasar.

The bishop was standing, still frozen in shock, the large dark stain around his crotch bearing witness to the fact that he'd very recently pissed himself. With hands trembling, he feebly tried to raise them, saying, "God will damn you for this, you devil!"

"God has damned me my entire life, bishop," Heinrich retorted. "Was it *you*?"

"Was . . . *what* me? You're making no sense! Stop this madness!"

"Did you conspire with these noble bastards?"

All Bishop Balthasar could do was shake his head, his chins jiggling.

Heinrich then aimed his gun at his old friend and mentor, Rolf Anders, who, even staring death in the face, seemed the calmest of the bunch.

"You must think this through, Heinrich. I am on your side," he said in a low tone.

"Shut your mouth, traitor!" Heinrich screamed. "You're under arrest for conspiracy, you old toad!"

"Conspiracy of what?" Rolf asked. "I have done nothing wrong."

Heinrich waved his gun to one of Ulrich's guards, motioning for him to take Rolf away. The guard grabbed Rolf by the arms.

"For conspiracy to commit treason," Heinrich told him. "For colluding with Baron Ludwig to overthrow me!"

Struggling with the guard, Rolf was too old to offer much resistance, though he kept trying anyway. "I did no such thing!" he yelled to Heinrich. "I've been your mentor—no, your friend—since you were a boy, Heinrich. Think this through!"

Then Hugo spoke, for the first time since the bloodbath began, tears streaming down his face. "Heinrich, my lord, please! Rolf is innocent!"

"Shut your mouth, Hugo! No one is innocent!"

Heinrich turned his dagger and pistol back to Tomas. Thumbing back the gun's matchlock, he said, "I know you've been conspiring with Balthasar, Tomas. I trusted you, but now you want me dead. All I ask is why?"

Tomas's reply was dry, though defeated. "I've never conspired against you, Heinrich."

Heinrich shook his head. "I've spied you speaking with Balthasar on multiple occasions. Don't lie to me!"

"The only thing I've ever spoken with Bishop Balthasar about was God, my lord. I swear."

Heinrich scoffed. "That's not good enough," he said, moving the barrel of his gun within inches of Tomas' face. Tomas closed his eyes.

"Wait, wait!" shouted Hugo. "Don't kill him, Heinrich, please!"

"Why in God's name shouldn't I?"

"Because you need him! After all this, you'll need a garrison commander who the people trust. Tomas is loved by the people. You'll need someone to protect you!"

"You think I can ever trust this man again? If so, you're more naïve than I thought, boy."

Hugo continued trying to reason with the man. "If your plan is to take Bergheim and Erftstadt . . . then you'll need an army—and a man to lead it, a man the people trust to lead them. Tomas is that man!"

Heinrich thought for a moment, his jaw clenched. Then he growled and slowly lowered his pistol. Which seemed to slightly ease the tension in the room.

"There is no *try*, Hugo," Heinrich told the boy. "Bergheim and Erftstadt are mine. The agreements were signed. There were no names mentioned in the agreements! I made certain of that. Just 'baronies' and 'territories.' I now own the parliament seat and the three villages. And the woman."

As Rolf was being led away by the guard, he turned back to Heinrich. "If you think it'll be that easy to take those cities, you are foolish," he said. The guard stopped in the doorway as Rolf continued. "After massacring the barons, you think the townsfolk will just let you come in and take their lordships?"

Heinrich eyed the old man with disgust. Waving his gun, he said, "Ulrich, take this old fool to the jailhouse and lock him away. Take the girl, Hedda, too, but leave her ledger. I'd like to see what the bitch was writing." Motioning to Tomas, he told Ulrich, "And bring this bastard with you, too. If I have to look at that blond, handsome face for a minute longer, I'll detach it from its neck."

Ulrich nodded vigorously. Apparently even the hardened torturer wasn't about to cross a man crazed enough to commit such carnage without warning. He accompanied his guards out with their prisoners: Hedda, Rolf, and Tomas.

Besides Heinrich, Bishop Balthasar and Hugo were the only two still standing. A moan sounded from the other side of the table as Lady Lucille began awakening from her faint. Ironically—given the purpose of the evening—Heinrich had completely forgotten about her.

"Beauregard!" Heinrich called out, as the butler dashed in from the doorway. He peered around the room, taking in the mayhem, though he didn't seem nearly as shocked as he should.

Turning to Beauregard, Heinrich said, "Take that hag and lock her in the cellar with the wolves."

"*With* the wolves, my lord?" the butler asked, arching an eyebrow.

Heinrich sighed. "Not *with* the wolves, dammit. *Next to* them." Then a cruel grin formed on his face as an idea came to him. "And when you're done with that, take her father's body and feed it to the hounds. That should cap off her night, eh?"

Beauregard's eyes glanced over the table again, at the two men slumped across from each other. "Which one's the father?" he asked.

"The fat one, without the head," Heinrich said.

"You'll excuse me, sir, but they're both nearly missing their heads . . ."

Impatiently, Heinrich pointed to what was left of Baron Josef.

"Right away, my lord," Beauregard said. He grabbed Lady Lucille by the hair and started dragging her out of the room, waking her further from her daze, her wails echoing down the hall.

"Balthasar," Heinrich said, his eyes landing on the shivering, piss-stained bishop. "Scurry out of my house before I kill you. Walk back to Bedburg and think about your future—*our* future."

"*Walk*, my lord? But look"—he pointed at the window, now foggy with small droplets running down it—"it's started to rain."

Heinrich arched his eyebrows. "Would you rather die?" he asked flatly. His adrenaline and rage were gone. Suddenly, he was exhausted, full, and drunk.

Balthasar didn't wait for more conversation. He fled the house as fast as his boots would take him, leaving wet boot tracks of urine behind.

Heinrich's gaze finally landed on Hugo. The boy was pale, wide-eyed, and trembling. "Hugo, my boy," Heinrich said, his voice now back to its fatherly, stern tone, "you'd better be right about Tomas. But for now, I won't ask you twice. Get out of my sight. I need to think."

Hugo wanted to say something. Dried tears streaked his face. But seeing Heinrich's face slowly turn from fatherly to furious, he thought better of it and bolted from the room.

CHAPTER TWENTY-TWO

DIETER

Dark thoughts plagued Dieter as he watched the eastern ramparts of Bedburg's city wall. He was hidden in the woods, where he'd been all night. After seeing off Wilhelm, Mary, and Salvatore, he'd stayed at the riverside to ponder his future. He knew the city would be far too chaotic for him to return any time soon.

But eventually he would have to go back, to meet up with William, Jerome, Martin, and Ava at the stonemason's old home. He'd agreed to meet them there, at the very least to let William Edmond know where his family was.

Dieter sat on an overturned tree trunk, bouncing Peter on his knee. The toddler gave him a strange look, as if to say, *I'm not a one-year-old anymore, father—you don't have to smother me like this.* But Dieter wasn't ready to let go of his son yet. He feared that if he did, even for an instant, the boy would evaporate into thin air and he'd never see him again. It was what seemed to happen to everyone close to him. So why should it be any different with his son?

As the first glimmer of sunlight peeked up from the horizon, he knew it was time to act, but he couldn't seem to get moving. Glancing back at the river, he was tempted to just float down its smooth, rippling surface and be rid of Bedburg forever.

The only thing in the world still important to him was right here with him.

So why go back?

His jaw tensed as he shook the thought from his head.

Because I can't be a coward. I've made promises. People are depending on me.

He thought back to the sermons he used to give at

Bedburg's church. Even then, he'd never had the kind of responsibilities facing him now. It was almost too much to bear.

He stared down at the top of Peter's head.

He doesn't deserve this . . .

Then, cradling his son in the crook of his arm, he stood. The air was already thick and hot on his forehead. It seemed to take every ounce of effort to move forward, but somehow he did. At the edge of the woods, he gazed off at the city of Bedburg as if seeing it for the first time. He squinted. The eastern tower looked strangely calm. No one was entering or exiting, which was either a blessing or a terrible omen.

But either way, it wasn't normal.

Maybe today was some holiday he'd forgotten about. At this hour of the morning, laborers and farmhands should have been crossing that gate in droves.

Where is everyone?

Then he noticed something even stranger: no guards in the tower.

But though troubling, it was also fortuitous. The perfect opportunity for him to re-enter the city unnoticed. Unfortunately, he also thought of what else entering could mean: that once in, he might never get out again.

He took a deep breath and willed his legs to move. They heeded his call, so he pulled up his hood and exited the woods, quickly heading straight for the gate two hundred yards ahead. Halfway there, he stopped. Second thoughts began clouding his decision. Glancing back to the woods, he wondered if this was the right thing to do.

Then he looked down into his son's eyes and saw his answer.

He proceeded on to the gate.

As he approached it, he realized his earlier observation had been correct. There was no sign of any guards. The city was completely undefended, at least from this entry point.

The thought angered him. Why wasn't Bedburg defending itself? If he'd had an army with him, he could have taken the entire city right then and there.

Stepping through the entryway arches into Bedburg proper, he found the streets deserted. He walked down the main thoroughfare, his head swiveling from side to side. Suddenly the fear he'd stifled bubbled to the surface. He felt sweaty, almost dizzy. He wasn't sure which was worse: expecting guards to pop out any moment to arrest him, or walking down empty streets that shouldn't be empty.

Not far from the stonemason's house he finally saw the first signs of activity. Two men burst out the doors of Cristoff's tavern and began stumbling down the street, clearly drunk, their arms wrapped around each other's shoulders.

Tucking Peter in close, he jogged to catch up with them.

"Excuse me! Gentlemen!" he called out.

One of them swung around with his fists up. When he saw Dieter standing there, one arm missing, the other holding a child, the man blinked through glazed eyes several times, then lowered his fists. "W-what's it you want, man?" he stuttered, trying hard to focus on Dieter. "You're gon' make us late!"

Dieter cocked his head to the side. "Late, my friend? For what?"

The man smiled a toothy grin at his friend. "Looks like we got another one been livin' under a tree here," he said, taking a step back and stumbling over himself, almost falling. "Can 'ye believe it, Marcus? I say, this is why this place's gon' to shit, it is." He thrust a wobbly finger in Dieter's direction. "All these un-uniformed . . . uninformed knaves!"

Dieter sighed. He allowed the drunk to berate him for a moment longer before finally saying, "If you'll just tell me what's going on . . ."

"You haven't heard?" the man spat to the side, barely missing his friend's shoe. "There's gon' be an execution!"

Dieter's heart dropped. He stepped away from the two drunks. The man who'd spoken to him slapped his friend on the back, then began pulling him along as the two stumbled away. Dieter turned, walking fast toward the stonemason's house, his heart pounding, his throat feeling like sandpaper.

As he approached the house, it too looked unusually quiet. When he reached the front door, he gently pushed and it creaked open.

Immediately, he could tell the place was empty.

Horrible thoughts flooded his mind.

Where's Martin and Ava? And William and Jerome? They should all be here by now!

Then, like a lightening bolt, the connection hit him: the empty house with what the drunk had just told him.

"There's gon' be an execution!"

Holding Peter tightly, he shot out of the house and took off running. Through alleys, down small streets, around curves, using every short cut he knew, to the town square.

The closer he got, the more people there were. And all heading in the same direction. Everyone knew. The news had been spread.

Which could mean only one thing: someone was sending a message to the city.

Watch these people die. Know that the next could be you. Or your family. Or any rebellious protestor or follower.

And that kind of message could come from just one person: Heinrich Franz, the only one with both the motive and power—the motive to send such a message and the power to bring everyone together like this on such short notice.

As he passed groups of people, he began hearing the murmurs and whispers.

"I hear he massacred them all," said someone. But when Dieter spun around to inquire, whoever said it was gone. He caught more bits of conversation.

"Murdered them in their sleep, is what I've been told."

"That Heinrich Franz is one cold bastard."

Frustrated, he touched a woman's shoulder with his stump. "Excuse me, Frau . . ."

The woman turned. It was Aellin from the tavern. Her black hair was damp with sweat, the curls plastered to her shoulders, like she'd run all the way from the tavern. Dieter smiled at the familiar face.

"Ah, Aellin! Nice to see you."

But for once, she didn't smile back. "Under the circumstances, priest, I think not."

"What's going on?"

"So . . . so much, it seems. You haven't heard? Where've you been?"

Dieter frowned. "Please, just . . ." he started.

"There's an execution underway—"

"So I've heard," he said. "But what's happened? I hear just bits and pieces, of deaths and massacres . . ."

"Heinrich Franz killed his rivals last night, at House Charmagne. The word is he invited them over for a feast and slaughtered them."

"Who? What rivals?" Dieter asked.

Aellin shrugged. "No one knows."

"Then how can you know it's true?"

Aellin stared at him as if he were a simpleton. "Because it's Heinrich Franz, Dieter."

Dieter paused, then nodded. "True enough."

Aellin began to walk away, but Dieter kept by her side as they both walked toward the square.

"This isn't anything the young pup should see, you know," Aellin said, nudging her chin toward Peter.

"I have nowhere to leave him—nowhere safe."

Aellin shrugged and turned away. She was done talking. Near the square the crowds grew denser and Dieter, looking to his side, realized he'd been separated from Aellin. As he made his way through throngs of people, a million thoughts raced through his mind. Nothing Heinrich might do, or had done, would shock him. After the man's earlier actions in Bedburg, while he was chief investigator, and then again during his triumphant witch-hunt in Trier, no level of violence or viciousness from the man would surprise him. In fact, in its diabolical way, everything Heinrich had done, and was doing, made complete sense.

He aches for power. But as a recluse he wants to rule from afar, behind closed doors, free from retaliation—from that dark, Gothic castle he calls home.

But what is his true goal? Power for power's sake? Or something more? Is there a master plan beyond just power and mayhem?

Dieter stood on his tiptoes to peer over the crowd. There, in the center of the square, he saw the familiar, ominous scaffold. On it, two nooses hung from two poles and two people were positioned behind each, their hands tied behind their backs, their faces hooded.

And there was Ulrich, standing between them.

Where is Heinrich Franz, the great lord of Bedburg? If this is his doing, he should be here!

Then Dieter remembered that Heinrich hadn't been at the last hanging either.

Perhaps he's given his trusty torturer Ulrich absolute authority over the city.

And perhaps I can use that against the both of them . . .

The hoods came off.

Dieter let out a stifled gasp and his knees buckled. If he hadn't been holding Peter, he would have fallen over.

Standing helplessly behind either noose was William Edmond and Jerome Penderwick—William, upright and stoic; Jerome, frightened and trembling.

Ulrich looked out at the crowd and began the spectacle.

"For any of you wishing to cause a commotion—that ends here!" he bellowed, stepping forward. Slowly, he fastened the nooses around each neck while he continued speaking.

"From here on out, any notions of revolution or uprisings will be dealt with swiftly and surely. Heinrich Franz has seen enough madness. And while he sincerely wishes for these executions to stop, they won't until all Protestant insurgents have been found, or have fled the city."

Jerome whimpered as Ulrich tightened the rope around his neck. His beady, bulging eyes took in the crowd. Somber and conflicted—unsure whether to silently acquiesce to, or be terrified by, what was happening.

Things are out of control here. Fear is pervasive. These hangings, once entertaining for the masses, no longer are. The citizens have had enough. If this proceeds, Heinrich Franz has made a tactical mistake.

Dieter wanted nothing more than to step forward and offer himself in place of the stonemason and surgeon.

After all, isn't it me *they are after?*

But then he glanced down at Peter. Stepping forward would mean more than just his own end.

Who will raise my boy? Sybil is gone. Aellin? No. Claus? No. And Martin and Ava are nowhere to be found.

But if I do nothing, I'm the worst kind of coward. I will have done nothing for these people who were my friends, who relied on me. And what of William Edmond's family? I promised them, swore an oath to rescue, shelter, and protect anyone who came to my door . . . Protestant, rebel, or other innocent.

Instead, I stand here sick with fear.

"Do you have any parting words before you meet your maker, Herr Penderwick?" Ulrich asked the shivering surgeon.

For a long moment, the man was silent. Then his quivering stopped and the fear on his face was gone. He looked up, clenching his jaw, and began speaking in a shaky voice:

"Do not d-d-despair, friends! My d-death is but one muh-muh-minor setback! Do w-what—"

Ulrich shoved him off the scaffold and the man dropped, his neck snapping in midsentence.

The crowd collectively gasped. Many cried out, a few fainted.

"His muttering was taking too long," Ulrich scowled to himself, now re-focusing his attention on William.

The grumbling from the crowd grew louder. This was no witch-burning. The rules had changed and the rulers had clearly lost their people's support.

"This is cold-blooded murder!" Dieter screamed before realizing what he was doing. Immediately, the crowd's eyes turned toward him. He'd made a grave mistake. His rage had overtaken his better judgment. Watching that poor doctor die, for no reason . . . it tore Dieter's heart apart.

But Ulrich ignored the outburst and looked at the stonemason, "And you, master mason? What do you have to say?"

William glowered back at the torturer, his eyes piercing through the man, so strongly that Ulrich actually looked away. A small victory, but something that would not be forgotten by the crowd or the historians who would later retell this sad, but defining, chapter of Bedburg.

"To my family, Mary and Wilhelm," William spoke to the crowd, "if you can hear me . . . I say to live on. I love you both more than life itself. God will take my soul and we will all one day be united in Heaven." Surprisingly, Ulrich let him continue.

"I cannot be sad about that. I am only sad that I shall never again gaze upon your mortal faces."

Ulrich put his hands on William's shoulders for the final push, but as he hesitated, William gazed out at the sea of worried, horrified, weeping faces, and said firmly, "To all of you, know that this is but a fleeting moment! History will happen. And rest assured that Bedburg will be its battleground!"

Then he looked to the sky, his voice taking on an unworldly resonance.

"Resist. The. Iron. Fist!" he shouted, as Ulrich shoved him off the edge.

And while his body dangled, his battle cry seemed to stay in the air, reverberating throughout the land.

Something had most definitely changed.

And as William's final message spread—remembered and repeated by the masses—the phrase was whispered and re-whispered. Every time a man was recruited for the cause, every time the cause was pursued, every time people gathered to seek justice and freedom, a new anthem was born.

From the simple mason who'd built the walls around the city.

From the man who'd been friend and family to all.

From the brave and peaceful warrior who'd died for the cause.

The battle cry of an unstoppable movement.

Resist the Iron Fist.

PART III

Savior of the Condemned

CHAPTER TWENTY-THREE

HUGO

Hugo sat on the bed of his small room in House Charmagne, alone. Two weeks had passed since the violent events in the dining room below, followed the next morning by the hanging of Jerome Penderwick and William Edmond in Bedburg's town square.

It was clear to everyone that Heinrich Franz was making a major vie for power around the territory. And the townsfolk of Bedburg were frightened.

Of more concern, a rising resistance had begun to take shape. Highway banditry was noticeably increasing around the city as Heinrich repossessed farms and estates from landowners unable to pay his steep taxes. Thievery and robbery had also reached new heights, along with a much higher murder rate.

And with much of the upheaval traceable to Heinrich's reign of terror, it was no surprise that most of the victims were Catholics.

Hugo ran his hand over the small carved horse he'd kept ever since he was a little boy. His sister Sybil had given it to him many years ago. Looking at the rough edges of its peg legs, and its soulless black dots for eyes, brought back a rush of memories. Peaceful times, living with his father and sister. Fearful times, when Tomas Reiner came to steal him away. And sad times, watching his father falsely accused of despicable crimes.

He was just a small boy when his life had been turned upside down, plunging him from the heights of a beautiful family childhood to the depths of misery and despair in the blink of an eye. His father tried, convicted, and brutally executed as the Werewolf of Bedburg. His family home abandoned, then reclaimed by Lord Werner and the county. His sister gone.

One day he hadn't a care in the world; the next day basic survival defined his entire existence. Still just a child, he was driven to the life of a beggar, rummaging around Priest's Circle and Tanner Row.

And then he met Karstan Hase and Ava Hahn and everything changed. He found a new family. They too were beggars and orphans, living on the fringes of society, which only brought them even closer. Three fast friends. Then they joined with another young scrounger named Daniel Granger, whose sharp mind and lofty ambitions helped give them a purpose. And with the addition of another lost lad, a lanky boy named Severin, the Vagabond Five was born.

For years they found success stealing from the rich, until Daniel got caught. Once he was gone, Severin took the lead, becoming more malicious, more dangerous, more careless. And the gang's downward spiral quickly snowballed.

Then one day Hugo spied his best friend Karstan kissing Ava, the woman Hugo considered his soul mate. And once again Hugo's world shattered. From that day on, he would never again trust Karstan. The affable, jolly, fat boy Hugo had once called his best friend became his enemy—and more like Severin, a truly dangerous force, a man to watch out for.

And now it seemed Karstan had become an operative of Ulrich, a position Hugo had once held. Hugo surmised that Karstan, apparently jailed for a crime he didn't commit, must have been offered freedom by the torturer in exchange for doing his bidding. At least everything pointed in that direction: Karstan had sounded the alarm when Dieter Nicolaus and his group were hiding in Martin Achterberg's family estate, forcing them to flee. And Karstan had also orchestrated the raid on Hugo's family estate after following Hugo and spotting Dieter and his company there.

And since the hangings of Jerome and William two weeks ago, Dieter's group had fallen quiet. Apparently, the deaths of the surgeon and stonemason had weakened the group's bonds. Dieter had gone missing, as had two of his followers that most concerned Hugo: Ava Hahn and Martin Achterberg. Ever since seeing those two embrace, Hugo's hatred for them had only intensified.

Sighing, Hugo laid his toy horse down on the bedstand. He'd done enough reminiscing and wallowing. It was now time for action. With Heinrich Franz absent and Bedburg in turmoil, the time was right for Hugo to resume his role as the city's temporary man of authority. Because Heinrich was the only person who could stop him, and he wasn't around . . .

He hopped from his bed, put on his coat, and headed out to the courtyard where he found Felix.

"Please bring the carriage around," he told the driver. "We're off to the Bedburg jailhouse."

Standing in the lobby of the decrepit jail, Hugo thought back to the interrogation of Jerome Penderwick several weeks back, shortly before the doctor met his unfortunate demise. As he'd watched Ulrich torture the man, he'd learned much about his friend-turned-nemesis, Karstan Hase. Most of all, that Karstan was apprenticing for Ulrich, but not for any love toward Ava, but rather to gain his freedom.

Perhaps he'd learn even more about the man here.

Looking around at the stone walls he pondered how most everything bad about the city seemed to always trace back to this horrible place. Hugo's thoughts were interrupted when Ulrich appeared at the top of the stairs, a lighted torch in his hand. Looking down at him, Ulrich said, "What is it you want, Hugo? No one has told me of your coming. And since you seem to be such an important presence around these parts nowadays, I find that a bit odd."

Hugo couldn't tell whether he was being sarcastic or threatening.

"I'd like to speak with your prisoners," Hugo said.

"Which ones? We're like a revolving door, this jailhouse. Old guests always vacating, making room for the new." The torturer smiled, the lines of his scar highlighted by the orange glow of the torchlight.

Staring up at Ulrich reminded Hugo of something else about

the man: how shocked he'd seemed when Heinrich had gone on his slaughtering spree the night of the wedding. Judging from Ulrich's expression that night, it was plain to Hugo that the torturer had not been complicit in that.

"You seem to have fallen into your position as Heinrich's subordinate rather easily, Ulrich," Hugo taunted his former master. "Despite how obviously shocked you were at his excessive display of violence that night."

Ulrich's smile twisted away. "You're one to talk, boy. You seem to follow in the man's shadows wherever he goes."

Hugo sighed. "I suppose we all walk in the shadows of Heinrich Franz . . ."

Ulrich nodded. "I suppose so."

"But I'm not here for that, Ulrich. May I speak with Rolf Anders? He's old, I know he can't be doing well, and likely won't last long."

Descending the stairs, Ulrich said, "You'd be surprised at what that man is capable of." As he walked toward the cells, he added, "You don't give the man enough credit. You clearly don't know where he's come from or been."

Hugo followed Ulrich past the first room at the bottom of the stairs. Glancing inside, he saw a girl in the corner of a cell, Hedda, Baron Ludwig's bespectacled scribe. She seemed so small and helpless, her knees pulled up against her chest.

"How's the girl getting on?" Hugo asked, motioning toward her as he passed.

"She's squirrelly but stout. I don't think I'll learn much from her."

"What could you possibly want to learn from her?"

Ulrich shrugged. "It's Heinrich's idea. To learn as much about Bergheim as he can from her. He seems to think she's the secret to it all, the answer to his political and military problems. So far, I'm not seeing that."

"If she has nothing to give, will you kill her?"

Ulrich shrugged again, indifferently. "That's up to Heinrich. If up to me, no. But, as you know, it's not."

They continued down the dark hallway, Ulrich waving his torch around, until they came to one of the last cells. Ulrich pointed inside. "There's the old man. I can give you five minutes with him."

"I appreciate it, Ulrich," Hugo said sincerely.

The torturer nodded and walked back the way he'd come.

Grasping the bars, Hugo leaned in as far as he could. "Rolf, can you hear me?"

There was movement in the far corner of the cell. Then Rolf's face appeared from the shadows. He looked like he'd aged ten years in the two weeks he'd been there. His white beard was filthy, the lines of his face deeper and longer.

"Ah, Hugo my boy, what brings you to my humble abode?"

Hugo's eyes lit up at Rolf's light attitude. "I wanted to see how you were, Rolf, how you're being treated."

Rolf let out a throaty chuckle, shuffling in closer toward the bars. When he got within a few feet, a rattling noise told Hugo that the old man had reached his limit from his chains.

"It's a jail, Hugo," Rolf said with a shrug. "Where the truth goes to die. But I'm well enough. And how are you, my boy?"

Hugo shrugged. "Heinrich is gone again, so at least that's a relief."

Rolf smiled kindly. "Do you remember when I told you to rule with love, not fear? Do you see why, now? Do you see what fear has done to that man's soul?"

Frowning, Hugo nodded. "I do, Rolf. And I promise I will heed your words if given the chance."

"Do not heed what I *say*, Hugo, but what you think is right!"

A long pause followed. Hugo heard clanking from other cells. Apparently the place was full, given the recent increase in banditry and thievery overtaking Bedburg.

"I suspect Heinrich has gone to Cologne?" Rolf finally asked.

Hugo nodded. "Though I don't know why."

"For support, of course," Rolf explained. "After what he's done, he now needs Archbishop Ernst's help to get him out of his predicament. He's always been one to act first and think later."

"Why does he need support?"

"He's surrounded by enemies—at least in his mind. And

while that once may have been merely delusional on his part, his actions have now made that a reality. By killing Baron Ludwig and Baron Josef, he's created enemies close to his borders. If he wishes to take those cities and become their lord, he's going to need help. He doesn't have enough support from Tomas Reiner's garrison alone. Perhaps he hopes to raise a fyrd and get aid from the freemen of the county."

"And where *is* Tomas Reiner?"

Rolf smirked. "In here somewhere." He looked out past Hugo toward the other cells. "Though I assume he'll be released shortly, once Ulrich is convinced of his innocence. They used to be friends, you know."

Hugo thought back to his journey in the mountains near Trier, when Tomas had executed their traveling companions. That had been Ulrich's idea. "Yes . . ." Hugo said, trailing off. "I'm aware."

Another lengthy silence ensued. Staring at Rolf, at his dirty face and beard, at his unsteady gait and undeserved condition, Hugo's eyes filled with tears. "Is there any way I can help you, Rolf? I wish I had the authority to release you, but I don't think Heinrich trusts anyone anymore . . . even in his absence."

Rolf reached out, his skeletal hand a foot from the bars. Hugo extended his arm through the bars, holding the old man's frail hand tightly. "There's nothing you can do for me here, Hugo. You know I did not betray Heinrich Franz. I am completely innocent of that charge. I helped raise that man from boyhood. My only offense is not stopping his dangerous actions when I could have. And now it is too late."

He stared intently at Hugo. "The only thing I wish for you is that you do not return here. Do not come back, do not see me again. Forget me and live your life."

A raspy cough erupted from Rolf's throat, spewing yellow and black phlegm from his mouth, spittle dribbling down his beard. His health was clearly giving out and it was all almost too much for Hugo to bear. "I can't promise that," Hugo said. "I'm going to do everything in my power to see you released. I owe you that much, Rolf."

"You owe me nothing and you'll do no such thing," Rolf

replied with surprising strength. "I'm going to die here. Heinrich will forget me. He sees me as a threat. It would show weakness for him to release me now. All I ask is that you do the same. Forget me."

As a tear trickled down Hugo's cheek, he heard hurried footsteps approaching—Ulrich coming down the hallway with a second set of boots close behind.

Tightening his grip over Rolf's hand, Hugo whispered, "I won't forget you, Rolf, but I'll do as you wish—"

The door at the end of the hall burst open and Ulrich stormed through, followed by Karstan Hase. Hugo released his hold of Rolf and stepped back, startled.

Hugo eyed Karston coldly. "What are you doing here, Karstan?"

Ulrich walked past Hugo, Karstan following, pushing Hugo aside. "I'm here to speak with my new prisoner, Hue. It's none of your concern."

"Your new prisoner?" Hugo asked, as Ulrich and Karstan marched into the next room of cells. Hugo watched Karstan stare into a cell, wrapping his hands around his belly and giving the prisoner a cruel smile. Hugo noted that Karstan had bulked up considerably, going from soft and round to hard and muscled. Almost a bigger version of Severin.

Karstan glanced back at Hugo, proudly nudging his chin toward the cell he was in front of. "Yes. Brought 'em in just the other day," Karstan said. "And we just got some welcome news, too, which I'd like to relay."

Hugo squinted to see who was in the cell. When recognition hit, his eyes widened in disbelief. Like staring at the past. He glanced around at the other cells.

Could this even be the same cell?

Off in the shadows of the cell stood Ava Hahn, shivering, her dark eyes darting from Karstan to Hugo.

CHAPTER TWENTY-FOUR

SYBIL

In the two weeks since Georg left for his position as the Hanseatic League's representative in King's Lynn, there'd been lots of activity in Strangers Shire. Their sleepy little village—once hidden within the huge countryside of Norfolk county, one of the largest counties in all of England—was definitely coming to life.

Daxton and Rowaine had gone with Georg, to make sure the first shipment of goods to Amsterdam and Germany arrived without any delays or mishaps. They knew the shire's growth depended on Reeve Bailey's textiles making it to their destination safely.

And with them gone, Sybil was alone and friendless, though she did manage to keep herself quite busy. Besides her daily mornings on Claire's porch playing the shire's miracle-worker—doling out prayers and medicines to soothe the local townfolk's woes, she also participated in many of the other activities going on in and around the now-bustling shire.

Under Leon Durand's command, the church was nearly complete, so Leon had begun working on Georg's tavern. As an added bonus, Leon had been given a fifty-percent stake in the pub in appreciation for all he and his wife had done for Sybil, Georg, Rowaine, and Daxton, so his motivation was high to complete it.

Elsewhere in town, farmers had begun felling trees for both lumber and to create more arable land around the shire's peripheries. Other farmers had quickly changed careers, at least temporarily, and were now builders, setting up foundations for structures that would surround the church and tavern.

They were even building Sybil her very own home—she

wasn't sure whether that was out of generosity, or just because Leon and Claire were sick of her staying with them. But either way, it was exciting.

And close to the river, a pressing-and-fulling factory was under construction, to complete the entire textile process so there'd be no need to travel to Norwich—the capital of Norfolk county—nearly twenty miles away. Next to that factory a granary was being built, along with sheds and barns for the growing population of livestock and cattle.

In short, the little village of Strangers Shire was turning into a proper town.

With Reeve Clarence Bailey becoming the biggest proponent of the building efforts. He'd borrowed huge sums of money from the Jews in Norwich to get his projects completed, and everyone knew that the success and future of everything—the new homes, the factories, the farming projects, the shops, and the welfare of all the shire's residents—hinged on the success of Georg, Daxton, and Rowaine's shipping excursions.

Sybil, of course, had become an important person in town. She was a leading figure in the shire's expansion efforts, many attributing the town's exponential growth to her mere presence. And among the many hats she wore was that of Town Meeting Organizer. So on a cold, sunny day—when the wind blew hard enough to hurt Sybil's face—she organized a town meeting to discuss the creation of a local fleece fair, so the people wouldn't have to travel to Norwich's marketplace to trade.

As usual, Reeve Bailey was skeptical of the proposal, nervous that the powers-that-be in Norwich would smite their efforts.

And he was partly right.

A barrister from a prestigious guild in Norwich visited the shire to explain that the law required town fairs to be at least twenty miles apart from one another, and that Strangers Shire was not that far away from Norwich.

"A town fair this close to Norwich," the little, white-haired man said in front of the large audience congregated in the town hall, "would be detrimental to Norwich, stealing business from it. Do you really want to anger the citizens of the capital city of this entire region? Powerful neighbors with the power to crush you?"

From the back of the room, Sybil stroked her chin, listening intently to the little man trying to do everything he could to ensure that the shire's town fair never saw the light of day.

Meanwhile, Reeve Bailey seemed frightened and conflicted. On the one hand, he had invested large sums of money in Strangers Shire and knew a town fair would greatly benefit the area. But he also knew that the last thing the village needed was to start a conflict with the shire's most prominent neighbor. Norwich already had too much of a presence in their community, with unwanted lawmen and patrollers regularly spying on them.

Just as the reeve was about to adjourn the meeting and quash the town fair, a man from the back of the room stood up.

"I have an idea that might benefit us all," the voice called out, as the audience turned to see who had spoken.

To Sybil's surprise, it was Corvin Carradine.

What is he doing here?

She hadn't seen him since he'd whisked Georg off to King's Lynn weeks earlier.

Corvin's eyes swept across the room, stopping at Sybil. Flashing her a warm smile, she involuntarily blushed. A man sitting next to Corvin then stood up. He wore a frilly white wig and the robes of a judge, and was holding a large book. Clearing his throat, he opened the book and said, "This village, Strangers Shire, is exactly eighteen miles from Norwich, correct?"

The audience collectively nodded, though they had no idea what the precise distance was.

Tracing his finger on a page of his book, he looked up. "So if we organize our town fair . . . two miles further, would that not suffice?"

The lawyer standing at the podium sputtered. "Well . . . while it's possible to do such a thing . . . I suppose . . . it would surely be in poor taste." He looked around at the crowd. "Using such an obvious *loophole*"—saying the word as if he'd just smelled something rotten—"would guarantee the ire from the lords and ladies of Norwich. They would not hesitate to crush—"

"But what if a tax were offered to those lords and ladies?"

Corvin proposed. "To appease them, in exchange for our not seeking out their customers and traders, and for allowing our town fair to stand?" He smiled. "We could offer them a small percentage of each sale. That way, we get our fair, and Norwich gets paid. Everyone wins."

A few people grumbled, but most nodded in assent.

"It would be a start," one man agreed, addressing the ones still grumbling about giving any of their hard-earned money to Norwich's greedy nobles.

"Besides," Corvin added, looking over at Reeve Bailey, "I'm sure you will be paying back your moneylenders, correct? Likely the very nobles in Norwich who would be benefiting from these new taxes!"

All eyes turned to the small reeve, who reluctantly nodded. "Eventually, yes . . . though I was hoping for more time, so we could grow our fair first."

"If our fair is to be small and non-inclusive," one farmer called out, "where would we get the buyers and traders? How could we hope to find success if we can't draw from the people of Norwich?"

Corvin smiled. "Luckily, Strangers Shire has a built-in attraction—one that's removed from fleeces or goods or accessories of any kind."

The crowd was puzzled, shaking their heads, looking to one another. Corvin glanced at Sybil with a knowing smile and suddenly she realized his point.

"What do you speak of?" Bailey asked with a dubious frown.

Corvin opened his arms toward Sybil. "Our very own *sorceress*." As everyone turned to follow his direction, a loud chorus of chatter broke out among the group.

"Nearly everyone this side of England has heard of the Pale Diviner by now," Corvin explained. "I've made sure of that," he said, winking at Sybil who turned away, wishing she could be anywhere but there right then.

A man called out from the crowd. "People will come from all over if promised an audience with the Pale Diviner!"

"Yes," agreed Corvin's barrister friend standing next to him with the big book. He gave the crowd a wolfish smile. "And,

Reeve Bailey, you could charge for each meeting with the soothsayer!"

The reeve stared at Sybil. Everyone stared at Sybil. Slowly she began shaking her head. This whole Pale Diviner nonsense had gone too far. She'd told Rowaine, Daxton, and Georg as much already—how she thought she was doing more harm than good and had grown tired of offering these poor people false prophesies and proclamations. It was never supposed to be a long-term affair. Now here Corvin was stoking the flames, promoting her fame throughout the countryside. She had never considered charging for her services, just the opposite. She had merely wished to offer the needy and desperate a sense of hope.

"What do you say, Sybil Nicolaus?" Reeve Bailey asked from the front of the room. "Are you comfortable wooing the people to our fair?"

With all eyes on her, she opened her mouth to speak, but her throat was too dry to push out the words. Debating whether to just leave, she didn't want to disappoint all these friends and neighbors now staring at her with their own need for hope.

Placing her hands in her lap, in a quiet voice she said, "I'll do it."

The meeting hall erupted in cheers. People leapt from their seats, pumping their fists and throwing hats in the air. Some embraced. This was going to massively increase their livelihoods and give their growing shire a real future.

The barrister from Norwich walked away from the podium, defeated, and left the shire without uttering another word, his thoughts no doubt on the grim task of announcing his failed mission to his superiors.

In the midst of all the chaos, Corvin had managed to inch his way beside Sybil. He put his hand on her shoulder and she jumped. "My apologies," he said, his voice smooth, like melted chocolate on Sybil's tongue. She tried to turn away to hide her embarrassment, but Corvin's touch had aroused her. Instead, she turned toward the fleeing barrister and noted, "I doubt that will be the last time we see that man."

Corvin ignored her comment. "Let's celebrate, my dear. This has been a decisive victory for the shire." He pulled her closer.

She could feel his breath on the nape of her neck. Weakly, she tried to change the subject. "Who is your barrister friend?"

Frowning, Corvin glanced at the man he'd brought to speak on his behalf, the one with the white wig and big book. "Just a man I hired from a guild in the League." He turned back to Sybil. "But enough about him . . ."

"I . . . I don't have my own house," she stuttered. "I have no private residence—"

"That's perfectly fine, my dear," Corvin purred. "There are empty stables all over the shire . . ."

He was a full head taller than she, with a most alluring smile. And though Sybil didn't trust a single hair on his body, that didn't quell her attraction for him. If anything, it made him even more irresistible.

She hadn't made love in many long months. She felt her forehead begin to perspire, her breathing growing rapid and heavy. Corvin held her close, his chest pressed against hers and suddenly everyone around them seemed to melt away. He ran a finger down the side of her neck and Sybil momentarily stopped breathing, goose-pimples shooting across her shoulders and down her arms. As he dipped his head toward her, his eyes closed and his lips parted slightly. Craning her neck up to him, she found his mouth and fused together for a long blinding moment of passion as time seemed to stand still.

Finally he pulled away and smiled at her, rubbing his nose against hers. "Come on," he whispered like honey, "let's find somewhere more . . . secluded."

She allowed him to take her hand and lead her away from the crowd and meeting hall. But it was as though she wasn't there, like her spirit had departed and she was watching herself from above. Hand-in-hand, she felt like a ragdoll, powerless, though not unwilling.

They quickly found a stable nearby in the midst of construction and, once inside, Corvin slammed the heavy door and, but for a few strands of light seeping through a seam of one wall, darkness overtook them. Corvin gently pushed Sybil against a half-built horse stall and slipped down the top of her dress. As he began caressing her breasts, she let out a soft whimper, feeling as if she were in a trance, her eyes wet and dewy.

But the moment began to melt away as his groping grew rougher. When his hand slid between her legs, the trance abruptly ended. She stared at Corvin, part confused, part angry. Then she realized why. The vision of Johannes von Bergheim was staring back at her—the young nobleman who had first defiled her not so long ago. Johannes had looked at her the same way Corvin was now. Her eyes narrowed and her face flashed with rage. "Stay away from me," she commanded, her tone cold and dead, as she covered her breasts with her hands.

And surprisingly Corvin obeyed, immediately ending his advance. Raising his hands in surrender, he took a step back. And suddenly his face was nothing like Johannes'. The man standing before her looked sincere, contrite, respectful, hurt.

Perhaps he's not the monster that Johannes was after all . . . or like most men. Maybe there is a good man here that truly loves me. But I can't love him back . . .

Oh, Dieter, I'm so sorry!

Then, just as she felt her resistance waning, a loud voice broke the moment.

"Where's Sybil Nicolaus?" it called out. "I need to speak with her, right away!"

It was a familiar voice.

Sybil's heart began racing. Quickly, she tied the top of her dress back over her bare shoulders and rushed past Corvin, nearly pushing him out of the way. Peering outside the barn door she saw Daxton Wallace with Rowaine at his side, marching down the road toward the meeting hall, calling out to passersby, asking them if they knew where Sybil was. Surrounding the two were several people she'd never seen before.

Turning back to Corvin, she whispered, "You stay here and be quiet. Or I'll tell them you hurt me. Do you understand?"

Corvin gulped and nodded.

Once Daxton, Rowaine, and their entourage were a safe distance from the barn, Sybil walked out and called to Daxton, "Here I am, Daxton. I was just tending to a friend's horse."

Daxton spun around and smiled widely, throwing out his

arms. Sybil jogged over to him, accepting his embrace and his peck on the cheek. Then Daxton pulled away and examined her. "Are you all right, Beele? You seem flushed."

She shook her head. "I'm fine." Then turning to the people around them, "Who are these people?'

"Our new friends," he said with a grin. He pointed at a small man dressed in little more than rags and furs, with strange blue drawings on his face and arms. "This is Salvatore." Then motioning to a stocky little woman, "And this is Mary and her son, Wilhelm."

The tall young man standing next to the woman smiled at Sybil. "Pleased to make your acquaintance," Wilhelm said. "We've heard so much about you on our travels."

Sybil cocked her head. "You have?"

Mary nodded profusely. "From your friends."

Salvatore, the strange-looking one, stepped forward and stared directly into Sybil's eyes. "You are the sacred Pale Diviner?" When Sybil nodded meekly, he said, "I must pick your brain and learn from your spiritual prowess, my lady."

Sybil surveyed the group and beamed. "It's a good thing I'm having my own house built, because we'd surely never all fit in Claire and Leon's!"

She took Mary by the arm and began walking, the rest of the group following behind. "Come, come," she said to the slightly frightened woman. "It's been so dull here. Please, tell me all about your adventures, and how you came to find this land of the Strangers . . ."

CHAPTER TWENTY-FIVE

HEINRICH

Following the slaughter at House Charmagne, Heinrich Franz went on vacation. He sensed he might be losing his grip on his power and authority and figured some time away might help him get re-grounded. That was his excuse anyway. His real reason for leaving Bedburg was more direct: he needed allies.

He had planned to kill the two barons, Ludwig and Josef, but when they'd arrived that night, he hadn't been sure if he would go through with it. He hadn't killed anyone—directly, by his own hand—in a long while.

Fortunately, the killings came easily and naturally to him. He thought back to that magnificent, sexually-charged tingle that had rippled through his body at the moment he stabbed the dagger into Baron Ludwig's shoulder; the coppery-tasting gusher of blood splashing on his face; the thick liquid pulsing across the table in all directions.

It had truly been a moment to cherish.

How he had loathed that snide, arrogant fool. As far back as Trier, when Heinrich had pretended to be Lord Inquisitor Adalbert, he'd formed a general dislike for Ludwig. And over time, the baron's exaggerated self-image of importance and superiority had turned Heinrich's dislike into outright hatred. Usually, Heinrich reserved such hatred for only a select few, casting off most others with simple indifference. For instance, he had no strong feelings about the witches and warlocks he helped burn in Trier—they were just numbers to him. Nor had he particularly despised Peter Griswold before executing him as the Werewolf of Bedburg—he'd simply needed a scapegoat to carry out Archbishop Ernst's message.

But Baron Ludwig was different. Heinrich couldn't pinpoint

why he hated the man so; it was just something that grew and festered with time. And once Ludwig finally sat at the table that night, Heinrich knew it would be his last supper.

On the other hand, his killing of Baron Josef had been something else entirely—nothing personal, just a means to an end. The truth was, Heinrich simply couldn't bear giving away his hard-earned land to a man he didn't know. And though he hardly recognized the names of the villages he was supposed to be giving up, that still didn't change the degree to which Heinrich abhorred the sense of entitlement that all high-born folk expected to receive.

He had also worried about the two barons for strategic reasons. They seemed to have become friends, more than mere acquaintances. And for Heinrich, that just wouldn't do. He couldn't be surrounded by powerful men who might *collude* with each other against him. Despite having no evidence to back that up, it was always better to be safe than sorry.

Heinrich smiled to himself as he reminisced about Lady Lucille that night, her precious expression of abject horror when her father's brains and skull had splattered across her face. If only he could commission a painting of that wondrous moment so he could relive it at will.

With both barons gone, and the ink of their signatures still fresh on the wedding agreements, Heinrich's position had improved greatly. He was still a married man—wedded to a Catholic wife—as Archbishop Ernst had wanted. But now he had two fewer potential enemies at his borders. And he could now take their lordships for himself, vastly spreading his influence. More importantly, with both Bergheim and Erftstadt under his control, he would be lord of the entire county.

And earn a new title: *Count* Heinrich Franz.

He liked the sound of that, grinning at the thought.

Before all that though, he had decided to travel to Cologne to discuss with Archbishop Ernst his next course of action, gauging Ernst's reaction to his new proposals, which he assumed would be accepting.

He also wanted to discuss his future in Bedburg. After killing the barons, he needed to make sure he was still in good standing with the rest of the nobility—that a powerful man like Lord Alvin, or a Godly man like Bishop Balthasar, wouldn't try to steal away his power or status.

Which was why he had invited Ulrich, Commander Tomas, and Bishop Balthasar to his wedding that night. They represented the three most influential people in the city and, thus, the most likely ones to potentially scheme against him. So he had needed to graphically illustrate to them what they were up against, that *no one* could keep secrets from Heinrich Franz.

And he was confident his plan had worked, noting the genuine fear on their faces that night despite their attempts to hide it.

It was a shame he'd had to arrest Rolf, but the old weasel had clearly outlived his welcome and worth. After all, it had been Rolf who had invited that madman, Salvatore, to his home. Then, when the lunatic's attempt to poison Heinrich had failed, Rolf had allowed him to escape! As long as Heinrich ruled, there was simply no room for such treasonous incompetence.

Isn't it strange how the people closest to you are the quickest to stick the knife in your back?

Ernst of Bavaria, the current archbishop of Cologne, had been born to the powerful Wittelsbach family. The youngest of three sons, he had been groomed for leadership and nobility his entire life. Usually, these were just the things Heinrich hated in a person, but not in the case of Ernst.

The oldest brother of the family, William, had become a powerful politician and the Duke of Bavaria. The next brother in line, Ferdinand, was a military man. But Ernst had instead chosen the ecclesiastic path. Perhaps it was because of that that Heinrich had always felt a sense of connection—as a man of God, Ernst was beyond Heinrich's reach, beyond the reach of mere mortals.

But whatever the psychological reasons, over the years Heinrich had grown quite fond of the archbishop. First, he admired the fact that Ernst was a man of action, like Heinrich.

Second, he was tall and handsome with the commanding presence of a born leader—which Heinrich liked to think, in certain respects, he shared with the man.

Heinrich wasn't jealous of the man. To the contrary, he simply wanted what the archbishop had, to be a part of his inner circle. Although the more he thought about it, the more he wondered if maybe there was something more he wanted than just friendship and admiration.

Late in the afternoon, Archbishop Ernst's courier came to gather Heinrich from the foyer of the castle. As usual, Heinrich had been kept waiting for hours. Apparently, there had been other matters that Ernst needed to take care of first.

A bit nervous, Heinrich followed the courier down the long hallway leading to Ernst's favorite conference room. Along the way, he examined the battlefield paintings and tapestries on the walls. As they approached the conference room, a small sheen of sweat formed on Heinrich's upper lip and mustache.

The courier pushed open the doors, then made the formal announcement of Heinrich's arrival. Archbishop Ernst stood next to the window, his back to Heinrich, his hands clasped at his waist. When he turned around, Heinrich's smile vanished. The archbishop's expression was grim, his frown pronounced, the skin around his eyes and lips tight.

It was an expression new to Heinrich. One that frightened him.

Could I have misread the situation this badly?

"Heinrich," the archbishop said in a stern voice.

"Your Grace," Heinrich answered, bowing his head.

Ernst motioned for him to sit in the chair facing his desk, which he did. Trying to appear calm, Heinrich couldn't stop his right knee from jiggling, exposing his apprehension. For a long while, the archbishop remained quiet, standing there with a gaze that penetrated Heinrich like a spear. Then he slowly walked to his desk and sat, still not speaking.

Say something, dammit!

But the silence continued, the archbishop's eyes never leaving Heinrich's.

He's enjoying this. Me suffering. Oh, how I covet that!

Another full minute of excruciating quiet went by before the archbishop, steepling his fingers in front of him, finally spoke.

"You've doomed us," he said, his tone deathly final.

Heinrich's eyes bulged. His mind reeled. "P-pardon, Your Grace?"

Ernst pounded his fist on the table, sending Heinrich's pulse racing.

"What were you thinking?" Ernst demanded. "Killing those two barons?"

Heinrich tried to speak but couldn't.

"You can't just go killing everyone you disagree with, you damn fool!" Ernst shook his head and looked down at the table. "I knew it was a terrible idea electing you as lord. I should have seen that it would reflect poorly on me."

Heinrich's heart sunk. "B-but . . . I did what you asked . . ." he said meekly.

The archbishop threw his head back in disgust. "*What I asked?* I never asked you to kill anyone! Especially not your neighbors!"

"I married that woman . . . a Catholic woman . . ."

"And killed her father!"

"They were planning my doom, Your Grace!" The instant his words flew out of his mouth, Heinrich heard how pathetically hollow they sounded.

Then another long moment of silence, the archbishop staring at Heinrich, blinking slowly. "Can you prove that?" he asked.

Heinrich hesitated, then gently shook his head, his shoulders drooping.

Waving an angry hand, Ernst bellowed, "I've had to deal with this catastrophe all day, and more. Why have you even come here?" Then thinking more about it, he added, "It's a good thing you have, so I can show the people the target of their ire."

Heinrich gulped. "I was hoping you'd be happy. That's all I wanted, Your Grace, to please you."

Ernst joined his hands on top of the table, then shook his head. "You could have done nothing more to make me *less* pleased, Heinrich, you foolish, foolish man. Was it your plan to just take their cities and call them your own?"

"It had crossed my mind."

"With no forethought into how you might do that?" Ernst shook his head again. "Imagine all the noblemen in Bedburg, vying for your position, scheming against you—"

Heinrich nodded. "I have. It is easy to imagine . . ."

"And now imagine *twice* that many people in cities you've never even stepped foot in *doing the same!* For every Baron Ludwig you kill, three more noblemen will replace him willing to fight for his power and position! You've completely fractured the infrastructures of Bergheim and Erftstadt. Where I once had stable allies in place in those cities, I now have"—he threw his hands up in the air, flustered—"I don't even know what I now have! Madness! Chaos!"

He squinted at Heinrich. "And for all we know, whoever rises to the top of the heap now may not even *be* Catholic!" In a lower voice, he said, "And all this because of your . . . your . . . insane *paranoia!*"

Heinrich was tired of being berated. His fear and self-pity were quickly morphing into something dangerous. It made him feel like a child again, his mother chastising him, beating him, for every small mishap. Clearing his throat, he sat up straight and spoke.

"Give me an army and I'll march into Bergheim and Erftstadt and establish peace," he said. "You have my word, Your Grace. I will win you back your cities."

The archbishop was shaking his head again, this time with eyes closed, as if Heinrich were an idiot to even consider that. "You don't understand the situation, Heinrich."

From outside the room, a familiar voice called out. "Uncle? Uncle!"

At the sound of the voice, Ernst looked up, then hurried to finish his conversation with Heinrich. "I don't have the authority to do such a thing—"

"Of course you do!" Heinrich retorted.

The voice outside was now shouting, getting closer. "Uncle!" But Heinrich ignored it, trying to make his point before he lost the archbishop's attention.

"You're the Prince-Elector and Archbishop of Cologne, for God's sake! One of the most powerful men in the Holy Roman Empire!" he told Ernst.

The door to the conference room burst open and a young man with a slight resemblance to Ernst stepped into the room. Heinrich recognized him. Ernst's nephew Ferdinand.

Before the nephew crossed the room, Ernst leaned toward Heinrich. "My constituents don't trust me with that much authority, Heinrich. Not after I let your debacle take place. Now, I would never win the votes in parliament to award me an army."

Heinrich scoffed. It had been Archbishop Ernst himself who had set up the parliament to begin with—to help streamline and better organize Cologne. And now he was telling Heinrich that his own creation would betray him? Heinrich made a mental note of that irony, vowing never to do anything so foolish, never to create something that could diminish, even eliminate, his own power in his own cities.

Heinrich switched to another tact. "I have two seats in Cologne's parliament that I've never been present to use. I can use *my* votes!"

By now Ferdinand was standing at the edge of the desk near his uncle. Smirking, he said, "While an amusing gesture Heinrich, it would not be *nearly* adequate."

Furrowing his brow, Heinrich stared at Ernst's young nephew.

I'd give anything to run my blade across that arrogant pup's thin neck.

Then he turned back to Ernst, his expression pleading.

The archbishop sighed. "Unfortunately, my nephew is correct. I'm growing old, Heinrich—"

"You're the best man to ever step foot in Cologne," Heinrich blurted, then blushed.

Ferdinand smirked. "Oh, isn't he adorable when he fawns, uncle?"

Heinrich stared daggers at the young man, as Ernst closed his eyes. Whatever the archbishop was preparing to say would be difficult.

"In light of what has transpired within the last few weeks,"

Ernst began, "I have decided it would be best if I stepped down from the archbishopric for a time . . . at least until things have calmed a bit here."

Heinrich was dumbfounded. Leaning forward, he said, "You've been forced to retire? By whom, the pope?"

Ernst chuckled. "No, no, it's nothing like that. I'd just like to see how my nephew can handle things. I will be watching intently, but from the peripheries."

Heinrich studied Ernst's expression. He looked tired, defeated. But he still didn't believe what the archbishop was telling him. Ernst was not a man to give up so easily—not unless forced to. And Heinrich could tell that the archbishop did not want this.

Could this really all be . . . my *doing?*

Suddenly Heinrich felt like crying. He hadn't wept in a long time, not since witnessing Odela burn at the stake in Trier. But now was not the time to show weakness or vulnerability. While he could do that in front of Ernst, a man he trusted completely, he certainly would never do it in front of his toadish nephew.

"Tell me what I can do," he asked Ernst in a harsh whisper. "Tell me how I can change your fate, Your Grace. I'll do anything."

"Come now, uncle, let's go," Ferdinand interrupted. "We have a meeting with those sugar sellers. I think I've brokered a deal, but it still needs your signature."

Archbishop Ernst stood. He eyed his nephew, then turned back to Heinrich. "You said you thought Baron Ludwig von Bergheim and Baron Josef von Erftstadt were colluding against you, to steal your authority?"

Heinrich nodded quickly.

"Then prove it," Ernst said with finality. Thrusting his finger in Heinrich's direction, he added, "Find me proof that they were a danger to the Empire—that they wanted to destroy Christendom as we know it, and maybe I can help you."

The task seemed impossible. Now Heinrich's face shared the same look of defeat. His cheeks sagged and his mouth fell open. But as Archbishop Ernst began to walk away, Heinrich regained his vigor.

"I'll do it," he called out. "You have my word, Your Grace! I promise I'll make this right!"

From across the room, Ernst turned to face Heinrich. "Good," he said, then his face turned dark. "But until you do, don't dare show your face here again."

CHAPTER TWENTY-SIX

DIETER

Dieter sat on the cold stone curb, his knees bent, his feet slightly hanging over the edge of the muddy sewer floor. He tried to keep his boots dry, but his present living conditions made that next to impossible. He bounced Peter on his knee, trying to keep the child calm, holding him close to his chest with his good arm. The nub of his other arm was buried beneath his dirty tunic to stave off the freezing chill. A few slivers of moonlight provided their only light.

"When can we leave here, papa?" Peter asked. "It stinks and I'm cold."

Dieter sighed. He looked left and right, where the tunnels continued in both directions into darkness so complete it looked like black curtains had been drawn. That, and the perpetual *drip, drip, drip* of rainwater and sewage leaking from above, kept Dieter edgy, uncomfortable, and scared.

His voice cracked. "Soon, son. Soon." Though he didn't know if that was true.

He felt like a coward, hiding away in his underground labyrinth of wet pathways and filthy tunnels. The place was a city under the city, offering nothing good—just nauseating refuse, sickness, and death. He worried for his son's health; if they didn't leave soon, Peter could easily catch something and never recover.

And if anything happened to Peter . . . his life would be pointless.

But as scary as it was down here, he was even more fearful of showing his face aboveground. That, too, would put his son in jeopardy as surely as a deadly disease.

He no longer knew whom to trust. He was relieved that he'd

helped Mary and Wilhelm to escape the city, but heartbroken about William and Jerome's capture and executions. Especially since he'd been the one to direct them on their fateful journey—instructing them to use Claus' underground entrance and exit at the tunnel's secret outlet under the jail. Of course he had no way of knowing that the jailhouse opening had been paved over. Still, in his mind he was directly responsible for their deaths.

I should have told William to go with his family. Instead, he ended up a helpless decoy. He didn't know the extent of Heinrich Franz's evilness—that the man would stop at nothing to get his way. I should have warned him better, emphasized the danger.

The only consolation had been the cityfolk's reaction to the public executions. The resistance movement was growing, due in no small part to William's now-notorious final words: *Resist the iron fist.*

Despite the people's understandable fear of Heinrich Franz, William's death had pushed them one step closer to the realization that the city was *theirs.* And that their only, and best, defense against such a ruthless, amoral ruler was to band together.

But Dieter knew his limits. He was no orator, nor a born leader. He didn't possess the fiery rhetoric of his predecessors, such as Pastor Hanns Richter. If he had such skills, he'd be able to rally the townspeople to his cause. A cause that was no longer a Protestant-Catholic fight, or power grab for land. This was a battle for freedom and life itself.

The revolution had definitely started, but it would have to proceed without Dieter. His personal situation was dire: Martin and Ava were both missing, ever since the executions of William and Jerome two weeks ago. And so he was literally alone—save for his thoughts and his child. And now living in the cavernous depths of Bedburg's underground tunnels.

The cold, hard truth was that Dieter was in no position to lead anything, much less a revolution.

But the people needed nudging. They needed someone who could help them see that they were indeed active, capable masters of their own destinies.

Hearing footsteps coming from the darkness, he tensed. He

knew he was cornered. Even with Claus' map in hand, he'd been afraid he'd get lost in the underground maze, so had kept close to this end of the tunnel where at least there was some light. But it also gave him nowhere to run.

He moved farther into the shadows, trying to hide as best he could, his hand over his son's mouth.

As the figure stepped into the dim light, Dieter sighed with relief. It was Claus, carrying a tray of food scraps with two cups.

"Priest?" Claus called out to the darkness. When Dieter emerged from the shadows, Claus nearly dropped the tray. Grinning broadly, the old man said, "I've brought you both some food, leftovers from Aellin's tavern."

"Your generosity is much appreciated, Patric."

Ever since Dieter had learned Claus' real name, and that he was Gebhard Truchsess' secret middleman in Bedburg, he'd refused to call Claus by anything other than his true name. Which of course irritated Claus to no end. But as long as they weren't in public, the old man seemed to tolerate it.

"While I was there," Claus said, "I saw something. Something you should see."

Dieter took a hard piece of bread from the tray, split it in two, and gave the bigger piece to his son. Biting into his half, he asked with his mouth full, "What did you see?"

"You should see for yourself." Claus looked around, eyeing the decrepit conditions. "And you should get you and your child out of this cesspool."

"Can I trust you?" Dieter dared to ask. "You aren't setting me up to be captured?"

Dieter figured that even if Claus didn't respond, he'd be able to read the look on his face. The old man was simply too honest to keep a secret. But Claus just frowned.

"You need fresh air so you don't go mad. I assure you there's no one there looking for you." Then he cracked a smile and took a quick sniff. "Although when you step into public, smelling as you do, you might attract the wrong sort of attention."

Dieter nodded but didn't smile. There was just nothing happy to smile about, even staring into the warm, kind eyes of

Claus.

"I can tell you this," Claus said with a wink and twitch of the nose, "Aellin won't get near you."

He waved Dieter onward. "Come now, just take ten minutes to see what I mean. You're lacking in company down here, and God knows I can't stay here much longer before I succumb to some mystery disease." Somberly, he added, "Your son can't, either."

Dieter nodded and rose from the curb. Following Claus down the tunnel with his son in tow, his eyes darted everywhere. A few minutes later, they came to the small ladder that led back up to Claus' secret trapdoor.

Nudging Peter up the ladder ahead of him, as soon as they stepped into the warm lobby of Claus' inn, the boy immediately ran to the fireplace, happily rubbing his hands in front of the flames to warm himself. Meanwhile, Dieter changed into a fresh set of clothing that Claus provided.

"They might be a bit small," the old man said, "but they're better than what you've got. Will you have a spot of tea before you go?"

Dieter was finally able to offer a thin smile as he shook his head. He looked over at his son, now curled up next to the fire. Reading his mind, the old man said, "Grandfather Claus will watch the boy."

Which unfortunately made Dicter flash back to the last time he'd entrusted his son with Claus at the inn. The result had been unspeakable violence right outside the inn's front door—a vicious battle that brought the loss of his arm, the death of Rowaine's lover, Mia, and the loss of his precious wife Sybil, whom he never saw again and was presumed dead from the witch burning in Trier.

Reading Dieter's thoughts, Claus smiled reassuringly, "Don't worry, everything will be fine. Just don't be too long."

Dieter left the inn and headed straight for the tavern, his hood pulled over his head. As usual, he kept to the shadows, though this time it wasn't necessary as the streets were deserted. When he got to the tavern, he stepped in and quickly moved away from the front door to avoid attention. From beneath his hood, his eyes swept the room.

Why couldn't the melodramatic old man just tell me what I'm supposed to be looking for . . .

Then he spotted it. In the corner of the room a man sat by himself, leaning over a mug, his shoulders sagging. Dieter walked up behind the man just as Aellin came up beside him. Grabbing his hand, she whispered, "He came in a little while ago."

"Alone?" Dieter asked, squeezing her fingers.

Aellin frowned and nodded. Then she pinched her nose and leaned her head back. "Jesus, priest, you smell like death died twice."

Ignoring her, Dieter walked around the man's table to face him.

Martin Achterberg looked up from his mug, his mouth parting in shock. He looked just as he had two weeks earlier: square-faced, scruffy chin, curly hair.

"Dieter!" Martin nearly shouted. Then he looked conspiratorially over his shoulders and leaned in, motioning for Dieter to sit.

"Where have you been?" Dieter asked, his voice stern and cold. He sat down across from him and waited.

Martin drained his ale, his eyes taking on a faraway sadness. "She's gone, Dieter." Tears welled in his eyes. "They took Ava."

"Who did?" Dieter asked.

Martin shrugged.

"And how? You two were on the same horse. Why are *you* here?"

Martin toyed with his mug, refusing to look Dieter in the eye.

"Martin? Say something."

"I'm ashamed," he blurted, his head bent low.

Dieter waited.

Finally Martin looked up. "We were going to leave, Dieter," shame filling his eyes. "Ava and I . . . we were going to quit this awful place."

Dieter quelled a stab of anger that melted into pity. The young man was clearly grieving. And it made sense. Martin and Ava were both young and had each gone through difficult times—one, branded a criminal his entire life and his family murdered; the other, an *actual* criminal for most of her life and an orphan.

But they'd found each other, wallowing in misery together. Of course they wanted to leave Bedburg and start a new life. Any such couple would.

"I understand," Dieter said softly.

"You're not . . . angry with me?"

Dieter gave him a sad smile. "How could I be, my friend? I'd be lying if I said the same thought hadn't crossed my mind as well, many times."

"But you've never acted on it . . ."

"Neither did you, apparently, or you wouldn't be sitting here."

Martin sighed. "We were stopped at the west gate. Jerome and William made it through the southern gate to Claus' inn. I assume they went underground, but I have no idea how they were caught."

"And how were you caught?"

"We were recognized at the gate. Karstan was waiting for us."

Dieter swore under his breath.

"They took Ava, and I escaped," Martin said, looking away toward the bar.

Dieter raised one eyebrow as he watched Martin. He dropped the subject and instead said, "Do you still want to help?"

Smiling, Martin nodded. "I want to *resist the iron fist.*"

"Where are they holding Ava?"

"In the jailhouse, I assume."

Dieter immediately began thinking of ways he could bargain with Ulrich. After all, he did have a history with the man, a tenuous one at best, but a history nonetheless.

Maybe there's something I can give him in exchange for Ava . . . something more valuable than one poor girl.

"Come on," Dieter said, rising from the table. "I've been here too long. People are starting to look this way."

"Where are we going?"

"I'll introduce you to my new home," Dieter said.

They headed back to the inn for Peter before taking the plunge into the darkness.

Fortunately, old man Claus couldn't bear the thought of young Peter staying in those nasty tunnels, so he'd insisted that Martin, Dieter, and Peter spend the night at the inn. Naturally he wouldn't hear of them paying for their rooms.

Dieter slept like the dead. He hadn't had a decent night's sleep in weeks. He awoke early, immediately aware that the bed next to him was empty. Panicking that Peter was gone, he looked down to realize that his son was safely asleep beside him.

So it was Martin who had left. But why and where?

He got up, stretched his aching joints, and looked out the window. The sky was dark purple and heavy, the sun still an hour from rising. Moving quietly so Peter could continue sleeping, he latched the door and made his way downstairs, finding Claus sitting at the front desk, chipper and humming to himself.

Sitting at the small table near the desk, Dieter asked, "Don't you ever sleep?"

Claus just shrugged.

"What's your secret?"

Claus furrowed his bushy white brow. "My secret?"

"I come down the stairs to the sound of you humming, rummaging around your desk, already starting your day with a jump. How do you do it?"

Claus smiled broadly, reaching for his cup. "Tea," he said.

Dieter chuckled, shaking his head. Claus brought a mug over for Dieter and sat down next to him. Slowly crossing one leg over the other and leaning back, the old man looked very grandfatherly.

"The secret to happiness is in the eye, or should I say the *mind*, of the beholder, my friend," he told Dieter. "I've discovered that if I act happy and give the outward appearance of happiness long enough . . . it eventually comes true." He smiled kindly at Dieter, who returned the gesture.

"You're a wise man," Dieter said, sipping his tea.

Claus raised a finger and shook his head. "I'm old—big difference there, Dieter," he chuckled. "But I have learned a thing or two in my day. Tell me, what makes *you* happy?"

Dieter thought about that for a moment. It had been a long time since the subject of happiness had crossed his mind. Lately, it seemed hopelessly far away, out of reach. He realized he hadn't been truly happy since Sybil. When he lost her, everything changed from happiness to survival—keeping his child safe, trying to stay alive in this deadly place.

"My son, and the memory of my wife," he said finally. "The only two things that have ever given me happiness."

"Ah, love and the memory of love," Claus repeated. "Two of the universal paths to happiness. Complicated, yet essential." The old man slowly helped himself up from his chair, sighing as his bones crackled.

Dieter stared at the man as he walked away. Claus was old and weary, showing signs that his days were few—his balding head sprouting dark patches of aging skin, his pace slowing, his back hunched.

"One day I would like you to tell me about yourself, Claus—where you've been and what you've done," Dieter said fondly.

Claus turned, chuckling as he feigned surprise. "Me? Now *that* would be a dull story!"

"Somehow I doubt it . . ." Dieter mumbled, thinking back to what he did know about the man, how he'd fought in the Spanish army and had been Georg Sieghart's superior officer.

But he left the military. Through choice or betrayal? And how did he end up here, as one of former archbishop Gebhard Truchsess's top intelligence aides? From soldier, to spy, to innkeeper? Quite the life.

Without warning, Martin barreled through the front door, shaking Dieter from his thoughts. Waving a small, wrinkled piece of paper in his hand, he eyed both men and smiled.

"We received a new note this morning," he said, almost out of breath.

Dieter pursed his lips, thinking out loud. "The first one since Jerome and William's capture and executions . . ."

Martin nodded. "Someone still wishes to help us."

Sighing, then draining his tea, Dieter stood up. Holding out his hand for the note, he said, "We could certainly use all the help we could get."

As Dieter read the paper, Claus said, "Well?"

Dieter sighed. "It's from the illustrious 'Mord' again. This time, marking *Cristoff Krüger*—the barkeep—as the next target."

"*He's* a Protestant infiltrator?" Martin asked, surprised.

Dieter shrugged. "Seems like everyone at that tavern is affiliated with the Protestant uprising in some way or other these days—"

"More like everyone in general," Claus added. "The rebellion is gaining favor among the masses. I see it in the way people carry themselves—whispering, shaking hands out in the open. Much different than before."

"Heinrich Franz is losing his grip over them," Martin said.

"Then let's loosen his hold even more," said Dieter.

After arranging for Peter to stay again with Claus, he and Martin left for the inn.

Approaching the tavern from a side alley, they hid behind a fruit-cart. Dieter peeked over the cart to watch the mostly-empty road that led to the tavern. Dawn was just breaking. A few people came and went from the tavern, mostly discarding buckets of vomit and piss from the night before, or drying out ale-soaked rugs.

Dieter saw no military or other guards in sight.

"Let's hurry before we're too late," Dieter said, quickly crossing the street, hoping they weren't walking into a trap. He trusted Martin, but he'd also learned not to trust anyone totally.

When he entered the tavern he didn't bother hiding his face. But once inside, he suddenly felt self-conscious and pulled his hood back over his head before stepping to the bar.

Even at the early hour, two regulars sat at the counter, their heads drooling over their ale. Cristoff was cleaning off mugs with a rag, looking nonchalant as usual.

His world is about to drastically change.

Dieter rested his arms on the bar, then whistled for Cristoff. The short man waddled over with a disgruntled look.

"My apologies for the rudeness," Dieter said in a low voice.

Cristoff frowned. He had deep bags under his eyes, probably from staying awake into the wee hours of the morning for most of his life.

"Usually it's only the whores that are whistled to, priest . . . not the owner of the tavern."

"We come with urgent news," Dieter began.

A loud crash shook the room, startling everyone but the two bar patrons at the counter. Upstairs, doors creaked open as people poked their heads out to see what the commotion was. Glancing over their shoulders, both Martin and Dieter's eyes went wide.

Three armed men entered the tavern, immediately stepping to both sides of the door as a fourth man entered.

We're too late!

Ulrich stood in the doorway.

The universally feared torturer and jailer swiveled his neck slowly, scanning from one side to the other. No one spoke as he slowly marched to the center of the room.

Dieter's heart pounded. Casually, he turned back toward the bar while trying to pull his hood tighter around his head. Martin did the same. Cristoff gave Dieter and Martin a scornful look, as if it was their fault for the intrusion, before he finally looked up and addressed Ulrich.

"Can I help you, Herr Ulrich?" he said, feigning calmness.

Ulrich's gruff voice rang out. "Yes, barkeep, I'm here to arrest a certain person . . ." he trailed off as he stomped toward the bar. "Ah!" he called out suddenly. "There she is!"

She?

"Aellin Brandt!" Ulrich barked, now looking up the staircase. "You are under arrest for treason, for conspiring to rebel against the lordship of Bedburg. Please step down here."

Turning to his left, Dieter looked up the stairs, keeping his face hidden. Aellin stood at the top of the stairs, her curly black hair in a bun. Her face flashed pure terror as she gripped the staircase railing with both hands. Dieter could tell by her eyes that she was considering making a run for it.

But to where? Out a window?

Please don't run, Aellin . . .

While Aellin remained frozen, Ulrich bounded up the stairs, more quickly than a man his size should have been able to do, and grabbed her by the shoulders. Aellin writhed from his grip, as Ulrich roughly pulled her down the staircase and out the door, his men quickly following.

"This is madness!" she screamed, her voice trailing off as they took her away. "I've done nothing wrong!" she yelled down the quiet street of a still-waking Bedburg.

Dieter considered what had just happened. Then realized something was wrong.

He reached into his tunic and found the crumpled note.

The message was wrong.

"Dammit," Cristoff said, pounding his fist on the bar top. "She's my best earner!" Then he returned to his chores like it was just another day. Glancing over at Dieter, he returned to their earlier conversation. "What urgent news did you have for me?"

Dieter was still staring at the message in his hand. Then he realized something he hadn't noticed before. He got up quickly, pulling Martin along with him, and returned to Claus' inn. There, he retrieved one of the earlier notes they'd received.

And noticed it immediately.

The handwriting was different. Noticeably.

Especially the curved lines of the signature, since it—*Mord*—was the only word found in both notes, and thus easy to compare.

"These notes were written by two different people," he said, looking up at Claus and Martin.

"We've been compromised."

CHAPTER TWENTY-SEVEN

HUGO

"I'm not in love with you, Hugo. I never was."

Ava's words hit him like a spear through the heart. Even locked in a cell, her tone was anything but submissive. Undeterred by her surroundings, the woman's words were unkind, combative, defiant. Hugo could barely speak, his face twisted. "B-but, when we were younger . . . in the Vagabond Five . . ."

With knees drawn up to her chest and her arms across her legs, Ava sat back against the wall of the cell and shook her head without emotion.

"I never thought of you like that," she said. "We were good friends, nothing more. I'm sorry if you think I led you on . . ."

That's exactly what you did! he wanted to shout. But Ulrich and Karstan were in the next room and he didn't want them to hear him grovel.

Shifting from heartbroken to angry, he squinted at her. "You're heartless, Ava. You played us against each other—Severin, Karstan, me."

She scoffed. "You're delusional, Hue. I never did any such thing! If anything, I tried to keep us all together, even when things began falling apart."

"So you never loved Karstan, either?"

Ava shook her head. "Of course not. That was a moment of weakness. I had just been freed of this place—"

"By me."

She sighed, ignoring the comment. "I wasn't in my right mind."

"You still aren't," Hugo spat. "You wouldn't know a good man if he stood right before you."

With a bemused look, Ava said, "Is that what you are, then? A good man?" She blew out a breath. "Any man who follows so closely in the shadows of that evil, despicable investigator—"

"*Lord*," Hugo interjected. "He's called *Lord* Heinrich Franz."

"For God's sake, he killed your father! How can you ever trust a man who's done such terrible things?"

"And he's been more like a father to me than anyone else—*including* Peter Griswold," Hugo blurted out, surprising himself at publicly voicing such disrespect for his own father. It was as if the words weren't his, like hearing someone else speak them.

Ava shook her head sadly, "He has you on a leash, Hugo. A puppy dog yipping at his every command. If you don't see that, then you're beyond help."

"You don't know anything, foolish girl."

"And that's always been your problem," Ava shot back. "You always know more than everyone else, you've got all the answers. Well Hugo, have you seen the city recently? Does it look like *Lord* Heinrich is doing a good job of keeping Bedburg peaceful?"

"We're in a war," Hugo muttered, his confidence waning.

"The Cologne War ended three years ago! That wicked man is stirring up trouble that shouldn't even exist. Darkness follows everything Heinrich Franz touches—including you."

Hugo shook his head violently, trying to shake off Ava's words. But the truth was, her points were strong and sensible. Bedburg was indeed in an uproar. The two sides, the Protestants and Catholics, hated each other more than ever. And there was no denying that all the latest upheaval was traceable to Heinrich's recent actions, not the least of which were the murders of barons Ludwig and Josef—two of the wealthiest, most influential men in the county. With no thought of possible ramifications. Solely on a whim.

But Hugo's doubts had to remain private. His survival depended on it. He certainly couldn't confess them to this foolish girl. So he stayed quiet and just stared at her. Which wasn't hard to do. Even in her filthy clothes, even in this grimy prison cell, she was still beautiful.

But she wasn't done destroying him. "Martin is twice the

man you'll ever be, Hugo," she said as he stared, her words crashing his world to pieces.

Gritting his teeth, he gripped the bars tightly, his knuckles turning white. Yet all he could say was, "You don't mean it."

With a rueful look, Ava answered quietly, "I do. You've turned into something I could never have dreamed of."

He inhaled, then let it out. "And I thought I knew you, too, Ava. But I couldn't have been more wrong. You're just like every other girl . . ."

Hearing his words come out, he realized how silly they sounded, like a wounded schoolboy.

Ava narrowed her eyes. "While you do Heinrich's bidding, Martin works to help people. Helping your sister's husband. When they rescued me from the streets of Bedburg, I realized something about myself."

Placing her hands on the cold floor for support, she slowly stood. "I never belonged with you, Hugo—the whole lot of you: Karstan, Severin, Daniel. We were fooling ourselves, just bringing misery to regular people, the same folk I'm now trying to help." She looked away. "I suppose I'm trying to redeem myself for the terrible things I've done, before I leave this awful city."

She turned back to him, stepping toward the bars, gazing into his eyes. "Unfortunately, I think you're beyond redemption," she said, and Hugo snapped.

"Say it again, you cold bitch," he snarled, his face coiled like a rabid dog.

And she did.

Leaning in even closer, she whispered, "You're beyond redemption."

"I'll kill you!" Hugo yelled, his arm darting between the bars, catching a handful of hair and yanking her forward. As her face smashed into the metal rods, her nose cracked and she screamed, blood spurting everywhere. Gagging, she sunk to the floor as a shout came from down the hall.

"That's enough!" yelled Ulrich, rushing over with Karstan steps behind. Grabbing Hugo by the shoulders, the jailer pulled him away as Ava quietly wept, her hands covering her bloody face.

"Jesus, Hue," said Karstan, eyeing the sobbing woman. "Why'd you do that?"

Hugo thrashed in Ulrich's arms, breaking the big man's grip and dashing down the hall and up the stairs.

A few hours later, Hugo was back in the comfort and safety of House Charmagne. Though exhausted, both physically and emotionally, he'd at least calmed down a bit. He'd never been that angry and it scared him.

Am I starting to take after Heinrich?

Being around so much death at the hands of Heinrich, Ulrich, and even Tomas Reiner, he knew he was unraveling, becoming desensitized to the violence. Thinking back, he could even pinpoint when it had started: that day he'd pushed Severin off the cliff—how easy it had been for him to do that, feeling virtually no remorse.

Perhaps I am *being blinded by Heinrich. What has he truly ever done for me? Given me a false sense of importance by making me his "liaison" or "emissary" or "regent" while he's away? Is that really anything?*

The mansion's butler, Beauregard, broke into his thoughts, approaching him in the hallway with a letter.

"A message from Cologne, young master," Beauregard said, before scurrying off.

Opening the envelope, Hugo sighed then read the short note.

Hugo,

You are the only person I can trust with the contents of this letter. Keep this information close to you.

I am indisposed in Cologne, trying to win back favor from Archbishop Ernst. Prior to his death, I believe Ludwig Koehler was attempting to conspire against our interests in Bedburg.

Help me find proof of that!

Go to the jail and free Tomas. Tell him to ready the garrison, that battle may be imminent. I fear the battleground will be Bedburg.

Do not trust anyone. I shall return shortly. Until then, I trust you to watch over our enterprises.

~HF

Ignoring his doubts from just moments earlier, Hugo smiled at the last two words of the letter.

". . . *our* enterprises."

A sign that Heinrich really did trust him? Though it left far more questions than answers.

Who will take over Ludwig's sword now that he's fallen?

If "battle may be imminent," where will these enemies come from?

And how do I prepare for that? I've never been in a war.

Can I truly turn to Tomas for advice?

Folding the letter back into its envelope, he tucked it away in his tunic. Then a thought struck him. He walked down the hallway to the stairs leading to the cellar and dungeon. As he descended the steps, he pinched his nose to avoid the foul odor. When he reached the bottom, the air was cold and damp. Tightening his tunic against the chill, he grabbed a lit torch from the wall and, once his eyes adjusted, headed for the cages.

Heinrich's wolves frightened him. He still didn't understand why the man kept such feral beasts as "pets." One of many things about Heinrich that made no sense.

In the corner of the room, Lady Lucille Engel sat curled up, hiding her face between her knees. Hugo called out, "Lady?"

Slowly, the woman lifted her head. Her face was dirty, her blonde hair greasy and plastered to her scalp. She hadn't bathed since her father's death weeks earlier, still wearing the wedding gown she'd had on that night, though the once lavish dress was now torn and covered in blood.

Yet through all the ugliness around her, for the first time Hugo noticed how attractive she was. Despite being in her early thirties, almost twice Hugo's age, her body was lithe and her cheeks slightly sunken in a sultry way.

As Hugo approached, she squirmed backward toward the wall. He stopped, putting his hands out in a calming gesture. "I'm not here to hurt you, my lady."

"I'm not a lady any longer," she groaned. "Since you killed my father . . . I lost that title."

"I'm sorry, Frau Engel. I did not know that was going to happen."

Lucille snorted. "You expect me to believe that?"

"Heinrich is a very impulsive man."

Tilting her head, she squinted up at him. "That's what you call your murderous, vile lord? *Impulsive?*"

Hugo looked down without responding.

A moment later, Lucille said, "I'm sorry, I . . . please don't shut down. I haven't spoken to anyone in weeks. How long have I been locked away here?"

Hugo looked up, feeling pity for the former noblewoman. Heinrich had done a heartless thing. Hugo looked over into the wolves' cage, noticing the dark blotches of dried blood smeared everywhere. Not content with simply murdering the woman's father, Heinrich had fed the man's body to the animals while she'd been forced to watch. It was yet another thing Hugo could not comprehend about his mentor: the need to torture someone after already winning.

He turned back to her. "Would you like to talk, then?"

Lucille gave an almost imperceptible nod. In contrast to her huge presence on the night of the wedding dinner, as she now huddled in the corner she looked so very small, a mere shell of her former self. Hugo's pity intensified. He stepped forward, moving very slowly so as not to alarm her. When he was three feet away he sat down on the cold hard floor across from her, laying the torch beside him, then resting his hands in his lap.

Lucille studied him for a long time. It seemed to go on forever until, feeling unsettled, Hugo had to look away, crossing his feet and toying with his boots. When he glanced back up, Lucille had a strange smile on her face.

"You are a peculiar young man, Hugo Griswold."

He tilted his head. "How so?"

"For some reason, I feel that I can trust you. I've been wrong before, mind you"—her head nudging toward the stairs, referring to Heinrich—"but I'm usually right about these things. *Can* I trust you?"

Hugo nodded dumbly, feeling like he was trapped under some sort of spell. He gazed into her eyes—amber in color, large and inviting. He glanced downward, to the top of her dress, to the clearly-defined curvature of her tight corset around her abundant chest. Catching him staring, she smiled. Embarrassed, he immediately looked away.

"Do you think you could do me a favor, Hugo?" she asked softly.

He again nodded, trance-like. Then he chuckled. "As long as it's not to break you out of here . . ."

"Of course not," she said. "Do you think you could get me a fresh dress? Surely your master has clean clothes for his many female guests . . ."

Hugo's head swiveled left to right before responding. "He doesn't really have any female guests."

Lucille put a finger to her chin. "I find that odd. And what about you?"

"Yes, I suppose it is odd."

With a twinkle in her eye, she clarified, "I meant, what about *your* female guests."

Hugo stammered. "I-I, n-no, no."

She giggled, an angelic sound that stirred Hugo. He couldn't take his eyes off her, his mind utterly blank.

"Was there a reason you came down to speak with me, Hugo? Or were you just lonely?" She paused, then, "Like me?"

Suddenly he couldn't recall why he'd come down. To ask her something? Then he remembered.

"Oh, yes," he said, trying to regain a more serious tone. "Do you have any idea who would attack Bedburg? I mean, if you were your father—"

"My father's dead," Lucille said flatly. "Your master made sure of that."

"R-right, my apologies. But, if you were in his *predicament*—"

"If you're asking whether or not my father was planning

something egregious against your city, you're asking the wrong person. My father never involved me with talk of battle and war. I'm sure he figured I wouldn't understand, or care."

"And . . . do you?"

"Do I what?"

"Care or understand battle and war."

Lucille shrugged. "I understand its necessity. But no, I don't care for it at all. You men and your weapons and strategies and barbaric nature . . . it's really quite dull."

"And what kind of things do you fancy?" Hugo asked.

"Clean clothes," Lucille said with a wry smile.

He let out a nervous laugh and again toyed with his boot. "O-of course, my apologies. Let me see what I can do . . ."

He stood, reaching down for the still-flaming torch on the ground. Looking into his eyes, Lucille said, "You don't seem like a terrible person, Hugo. Unlike your master."

"You mean your husband," Hugo retorted, immediately regretting his words.

But Lucille took the jab in stride. "Heinrich Franz will never be my husband. To me, he'll never be anything more than a murderer."

"And what about me?" Hugo asked.

She tilted her head, mulling the question over. "I'm not sure yet what I think of you, Hugo Griswold," she replied. "Only time will tell . . ."

His heart began racing as Lucille waved him off.

"Now go, I beg of you. Please find me that fresh dress."

Hugo nodded then hurried away. As he headed up the stairs, he imagined Lucille watching him from behind, increasing the pace of his pounding heart. When he reached the top, he closed and locked the door behind him, then leaned back against it, sighed, and sunk down to the floor.

He was no longer thinking of Ava. In fact, she was the furthest thing from his mind.

But a woman had taken over his thoughts.

And he was feeling something powerful.

Immensely more powerful than anything he'd ever felt.

CHAPTER TWENTY-EIGHT

SYBIL

Sybil quickly grew fond of the newest members of Strangers Shire—her guests, Mary, Wilhelm, and Salvatore.

Mary and Wilhem were a very close mother and son. Wilhelm's kindness and support for his mother reminded Sybil of a younger Dieter. It seemed *everything* reminded her of Dieter these days, now that he'd been missing for so very long and was likely dead. Wilhelm was also physically similar to Dieter, both lean and tall, with handsome faces and brown, short-cropped beards.

And Salvatore, the tattooed druid who spoke in unintelligible riddles, was unlike anyone Sybil had ever met. Though his words held more flare than substance, he seemed a kind man. And when he explained that he was a *benandanti*—a "spirit wanderer"—Sybil couldn't help wondering if maybe *he* might be more suited as the village's soothsayer than she was.

Mary spent most of her time either preoccupied with Claire and her child, Rose, or working with her fabrics. Since she was already well versed in threading wool, she was a fast study in textile-making, staying indoors most days, head bowed, hardly uttering a word, working her distaff.

Sybil found Wilhelm sitting on the grass behind Claire's house, working with his dyes. His new responsibilities included extracting the natural reds, oranges, and browns from unused tree bark and other plant parts, and he seemed to relish his work. Sybil watched over his shoulder as he mixed a bucket of color. Next to it was another bucket filled with clear liquid.

"Where did you learn to do that?" Sybil asked, startling him.

He stopped stirring and, without turning, submerged his hand into the bucket of clear liquid. "I was apprentice to a man in my hometown," he said, dabbling a few drops of the colored dye onto the knuckles of the hand he'd just dipped into the clear liquid. Sybil was mesmerized. He then reached down to a flint stone laying beside him and sparked it against some wood pieces, creating a small flame. Quickly, he touched the hand he'd dabbled the dye onto across the tiny fire, and it exploded over his hand into a bright blue flame.

Sybil gasped, but Wilhelm seemed unperturbed, closely studying his flaming hand. The fire seemed to curl around the red dots on his knuckles. Then he shook his wrist in a quick, practiced motion, and the fire was instantly gone, leaving his hand apparently unburned.

"By God!" Sybil exclaimed, covering her mouth. "What did you just do?"

Wilhelm chuckled. "Seeing how flammable the dyestuff is. This solution"—he nudged his chin toward the colored dye bucket—"must be more flame retardant before I apply it to the textiles. That way, the resulting fabric will be, too."

Sybil cocked her head to the side. "How does your hand not burn?"

With another light laugh Wilhelm explained. "The clear liquid is alcohol and water. The water is drawn to my skin, conducting the heat away from my hand, while the alcohol keeps the flame lit."

Sybil was amazed. "And you can recreate that?"

Wilhelm nodded. "I can't keep it going for long, or else the water will evaporate and my skin will be the only surface underneath the fire . . . but yes, I can recreate it. Why do you ask?"

Sybil just shook her head. "When Daxton called your family the 'stonemasons,' what did he mean? Stonemasonry has nothing to do with what you're doing here."

Wilhelm sighed, slumping his shoulders. "My father was a master stonemason, but I was never passionate about that, so I became a dyemaker. At first he disapproved, thought it a foolish endeavor, until he realized I was earning almost as much as he was. Then he became supportive."

Sybil smiled. "Is that why your mother is so downcast?

Because your father is not here?" she asked, as diplomatically as possible. From the bits and pieces she'd heard about Wilhelm's father, she surmised he was either dead or missing. She walked around and sat beside the young man on the grass.

Wilhelm nodded without looking up. "Father is missing. He helped us escape, but I worry he didn't make it out alive, though I don't have the heart to tell mother that. It would crush her. I just pray for the best."

"You're a good son," said Sybil, causing Wilhelm to finally turn to her. "When you're in a foreign place like this, it's definitely best to keep hope alive. If you're a worshiper, direct your questions to God."

Sybil had her own feelings about God but thought it best to keep them to herself. It would do no good to dishearten this nice young man.

"I appreciate that, Frau Sybil," Wilhelm said, "and I believe our rescuer would agree with you. Prayer is best in situations such as these." He smiled sadly. "Who knows, my father could come walking down that road any day now."

Sybil nodded. "Yes, don't lose hope. It could just be that it takes your father longer to get here than it did you and your mother."

"Aye," Wilhelm agreed, "thanks to meeting Daxton, Georg, and Rowaine in Amsterdam, we were lucky to get here so quickly." Wilhelm smiled, as if thinking back to when he and his mother had first met their rescuers. "We'd been instructed by our original rescuer to seek a ship to Norfolk, from Amsterdam, then go to a shire lorded by a reeve named Clarence Bailey. But at first, no one knew where that was . . . until 'the Pale Diviner' was mentioned."

Sybil's face reddened, blushing at the speed with which her new reputation had apparently circulated. Changing the subject, she asked, "You sought refuge here from persecution, you've said?"

Wilhelm nodded. "The *Lion's Pride* happened to be at the right place at the right time."

As it had turned out, Daxton, Georg, and Rowaine had just finished transporting their first batch of goods belonging to

Reeve Bailey to Amsterdam when they'd run into Wilhelm, Mary, and Salvatore. From there, the textile shipment would continue down the waterways to Germany and ultimately to Cologne. The archbishop in Cologne would never know that his best clothing shipments had come illegally from England.

And since Wilhelm, Mary, and Salvatore were seeking passage from Amsterdam to the same harbor in England that the *Lion's Pride* crew was headed, it had seemed like divine intervention when they'd crossed paths. Especially when it turned out that, not only were they all headed for the same port, but for the very same shire as well.

"I don't believe in coincidences," Sybil said. "So keep your prayers alive, just like I'm sure your father is doing right now."

Wilhelm smiled. "It certainly is what our liberator would have sought from us—to keep praying. He was a priest, after all."

Sybil nodded slowly, then furrowed her brow. "The man who originally rescued you was a priest?"

Wilhelm grinned. "Well, a former priest, I suppose. But everyone still called him that and treated him as one. I think once you've lived that life, you never truly escape it."

Sybil was quiet for a moment. Then, as she watched Wilhelm stir his dye, her adrenaline began to pump. Clearing her throat, she asked, "Where was it you said you escaped from, Wilhelm, before arriving in Amsterdam? Your hometown?"

"A place called Bedburg, madam. A small city in Germany."

It couldn't be him.

With her heart racing, she said, "And the man who rescued you was a priest . . ."

Wilhelm nodded, focusing back on his bucket. "Yes, madam, a one-armed priest," he said nonchalantly.

One arm? Then clearly it could not have been my two-armed husband.

But she asked the question anyway. "What was this one-armed priest's name, Wilhelm? The one who rescued you."

"Well, I never learned his surname. But his first name was Dieter." He looked up. "Are you all right, Sybil? You look ill."

It took several minutes to regain her composure. After lying to Wilhelm that she was fine, she stood up and walked around the grass, gazing out at the countryside, trying to understand how the impossible could be possible. Finally, she sat back down and quietly watched Wilhelm work for a while.

After a time, she asked, "I hope you don't take this badly, Wilhelm . . . but what was this man trying to accomplish by saving you?"

Wilhelm scratched his neck, then shrugged. "I'm not sure. I suppose he was simply a good man. We weren't the first people he'd rescued. He is somewhat of a legendary figure in Bedburg, my lady."

With a bemused look, Sybil chuckled. Hearing all this now—after so long hearing nothing, after thinking her husband dead—it was all so difficult to process.

Several minutes passed, then Sybil spoke in almost a whisper. "*Legendary?* How so, Wilhelm? Please, tell me everything."

Wilhelm stopped working and looked at her carefully. Clearly, there was more to her questions than simple curiosity. He thought for a moment exactly how to answer her. Finally, he said, "There's a nasty uprising happening in my homeland, I'm afraid. One side calls it a rebellion, the other a revolution. Dieter is one of the leaders of that revolution."

He always wanted a calling. Perhaps this is God's answer to his cries!

Wilhelm tilted his head. "Your demeanor has changed, my lady, if you don't mind my saying. Why are you so curious about this priest?"

Sybil sighed. "Because, Wilhelm, Dieter Nicolaus is my husband. "And thank you," she added, leaning over and planting a big wet kiss on his cheek before hurrying off.

Rowaine was equally ecstatic hearing the news about Dieter.

Lying in bed, nursing her sore back, she jubilantly sat up. "If he's in danger, we must rescue him!"

"I agree. We must!" Sybil said, turning to Daxton who'd been eavesdropping in the doorway. "How quickly can we set sail on the *Pride*?"

Daxton scratched his favorite spot on his bald head. "Er,

well, Georg is with the ship in King's Lynn, preparing it for their next voyage."

Rowaine nodded. "Father told me he had a huge shipment to arrange, headed for the same place."

"Amsterdam?" Sybil asked.

Smiling, Rowaine nodded. "And Germany beyond. But if we hurry, I'm sure we could get to King's Lynn before he sends it off."

Sybil's mind was still reeling, thinking of seeing Dieter again. "I can be ready by nightfall," she said, unconsciously clenching and relaxing her fists. "I have little to pack."

"We could make it there within a day if we hurry," Daxton said. "Perhaps we can catch Georg before he sends the ship off."

"We?" Sybil asked. She and Rowaine were both staring at him.

"Of course," Daxton replied. "Obviously I'm going with you. The rough seas are no place for an excitable, beautiful wom—"

"Don't even finish that sentence," Rowaine barked, holding up her hand. Daxton knew enough to heed her warning. Rising from her bed, Rowaine put a hand on Sybil's shoulder. "I'm joining you as well."

Sybil smiled sadly. "It will be dangerous . . ."

"More dangerous if you go alone," Daxton countered. "And besides, even though I passed off the *Pride* to Georg for our work in King's Lynn, that was just *temporary*. I'm still her captain. And you won't be sailing anywhere without me!"

"Nor me," Rowaine added.

Daxton spoke with finality. "I can use this opportunity to gather up Darlene and Abigail, my wife and daughter. It's been far too long since I've seen them. I'd like to bring them here so we may settle in Strangers Shire."

"And I," Rowaine said, her eyes growing dark, "still wish to serve justice to my mother's killer. And now I can resume that quest, with my legs working again."

Sybil smiled. How could she deny her friends? Especially when their reasoning was so sound? Besides, it was naïve to believe she could rescue Dieter by herself, knowing nothing of the sea or the rivers leading to Bedburg. Then her face grew serious.

"Wilhelm tells me the Protestants are rising up," she said.

"As they always will, so long as there are any of them left alive," Daxton added.

Rowaine looked out the room's single window. "We'd better get ready. We've only an hour or so of daylight left."

So the trio set to work packing their things for their trip to King's Lynn and, eventually, on to Amsterdam and Germany.

And hopefully their *final* voyage across the North Sea.

As it turned out, *everyone* seemed to want to join Sybil on her adventure—despite the dangers. And those dangers would indeed be great:

First would be the trip up to King's Lynn to the *Lion's Pride*. Then, the sail across the North Sea to Amsterdam. And finally, navigating through the rivers that snaked through Germany to eventually extract Dieter from a war-torn city.

Yet no one was deterred, each having his or her own agenda:

Daxton wanted to captain his ship again, and retrieve his wife and daughter.

Rowaine sought vengeance against her mother's killer, as well as a chance to polish up her navigational skills.

Wilhelm and Mary wanted to rescue their father and husband, William—and if he wasn't in Bedburg, at least find out where he might be. Plus, they felt a strong kinship and indebtedness to Dieter for all he'd done for them.

And then there was Salvatore, who had found Strangers Shire entirely too dull, and also wished to follow Sybil to learn more of the Pale Diviner's ways—while staying far away from Heinrich Franz.

And lastly there was Corvin Carradine, who simply thought the adventure sounded exciting. He likely maintained hopeful thoughts of seducing Sybil along the way.

Early next morning, after riding hard all night, when the

seven of them arrived at Georg's dark warehouse in King's Lynn, he was rolling barrels and placing them onto a cart.

"Perfect," he said, once the situation was explained to him. "Then I'm going too." Within minutes he'd found a local friend who gladly accepted his offer to lease his position as the Hanseatic League's port representative, pending his eventual return.

As the group stood in the warehouse, ready to load the ship, Georg slapped the side of one of the barrels. "I have plenty of these filled with sugar, headed for Cologne. Apparently it's another commodity the archbishop would rather buy in secret—for cheap—from rivals across the sea."

When the barrels were loaded onto the *Pride*, the group was shocked to discover that the hold was already crammed with caskets and chests loaded with arquebuses, pistols, spears, and armor.

"Where is all this headed?" Corvin asked, gesturing to the weapons.

Daxton bent down to inspect one of the tags. "Let's see . . . Bergheim, Germany."

"That's Bedburg's neighbor," Sybil said.

"Seems someone is expecting a war," Rowaine said.

"I suppose we all should be expecting one," Daxton said with a smirk, cracking his knuckles.

An hour later, with the sun just emerging above the horizon, waiting to spring another day, the crew of eight set sail out of King's Lynn, toward their fate.

CHAPTER TWENTY-NINE

HEINRICH

Heinrich sat at the window, staring out into the darkness. He was alone in a small cabinet room in Cologne Cathedral that overlooked the city. Below him, dots of flickering orange light lit the foggy streets in random places, like faraway stars twinkling.

He'd never much cared for the bustling metropolis, but this was where the power was. Appeasing the city's masters was the only way for him to get what he wanted.

And what were his wants?

Originally, to placate and impress Archbishop Ernst, one of the most powerful and influential men in the entire Empire.

But once Heinrich was given his lordship of Bedburg, his greed and ambition swelled, becoming unstoppable like lava flowing down a volcano. He realized that he was destined for much more than just Bedburg. He needed to grow his lordship, conquer the surrounding cities, and rise in the ranks of nobility.

Yes, rise to the ranks of that same nobility he'd always despised. But he rationalized that it was different in his case because, unlike the noblemen he hated, he had *earned* his authority—on his merits, not through birthright.

But right at that moment, staring off into the vast expanse of the sleeping city, his wants felt different. As did his emotions.

He'd never known his father, and his mother and brother had both died when he was young—it was irrelevant to him that he may have been the cause of both deaths; all that mattered was how lonely he'd been for so much of his early life. Originally, that void had been filled by Odela Grendel, all those years ago when she took him in after his mother was burned at the stake.

But ever since then—maybe because of the family he never

had, maybe because of his fondness for power, or maybe a little of both—he realized that someone else had filled that void. A man. A man he cared for dearly.

Ernst.

And he also knew it was far more than just caring. Far more than respect and gratitude for all he'd done for him. No, that tug at his heart, that ache in his soul, was something different. Something much stronger.

Love.

And even if that love wasn't reciprocated, it still burned with such passion that he knew he must defend the man at all costs.

For it had been Heinrich's blunders and violent impulses that had caused the archbishop to now face dethroning. This great man—who had fought a war to earn his high position in the Counter-Reformation, who was an unparalleled champion of the Catholic cause in Germany, who had fought his entire life against the teachings of Martin Luther and John Calvin, who had given Heinrich everything, and yes, who had turned Heinrich into a monstrous killer—this great man was now in jeopardy of losing everything because of Heinrich.

Which left Heinrich no choice. He had to ensure that Ernst's power was restored. That his name was returned to its rightful place of glory.

This was more than a mere assignment or obligation.

This was his *responsibility*. His reason for being.

To seat Ernst back on his throne. To return him to his proper place of respect.

For now, and for all of history.

But he didn't know how.

Then, as his eyes swept across the sleeping city before him, he recalled the last words Ernst had spoken to him.

Prove it.

He'd challenged Heinrich to prove that Ludwig von Bergheim and Josef von Erftstadt had in fact been plotting against Bedburg before their deaths.

But could he? And was that even true? The two barons could have been totally innocent, never plotting against his lordship or his city.

Could my thoughts have been delusional? Could my illusions of grandeur have torn me asunder, turned me paranoid, made me do terrible things, all because of my lust for power?

Turning away from the window, his gut told him he'd been right. Those men had been enemies. He just knew it.

But how could he prove it?

On the desk next to him sat a stack of books. His eyes scanned the titles—a treatise on war, another on politics, another translating the Protestant Bible—apparent favorites of Ernst that he read at his leisure. But the book on top was one Heinrich had brought with him from Bedburg on a whim. It was the ledger from Ludwig Koehler's scribe and assistant, Hedda. The one he'd confiscated after slaying her lord.

Suddenly he had an idea. He took the ledger from the stack and, sitting down at the desk, opened it. He moved a small candle burning in a dish closer, so he could read more clearly, and began poring over the pages of the book. Some contained numbers and columns and graphs he had no interest in. But others were filled with conversations Hedda had transcribed between Ludwig and the people he did business with.

He began to read the transcriptions. Scooting his chair in closer, he lost track of time. Before he knew it, dawn was approaching.

Leaning back in his chair he yawned and rubbed his eyes. But just as he was about to close the ledger, a single word on the opened page caught his eye.

Mord.

Bubbling anger rose as Heinrich's jaw clenched. He'd seen and heard that word many times since becoming lord of Bedburg. It was an alias, a pseudonym, of an unknown bastard trying to save the Protestants and other rebels from their doomed fate. It had been Ulrich who had first brought the name to his attention, on notes apparently written by the rogue.

In Heinrich's efforts to shape his control over the citizens of Bedburg, he'd devised numerous strategies for rooting out non-Catholics. Since his time before becoming the lord of Bedburg, back when he played the role of Chief Inquisitor Adalbert in Trier, Heinrich had acquired a knack for learning secrets circulating his town. And under the authority of Archbishop Ernst, he'd mastered that art, becoming a vicious inquisitor in his own right, in his efforts to help keep his city a Catholic majority.

And that required names. Names of those to be imprisoned or executed, brought to him in several ways: in hushed tones from concerned Catholics; through confessions with Bishop Balthasar; from backstabbing landowners willing to give up their neighbors in exchange for their land; and from tavern-dwellers and alleyway rumormongers.

But someone—this *Mord*—had been thwarting those efforts. And to Heinrich's infuriation, this person was apparently a better schemer than he was, having somehow created a system which figured out in advance who Heinrich would brand as traitor, witch, or Protestant. As a result, too many insurgents were managing to escape the city without facing their deserved punishment.

So Heinrich was very interested in this *Mord* person.

And by God, Baron Ludwig was actually having a conversation with this bastard!

He continued reading the transcript of that conversation:

Mord – Give me what I want and your city will be safe.

L – What guarantees do I have of your success? It's my neck in a noose if you fail . . .

M – My superior will reward you handsomely. You don't even have to take part in the battle.

L – That still doesn't abate my worries.

M – Allow my lord's men to settle in Bergheim, Ludwig, and you will soon find yourself a prosperous man.

L – You promise me Bedburg?

M – We have no need for Bedburg. Cologne is our final destination—Bedburg is merely a stepping stone.

L - Because you can't stay hidden in Bergheim forever.

M – Precisely. My lord requires a central base of operation for all of our efforts against Cologne. Once Bedburg has fallen, it will be too late to rid us from the principality—we will be an established power.

L – And once Gebhard has reclaimed his throne . . . (trailed off unintelligibly)

M – Once my lord has Cologne, Bedburg and the districts west of Cologne will be yours, in payment for your allegiance and for sheltering his troops. All we ask is that you open your gates to us and house and feed us while the army builds.

L – Sounds like an expensive proposition.

M – The rewards will far outweigh the expenditure. My lord promises that.

L – We shall see. I'll have my answer for you within the fortnight.

(hands shaken)

By the time Heinrich got to the end of the passage, his throat was tight, his lips dry. Flipping quickly through the book, he discovered that passage was the only one with no date attached. And it was clear why: the words spoken were treasonous. Which explained Hedda's use of letters, rather than full names, except for that initial mention of *Mord* at the beginning, presumably to reference for the baron which conversation it was.

In fact, the only reason Heinrich could imagine the baron asking Hedda to transcribe something so incriminating would be to document for "L" what his compensation would be under the agreement in the event of a later dispute.

Slamming the book shut, Heinrich tried to absorb what he'd just read.

That bastard Ludwig has indeed been plotting against me!

He'd found it! He had his proof.

Jumping up from his chair, he punched his hands above him in victory. Though it was near morning, and the city—and Ernst—were still sleeping, he was too energized to let this groundbreaking news rest. Grabbing the ledger, he tucked it into his tunic and, wrapping both hands around it, headed up the stairs to the throne room.

Archbishop Ernst was not happy. Emerging from a hallway hunched over and still in his sleeping gown, his eyes were red and half-closed. Rubbing the crust from his eyelids with one hand, he held a candle close to Heinrich's face with the other.

"What is the meaning of this early intrusion, Heinrich?" When he squinted more closely at the man, he added, "And why are your eyes so big?"

Unable to contain himself, Heinrich smiled broadly and dramatically presented the ledger. "The proof you told me to bring you, Your Grace. I've found it."

"What the devil are you talking about?"

"In these pages! The proof we've been looking for! The proof you asked me to find, to regain your electoral seat." He shook the ledger for emphasis, proclaiming, "Baron Ludwig Koehler von Bergheim *was* plotting against me, Your Grace. And against *you*! He was arranging for the Protestant army to encamp in Bergheim in secret, while they readied themselves to attack Cologne."

Ernst's eyes grew wide, all sleepiness gone. He snatched the ledger from Heinrich. "Can it be true?"

Heinrich stepped beside him and opened the book to the correct passage. As Ernst read through it quickly, his face lost all color.

"God preserve us . . ." he muttered.

"So you see?" Heinrich said, "this is the evidence you need, to take your seat back from your nephew, yes?"

The archbishop nodded slowly, his face blank, his mind working feverishly. He looked up at Heinrich. "Who's *Mord*?"

"I'm not sure. At least not yet. But let me worry about that, Your Grace."

Ernst sighed. Scratching his forehead, then running his fingers through his hair, he said, "This could be disastrous. I . . . I must warn someone—everyone!"

Cupping a hand to his mouth, Ernst yelled down the hallway for his couriers. Three boys instantly appeared. Ernst quickly directed each one on a different mission and they scurried off as fast as they'd appeared. Then Ernst headed for the door. Before he got there, Heinrich shouted, "M-my lord!" and the archbishop turned back around.

"What about me, Your Grace?" Heinrich asked sheepishly.

Ernst glanced off for a moment and thought, then looked back at Heinrich.

"Oh, yes, yes, very well, Heinrich. You have your army. Now go defend my city, before it's taken from us both!"

As soon as Ernst vanished from view, Heinrich smiled wolfishly. Now he had the support he'd wanted. The power to fight against the Protestants, who now it seemed were apparently at his doorstep.

But you make one mistake, my lord, my love . . .

Bedburg is my *city.*

Heinrich's carriage exited Cologne through its western gate. Ordering his driver to go faster, he regretted that Felix wasn't driving. But as long as he kept reminding this new coachman to hurry, they'd hopefully still make it back to Bedburg by nightfall.

As they sped through the countryside, one thought kept swirling through Heinrich's brain: *Who is Mord?* He opened the ledger again and re-read the passage between "Mord" and Ludwig. Then he read it again. And again, until his head hurt.

Perhaps it was that headache, or the steady beat of the sun through the carriage window, that cleared his mind. But whatever it was, when he finally closed the ledger he had his answer.

An operation of this magnitude, storing and hiding an army right under my nose . . . would take a man with a sound military mind. Only a man with that kind of training could control all aspects of such a far-reaching mission. He'd need to know how much food and supplies to bring, how many rifles and horses were necessary, calculate how long to stay in Bergheim.

Very few people knew of my plans to arrest the Protestant rabblerousers. I've made sure to keep that information close to me. But there is one man who did know—either directly from me, or from reading Ulrich's ledger.

The same man responsible for arresting those people.

The same man I see going to church everyday—undoubtedly working with the bishop, that sly bastard.

The very man I just ordered to be released in my letter to Hugo.

The same man who would lead my army.

Tomas Reiner is Mord!

CHAPTER THIRTY

DIETER

The newest note from "Mord" had named Cristoff Krüger, the tavern owner, as the man needing to be rescued. But it had been Kruger's top-earning worker, Aellin Brandt, who had actually been arrested for treason.

Dieter tapped his chin thoughtfully.

He, his son, and Martin were now in a small room that Claus had graciously provided them at his inn. Sitting on the edge of the bed, Dieter had the two "Mord" notes he'd been comparing spread out next to him. Every so often he'd look up from the messages and peek out the curtained window to the street below, crowded with citizens milling about and town guards patrolling.

Now that it was clear that this latest note had been written by someone other than the "Mord" who had signed the earlier messages, Dieter had to figure out why it had been delivered and why the information in it had been wrong.

Had the misinformation been accidental or intentional? Was this new "Mord" someone trying to help who just happened to have bad information? Or was it someone intentionally trying to mislead? And if so, to what end?

And was this new "Mord" even a person, or something more sinister?

With so many questions, Dieter didn't know where to begin. Frustrated, he shook his head. Up until this last note, the messages from "Mord" had been his strongest weapon against Heinrich and his tyranny. So he'd never questioned where they came from. As long as they proved truthful and helped, there was no need to.

But now things were different. He was angry, of course, but more than that he was ashamed. He should have determined the identity of the letter-writer before it had come to this. Because now, not only was his strongest weapon rendered useless, but his strongest ally was gone. Aellin had proved invaluable. She was cunning, aware of everything going on in Bedburg—and what she didn't know, she had ways of finding out—and had helped him save numerous condemned Protestants and rebels.

And now Dieter feared for her life. He knew how far Ulrich would go to extract information from the poor girl. And though Aellin was one of the bravest and most loyal women he'd ever known, she was also still human. A person could only be put through so much agony before cracking and revealing secret sources and pertinent intelligence.

Which made Dieter wonder how much Aellin really knew. And where her true loyalties lay. Did she know, or at least have an idea, who "Mord"—either of them—really was? Did she know where he, Dieter, was now hiding? *How long do I have before my position is discovered?* And how much did she know about this supposed Protestant rebellion?

Dieter remembered that Aellin's friend and co-worker, a redheaded wench named Josephine, had been accused of supporting the Protestants before she'd been killed by Heinrich Franz. And Aellin's former boss, Lars, the tavern owner before Cristoff, had also been a Protestant backer. Did that mean Aellin's loyalties were similarly aligned? Or were such past relationships meaningless in determining one's beliefs?

As his thoughts drifted from one unanswered question to the next, he considered his next move. He'd become increasingly scared of going outside, especially in the daylight. He didn't want to put any more people in danger, not to mention his own safety. As his son's sole means of support, he couldn't afford to take any more chances. If something were to happen to him now, his boy would have no one: Ava, who'd done her best to act as the boy's surrogate mother, was now missing; and Claus, as kindly and well-intentioned as he was, was still old and in no condition to care for a young child.

Dieter sighed. Whatever he did, he had to be careful.

He looked over at Martin who was sitting on the floor on the far side of the room watching Peter walk in circles to make himself dizzy, as young boys do. When the toddler finally tumbled innocently to the ground, giggling, both Dieter and Martin shared a pained grin.

"What do you think about all this?" Dieter asked Martin. "Do you have any suggestions? You know Heinrich Franz and Bedburg as well as I do."

Martin's mouth turned down. "I feel just as lost as you, Dieter. I don't know what to do. We certainly can't trust the notes anymore, and if we can't trust them, what do we have?"

"So you're saying Heinrich has won?"

Martin shook his head. "As long as you remain free and alive, I do not believe all is lost. You give hope to the townspeople—the marginalized, the restless, the rebellious."

"I'm not sure that's true any longer," Dieter said, peeking out the window again.

"I do. People still see you as a beacon of faith and trust, even if they must say so in whispers. I daresay you're more accepted than the lord of Bedburg."

Dieter hadn't really thought of things that way, so Martin's words gave him a glimmer of hope. "Do you have any idea who could be compromising our letters and giving us false information?"

Martin shook his head, still watching Peter on the ground.

A light knock came at the door. Dieter and Martin exchanged a look, then Dieter quietly got up and hid behind the door. "Yes?" Martin called out, cracking the door enough to peer out.

It was Claus with a young woman beside him. She was petite and pretty, and wore large spectacles. In Claus's hand was a tray of food: more stale bread, cheese, and warm ale. Handing the tray to the girl, Claus smiled then walked away, leaving the girl to bring the tray into the room. As she entered, and Dieter registered who it was, his eyes widened. It was Hedda, Gustav Koehler's former secretary and scribe.

She set the food tray on the bed, smiling down at Peter who stood up and attacked the food like a rabid wolf.

"What's the meaning of this, woman?" Dieter asked, walking out from behind the door. "What are you doing here?"

Hedda turned toward him. She seemed to have aged a great deal since Dieter last saw her. It hadn't been that long ago, less than a year, outside this very inn, the night of the fateful battle between Gustav's men and Rowaine's pirate crew, when Dieter's wife, Sybil, was taken from him. Although that deadly confrontation had been triggered when it appeared young Peter was in jeopardy, it turned out to be a ruse. Gustav had used Peter as bait to capture and escape with Sybil instead.

Which then of course led to Sybil burning at the stake, or so Dieter thought.

So Dieter had plenty of reason to despise Hedda. She'd not only aided Gustav, she'd also been complicit in what eventually led to the loss of his wife.

"I come bearing good news," Hedda said, glancing at Dieter, then looking away when she saw his expression of utter disgust. Turning to Martin, she said, "I'm here to help."

"Say your piece and be gone," Dieter told her.

Martin exchanged a hard look with Dieter. Although Martin had also been in that battle with Gustav at the inn, for whatever reason he was more forgiving of this girl. "We can take whatever help we can get, Dieter."

Dieter didn't reply, his gaze fixed on Hedda.

"I come from Bergheim," she said. "Following my Lord Ludwig's murder, I was thrown into Bedburg's jailhouse, then released a few days ago and sought refuge in Bergheim, where I thought it to be safe."

"I hope that place burns to the ground," Dieter mumbled, "just like my church in Norfolk."

That had been another evil perpetrated by Gustav, the burning of Dieter's church.

Hedda sighed. "I'm sure it will, in due time, with or without my help. Because of what's headed there."

Martin cocked his head. "What do you mean?"

Hedda pushed her spectacles up the bridge of her nose. "An army is building in Bergheim, in secret. Their goal is a military coup to take Bedburg and the surrounding cities, and eventually Cologne itself."

If the goal is to take Cologne, there can only be one man leading such a company.

"Gebhard?" Dieter asked, his body tensing.

Hedda furrowed her brow. "Yes, priest, the former archbishop of Cologne has returned to take back what he believes is his rightful, God-sent office."

"What happened to Bonn? When I visited there, it looked like he was garnering troops at that location."

Hedda shook her head. "He was garnering *support.* But Bonn was never a serious contender for his garrison. It's too close to Cologne and he feared being discovered by Ernst."

"How is Bergheim any different?"

"With my lord killed," Hedda said, "Bergheim is in turmoil. Gebhard has smartly used that as an opportunity to rouse the troops. He's found support from the squabbling nobility. Even *they* can put their differences aside when it comes to battling a common enemy—a lordkiller, no less. So with monetary and political support from Bergheim, Erftstadt, Bonn, Kerpen, and other regions, plus military support from his bishopric in France, he's about ready to move on Bedburg."

Dieter mulled that over for a few moments. Finally, he said, "Why are you telling us this? What reason do you have to help *me?*"

"No reason other than Gebhard wishing me to."

"So you're a Protestant now?"

"No. I share sympathies with the nobles of Bergheim. It is my home. Any man capable of slaughtering two powerful barons over dinner is truly mad. And cannot go unpunished. If he is not stopped, Heinrich Franz will only grow more powerful. As I've said, we all now share a common enemy."

"Gebhard wishes to take Bedburg from Heinrich," Dieter mused, "so that he can eventually move on Cologne and Archbishop Ernst." Then he shook his head. "But I still don't understand my place in all this."

"Gebhard wanted to forewarn you of his coming. He'll need support from the citizens of Bedburg and he believes you can marshal that support. He only wishes your ear and allegiance."

"My only allegiance is to God," Dieter retorted. "No man has my oath." Then, softening a bit, he added, "But I will assist

Gebhard. After all, he introduced me to Patric Clauson, who before then I knew only as 'old man Claus.'"

Hedda smirked.

From the far side of the room, Martin asked, "Now that Ludwig is dead, who is slated to become lord of Bergheim?"

The woman shrugged. "It's unclear. We'll see how the dust settles once Gebhard's campaign plays out. But currently there are plenty of shrewd and wealthy noblemen vying for the position. With both of Ludwig's sons dead, there is no issue of inheritance."

"I foresee a bloody future for Bergheim," Dieter said quietly.

Hedda nodded, adding, "I see a bloody future for the entire principality of Cologne, priest."

"When should we expect Gebhard to make his move on Bedburg?" Dieter asked.

"He plans to march two days hence."

"Does he have any specific instructions for me? I am rather limited in my ability to step outside this inn, much less rally support for him."

"He trusts you will know what to do when the time comes. Just keep your ears open and when he *does* arrive, try to sway the citizenry to his cause." She looked over at Martin but continued talking to Dieter. "And if your hands are tied," she nudged her chin toward Martin, "perhaps you can use this one to relay the message to the townsfolk."

Hearing that, Martin's first impression was one of alarm, his eyes involuntarily widening. But after considering it for a moment, he slowly nodded his approval. "I can do that—"

Dieter cut him off. "You've done quite enough," he said, closing that option. "I suspect your face is now as recognizable as my own, since it's well known that you travel by my side."

Martin frowned. "Please, Dieter. I'd like something to do, something to distract me from Ava . . ." His voice trailed off.

Hearing mention of Ava, Hedda perked up. "Ava Hahn?"

Martin jolted to attention.

"She's in the jailhouse," Hedda told him. "Before I was released, a big round man brought her in as a prisoner."

Dieter glanced at Martin, then turned back to Hedda. "Tell

Gebhard of my acquiescence. But also warn him I will do all I can to prevent a bloodbath in Bedburg. This town has seen too much of that already."

"Some things never change," Hedda replied.

She and Dieter exchanged a long stare and awkward silence. Finally, she gave him a curt nod and walked to the door. Before exiting she turned back to him.

"Try to stay alive," she said before shutting the door behind her.

Dieter sighed, then nodded to the closed door.

As Hedda's footsteps faded down the hall, Martin and Dieter quietly digested the new information.

Martin broke the silence. "Can we trust her?"

Dieter walked to the window and peered out between the curtains. "I see no reason why Ulrich would release her unless he thought her useless. Though I can't say for sure."

"Ulrich could have forced her to spy," Martin said.

Dieter turned from the window. "How did she find us? Unless you told her?"

"Absolutely not!"

Dieter considered that for a moment. "Then how else could she have found us unless she actually *had* gone to Bergheim and received word from Gebhard about my seeking out Claus." Raising his eyebrows at Martin, he added, "Remember, the Catholics here still don't know of Claus' sympathies for the Protestants, that he secretly provides them sanctuary."

Martin leaned back against the wall. "I suppose you're right," he said. "Then what do we do? I feel so trapped in this damned place."

Dieter stared at his son for a few moments, watching him examine a piece of cheese, then peek out at the two men through the holes of one of the slices. The thought of again leaving Peter suddenly overwhelmed him.

Then he got a strange look in his eyes, as if a major decision had been made.

Turning to Martin, he said, "You say you want to help?"

Martin nodded enthusiastically.

"Then I will have you deliver a message to Ulrich."

Martin was intrigued. "Saying?"

"Explaining the terms of my surrender."

Martin's mouth fell open.

"By the Blessed Virgin, what are you talking about?"

"They will kill Aellin and Ava, Martin," Dieter explained. "I can't have that on my conscience. Those two have been invaluable to our cause. Should they die, our entire operation could crumble—"

"It certainly will crumble if *you're* gone, Dieter. You're speaking nonsense! I never expected to hear you say you're willing to lay down and die—"

"I never said I was—"

"You're throwing your life away—practically putting Ulrich's noose around your neck for him! They'll never let you leave that jail." Martin shot Dieter a look of anger and sadness, the corners of his eyes welling with tears.

"I have a plan, Martin, but I must make sure Aellin and Ava are safe, first. When that is done, I want you to marry Ava. Be a good husband, as I wished I could have been. Have children. They are the most important thing you will ever achieve, our only true legacy."

A flood of memories suddenly washed over Dieter: he and Sybil in Ulrich's jailhouse. Georg Sieghart rescuing them. And how Dieter had promised Georg that he'd do the same thing with Sybil that he was now asking of Martin.

But Martin was still bewildered. As he watched Dieter get lost in his thoughts, he began inhaling and exhaling loudly, his fists clenching. When he saw Dieter calmly smile to himself, he couldn't take it any longer.

"You're talking like you're already dead!" Martin yelled.

Breaking his trance, Dieter gave Martin a kind smile. "I'm tired of this fighting, Martin."

The young man thrust a finger out. "You're being selfish, Dieter."

Dieter's eyebrows rose. "How do you mean?"

Martin walked behind Peter on the bed and silently pointed down at him, signaling his answer.

Understanding his point, Dieter said, "You and Ava will

oversee my child, if you would . . ."

"Of course! But . . ."

Finishing his sentence, Dieter added, ". . . for a time."

Martin still didn't understand. "Dieter, please! Minutes ago you were ruminating over not going outside for fear you'd orphan this fine young man here," he pleaded, nodding to Peter. "And now you suddenly want to surrender and face summary execution! Have you gone mad? What has changed in those few minutes?"

"Hedda's message," Dieter answered quickly, emphatically. "Now that I know Gebhard will be here in two days, the best chances my son has for a 'living' father is to surrender and wait, rather than keep hiding and face certain death by any guard on the street!"

Dieter walked over to Martin and placed his hand on his shoulder. "Plus, my surrender will ensure that Ava and Aellin will be free."

Martin closed his eyes tightly, trying to accept this new reality.

"So all I'm asking is for you to watch over my boy *for a time*," Dieter repeated. "I don't plan on dying. At least not in the foreseeable future. I will turn myself in so that the Catholics are relaxed. Then once Heinrich has me in custody—"

"He'll kill you."

Dieter shook his head. "No, not at first. He will use Ulrich on me. He needs information, about the rebellion. But more importantly, my surrender will end his need to continue his searches and seizures, his reign of terror. It's me he wants, Martin. And once he has that, he'll put down his guard." Dieter looked off somewhere unseen. "He'll have Ulrich work on me for what I know." Looking back at Martin, he added, "And surely I can outlast two days of that. And by then, Gebhard will be here."

Martin still looked bewildered.

"Don't you see?" Dieter continued. "As long as Heinrich is caught unawares, Gebhard will crush him! With both Heinrich and Ulrich focused on me, they will be blind to what's happening around them. I have every confidence that Gebhard will save me once he takes control of the city."

"That's your brilliant scheme?" Martin scoffed. "Relying on Gebhard? The man responsible for the Cologne War? Do you forget that he once was a Catholic elector? One of the most influential men in the realm? Then only converted for the love of a woman?" Martin shook his head in disbelief. "He's been an archbishop, a traitor, an outcast, and now a bishop again. And this is the man you place your trust in?"

Dieter sighed, then shrugged. "I can see no other way to serve both objectives: help Gebhard and free Ava and Aellin. Just please Martin, do this for me. It will benefit everyone."

Martin wagged his finger, then, exasperated, held his breath for as long as he could before finally exhaling loudly. "If you die because of this, Dieter . . . I'm going to haunt you in the afterlife."

Dieter smiled kindly. "You shouldn't be so attached to me, Martin. It's odd to hear things like that from you."

"You are one of my only friends—the only person who's been kind to me."

"Well, soon you will have one even closer. Elope, marry, have children. And leave here! Are we in agreement?"

Martin's shoulders slumped. He held back a sniffle and wiped his nose with the back of his arm. Finally, he nodded.

"I want to hear the words, Martin. Tell me what you're going to do."

Martin sighed, looking up to meet Dieter's eyes. He seemed strangely guilty—strangely off—about something. "I'm going to offer your terms of surrender: yourself for Ava and Aellin."

"And then?"

Blushing, Martin could no longer keep eye contact with Dieter's intensity. "And then I'm going to marry Ava and start a family with her."

Dieter nodded. "Away from here, Martin. Promise me you'll leave this dark shadow of the past behind."

Still without meeting Dieter's eyes, Martin bobbed his head slowly. "I promise Dieter. I promise I'll live the life you wished you could live."

Dieter smiled back.

Though he had no reason to.

His fate now rested in the hands of the two most dangerous men he'd ever known.

Ulrich the Punisher and Lord Heinrich Franz.

CHAPTER THIRTY-ONE

HUGO

Beauregard held up an elegant, blue silk dress he'd found somewhere in the maze of rooms within House Charmagne. Hugo's eyes lit up. The dress looked strangely familiar.

"That's the one," he said, emphatically. He took the garment from Beauregard and, holding it close, paraded down the red carpet toward the cellar as morning sunlight streamed in from the hallway windows. When he got to the stairs at the end of the hall, he was in such a rush to show her his find that he took two steps at a time all the way down.

Lucille was resting against the cellar wall, eyes closed, a single torch illuminating her grimy face. When she heard the door open and Hugo's steps down the stairs, her eyes popped open and she turned to look.

Hugo's hands were behind him, like a little kid hiding a surprise, but his dumb grin gave it away. Lucille couldn't help but smirk at the foolish, yet earnest, young man's expression.

With a flourish and bow, he exposed what he was hiding, presenting the dress to her.

"Oh, Hugo, it's perfect," she cried out, clasping her hands together. "Where did you find it?" she asked, taking his offered hand to rise to her feet.

She took the garment and gently ran her hand down its seams.

"My butler," Hugo replied. "I have no idea who it belonged to, but I think it will be perfect for you."

"Very much so," she said, offering a most charming smile. For a long moment, they gazed into each other's eyes, until the silence became awkward. Finally she glanced away, focusing somewhere toward the ground. "Shall I try it on?"

"Ah, y-yes, of course," he said, somewhat surprised she hadn't just waited for him to leave. He turned around to give her privacy, then heard the rustling of cloth and the unclasping of straps.

"You can turn around now."

He spun around and was instantly stupefied.

Lucille stood naked before him.

His face twitched, his eyes bulged, his body shuddered.

And of course he was speechless.

Standing there like a fool, he just took it all in.

Her shapely body, fair and pale. Her swelling breasts, full with dark nipples hardened in the chilled air. Her blonde hair tumbling past her delicate neck and shoulders. The thin mound of delicate fuzz declaring her womanhood.

Hugo had never seen such a perfect female specimen in his life.

Not knowing what to do with her hands, Lucille smiled modestly, then clasped them tentatively in front of her. Finally she looked away, only slightly embarrassed.

As Hugo continued mindlessly gazing, she began to walk toward him, slowly, stopping just inches away. She was slightly taller than he, so she gently took his chin and lifted it toward her. Then she leaned in and kissed him.

Hugo sucked in his breath as her warm, tantalizing tongue darted smoothly into his mouth. He was immediately aroused. The kiss soon became much more as she pushed herself forward into him. When his back touched the wall, she moved down his neck, then pulled open his shirt and continued down his chest and stomach. All Hugo could do was breathe deeply, frozen in place. He stared up at the ceiling as she knelt down, opened his pants and took him in her mouth. Clutching a handful of hair, he groaned loudly before losing all control.

It was over quickly. Softly, she dabbed at her lips, then looked up and smiled, motioning for him to lie down beside her. Using the torn and bloodied white wedding gown she'd taken off as a makeshift sheet, they lay together while Lucille stroked his chest. Within minutes she had him ready again, this time mounting him as he lay on his back. Leaning forward so her breasts made teasing, intermittent contact with his chest, she slowly began grinding into him, picking up rhythm while her sultry eyes remained fixed on his. His mind left his body as her animal wetness flowed over him like a wave of solid heat. Her pitch quickened, then grew feverish, and they both climaxed together in a rush of groans and whimpers and grunts.

When their heavy breathing began to slow, Lucille rolled off and cuddled against him, gently placing his head across her breasts as he drifted off to a beautiful place. The last thing he remembered was marveling over the wonderment of both losing his virginity and finding true love simultaneously.

Unfortunately, he woke up alone.

He was naked.

His mind a hazy recollection of lustful memories, fading quickly like a distant dream. He was still on the floor, the muddled white wedding dress beneath him only partially insulating him from the cold floor. His eyes scanned the room. The new blue dress was gone.

As was Lucille.

What started as a feeling of immense satisfaction quickly soured into confusion, then anger, then panic. He pushed off the ground and hastily pulled on his clothes while his eyes darted back and forth across the room. The torch still flickered on the wall by where they had made love.

But suddenly that love melted into humiliation.

How could I have been so stupid, thinking such an unbelievable woman would fall for someone like me? Someone half her age?

He hurried up the stairs. Running down the red-carpeted hallway, he called out for Beauregard.

The butler's head popped out of a sideroom, a baffled look on his face.

"Young master, what has happened? Your hair! Has there been an incident? Should I call for assistance?"

Hugo impulsively smoothed down his hair, brushed off his wrinkled shirt, then grabbed Beauregard by the shoulders. "Have you seen the Lady Lucille?"

The butler squinted at him. "No, sir. I haven't. You mean

she's not in the dungeon?"

Hugo groaned, shaking his head. He let go of Beauregard and bolted for the front door which was slightly ajar, throwing it open. The blazing sunlight instantly blinded him. Shielding his eyes, he called for Beauregard to fetch Felix. A few minutes later, the young driver brought the carriage to the front of the house.

Hugo hopped in and they sped off down the cobblestone road, past rows of trees and statues.

"Where to, my lord?" Felix asked.

Hugo yelled over the *clop-clop* of the horses' hooves. "Bedburg."

His eyes surveyed the countryside, searching as far and wide as he could through the carriage window. But Lucille was nowhere.

As they drove on, his anger started to subside and a different, more-positive thought began to form. Slowly, his mouth curved into a sinister smile.

Who cares if she escapes?

But then an image of Heinrich replaced that thought and his smile faded.

He will kill me!

He put his face in his palms, clenched his eyes shut, gritted his teeth, and violently launched himself backward into the leather seat.

There was nothing to be done. If he called a search party, his stupidity and humiliation would be known to all.

So he let his mind return to the less-negative perspective.

Maybe it's not the worst thing that she escaped . . . before Heinrich killed her anyway. After all she's already been through . . . the murder of her father . . . and her father-in-law . . .

He tried to slow down his thinking, relax, taking in long steady breaths.

She's lived through so much chaos and death. Perhaps this is for the best. As long as she doesn't come back, which I doubt she will. Perhaps someday I could even find her. She was truly magnificent, regardless of her motive. And under different circumstances, who knows . . .

The only thing he regretted was being manipulated. Then again, it had been a most wonderful experience, perhaps the highlight of his short life. There was no denying that.

What's done is done.

And suddenly, inexplicably, he had the crazy urge to speak to Ava again. This brief but spectacular experience he'd shared with Lucille had changed him. He was a man now, he'd finally experienced love. And facing Ava in this new light excited him.

He yelled to Felix, "Take me to the jailhouse!"

He would speak to Ava—though he had no idea what he'd say. Or he would speak to Ulrich, the man most symbolizing the exact *opposite* of love.

As he neared the jailhouse, he finalized what he would say to Ava. It would not be pretty. He decided she needed to know that he'd found someone else, that she needn't worry about him fawning over her any longer, and that she could rot in Hell for all he cared.

He realized that the words—admittedly untrue—sounded somewhat pathetic, but he needed a target for his current hodgepodge of emotions.

Felix dropped him off near the side of the jail at the stroke of noon. Rounding the corner on the way to the gate, Hugo felt a certain new zest in his step. It was amazing what a good woman's love could do to a man. When he looked up, he stopped in midstride. Directly in front of the jailhouse gate, on both sides of the street, a spectacle was playing out. He quickly moved into the shadows to watch.

A small group stood in front of the jail gate—Ulrich in front, and Ava and a popular barwench, Aellin Brandt, behind him. Two guards surrounded the women who clearly were being handled as prisoners. Aellin had her arm around Ava's shoulder.

Across the street a much larger group had gathered. Standing in front of a horde of farmers and townsfolk stood Dieter Nicolaus, who was calling out to Ulrich across the road from him.

"I told you I'd be here," Dieter was saying.

"And I knew you would," Ulrich responded. "That's

something I respect about you, Dieter Nicolaus—a man of your word."

"I don't need your admiration, torturer."

From behind Ulrich, Aellin shouted out. "Don't do this, Dieter!"

Ulrich spun around, ready to backhand the woman, but Ava stepped in between and Ulrich backed off. From that angle Hugo caught a glimpse of Ava's face, still caked in blotches of dried blood, a large bump below her left eye and a broad bruise covering her entire nose. Hugo felt sick to his stomach knowing those injuries had been at his impulsive hand.

"It's too late, my dear," Dieter called back to Aellin with a wistful smile. Spreading his arms wide, he yelled, "So, Ulrich, will you be good to your word, in front of all these people? You remember our deal, yes?"

Hugo couldn't imagine what kind of deal this could be. But whatever it was, Dieter was being smart. Making Ulrich announce the terms to everyone around. Clearly this was a deal Dieter wanted. Hugo could only assume it had to be something that, in the coming days, would be spread to every ear in the city.

"Yourself for Ava Hahn and Aellin Brandt," Ulrich recited, thrusting his thumb over his shoulder at the women. "In exchange for you, I send these bitches home."

Hugo was shocked. Why would Dieter be doing this? What was happening?

Dieter nodded approval to Ulrich.

"I am a man of my word," Ulrich announced.

"You may not be good, Ulrich," Dieter said, "but I believe you speak the truth when you say it."

From somewhere behind the large crowd of citizens, a voice yelled out, "Unfortunately, it's not up to him."

All eyes turned to see who had spoken. Then the crowd began to part, making room for the speaker to walk through.

Hugo gasped, as did the crowd, as Lord Heinrich Franz stepped forward, his hands on his hips, smiling broadly.

"Lord Heinrich," Ulrich muttered from across the street, clearly surprised at his lord's grand entrance.

"Actually," Heinrich beamed, "it's Count Heinrich, my dear

punisher."

Ulrich scratched the scar on his face, then motioned toward Dieter. "I've promised them a trade, Your Grace. A very favorable exchange. If you'll just come speak with me in private for a moment . . ."

Heinrich held up a gloved hand to silence Ulrich, then shook his head. "That won't be necessary, Ulrich." He clapped his hands together, once. Instantly, a flurry of action disrupted the street as guards poured in from all directions. Within seconds Dieter and the citizens were surrounded, while across the street more guards circled Ulrich and the two women.

Heinrich smiled menacingly at the jailer. "You were never given the authority to set any of these prisoners free, Ulrich." Addressing his guards, he ordered, "Arrest the treasonous priest here and throw those two whores back in their cells."

An outcry rose from the peasants, but there were too many guards, so everyone heeded Heinrich's orders. The guards grabbed Ava and Aellin by the arms. Writhing against her captors, Ava shouted to Ulrich, "You promised, you bastard!"

At the same time, guards took hold of Dieter, who offered no resistance, his shoulders sinking in defeat. As he was led across the street, his eyes found Hugo in the shadows and locked onto him for a moment before he was pushed forward toward the gate, disappearing into the dark recesses of the jailhouse.

Heinrich then turned and walked back the way he'd come, never noticing Hugo from a distance. The crowd dispersed, mumbling bits of displeasure but nothing more. Within minutes, only Ulrich was left alone in the street, shaking his head, while Hugo remained out of view along the side of the jailhouse.

Witnessing what he'd just seen had erased all of Hugo's earlier thoughts—his wondrous first sexual experience, his anger and humiliation over Lucille, what he'd planned to tell Ava. For an instant he considered just fetching Felix and the carriage and retreating to House Charmagne. But he knew Heinrich would return there as well. And the last thing he wanted right then was to face the man.

And then a strange thing occurred. Hugo was suddenly overwhelmed with sorrow and shame. Not for himself, but for those he'd just seen—for the two women unceremoniously dragged away; for Dieter who'd just tried to do the honorable thing by exchanging himself for the women; and for Ava, or rather his shame over his selfish plan to torment her over a sexual conquest that was really nothing more than a determined woman's justifiable manipulation of a weak, inexperienced idiot.

And he knew he had to apologize to Ava—for everything he'd done to her, for treating her so savagely after all she'd been through. So with both reluctance and resolve, he walked from the shadows toward the cold jailhouse.

He was halfway down the second hallway when he heard their conversation. Apparently the prisoners had been jailed in adjoining cells, or at least Ava and Dieter, because he immediately recognized their voices. He stepped quietly past a room with its door cracked open just an inch or so, then stopped when—far enough back so the prisoners couldn't see him—he could hear their voices more clearly.

"Please, Dieter," he heard Ava say. "I beg of you . . . don't be angry with him."

Dieter sighed. "I'm disappointed, Ava, but I've already forgiven him."

"You have?"

"Yes. If I'm being honest, in my heart . . . I already knew."

"He did it for me," Ava said desperately, her voice choking with tears. "He's a good man, Dieter. You know that."

"Yes, I do," Dieter replied, his own voice thick with sadness.

"It was never his intent to betray you."

"I know, Ava."

Hugo wasn't sure what they were talking about.

There was a moment of quiet, where the only sound was Ava's gentle sobs. Then Dieter said, "Tell me how it happened."

"Are you sure?"

"Please. I'd like to know."

Ava sniffled, then began. "When Martin and I were captured at the western entrance, he was given an ultimatum for my release. Oh, Dieter, but I do think he loves me."

"And you?"

"I do. I just wish I could tell him . . ."

Dieter cleared his throat. "Please continue."

"Somehow the punisher knew that Martin was working with you. He showed me the notes—now that I think on it, it must have been Karstan that stole that first note, the one with the Jacobos mentioned. Remember when he came seeking shelter in our home?"

"I already put that together, my dear," Dieter said. "That Karstan deceived us."

"Yes, well, that bastard gave the note to Ulrich. Who showed it to Martin, telling him that if he ever wanted to see me again alive, Martin had to forge new letters. His goal apparently was to send us on a fruitless hunt—"

"Which worked quite handily, fool that I am," Dieter muttered.

Ava coughed. "By giving the wrong name on the note, Ulrich hoped to drive you out of hiding and capture you in broad daylight. He knew your honor and dignity wouldn't allow you to let someone suffer a burning if you could possibly save him or her . . ."

"And I fell right into his trap . . ."

Ava sounded confused. "B-but, you weren't captured. What do you mean?"

"Martin and I were at the tavern when Aellin was captured. Ulrich never saw us."

"Oh, dear . . ." Ava said, trailing off. "S-so, you see, Martin was told that if he *didn't* aid Ulrich in capturing you, I would be tortured and killed. He had no choice, you see?"

"Yes, Ava, I understand now."

Then they were silent.

Hugo waited for more but nothing came. Just as he was about to step forward and announce himself, he heard another voice from the room he'd just passed, through the partially open door.

"We told you not to show your face in Bedburg again if you wanted to live, you stupid whore!" a gruff voice scolded.

Hugo recognized it. Karstan.

He inched closer to hear better.

"But instead of leaving town like a good girl," Karstan chided, "I find you wandering the streets by old man Claus' inn! I think it's time for a little lesson, woman."

Hugo winced at the sound of a loud slap, then a muffled cry, then garbled words and more whimpering.

"Hugo?"

He spun around. Peering through her bars down the hall, Ava was staring directly at him. He opened his mouth to speak, but no words came out. Locking eyes with her for a moment, wishing he could speak but unable to, he turned and hurried off. As he walked past the door where he'd heard Karstan and the woman, louder and more frantic scuffling and shrieks made him stop. He stepped back and inched open the door.

Then froze in shock.

Karstan was on top of a woman, a small figure, her feet kicking wildly, her arms and body writhing, crying out under Karstan's considerable weight. The big man was holding down the woman's wrists with one hand, while fumbling with his pants with the other.

The girl cried out, "Stop it! Get away from m—" as the hand Karstan was using to pull down his pants suddenly slammed across the woman's face.

Then everything went blank and Hugo saw red. Clenching his teeth so hard he felt they would crack, he instinctively reached around his waist to discover he had no weapon. Glancing back into the hallway, he rushed for the torch hanging from the wall, grabbed it, then raced into the room, kicking the door back with such force the knob embedded itself in the wall. As Karstan looked up and over his shoulder to see what was happening, he had a split-second to make eye contact with Hugo before Hugo shoved the torch, flame-first, into his face.

The big man shrieked in agony as the fire sizzled into a bright orange cloud across the entire front half of Karstan's head. The man's hands instinctively shot up to his face as his body jerked involuntarily in hopeless defense.

When Hugo pulled the torch away, Karstan's face was

unrecognizable. His screams quickly faded as his mouth disappeared into a scorching mound of blackened ooze. Ulrich rushed in just in time to see Hugo plunge the blazing torch back into the melted mass that was once Karstan's face again and again, until there was nothing left but a dripping blob of twisted, hissing black and pink flesh. Karstan's body sank to the floor, twitching in its last death throes.

Hugo, still holding the lit torch in front of him, spun around to Ulrich, who was frozen in place. Pieces of burnt skin smoldered in the flaming bristles of the torch, the stench of cooked fat and hair and flesh overpowering.

"I'm taking whoever this poor woman is and we're both leaving here, Ulrich," Hugo said.

Ulrich just glared at him, not moving.

"If you've ever cared a stitch about me, Ulrich, you'll let us pass."

Ulrich's hand was at the hilt of his sword, his brow furrowed, his facial scar pulsing. He locked eyes with Hugo for what seemed like forever. Then, abruptly, the tension lifted as Ulrich spread his arms wide, giving Hugo a bemused look before stepping back.

Hugo took the woman by the hand. Her spectacles were bent across her face. She smoothed her dress back down over the lower half of her body, then stood up.

Turning toward her, Hugo said slowly, "I recognize you . . . you're . . ."

"Hedda," the girl said uneasily. She tried to straighten her glasses, then quietly said, "Thank you for rescuing me," and walked out with Hugo hand-in-hand.

"You're welcome," he whispered, passing by Ulrich, who gave the boy a wry smirk.

CHAPTER THIRTY-TWO

SYBIL

With help from Georg's new connections, Daxton managed to maneuver the *Lion's Pride* past the heavily guarded waters of Amsterdam's harbor, keeping to the southern coast beyond The Hague, then around the Hook of Holland. From there, they traveled deep into the European mainland, through the northern channel of the Waal River, and south down the Rhine.

After nearly two weeks of negotiating dangerous waters and paying off shifty-eyed patrolmen and bridge-watchers, the *Pride* had gone as far as it could, docking in Düsseldorf, the capital of North Rhine-Westphalia, just thirty miles north of Cologne.

Georg paid a handsome fee to hide the *Pride* among the less-desirable ships in the harbor, so that it wouldn't be recognized or vandalized. Without its notorious red lion flag flying, it was just another anonymous ship in a harbor of hundreds.

Once docked, Daxton rented a horse then headed back west toward the Netherlands to find his family. He gave the women of the group hugs, firm handshakes for the men, and set off into the sunset on a Thursday. The plan was for Sybil and her companions to travel on to Bedburg, rescue Dieter, then escape the city. They'd all rendezvous back in Düsseldorf within the week, board the *Lion's Pride,* and sail back the way they'd come, to freedom and Norfolk and the peace and quiet of Strangers Shire.

By Saturday evening, Sybil and the rest of her company were closing in on Bedburg. They'd hiked south along the Rhine, staying parallel with the river as it twisted down the countryside, then cut west several miles before Cologne.

As they traveled through the night, feet aching and minds

foggy, Sybil began noticing a brown cloud in the distance, growing larger, with hundreds of orange and yellow dots twinkling within it, like stars in the sky. Squinting into the darkness southeast of their position, she realized the dots were moving in a westerly direction from Cologne.

"Looks like an army," Georg said, coming up beside her, pointing. "That haziness and spots of light are the dirt of disciplined marchers carrying torches."

Rowaine came up beside them and nodded, then bent forward, resting her hands on her knees. Though she'd had time in Norfolk to strengthen her legs, she still wasn't prepared for such a harrowing trek through the German countryside. But her stubbornness had kept her from complaining despite being the one most in need of rest along the way.

Lifting her head, she said, "They're headed west, toward Bedburg."

"Same direction we're headed, my friends," Corvin said, bringing up the rear of the group, along with Wilhelm, Mary, and Salvatore.

"If we could sneak into the astral plane," Salvatore muttered, nodding to himself, "we could surely outrun them."

Georg looked out, shielding a hand over one eye and swiveling his head from the nearby hill back toward Bedburg on the horizon, mentally calculating the distance. "No need for your mythical nonsense, warlock. We'll get there before they do. But we should make haste."

Salvatore snorted. "I'll still travel to the army in my dreams when we rest tonight. Perhaps I can slow them down."

Rowaine glanced out of the corner of her eye at the strange man with the blue tattoos. "Magic or not," she said, "they'll be at Bedburg's doorstep by mid-afternoon tomorrow."

"Or sooner," Georg added.

"Then let's not tarry," Sybil said, heading down the hill.

Everyone followed.

They walked in silence for hours, up and down hills and around overgrown bends in the road. Eventually, Sybil could smell birch trees and the familiar stench of tanning leather in the air.

"We're getting close," she told her entourage.

"What do you suppose they're doing, Beele?" Wilhelm asked, referring to the army moving westward, a question clearly on everyone's mind. Because three of their group—Wilhelm, his mother, and Sybil—had once called Bedburg home, seeing an army moving in that direction carried special significance to them.

"God only knows," Sybil said, shaking her head. "I've been gone from Bedburg for too long—I can't even imagine the tribulations the city has gone through since my escape from there."

"With Heinrich Franz as lord," said Mary, "anything's possible."

Several in the group grumbled in agreement.

"If the army is coming from Cologne," Georg noted, "there are only two possibilities. Either Archbishop Ernst is attacking Bedburg, or defending it."

"Or," Rowaine offered, "the army could just be passing by Bedburg, not heading there at all."

Sybil snickered. "You don't know Heinrich Franz as I do, Row." She shook her head. "No . . . that army is clearly bound for Bedburg."

Sybil's gloomy prediction quieted the group for a while.

When they finally reached the far outskirts of Bedburg proper, they passed the northern tip of Peringsmaar Lake, just east of the city, before the farmlands finally gave way to forest. Walking along the edge of the woods, they kept inside the treeline to avoid detection by any scouting parties.

Passing a short length of river, Wilhelm said, "This is where Dieter sent me and mother off," pointing down the waterway.

Sybil perked up, interested in any detail about her husband.

Mary nodded. "He'd somehow gotten a boat, hidden under some canopies. Almost like he'd prophesied our arrival and escape . . ."

"I have no doubt he did," Salvatore said confidently. "That man had a bright, dazzling aura about him. Much untapped energies in the spiritual arts—even if he doesn't realize it."

Sybil was about to retort but felt Rowaine's hand on her

shoulder. Rowaine gently shook her head and Sybil sighed. Let the druid live his dreams. Arguing with insanity was itself insane.

It was deep into the night when they reached the end of the woods. Through a circle of gnarled tree branches, the party surveyed the city wall beyond, watching for movement.

"It looks inviting," Georg commented. "Strangely calm. . ."

"Though I doubt it will stay that way once word comes of the approaching army," Sybil whispered.

Corvin smirked. "Shall we warn them?"

After some nervous chuckles, they pushed out into the open countryside toward Bedburg. As they approached, the city walls loomed higher and higher. The iron gate was open, two guards manning the archway, spears ready, checking entering and exiting merchants and farmers as they passed through. Sybil hoped and prayed that their group, dirty and tattered from their long trek, looked like any other group of fieldworkers coming in for the night.

And sure enough, the guards barely took notice before allowing them through without incident. Considering all but Corvin were known fugitives, Sybil was slightly shocked, but pleasantly surprised, at how easy it was to enter. But to the lazy, overworked guards, they were just another set of everyday commoners. Little did they know, Sybil mused to herself, that the seven of them were exactly who the guards were supposed to be guarding *against*—Protestant sympathizers, Heinrich's former companions-turned-enemies, the former captain of the *Lion's Pride,* and the "Daughter of the Beast."

The group walked down the street together as a unit—their faces masked in grim determination, their nervousness gone. During their entire two-week journey, they'd carefully planned this arrival, everyone well aware of his or her part in their upcoming play.

As they proceeded down the road, taking up the whole width of the street, peasants parted to give them room to pass, while town guards gave them no more than scant glances. A few whispers could be heard as passing citizens talked in hushed tones, possibly recognizing one or more of them, especially the three former local residents.

But no one blocked their passage.

When they arrived at the tavern, they stopped. The familiar raucous sounds of drunken behavior filtered out the pub windows and could be heard long before they got there.

Georg produced a long dagger from his waistband. Rowaine clicked back the hammers of her hidden pistols. Wilhelm took off his backpack and, kneeling near the tavern door, began rummaging for his equipment, Mary beside him. Salvatore's yellow eyes opened wide as he clenched his fists and took on the look of a blue-tattooed, rabid animal. Corvin stood inches away, cracking his knuckles then shaking them at his sides. Sybil took a position near the back, waiting.

They all looked to Sybil for their signal.

She nodded once.

Georg shoved the door open and was the first to enter, followed by Rowaine. Not a single eye from the drunken patrons moved to the door. Then Salvatore walked in and his strange appearance did garner a few peeks. But it wasn't until Corvin stormed in, jumped onto the closest tabletop, and kicked over a mug of ale, that the group got the packed crowd's immediate attention.

Cristoff, tending bar, cut off his conversation. "Hey!" he shouted, "you're going to pay for that!" pointing to the shards of mug scattered about. "And get off the table, man! Have you no manners?"

The invading group ignored him.

Georg and Rowaine surrounded the table Corvin stood on, dagger and pistols in hand, though not yet pointed at anyone.

"Citizens of Bedburg!" Corvin bellowed, throwing his arms up in triumph. "I come to you as a citizen of the world! A nomadic traveler from many miles away. I come to you as a man, much as yourselves"—his hands sweeping across the room—"as a man . . . who has been wronged."

A few heads tilted. Everyone, despite their inebriation, was listening.

Who was this man? How had he been wronged? Why was he standing on the table?

After a momentary pause, Corvin continued.

"Whether you know it or not, each and every one of you in this room has been wronged. Damaged. Beaten. And only one person is responsible for causing so much grief, a single entity who has harmed all of Bedburg so dastardly."

Several patrons began losing interest, grumbling and shooing away the blowhard. Unfazed, Corvin got to his moment of truth.

"I speak, of course, of the evil, cruel, *bastard* . . . Heinrich Franz."

That stopped everyone, the actual mention of the man's name. Some literally sucked in their breath. Probably not in years had anyone had the nerve, the courage, the foolhardiness, to publicly denounce the former chief investigator of Bedburg who was now lord and count of the entire region.

Either this man was very reckless, very heroic, or had a death-wish. But either way, Corvin had everyone's undivided attention.

"There isn't a single one of us who has not been affected by Heinrich Franz's carnage. As chief investigator of the city, he rounded up countless innocents and burned them at the stake. There was nothing we could do then. And was he punished?"

"No . . ." someone muttered.

"*No!*" Corvin emphasized. "He was rewarded!" He threw up his hands, his brows forming a straight, angry line. "And as lord of the city, his crimes have only multiplied. Yet he works under the guise of absolute authority. Any person he sees as a threat to that power, he kills"—running his finger across his throat—"not because he has any God-given authority, but because he is... *fearful!*"

He waited before speaking his next line, eyeing as many in the crowd individually as he could. Then he spoke it loudly and clearly.

"I stand before you today to tell you that Heinrich Franz is a coward!"

"Yes!" a man dared to yell. A few others nodded with him.

"He has killed our friends; he has chased our brothers out of the city; he has raped our sisters. He believes he controls Bedburg. But . . . could Bedburg run without *us?*"

Now the crowd was engaged, heads shaking, grumbles

growing louder. Corvin bent his knees slightly, taking on a battle-ready pose.

"Even now, he has an army of reprobates descending upon us, upon this city!"

Corvin didn't know if that was true but it was good theatrics. Several in the crowd gasped at the news of the supposed incoming invasion.

"You see, my friends, Heinrich Franz believes we will bend to his will . . . he believes his power is absolute and infallible. He thinks he is untouchable. He did so when he butchered Peter Stubbe—do you remember him?"

A few nodded slowly, unsure where the speech was going. One man got up to leave, apparently bored, but was quickly seated by Rowaine's pistol.

"Yes, Peter Stubbe. An innocent farmer and stalwart citizen of Bedburg—murdered for his beliefs. Wrongly labeled the Werewolf of Bedburg, it was proved that Heinrich conspired with the bishop and that Peter Stubbe was in fact *innocent.* But did the murders stop?"

"No!" a man yelled, shaking his fist. "They got worse!"

Others joined in, nodding and growling.

"Indeed, my friend! *It. Got. Worse!* And that is because Heinrich Franz is a tyrant, a despot hellbent on the destruction of morality and honor. He kills because he fears what people will do to him, what people *think* of him! And the killings go on, the days get worse, and Bedburg sinks into Hell."

"But he's our lord!" a man cried out. "What could we possibly do? You just said it. He has the *army!*"

Corvin offered a thin smile. "I'm glad you asked, my friend. Because that is the true reason I have come here today."

"Who are you?" someone asked. "I've never seen you in my life."

Corvin tightened his hands into fists. "I am just a man who has been pushed to the brink of my conscience. I am a man who is tired of Heinrich Franz's deplorable deeds. I am just like every one of you." He pointed to a few faces. "And I'm here with friends—people you may recognize, who have been persecuted without mercy by that devil."

Standing back to his full height, Corvin punched a fist into his open palm. "You see, my friends, Heinrich Franz believes he is above the Almighty. He thinks he can do any evil he wishes. But Heinrich Franz is not above the laws of *God!*"

Behind the bar, Cristoff crossed himself. "Amen," he said in a low voice.

"And I have come with someone to rally us to God's cause. Imagine, if you will, a Bedburg that does not answer to a tyrant. Imagine an army that arrives here and finds it has no lord to serve. What would happen? I'll tell you. That army will crumble. For even if Heinrich has many men at his disposal to carry out his foul deeds, the citizens of Bedburg are legion! *We* hold the ultimate authority—God's authority—because the city cannot exist without us." He looked from face to face. "But it *can* and *must* exist without Heinrich Franz."

People were excited now, leaning forward in their seats, standing, talking to one another with an energy absent just minutes before.

As if an afterthought, Corvin added: "And we *will* exist without Heinrich Franz. I promise you that."

One man pounded his fist on the table and snarled. Another punched his mug of ale into the air, yelling obscenities. The mob was loud and angry. But Corvin wasn't nearly finished.

Raising his hands in the air, he said, "The alleged Werewolf of Bedburg—an innocent man named Peter Stubbe—his soul lives on through his offspring. And I don't mean his son, who you all know as Hugo Griswold . . . I mean through his *daughter.*"

A collective gasp could be heard as hands covered mouths.

"Yes, the Daughter of the Beast has returned to Bedburg!" Corvin screamed. "To seek vengeance for her father's wrongful death! She has returned to serve as the spirit for your loved ones, for the sons you have lost to Heinrich's battles, for the daughters you have lost at the stakes! Heinrich Franz believes he is above God, but we the citizens will show him otherwise!"

The tavern door shot open. Two guards ran in, spears at the ready. One shouted, "What the devil is going on here?" as Rowaine stepped forward with two pistols aimed at both guards. Georg moved next to her, his dagger out and ready. The crowd collectively held its breath while the four faced off, ready to attack each other.

But Corvin would not be silenced. Reaching a crescendo, he yelled at the top of his lungs, "Citizens of Bedburg, I give you the Daughter of the Beast!"

He spun around and threw his hands out toward the door, adding, "She has returned to us as the Pale Diviner—God's holy crusader against tyranny. Our Angel of Resistance!"

A figure stepped through the doorway.

The crowd stared in stunned silence, stopped cold by the sight.

Before them stood a divine creature clearly from another world. A woman in a sleeveless garment, her arms outstretched and ablaze in brilliant orange flames.

A Norse Goddess from a mythological kingdom.

Without a word, people cleared the way as she slowly raised both flaming arms above her.

"God have mercy!" a man cried, crossing himself.

"Preserve us, oh Lord!" said another, joining his hands together in prayer.

"She's aflame in the Holy Fire!" someone screamed.

Both guards dropped their spears and dashed out of the tavern.

Showing no pain or expression, Sybil gazed around the room, her pale eyes and intense frown captivating the spectators.

Her appearance having had its intended affect, with a fluid, well-rehearsed flick of both wrists, the flames were instantly extinguished. Another collective gasp spread through the crowd as she slowly lowered her arms to her sides.

Her skin appeared unscathed, the only remnant of the spectacle were a few lingering puffs of smoke floating near the ceiling.

After several long moments of shocked silence, almost as if the crowd was catching its breath, the entire tavern spontaneously burst into cheers. One man fainted. Several others knelt before her like a heavenly deity.

"We will march on Castle Bedburg," Sybil proclaimed solemnly. "We will find Heinrich Franz, and we will put him through the same gauntlet he has put so many of us through. And you will all join me!"

Once another round of cheers ended, a man said, "B-but, my holy lady, Lord Franz doesn't stay at Castle Bedburg. He stays at his estate in the countryside."

Sybil tried not to act surprised, though she was. With her best mask of spiritual fury firmly etched on her face, she started to respond but before she could, Cristoff shouted from behind the bar: "And what about your husband, my lady? He has been a savior to so many of us."

The comment broke through Sybil's mask. Confused, she questioned, "My husband? But . . . he's alive?"

"Yes, my lady, he's alive! Thrown in jail just this afternoon. By Heinrich!"

"With Aellin!" added another. "Poor Aellin!"

Suddenly Mary, who'd been standing outside, popped into the room. "What about my husband? Master stonemason William?" she asked hopefully.

Cristoff frowned. "Dead, I'm afraid, Frau Edmond. Another atrocity of our lord. Hanged two weeks ago."

Unable to control her anger, Sybil snarled to the crowd. "Gather your comrades, my friends. Tonight we free those who have been lost to us, their bodies and their souls. And we march upon Heinrich's country estate to demand justice for all his evil!"

With that, she turned and stormed out of the tavern, the entire crowd following in her wake. As she exited, she glanced to her side. Wilhelm was kneeling quietly by his backpack, repacking his alcohol mixture, his face streaked with tears at the news he'd just heard through the tavern door. A bittersweet moment for the young man—thrilled knowing his "magical" fire potion had successfully motivated the crowd, yet devastated to learn of his father's execution.

The mob, more than thirty of them, marched down the dark city streets behind Sybil and her group, gathering more followers as they moved on. By the time they reached the jailhouse they were at least a hundred strong, angry and determined.

Near the jailhouse gate a man was leaning against the side of a carriage.

Ulrich.

At the sight of the approaching mob, he backed away and slapped the side of the coach to send it off. As he turned toward the crowd, two guards rushed to his side. Then, as the crowd grew, the guards saw the Pale Diviner leading the way. By now, everyone had heard of Sybil's awesome powers and no man was worth facing God's wrath over—not Ulrich, not even Heinrich Franz. Quickly, the guards scattered, leaving Ulrich by himself.

But Ulrich feared no one, not even God. Especially not a foolish girl with nothing more than simple parlor tricks at her disposal.

The torturer stood stoically in front of the gate, barring entrance. Unsheathing his heavy sword, he stared menacingly at Sybil, who returned the look.

The crowd quieted.

Georg Sieghart came forward and raised his hand to stop the crowd from further action. He had no desire for a bloodbath.

Georg looked at Ulrich. "Remember me?"

Nodding, the jailer's devilish grin grew wider. "The same man who freed this witch and her husband the first time. I'll never forget the bruise you gave me. Nor the lashing for allowing those two to escape."

Georg pulled his long dagger from his belt. It was about half the length of Ulrich's sword. He spread his arms wide, shifted into an attack position, then took another step forward.

Ulrich snarled and Georg charged.

The horrific clashing of steel echoed as their weapons met—Ulrich slashing down, Georg bringing his weapon up to block it.

As their battle got underway, Ulrich's strength pushed Georg back with each blow of his sword. But Georg was faster—surprisingly swift for a man his size. Deftly, he weaved his long dagger in and out of Ulrich's defenses in quick succession, nearly catching the torturer off-guard several times. Finally, Ulrich recoiled and swung his blade horizontally, trying to take off Georg's head. Georg ducked low and stabbed Ulrich in the leg, a shallow thrust that barely drew blood.

Ulrich growled loudly and shot out his bare fist, catching Georg under the chin, snapping his neck back and sending him reeling backward.

"Father!" Rowaine cried, stepping forward and unholstering her guns. But the two combatants were moving too fast. A shot at Ulrich could easily kill Georg instead.

Ulrich clutched the hilt of his blade with both hands and lunged forward, thrusting the steel toward Georg's heart. Still stunned from the blow to his chin, Georg managed to focus just in time to bob away from Ulrich's thrust, then Ulrich tried to backhand him with the sword, but again missed.

As both men regained their balance, Georg flanked the torturer and stabbed quickly, the tip of his dagger nicking Ulrich's hip bone, painful but not debilitating. Ulrich cried out, then, teeth clenched, stepped forward into Georg's guard, grabbing the back of the man's neck and bringing his sword up, underhanded, for a gut kill.

But Georg was quicker. He jabbed his dagger down, its point cleanly piercing through Ulrich's wrist and coming out the other side. As the dagger blade remained firmly embedded in Ulrich's wrist, the jailer's grip weakened around his sword, causing it to barely puncture Georg's belly.

Ulrich tried vainly to force the sword deeper into Georg's stomach but Georg just grimaced and wrestled it away, stepping back with Ulrich's blade. Ulrich, now weaponless, lurched his body forward, trying to catch Georg off balance but Georg, blood seeping from his stomach, swept Ulrich's sword in a quick overhand motion, the tip tearing across Ulrich's throat as the torturer stepped forward, his momentum adding to the strike.

Blood and cartilage poured out of Ulrich's neck as his eyes bulged and his color faded. He fell forward with a heavy thud, Georg's dagger still protruding from his wrist, and didn't move.

Georg grunted, then dropped the sword and clutched at his bleeding stomach, going down on one knee as Rowaine rushed to his side. No one came to Ulrich's aid.

Sybil ran for the gate. Pushing open the jailhouse door, she sped down the stairs, calling out for her husband, "Dieter? Dieter!"

No one responded.

She dashed through the first hall, then barreled down the

second. As she passed different jail cells along the way, a small form came forward, clutching the bars of one of the end cells.

"Is that . . . Sybil Griswold?" the shadow asked.

Sybil jumped back in alarm. "Who's there?"

A small white smile gleamed through the shadows. Though the man looked half dead, Sybil recognized his bearded face.

"Rolf Anders," the man began to explain, then with a wistful grin, added, "Former regent of Heinrich's countryside estate." Seeing Sybil's serious expression, he stopped his introduction.

"Where's my husband?" Sybil asked, skipping pleasantries.

"Sybil?" another voice called from the next cell. Sybil stepped back to see Ava Hahn standing by her bars.

"Oh my," yet another woman yelled. "I hope you brought that damn fiery mermaid with you!" Sybil recognized the voice as Aellin's, the wench from the tavern who had helped her find Odela many months earlier.

"My, my," Rolf chuckled. "Quite the reunion."

Sybil turned back to him. "Please, where's my husband, old man?"

His smile vanished. "Heinrich Franz left with him less than ten minutes ago. In his carriage. I heard them leave."

Sybil cursed under her breath. "Where?"

"To House Charmagne, of course." Rolf seemed to shrink from Sybil's gaze. "I must warn you, my lady . . . I believe your husband is in dire peril."

Sybil sighed. She heard footsteps coming down the steps from the lobby. Corvin appeared with keys in his hand, presumably taken from Ulrich.

Once Sybil and Corvin had freed Rolf, Ava, and Aellin, they all hurried for the stairs, then out the jailhouse door into the night.

When they reached the gate, they stopped abruptly.

Tomas Reiner and nearly fifty soldiers stood between them and the large mass of tavern patrons and townsfolk, blocking their path. Though the mob of citizens was at least twice the size of Reiner's group, the soldiers had much deadlier weapons, so the crowd kept their distance.

"I cannot let you pass, I'm afraid," Tomas declared to

everyone. Addressing Sybil's group trying to leave the jail, he said, "Not you," then turning to the mob in the street, "nor the rest of you."

"Shit," Sybil muttered. She whispered to Corvin, "Do you have anything to say?"

Corvin cleared his throat, the color in his face draining. Carefully eyeing the swords and rifles of Tomas' men, he slowly stepped forward. "I s-suppose I can think of something . . ." he whispered, trailing off as he reached the front of the group.

Loud, running footsteps interrupted the moment. A town guardsman, out of breath, ran up to Tomas. "C-Commander, we have trouble!" the man cried, thrusting a thumb behind him.

Tomas shot a dangerous look at the man.

"An army's reached our southern gate," the messenger told him. "I don't know how they got there without warning, but they're there, my lord. Sure as day."

The soldiers in Tomas' ranks began mumbling to one another, relaxing their poised weapons. Suddenly there were more important things to worry about than the peasants in the street or these escaping prisoners.

Salvatore came up beside Sybil. "It can't be the army from Cologne . . . they shouldn't be here for hours. I saw their masses in the spiritworld, they can't be here before daybreak, at the least."

Sybil rolled her eyes. As much as she liked Salvatore, she wasn't going to rely on his "spiritworld" at the moment.

"Dammit," Tomas spat. To the messenger, he asked, "Can you tell where they come from?"

The soldier shrugged. "Perhaps from Bergheim, my lord."

Tomas frowned, then looked long and hard at Sybil. Though she may have imagined it, she thought she saw Tomas give her an almost imperceptible nod, before turning to his soldiers.

"Let's go, men. Rouse the garrison! We have enemies at our back door!"

And with that, they were gone.

CHAPTER THIRTY-THREE

HEINRICH

"How long have you been working with Tomas, priest?"

Dieter, sitting across from Heinrich in the carriage, didn't answer—his face a mask of absolute blankness, no expression, complete indifference, as if he hadn't heard the question.

Each stared at the other, both of them gently swaying from side to side as the coach bounced along the country roads outside Bedburg. After a long silence, filled in only by the clopping of hooves along the uneven road and Felix's occasional shouts to the horses, Heinrich finally looked away. He had no idea what was going through the priest's mind.

He sighed and tried again. "I know that Tomas Reiner, my own garrison commander, is 'Mord'—the writer of the notes your resistance group has been receiving."

At that, Dieter flinched slightly, a twitch at the corner of his eye, but enough of a tell to make Heinrich notice.

So he doesn't know who it is . . .

But even if Dieter didn't know who had authored the notes, he could still be of value. He was, after all, a recognizable figure in his own right. Some in town even considered him a saint of sorts. A rescuer of the laymen. A Robin Hood figure.

Of course Heinrich didn't buy any of that. To him, Dieter was just a man thrust into a dangerous situation doing the best he could.

If it were up to him, knowing what he knows now and where it has gotten him, I doubt he would have agreed to become this champion of the weak.

"When did you first receive Tomas' messages?" Heinrich asked.

This time Dieter answered. "Months ago," he said in a low voice. "I don't remember the exact date."

Not much, but it was something. Heinrich tried to keep him talking. "I also know that the army at Bedburg's doorstep belongs to Gebhard von Truchsess," he told Dieter. "Don't bother denying it."

"I don't."

"You won't escape from this," Heinrich said.

Dieter gazed into Heinrich's eyes. "What do you want with me, Heinrich?"

"Information. I found out from Hedda's ledger that Gebhard has an army and had been conspiring with Baron Ludwig before his . . . untimely death." Jarred by a particularly brutal bump, Heinrich shifted in his seat. "And that is where you come in. I associate with Archbishop Ernst, you see—"

"Yes. It is well known that you are the archbishop's lackey."

Heinrich smirked. He was getting under Dieter's skin. That usually brought results. He continued. "Ernst and Gebhard are dire enemies, have been since the Cologne War broke out. But I'm sure you're aware of that, too."

Dieter said nothing.

"With Gebhard being a Calvinist leader, and yourself being such a prominent Protestant in Bedburg, I find it hard to believe you weren't working together. You seek the same ends, after all."

"I seek to save people from your viciousness and tyranny. That is all. Gebhard seeks a throne of lies."

"So you claim that you're not allies?"

"I sought his help once. He refused me."

"A shame."

"I thought the same."

Heinrich rested one leg over the other, trying to act relaxed, though his mind was awash with many thoughts.

If that's true, then my plan could be foiled before it even begins . . .

No, I doubt this priest would admit to his treason just from my asking.

"I don't believe you, that you're not working together," Heinrich challenged.

But by now, Dieter had guessed Heinrich's plan. "If you propose to hold me as bait over the former archbishop," Dieter said, tilting his head to the side, "I'm afraid you're going to be sorely disappointed."

"So it wasn't your idea to confine yourself to my prison in hopes that Gebhard would rescue you once he took Bedburg?"

"Gebhard wants Bedburg so that he can control more territory around Cologne. That's always been his goal, as you well know. So, yes, it crossed my mind that if he entered Bedburg, the Protestants you jailed might be freed. But me, personally? I'm not that important to him."

"I doubt you would abandon your son for such a slim hope at freedom, priest."

Dieter scowled. "Don't speak of my son, you devil."

Heinrich smiled. "I think you were given more of a guarantee than you admit. That if Bedburg fell to his army, you'd be freed."

Dieter shrugged. "Think what you want. I'm telling you, he won't go out of his way for me."

"If you mean he won't travel all the way out to House Charmagne to free you, then, yes, I agree. He has more important things to focus on."

"Indeed."

"Well, I grant you that it was a courageous wager on your part—risking your freedom and life for the lives of your friends. I admire you for that. But it won't succeed." Heinrich's gray eyes darkened. "You may have friends in Bedburg—even in the lowest depths of the dungeons and jails. But where we're going now, you have no allies."

Dieter shrugged again, his mask of indifference on again.

And it riled Heinrich. His plan was to scare Dieter into talking, like he'd done to so many others. But this man was a hard nut to crack. Fearless. Impossible to decipher. Someone who could easily be hiding more tricks up his sleeve.

"If you think I'm defenseless against Gebhard's siege," Heinrich said, "you are mistaken."

The carriage began to slow. Dieter leaned toward the coach window and peeled back the curtain, telling Heinrich, "So you plan to fight Gebhard? I am surprised. Here I thought you'd just hand him your seat."

The sarcasm irritated Heinrich. The man could get under *his* skin as well. "Archbishop Ernst awarded me an army to fight Gebhard on his behalf," Heinrich said.

"Congratulations," Dieter answered, turning away from the window.

Heinrich touched his mustache and thought.

Who will lead my army if not Tomas Reiner? Since I'm certain he is my betrayer, I must see to his end promptly. But who will that leave in command of his garrison? Perhaps I should send messages to Ernst and his allies. Perhaps Ulrich is worthy for the job.

Both of them pitched forward when the carriage came to an abrupt stop. They'd reached Heinrich's mansion. Felix opened the coach door for his master and offered his hand. Heinrich waved it off, then stepped out on his own. He stretched deeply and took in the night. It was dark and chilly, only a few stars showing.

Dieter followed him through the large front door, the warmth from the interior torchlights instantly soothing his chilled bones. Heinrich rubbed his gloved hands together as he led Dieter down the foyer.

"Where do you want me?" Dieter asked him from behind.

"By my side, priest," Heinrich replied without turning around. "I won't have you leaving my sight."

Dieter must have figured he'd be locked away, so he wasn't quite sure what to make of this development. But he knew enough about the man to be suspicious, not grateful. When they entered the dining area, Beauregard was preparing the table with plates and silverware.

Heinrich snapped his fingers. "Beauregard!"

The butler stopped, standing ramrod straight.

"Go check on Lady Lucille for me," Heinrich instructed. "I haven't heard from her in some time. I'd like to sup with her and my Godly friend here. Perhaps we can come to some mutual agreements."

"You keep the lady of Bergheim your prisoner?" Dieter asked.

Heinrich frowned. "*Prisoner* is a harsh word. She's my … permanent guest," he smiled, "who happens to be staying in the dungeons. She *is* my wife, after all, and has little waiting for her back in Bergheim anyway. In truth, the only reason she remains lady of Bergheim, as you put it, is because I'm the baron there."

He turned, noticing that Beauregard hadn't moved. The butler's stiffness was normal, but his darting eyes weren't.

"What are you doing, Beauregard? Did I not give you an order?"

The butler gulped. "Er, I apologize, my lord, b-but . . ."

"Out with it, man."

"Lady Engel has escaped, my lord."

Heinrich sucked in a breath, then stepped back. "Impossible! There is no exit from the cellars. And the door was under lock. Do you mean to tell me *you*—"

"No, my lord!" Beauregard quickly shook his head. "It was not my doing. It was the young master—"

"*Hugo?*"

Beauregard nodded. "He went to fetch clean clothes for her, and she somehow fled."

Without warning, Heinrich began to laugh. Shaking his head, he chuckled, "That young fool!"

Except that meant that now Heinrich would have to find the damnable woman. She certainly was proving to be much higher maintenance than he'd bargained for. Yet still, he couldn't help laughing at the absurdity of it all. She was as beautiful as Hugo was young and naïve. He'd noticed Hugo's smitten expression whenever he was around her. So he wasn't that surprised to learn of the boy's susceptibility at the hands of a manipulative, wily woman.

Did I not do the same thing with a woman nearly twice my age when I was younger?

Which made him think of Odela, causing him a sharp pang of heartache that he quickly suppressed. Waving off Beauregard, he said, "It's no matter. Continue setting the table. I will dine with Dieter alone—"

A noise from above cut off his words. Feet creaking on floorboards upstairs. Skewing his brow, Heinrich turned to the butler. "Who else is in the house?"

The butler shifted his feet uncomfortably. "Er, no one else, my lord, to my knowledge."

Heinrich glanced at Dieter before turning back to Beauregard and squinting. Then, without a word, he stormed out of the dining room, motioning for Dieter to follow. When they reached the stairs, Heinrich began climbing them lightly, making sure not to sound any squeaky floorboards. At the top of the steps he heard the same sound again, this time closer, behind the first closed door. He reached for his knife and crept down the hall, whispering back to Dieter, "Stay here. And don't let me lose sight of you, or I'll take off your ear."

He walked quietly to the closed door, putting his ear against it. He heard a soft conversation.

". . . that one might be too late . . ." a female voice said. Though definitely not Lady Lucille, it did sound familiar—the nuance and tone—but he couldn't quite place it.

". . . I must try . . ." a male voice replied. *That* one he definitely recognized. He shoved open the door, startling the two inside. The woman was sitting on the edge of the bed and let out a *yip* before putting her hand to her mouth. Hugo, leaning over the small desk in the room, quickly straightened up when Heinrich burst in.

"You!" Heinrich said, low and menacingly, pointing to Hedda. "What in Jesus' name are you doing here with my emissary?"

Hedda stammered, but couldn't speak. She tried adjusting her skewed glasses but with little success.

Hugo held out his hands. "H-Heinrich, I can explain."

Heinrich's face was bright red. He yelled at Hugo. "You realize this woman has been fostering the alliance between Gebhard and Baron Ludwig, don't you?"

The young man turned to Hedda with a look of surprise, as he moved in front of the desk.

"I was just the transcriber, Hugo!" Hedda pleaded. "It's not true!"

"Before we deal with her," Heinrich said, sheathing his dagger, "I have more pressing issues. I need your advice on something, Hugo."

Hugo inched awkwardly forward from the desk. "M-my

advice, my lord?" Hugo asked, his expression off somehow.

Heinrich nodded slowly, noticing the young man's peculiar stance. "Yes, on how to deal with Tomas Reiner. I've uncovered the truth about his treachery and . . ." he trailed off, watching Hugo's confused reaction. "Ah, I'll explain it all over supper. Come now—and expect retribution for what you did with Lady Lucille, boy."

Motioning to Hedda, Heinrich said, "We'll lock this one in here until we've feasted. We can decide what to do with her then. Where did you find her, anyway? Ah, it's no matter." He waved off his question and turned to leave.

That's when he noticed that Hedda, too, was acting strangely, glancing repeatedly at Hugo, who was still in front of the desk, unsure and shaky, his hands clasped behind his back.

Scratching his cheek, Heinrich's eyes swept from Hedda to Hugo, then back again. He walked up to Hugo and stood a foot away, expecting him to glance down or back away. Instead, the young man uncharacteristically stood his ground.

Heinrich's face twisted into a snarl. He put his hand on Hugo's shoulder and said, "Get out of the way, boy. What on earth are you doing h—"

He stopped speaking. He stared behind Hugo at the desk, where a small piece of parchment had been scribbled on. Next to it was a jar of ink and a pen. He reached over and bent down, squinting. He studied the paper, but his eyes weren't what they used to be so he moved in closer . . .

Then he gasped. His heart sank to his stomach, and every hair on his body began to tingle. He vision blurred, he felt faint. He stared at the unfinished note:

Dieter Nicolaus—

~ Mord

He gently picked up the paper. With his mouth open, unable to speak, he faced Hugo.

I treated him like one of my own!

No! Why couldn't it have been Tomas?

Hugo wouldn't meet Heinrich's eyes. He stared at the ground, clenching his jaw, sucking in his cheeks. Then without a word, Heinrich turned and left the room—dazed, dizzy, heartbroken.

The ultimate betrayal.

Dieter was still waiting at the end of the hall. "What happened?

Heinrich thrust the paper at Dieter. "Congratulations," he muttered. "It seems you have friends in higher places than I ever imagined . . ."

He limped past Dieter while Dieter took in the note. Shocked, Dieter rushed after Heinrich down the hall, nearly running into him when the man stopped abruptly. Then Dieter saw that familiar, horrible look in Heinrich's eyes. The beast within.

Ripping out the dagger from behind his back, it all suddenly became clear to Heinrich. The fate he'd planned for Tomas must now be bestowed on Hugo. He had no choice. He marched back down the hallway toward the door he'd just exited, shaking his head, his face a mix of pain, sorrow, and rage.

But this time, Dieter ran after him. "W-wait, Heinrich, think about this!" He grabbed the man's arm as Heinrich reached for the door. Heinrich spun around and punched Dieter in the face, dropping him to the ground with a bloody nose.

Throwing open the door again, he stepped inside, his dagger raised. Hugo and Hedda were on the bed together, embracing.

"No!" Hedda cried.

Hugo jumped to his feet and pushed Hedda behind him, his eyes steely and dark. He held his breath as Heinrich loomed over him with the dagger, so close that Heinrich could see the dagger's reflection in the young man's eyes. As Heinrich prepared to strike, his vision blurred and he paused his attack. He looked at the brave, frightened young man—his protégé—one last time. Then . . . a glimpse of something clicked in his mind.

Looking over Hugo's shoulder, on the shelf next to the bed, he saw a shape that sucked the fury from his soul. He looked back at Hugo, confused.

"W-where did you get that?" he muttered, eyeing the toy on the shelf.

A doll, carved from wood, yellow and brown, with little black dots for eyes.

A horse.

Hugo spun around, confused. "That doll?"

Heinrich nodded numbly. The arm holding the dagger dropped to his side. Hugo reached over the bed and took the wooden horse. With a faint smile, he said, "My sister carved it for me when I was a babe . . . It's the only innocent memory I have of her."

Memories rushed back to Heinrich, his past, shadows he'd tried to obliterate . . .

His older brother, Oscar. Standing on the side of the riverbank. Watching him climb the slippery rocks—balancing like a court jester.

"Please, don't tell her, Oscar!" little eight-year-old Heinrich had cried after being exposed in his mother's gown. *"What do you want?"*

"You know what I want!" Oscar had said.

What Oscar had wanted that day was a toy that Heinrich's *father*—not Hugo's sister—had carved for him. The only memory Heinrich had of his father, a man he'd never known.

A wooden horse. With little black dots for eyes.

Heinrich had always kept it with him, wherever he went.

Until he met Odela Grendel, the woman who had stolen his heart. He'd impregnated her, a feat he thought impossible at the time due to Odela's advanced age. And when the baby was born and Odela had disappeared with the infant, so too had Heinrich's childhood doll . . .

The same horse that Hugo now had in his hand.

Dieter was now standing between him and Hugo, shouting something at him. But Heinrich's face felt numb, his ears deaf. He stared over Dieter's shoulder into Hugo's scared eyes.

I treated him like my own.

Because . . . he is *my own.*

Dumbfounded, Heinrich turned and walked out of the room.

Shutting the door behind him, he locked it from the outside, leaving Dieter, Hugo, and Hedda inside.

Then like a ghost he walked through the hall and down the stairs.

At the bottom, Beauregard stood, waiting. The butler started to speak, but saw Heinrich's expression and said nothing.

Then Heinrich heard it before Beauregard could tell him.

Voices. Shouting. Outside.

An angry mob.

Or an army.

Turning to the window, Beauregard whispered to Heinrich in a shaky voice.

"W-we have . . . visitors, my lord. Many, many visitors."

CHAPTER THIRTY-FOUR

DIETER

Dieter studied the confused look on Hugo's face. The boy still had no idea what had just happened. Heinrich, poised to kill, suddenly retreating with an expression Hugo had never seen on the man.

It had taken Dieter but an instant to recognize that expression on Heinrich's face—from anger and betrayal when first seeing the "Mord" note, to shock then confusion, and finally emotional overload when the truth finally dawned on him. The man went from bloodthirsty rage to paternal despair in seconds, all from something he'd seen on the shelf.

It had been a truth Dieter had known for a long while. But it was never his place to divulge it to Hugo. Not only was he not family, but he had also promised his wife that he'd never tell her brother the truth. In fact, he had been with Sybil when she'd first discovered her brother's true bloodline.

But that truth had just now almost cost Hugo his life. And no secret was worth that.

Hugo was still holding the carved horse, seemingly in a daze. Dieter put his hand on the boy's shoulder. He was still trembling. And that's what he looked like to Dieter at that moment—a terrified twelve-year-old boy, trying to make sense of what he'd just seen. Gone was the prideful arrogance he'd carried around with him under Heinrich's wing.

Dieter looked down at the wooden horse in Hugo's hand. "Tell me about the toy, Hugo." His voice was calm and reassuring, his hand still on the boy's shoulder.

"What just happened?" Hedda wondered aloud, baffled that Hugo was still alive and breathing. She swiveled from Hugo to Dieter, but both men's eyes were locked on each other as if she weren't there.

"Sybil made it for me when I was a child," Hugo said quietly.

"Did you ever see your sister carving it? Or working on it?"

Narrowing his eyes, Hugo thought for a moment. Then he shook his head slowly. "Not that I remember, no."

Dieter dipped his eyes away from Hugo and inhaled sharply. And as delicately as he could, he told him.

"Hugo. I . . . don't think Sybil made that doll for you. I'm sorry to tell you this. I think she just wanted you to believe that. Trying be a good, protective sister to her new brother."

Puzzled, Hugo asked, "Why does that matter?"

Dieter walked to the edge of the bed and sat. He leaned forward and joined his hands in front of him, staring up at Hugo. "Because I think that doll belonged to Heinrich Franz. When . . . *he* was a child."

"That's impossible!" Hugo exclaimed. "I didn't even *know* Heinrich when I was a child or when he was . . ." Suddenly his words trailed off as the realization slowly hit him.

Dieter said nothing, letting Hugo put the pieces together himself. Minutes earlier, when Hugo had been staring death in the face, he'd been incapable of rational thought. Now, however, he was much calmer and could think through Dieter's words and Heinrich's actions, and follow where they led.

Finally, he looked into Dieter's eyes with a knowing expression.

Dieter only nodded. Then, after a long moment passed, he said quietly, "I swore an oath to Sybil not to tell you . . . I'm not family, and she wanted to be the one to inform you, when and if the time was right. If ever. I actually believe she may have thought it best to allow you to live your entire life *without* knowing such pain."

Speaking from his heart, he tried to reassure the boy. "Believe me, Hugo, when I say that she was only trying to protect you. From a life of pain, and shame, and confusion. She was only doing what she thought was right. But now that she's gone—"

"Then let me hear it from you, Dieter. Say the words."

Staring at the ground, he did. "Heinrich Franz is your

father."

The boy showed no reaction, the statement just confirming what he'd already figured out. But as he gazed around the room in a disoriented haze, something Dieter just said suddenly registered on him. He looked at Dieter.

"What did you just mean, 'now that she's gone'?"

Dieter frowned. "You know what I meant, now that she's dead . . . in Trier."

"What are you talking about?"

Dieter furrowed his brow.

Hugo shook his head. "Sybil isn't dead. My sist—your wife—is very much alive!"

"What in God's name do you mean?"

Hugo gave Dieter a puzzled look. "Haven't you heard the rumors around town, the stories, about the 'Daughter of the Beast'?"

"Of course I have. But that's all they are—rumors."

Hugo shook his head. "It was an act of God, no doubt. Surely, she should have burned to death at the stake in Trier. *But she didn't!* When the hood was lifted . . . an old woman had taken her place. An old woman died that day, Dieter, not Sybil. I assure you. And while I don't know where my sister is . . . I do know she did not die on the stake in Trier."

Dieter was speechless. He coughed, trying to compose himself. He sat back on the bed with a heavy thud. "All this time . . ."

Hugo was still thinking back to that day in Trier. He looked up at the ceiling, recalling a distant detail. "And when that old crone burned, screaming like a white-haired banshee, Heinrich seemed very upset. He was dressed as Lord Inquisitor Adalbert at the time, but he raced from the pulpit when that woman died. I always wondered why . . ."

And because Dieter had more pieces of that puzzle than Hugo did, he quickly put them together. Looking at the boy, he spoke softly. "Hearing your description of Heinrich's reaction that day, Hugo, I'm convinced that that woman you speak of—that white-haired banshee—was likely your mother. Your biological mother at least. Her name was Odela Grendel,

Heinrich's lover when they were younger. They had a child—you—and Odela stole you from Heinrich when she learned of his murderous ways. She was terrified for your safety, so she took you to a family that she came upon during her blind travels.

"A family that had just buried their own stillborn babe. The Griswold family—*your* family, Hugo—Peter, Sybil, and the woman you were told was your mother, who died shortly after her baby's stillbirth."

Hugo stared at Dieter, tears glistening his eyes. "Peter . . . Sybil . . . mother . . . they weren't my real blood?"

Dieter's face hardened. "No, Hugo, they were *better* than blood, they *were* your family. Peter *was* your father and Sybil *was* your sister. Don't ever forget that. 'Family' is who loves and raises you. Peter Griswold raised you to be the man you've become. Peter Griswold was a fine, wonderful soul, whom you should be proud to call your father. He was the namesake for my very own son—"

The mention of his son Peter stopped Dieter cold. He choked up, feeling guilty that—what with Heinrich's ferocious rampage and Hugo's last-minute reprieve from death—he'd almost forgotten about his own precious child.

Will I ever see you again? God! Please let me see my son!

But the overload of information was unraveling Hugo's emotions. "He 'raised me to be the man I've become'?" Hugo bellowed, throwing up his hands. "Just look at what I've become, Dieter. A killer! An operative for a *monster!*"

The outburst took Dieter by surprise. After seeing how close Hugo and Heinrich had become—virtually "mentor-protégé"—he never imagined hearing Hugo describe his master as a monster. Maybe he'd been misreading Hugo all along. Which made him think of something else. He reached into his pocket and pulled out the note Heinrich had handed him.

Dieter Nicolaus—

~ Mord

Yes, the handwriting was the same as on all the earlier ones.

Hugo had been writing the warning messages!

By God!

"Why did you do it?" Dieter asked, showing him the note.

Hugo shrugged. He glanced at Hedda, still huddled in the corner, quietly observing the spectacle playing out between the two men. She tilted her head, as if wondering the same thing as Dieter.

Hugo exhaled loudly. "After Trier, I became wary of all the killing I'd borne witness to. On the way to that Godforsaken city, I befriended a minstrel, Klemens, and his dog . . . Mord. That minstrel died, thanks to me—I did terrible things in Trier, Dieter, and I felt I had to atone for those sins." Hugo spoke slowly, deliberately, measuring his words as if he'd never truly understood his own motivation until now.

"My first act of atonement was helping the people of Bedburg. When I came back here, I decided Bedburg was my home—my rightful place. I had been so curious to see the outside world. Yet once I found it to be so cruel and unforgiving, I no longer wanted a part in it." He gave Dieter a tight smile. "And when you took the mantle as the champion of the people, it was mere coincidence. I had planned to help the next natural leader, using my new position by Heinrich's side. But I never expected that person to be you, Dieter. Though I was very proud that it *was* you, and knew Sybil would be pleased, too."

Dieter's face reddened.

Pointing to Hedda in the corner, Hugo said, "I'd met Hedda briefly in Trier, when she was working for Baron Ludwig and while I was operating under Heinrich's directive. There, we formulated a rough scheme, yes?"

Hedda nodded, leaning back against the wall and stretching out her legs. "Hugo was a natural-born renegade," she added, "having grown up on the streets of Bedburg. So while he worked under Heinrich and gained his trust, he had a near-constant flow of information coming to him. And he relayed that information to two people, via those anonymous letters—me and you."

Dieter ran his hand through his stubbly beard. "So you learned of future Protestant targets straight from Heinrich's mouth?" he asked.

Hugo shook his head. "Not entirely. Also from Ulrich's ledger, and from Tomas, who was usually the one ordered to make the arrests. And even from Bishop Balthasar." He smirked, somewhat proud of himself. "For claiming to be so discreet, Heinrich really wasn't too guarded or cautious about his secrets."

Dieter thought back to the carriage ride he'd just shared with Heinrich. "So you two put this army together, then? The one Heinrich spoke to me about—Gebhard Truchsess' army?"

Hedda and Hugo looked at each other, then both shook their heads.

"Gebhard had always planned to attack Cologne," Hugo said. "He's been planning it for nearly a decade."

Hedda smiled. "We just . . . nudged him in a certain direction."

Dieter chuckled, shaking his head. This young man and woman—Hugo was five years his junior, Hedda nearly his own age—were much sharper than he'd ever imagined. "You nudged him toward Bedburg?"

Hugo shrugged. "We hoped he'd want to take a town close to Cologne, especially if he had help."

Hugo spoke without arrogance or pride—in an honest, humble tone Dieter hadn't seen in the boy before. He'd always assumed Hugo took after his biological father, that he'd let power go to his head. Now he realized how wrong he'd been. Another question came to him.

"And what about Tomas? Why do you think Heinrich was so sure he was 'Mord'?"

Hugo scratched the back of his neck.

"At one point or other, Heinrich suspected *everyone* of betraying him. His rampant paranoia has become notorious. I reckon he thought that, because Tomas was a military man and garrison commander, he must have opened the gates for Gebhard, possibly set up the supply lines. And since Tomas met with Bishop Balthasar, there was more reason to suspect he'd colluded with the priest."

"It sounds to me that Heinrich Franz's paranoia has traveled to the edges of delusion," Dieter said, drawing smiles from both

Hugo and Hedda.

"I'm sure he seems perfectly sane in his own mind," Hedda commented.

"As do most, my dear," Dieter added. "I doubt anyone crazy has ever thought they were."

Hugo smiled, then continued explaining Tomas. "Like myself, maybe even more so, Tomas has become very repentant of late. Especially since his actions at Trier. I believe remorse and regret have greatly affected him. He's now married with a beautiful baby boy. He gives penitence at the church at least three times a week. *That's* what he so often meets with Bishop Balthasar for."

After a long silence, as each of them considered the significance of their conversation, Dieter finally said, "You're a very brave young man, Hugo. I just wanted you to know that. It takes a strong will to do what you have done."

Hugo sighed, waving Dieter off. "You would have done the same, had you been in my position. I just did what I thought was right."

"But that's the point, isn't it, Hugo?" said Hedda. "Not everyone would do what's right. I must agree with the priest here." She stood and slowly walked to the bed where Hugo sat, sitting next to him in silence.

A loud boom broke the quiet. Dieter spun around. The noise got louder. Hugo stood and ran to the window, Hedda and Dieter following.

They stared down at the courtyard in shock.

"Where did they all come from?" Hedda mumbled.

"Lots of them," said Hugo.

A huge crowd had gathered in the courtyard. They were rowdy, loud. Some looked angry, others drunk.

"How did they get in?" Dieter wondered.

"They must have broken down the front gate . . ."

As the chorus of shouting and yelling grew louder, so did the mob's actions. Arms swung wildly in the air, some holding pitchforks, others torches, still others waving swords and axes.

This was no military force, and not a part of Tomas' garrison.

This was a peasant army. This was an uprising.

This was a revolution.

Dieter smiled to himself. This was exactly what he'd been fighting for all this time. While two armies squared off against each other back in Bedburg proper, out here in the darkness of the countryside was where the *real* passion burned. The power of the people! The honest dedication of the masses to the worthiest of causes: fighting tyranny and injustice. Agitated peasants and farmers and common folk, joining together, throwing aside their differences, to fight the common enemy—the evil that was Heinrich Franz.

Dieter put a hand on Hugo's shoulder, causing him to flinch. "You must continue to be brave, Hugo," he said in a solemn voice. "For all our sakes."

Hugo held his breath as he watched the scene below intensify. There was so much to think about, so much at stake. How Heinrich would react. How Bedburg's army would react. Whether these angry citizens had any chance against professional soldiers. It was all so overwhelming.

"I don't know if I can, Dieter," Hugo replied. "I think I might have used up all my bravery. I'm so tired . . . and not the person people think I am."

"That's the beauty of it, Hugo. You can reinvent yourself when this is done."

Hugo winced again, recalling something from the distant past. "Severin said something like that, right before . . . Trier," he muttered to himself.

"Who?"

"Never mind." Hugo brushed off the thought.

"Regardless," Dieter continued, "you must remember that you have a responsibility to these people. They may be drunk with rage and drunk with liquor. But either way, they need a leader. They are loud because they must be. That's the only way they will be heard. But it will take a brave man, someone quiet and observant, to be their guide. And that must be you, Hugo!"

"I rather think they're here for *your* sake, Dieter," Hugo said.

Dieter looked down and smiled. "My time is done with these people, Hugo. I've led them as far as I could—beyond the gates of Hell itself. But only you can bring them out, back to the land of the living."

"Why are you saying such things, Dieter? You're scaring me."

He was saying those things because of what he saw. Down in the courtyard.

Her. He was sure it was.

Sybil.

Standing near the front of the crowd, managing the anger and emotions of the mob with a masterful display. Then he saw others he recognized.

Georg Sieghart and Martin Achterberg and Ava holding Peter!

Praise the Lord! Peter is safe.

"It's okay to be frightened, Hugo," Dieter said quietly. Then he pointed. "Don't you see her? Down there, your sister?"

After a moment, Hugo's face lit up. "By God, there she is!"

"Do you see how she is the only quiet one? Gauging the reactions, deciding her next move? That is because she is like you, Hugo. You come from the same stock."

Hugo didn't respond. He just kept watching the scene below.

"You do!" Dieter continued. "You were raised together, in the same household, by the same father. Do you see the fear in her eyes? In her posture? But she refuses to back down despite that fear. Only a foolish person is not frightened in the face of adversity, Hugo. Your sister is no fool! It's better to be courageous and scared than arrogant and cocksure. Your sister understands that, clear as day."

He paused and turned Hugo around by his shoulder to face him. "Do *you* understand?"

Hugo narrowed his eyes, then nodded once, firmly. Locking eyes with Dieter, he asked, "If you've led your flock as far as you can take them . . . what will you do now, Dieter?"

"He'll come with me. That's what he'll do."

The voice pierced the room, harsh and abrupt.

Heinrich Franz stood in the doorway, frowning at his three prisoners.

CHAPTER THIRTY-FIVE

In the chilly night air, Sybil stood in the courtyard of House Charmagne, surrounded by her friends and allies. The large enclosure was bordered by the unmanned gatehouse they'd just passed through, dark rows of trees on both sides, and the mansion and its entry doors directly in front of them.

Sybil had managed to get her ragtag mob this far thanks to the help of her friends and a few pyrotechnic tricks. The crowd believed her to be something she was not. Yes, she'd put on a farce. But it was a necessary means to a righteous end.

At Sybil's sign, the group of about thirty-odd peasants and farmers headed forward. Georg, clutching his bandaged stomach, limped beside Wilhelm, his arm slung over the young man's shoulder for support. Mary, Martin, and Ava followed behind them, Ava holding a scared Peter Sieghart close to her chest, trying to hide his small head from all the activity around them. Corvin walked on one side of Sybil, Rowaine on the other—Rowaine's eyes continually roving between the house, the crowd, and their surroundings, looking for signs of danger. Salvatore was off somewhere by the trees, inspecting one of them for something.

The peasants approached the mansion's large oak doors, adorned with snarling wolf handles, and began banging with whatever they had: fists, feet, hammers, hoes, swords, axes. The doors were strong and high, but not reinforced for prolonged battery. They *would* fall. It was just a matter of time.

As the peasants' shouting and cursing grew louder, Sybil looked around. Far in the distance, off by the horizon, she could see the first signs of smoke and orange flames rising from the walls of Bedburg. The battle for the city had begun—Bishop Gebhard's company pitted against Tomas Reiner's garrison.

Sybil knew that the group's energy and enthusiasm wouldn't

last. As the obstacles before them mounted, they'd begin to waver, their passion wane. Soon they'd grow tired of beating on these thick wooden doors. They'd been awed by Corvin's masterful oratory and Sybil's intense, blazing display. They'd been angered by years of abuse from their lords, especially the resident of this manor, Heinrich Franz. And they'd been incensed at the news that their savior, Dieter Nicolaus, had been captured.

But these were not trained, disciplined military men. They were farmhands and landowners and merchants. Once they took stock of their position this far from home, in the midst of strangers, with their lives at stake, their support would quickly ebb. Sybil knew that, and so did her collaborators. A few of the peasants had already begun grumbling in hushed tones, glancing over their shoulders at Sybil and her company.

Leaning close to Rowaine, Sybil asked, "Do you believe there's a way to hurry this up? That door must fall, soon!"

"We don't have the tools for a proper siege, Beele," Georg said, grimacing while keeping the pressure on his bandage. "We must work with what we have."

"The doors will fall, Beele," Rowaine said reassuringly. "I promise."

Sybil studied the progress the peasants had made. Parts of the surface were beginning to splinter, albeit barely. Wilhelm gently took Georg's arm off his shoulder and walked up to the front. Addressing the men beating on the doors, he shouted, "Attack the sides! Near the hinges!" Turning back to his comrades, he shrugged with a weak smile. "My father worked on such structures all his life. The doors may not be stone, but the concept's the same: the center is reinforced, but the surrounding foundation is not. If we can damage the doorframe, it should fall faster."

With some additional instruction from Georg and Wilhelm, the mob began aiming their strikes along the doors' edges, especially the corners where the right angles met. The change in focus had an immediate impact.

Within minutes, the doorframes began crumbling against the weight of the attackers. They struck high and low, thumping and smashing with their crude tools.

Salvatore turned from the tree he was inspecting and yelled, "We could craft a battering ram from one of these tree trunks."

But Wilhelm shook his head. "It would take too long to fashion a ram, Herr Salvatore. And it won't be necessary," he said, "look!"

The first hole was now visible in the upper corner of the right door. The attackers focused on that area, people falling over each other as they pulled and banged away. A few yelled deep-bellied *hoorahs* as they worked to fell the rest of the door.

Sybil joined her hands in a prayer-like gesture. "It's going to work," she said softly.

Two minutes later, the hole had widened. A low orange glow seeped through, bathing the peasants in warm light. They kicked and prodded and pulled on the fractured structure, until the hole was finally big enough for a few arms to stick through. Georg ran up, pushing some of the others aside, grunting when his wounded belly bumped up against them. With his jaw clenched and the veins on his neck pulsing, he reached inside the door and lifted something heavy away from the back of it. When it dropped to the ground with a loud *thump*, he and the crowd roared. It was the heavy beam crossing the doorway to block entry. With it gone, a hard shove pushed the damaged portal wide open as everyone stepped back, suddenly falling quiet at what they saw waiting for them inside.

At the far end of the long, red-carpeted hallway, halfway up a massive staircase, Heinrich Franz faced them. Standing beside him was Dieter, grimacing, his hands apparently tied behind his back, Heinrich's arm wrapped tightly around his neck. In Heinrich's other hand was a dagger, pressed firmly against Dieter's throat. A few steps below them, Beauregard, the butler, stood in his pristine suit, his stiff-backed posture perfect. Cradled against his shoulder was a large arquebus pointed directly at the front doors. One step up from the butler, in arm's reach, an iron weapons stand was filled with several more rifles at the ready.

Sybil stepped through the broken door, followed by Georg and Wilhelm and the rest of her friends. Fearlessly, she stared straight ahead at the men and their weapons on the stairs, while the rest of her mob clamored through the splintered doorway, filling up all available space in the large entryway. Once everyone was inside, she began walking toward the staircase. Georg, Rowaine, and Wilhelm took up positions alongside her, while the rest of her group—Aellin, Ava with Peter, Martin, and Wilhelm's mother Mary—formed a second row immediately behind them.

As they proceeded forward, the crowd followed.

"Halt, fiends!" Beauregard barked as the crowd ignored his words and continued moving forward behind Sybil. The butler fired his weapon, aiming past the leaders, and a man in the crowd dropped, clutching his chest.

"Anthony!" another peasant shouted, rushing to his fallen friend. Kneeling beside him, the friend touched the dead man's chest, his fingers coming away with slick blood from the man's fatal wound. Looking up, the man seethed. "You killed Bedburg's best blacksmith!" he shouted.

Beauregard had already discarded his arquebus and was reaching for another.

"And he won't be the only one to meet a grisly end if you don't cease your advance at once," Heinrich growled.

The fatal gunshot had stopped the mob. Sybil's heart sank as she surveyed the bleak situation, swiveling from her terrified husband up on the stairs to the nervous peasants around her. She knew she was quickly losing the crowd's momentum. Seeing one of their own die, they had no real, personal vendetta against the count, other than a common dislike for the man.

So while the main crowd stayed in place, grumbling, Sybil took two more steps forward, her body reacting before her brain could. Her friends moved forward with her, bravely facing their enemy together.

At the sight of the seven adults standing before him, banded together in two tight rows, something in Heinrich's manner changed. The faces he saw had all been his victims—actual recipients, directly or indirectly, of his cruel reign of terror. And their steadfast look of determination shifted his own expression from one of smug assurance to anxious uncertainty.

Noting the subtle shift of confidence in the man's face, Sybil shouted, "Hand over my husband, you monster!" which quieted the jittery crowd behind her. Yet again she began to walk forward. She was now less than twenty paces from the foot of the stairs, stopping only at the click of Beauregard's weapon being cocked.

"Beele, don't!" Dieter shouted, sweat pouring down his face.

She froze and held her hands out to stop her group from continuing. Gazing into her husbands terrified eyes, she saw him look from person to person around her. And she understood his fear. It wasn't for his own safety, but rather for the lives of his loved ones.

For his wife.

His son.

And Georg—the man who had rescued him so many times.

And Rowaine—the captain who'd ferried him and Sybil from Gustav's grasp.

And Mary and Wilhelm—the family he'd helped escape, having failed to rescue their husband.

And Martin and Ava—his closest friends and accomplices during all these months of helping the Protestants.

So for Dieter's sake—for his peace of mind that his loved ones would not die in front of him—Sybil remained where she was, though it took every ounce of strength to do so.

"What is it you want, Heinrich?" she called out.

The count of Bedburg spoke matter-of-factly. "You'rc all going to turn around and leave, or I will kill your champion."

Sybil surveyed the room, trying to figure out her next move. As she panned the area above the stairs, her mouth fell open, though she quickly closed it to hide her surprise. Staring down at her from a corner of a balcony railing, partially hidden from view, were her brother Hugo and that bespectacled scribe, Hedda.

What in God's name were they doing there?

Then she remembered the gossip she'd heard. That while she'd been away at Norfolk, Hugo had become an accomplice of Heinrich Franz. She hadn't believed it, thinking it nothing more than stupid rumors. She could never imagine her little brother having anything to do with such a vile man.

But now the cold, hard truth was staring down at her. And it broke her heart.

When she looked up again, Hugo and the woman were gone.

"If you come any closer, his blood will be on your hands," Heinrich yelled, his blade so tightly pressed against Dieter's throat that a small trickle of red began to run down his neck. Dieter winced as Heinrich, in a low voice, called down to his butler. "Is everything ready?"

"Yes, my lord," Beauregard replied without lowering his weapon or breaking eye contact with Sybil and the crowd.

The situation seemed to be at a stalemate. Until something amazing happened. Whether it was good besting evil, or just the downtrodden finally reaching their breaking point, suddenly the mood of the crowd seemed to shift. Something deep within the hearts of all these good people—hard-working folk all victimized by this tyrant—seemed to rise to the surface, melting away fear and uncertainty. It started when a brave voice in the crowd spoke up.

"Every man and woman here has been affected by the deeds of Heinrich Franz!" the voice shouted. "Think of your families and friends."

It was a farmer, holding a hand shovel. Looking over at another stocky peasant across from him, he said, "Jonathan Meier, your cousin the tailor was swept away in a land dispute that wasn't of his making."

And that started it.

The man he'd just spoken to slumped his shoulders and replied, "He lost his hand and his livelihood over nothing . . ."

Then another, further back in the crowd, yelled, "Cristoff Krüger, you lost your mistress Josephine, your employer Lars, and nearly your most valuable employee, Aellin."

Then Dieter joined in from the staircase. "Stephen Burmack, Oliver Thorpe, Dietrich Simonson . . . everyone here! Not a one of you has been free from this man's whims."

"Quiet your tongues, all of you!" Heinrich ordered, thrusting his elbow into Dieter's side. In a wordless gasp, Dieter went down on one knee. Sybil clenched her fists but didn't move.

"That's enough of this traitorous rhetoric!" Heinrich yelled at the mob. "If you value your lives, and this man's, you'll quit this place at once! Otherwise I'll see that you're all hanged—"

"Your executioner is dead, Heinrich," Georg called out, standing next to Sybil.

"There will always be men willing to dislodge the heads of traitors, Herr Sieghart," Heinrich responded.

"You are the traitor to Bedburg, Heinrich Franz!" Wilhelm screamed, thrusting a trembling finger up the stairs. "We make the city operate, while you reap the rewards of our toil! My father died at your executioner's hand, and for what? For nothing more than a rumor that he was a man against you!"

This got everyone even more enflamed. Wilhelm was one of their own, a local laborer.

Heinrich snarled. "Your father sought to bring Catholicism to its knees, boy."

"You have no proof of that!"

Dieter rose unsteadily, refusing to be silenced. "Heinrich is a man who acts without evidence or morality. Do not fear the coward who is afraid himself . . ."

Another punch deflated him. He doubled over and gurgled as Heinrich pulled up with his forearm against Dieter's neck, choking him silent. Dieter began frothing and writhing.

"Stop it, you're killing him!" Sybil screamed, tears welling in her eyes.

"Something I should have done a long time ago. If I had, perhaps I wouldn't be in this predicament," the count said, as the crowd once again began to advance.

"That's enough!" Heinrich screamed, his voice more fearful than confident. "Not another step forward, or your savior dies!"

And with that, Heinrich let out a loud, piercing whistle, silencing the mob. Seconds later, a strange pitter-patter could be heard from somewhere on the second floor. Before the crowd had time to make sense of it, the first black shapes emerged. Wolves, six of them, snarling, began to descend the stairs and surround Heinrich, Dieter, and Beauregard. With teeth bared and the low buzz of their growls vibrating in their chests, they appeared feral and ready to kill. When they got to the foot of the stairs, Heinrich snapped his fingers and the wolves instantly reared back on their haunches and sat at full attention, their yellow teeth dripping with saliva, anxiously waiting for their attack command.

"Dear God," Georg muttered, taking several steps back, as did everyone else. It was the first time Sybil had ever seen fear on the big man's face. Which only frustrated her more. The crowd was retreating, the tide changing, their cause weakening. Without thinking, she spontaneously yelled out, "I will forfeit my family estate to the man who brings me Heinrich Franz's head!"

Heinrich let out a short burst of laughter. "You can't give what doesn't belong to you, witch!"

"I can once you're dead, you devil," she replied, narrowing her eyes. "Then it rightfully reverts back to me." It was enough to stop the crowd's retreat.

Then Martin then stepped forward. "I, too, will give my family estate of Achterberg to anyone who kills that man." The rumblings of the crowd increased.

"You're all mad!" Heinrich bellowed.

Then Wilhelm raised his hand. "Let us give this vile man what he tried to sneak on the citizens of Bedburg! My house of Edmond for his head!"

Heinrich pulled Dieter in close and poised his dagger by his jugular, but it had no effect. The mob charged forward. Beauregard let off another shot from his second rifle, this one striking Wilhelm in the leg. The dyemaker clutched the wound and fell forward, his mother rushing to his side.

Heinrich growled then snapped his fingers again. The wolves all rose, fully re-energized, ready to attack. Then everything happened so fast, Sybil would hardly be able to recount the exact sequence of events later. As the snarling wolves descended upon the peasants, a flash moved to the front of the group.

Salvatore the *benandanti* stood bravely between the crowd and animals, calm and happy. As the wolves surrounded the man for the kill, Salvatore's arms flew up in a flurry, like he were conjuring a spell, and he let out a whistle, much higher-pitched than Heinrich's, bringing everyone's hands to their ears.

Instantly, the wolves stopped in their tracks, mid-charge, sliding down on all fours, staring submissively up at Salvatore, their purple tongues lolling to the sides.

Everyone stood stunned, except of course Salvatore who merely smiled and gave a curt nod to his audience.

Dieter took this divinely auspicious moment to shout, "My friends, do not fear the man with hate in his heart!"

With his last line of defense neutralized, Heinrich raised his leg and, with a swift and powerful kick to Beauregard's back, sent the butler careening down the staircase. His gun fired wildly in the air as his head slammed hard into the railing, crumbling him into an unconscious, bleeding heap at the foot of the stairs.

Immediately, several peasants ran past the still-docile wolves to the unconscious butler, pummeling the man's skull into an unrecognizable mass of bone and gray matter with their crude farming tools and makeshift weapons—showing no mercy for the man who moments earlier had killed one of their own for no reason. Meanwhile, the rest of the mob, led by Sybil and her friends, walked around the bloody scene toward Heinrich and Dieter who had now ascended to the top of the landing.

Taking one last look at the angry group approaching, Heinrich shouted, "I warned you all!"

And Dieter locked eyes with Sybil, a calm, gentle smile on his face. It was a smile that told her not to worry.

That he was at peace.

That he had done all he set out to do: revolutionize the townsfolk of Bedburg, and lay eyes on his beloved wife and son.

Sybil felt tears stinging her eyes. She reached out her hand, willing herself to touch Dieter's hand one last time, even though he was far from her grasp.

Then, with a swift and precise slash, Heinrich dragged his dagger across Dieter's throat and threw him down the stairs into the onslaught. Blood spurted everywhere, spraying across the wall and stairway. Bouncing helplessly down the stairs, Dieter's hands still tied behind him, his body twisted and jerked before coming to rest near Sybil's feet.

"NO!" Sybil shrieked, dropping to her knees. She let out a bloodcurdling scream that could be heard in the heavens, as the crowd looked on in stunned horror.

Georg, Rowaine, and Wilhelm raced to comfort the dying

man, kneeling beside Sybil. But Dieter's eyes were already still and lifeless, his blood pooling under him and spilling down the remaining steps.

And with that, the crowd went wild, forging up the stairs, around and over their fallen hero and his mourning loved ones, to dispense justice upon his murderer.

But Heinrich was gone.

As the crowd pushed its way up the stairs, too many bodies bottlenecked their advance, giving Heinrich enough time to escape down the hall. When he came to the room that he'd locked Hugo and Hedda in, he kicked open the door.

No one was there.

Slamming the door shut, he ran to the window and looked out. The shouting and pounding of feet got louder down the hall. He lifted the window up and a cool breeze swept across his face. Jumping over the windowsill, he rolled onto the roof, then crawled to the edge, just as the first peasants burst into the room.

Cristoff, the tavern owner, immediately ran to the open window. He poked his head out to see which way Heinrich had gone. Glancing to the side, he spotted Heinrich slinking away and turned back to tell his comrades. But he never got the chance. A shot rang out from Heinrich's pistol, catching the left side of Cristoff's forehead, slumping him across the windowsill as his head dropped forward. Martin and two others ran to his aid, pulling his body back inside. At the sight of the dark, bloody dot above his left eye, Martin roared, then leapt out the window, hitting the roof in a run and following the crumbling roof plates that Heinrich had left in his wake.

When Heinrich reached the far end of the roof, away from the window's line of sight, he scooted his toes to the edge and peered down at the fifteen-foot drop to the ground. A carriage was parked not far from the drop, its driver, Felix, keeping the horses in line with his whip as they neighed and snorted. Heinrich glanced back over his shoulder as Martin rounded the corner, approaching as fast as he could on the unsteady roof tiles. Turning onto his hands and knees, Heinrich lowered his legs slowly over the side of the roof, gripping the roof's edge tightly with his fingers. He inhaled deeply, then pushed off with a gasp, his body plummeting to the ground for what felt like eons.

Hitting the ground hard on his feet, he felt a crunch of pain through his ankles and shins. He hobbled toward the carriage, which had already begun rolling away under Felix's direction.

As Martin neared the edge of the roof where Heinrich had dropped from, he reached to the back of his belt and pulled out his only weapon, a dagger. Watching Heinrich half-limp, half-run to the carriage, Martin cocked his arm back and flung the knife as hard as he could as Heinrich reached for the carriage's side door.

The dagger punched into the side of the carriage, two inches from Heinrich's head. Martin cursed as he watched Heinrich and the coach disappear into the misty fog.

All was quiet inside the carriage, a welcome respite from the madness outside. Dark curtains covered the windows rendering the interior black as night. Shuddering off his adrenaline, Heinrich closed his eyes and leaned back against the seat. After several deep breaths, he began to smirk.

He'd made it.

"Hello, *father*," a voice said, shattering his quiet.

His eyes shot open, staring across the carriage into the darkness. As he squinted and his eyes acclimated, two figures took shape.

Hugo and Hedda, sitting across from him.

Baffled, he sat up in his seat, his eyes moving from Hugo to Hedda, then back to Hugo.

"Hello, *son*," he said, feigning calm. "I'm glad to see you came to your senses about this entire ordeal," he said, shaking his head.

"Yes, father, I have come to my senses."

Heinrich nodded. Then both were quiet.

Hugo noticed his father's hand slowly slipping around behind his back. They locked eyes for a moment—the young man's big and brown, his father's narrow and gray. Then, while his father's expression remained pathologically serene, Hugo saw the glint of steel. But the younger man was quicker—and well-trained by Ulrich. He lunged forward with his own dagger as Heinrich's knife, still bloody from its work on Dieter, swung around just as the carriage hit a bump, sending both men to the carriage floor.

"Hugo!" Hedda cried, watching helplessly as Heinrich's knife arced from the side, aiming for Hugo's intestines. But Hugo's left arm shot out at the last second, catching Heinrich's wrist, as his right hand plunged his own dagger into the right side of Heinrich's chest.

Heinrich gasped, then pushed his own weapon forward, stabbing Hugo in the side, before reeling back and howling like one of his wild wolves. Hugo pulled out his blade and thrust it back in, this time catching Heinrich in the stomach.

Between clenched teeth, blood began oozing from Heinrich's mouth. Suddenly realizing he was fading fast, his expression shifted from unbridled rage to the grim reality that he was losing strength. His dagger dropped from his hand. But Hugo's fury was relentless. Fighting back his own pain, he struck Heinrich a third time, this time piercing his father's black heart.

At the moment of contact, Heinrich's eyes seemed to brighten in amazement, staying fixed on Hugo's, until his mind recognized the battle was over and his eyelids began to flutter. Then his body shuddered one last time before the beast took his final breath and was no more.

Hugo slumped in his seat, trembling, blinking uncontrollably, breathing heavily. At the next bump in the road, he lurched to his side and Hedda reached over to him. "You're hurt!"

He wanted to be strong, especially at this pivotal moment, but he was dizzy. Suddenly, he couldn't breath, his heart pounding in his ears. He reached for the seat for support and as Hedda screamed, he crumbled to the floor.

CHAPTER THIRTY-SIX

The battle raged on at Bedburg. From atop the southern ramparts of the city, Commander Tomas Reiner directed his men, waving his sword in one direction or the other to indicate which way they should go.

A small group of Protestants had dashed through the gate into the city, taking refuge in a shadowy alcove. Tomas' men—devout Catholics with fury in their eyes—had surrounded them. Tomas watched as the religious warriors butchered each other, until it was impossible to distinguish one side from the other.

With grim resolve Tomas followed as the gory scene unfolded, so absorbed he almost forgot to pay attention to what was happening right in front of him. Two Protestant soldiers had cleared the ramparts, jumped onto the balcony from the other side of the wall, and dispatched an unsuspecting Catholic soldier with an axe.

Tomas' only warning came when someone called out his name. At the last second, he looked up as the man with the axe, his eyes red-rimmed and savage, reached back to throw it. Tomas ducked and the axe flew over his head, but just barely.

Tomas gritted his teeth and charged the man, shoving his long blade up into the man's stomach. Yanking down hard, he split open his flesh, his entrails dangling out his belly. The man howled as he tried to reach down and gather his guts but Tomas kicked him in the side and he flew over the rampart ledge.

Another soldier approached Tomas, but faltered when he saw his friend fly off the ledge. Tomas took the opportunity to lunge, raising his blade high. The man shrank back with his own blade up, ready to parry. But Tomas shifted the downward angle of his attack and came in sideways, stabbing into the man's left armpit and piercing his heart.

Tomas soon realized that most of the men he faced weren't soldiers. At least not professionals. They were laymen roused by the ambitions of Gebhard Truchsess, who promised them fortunes and wealth if they backed him. But they hadn't expected to meet such fierce resistance.

Gebhard had lied to them about Bedburg's able defenses. Tomas was a born military man. Even when he wasn't acting as a bodyguard or escort, he'd always maintained his fighting prowess by practicing in the dueling rings. And his garrison consisted of like-minded men, not peaceful farmers or traders, but practiced killers raised and trained at war and carnage.

Tomas and his men were truly a force to be reckoned with—as the dead Protestants who'd just tried to attack him had come to find out too late.

Suddenly a trio of attackers appeared. They glanced at one another, apparently deciding which one would step up to Tomas' flashing blade. When none did, Tomas decided for them. Stepping into the guard of one man, he easily sliced down the man's chest, causing his two friends to turn and run as Tomas screamed, "Cowards!"

Then another approached, swinging his sword wildly toward Tomas. As the two parried, the man's comrade knelt down and began rummaging through the pockets of a dead soldier. Suddenly Tomas' eyes went wide when the comrade came up aiming a pistol at him. A deafening *boom* went off and Tomas wondered where he'd been hit. But then the man aiming the gun fell to the ground, clutching his chest. Glancing back, Tomas saw a Catholic soldier had come to his aid and gave him a curt nod of thanks.

Turning back to the man he'd been parrying with, who seemed temporarily frozen by the gunshot to his friend, Tomas lunged with dangerous precision, skewering him under the ribs. Before the man fell, Tomas stabbed him twice more in rapid succession, killing him before he hit the ground.

Somewhat out of breath, Tomas returned his gaze to the battle down by the southern gate. With a sigh of relief, he saw that his men had successfully fended off the Protestants, sending them to a hasty retreat, though many were cut down as they attempted to flee back out the southern gate.

Tomas looked further down the battlefield, to the green

plains beyond the walls of Bedburg. Though he'd successfully staved off the first round of attacks from Gebhard's Calvinist army, they were still gathering in force down the hill from Bedburg, wheeling in cannons, to ready another assault.

This was not what Tomas wanted to see. Once Gebhard realized his army had nearly twice as many soldiers as Tomas' Catholic garrison, he would order a full assault. Tomas knew he couldn't meet such an attack head on. He could only act defensively. It would be suicide to send his men directly out against the much larger Protestant army. Eventually his forces would be overwhelmed and scatter.

If something didn't happen soon to change the landscape of the battle, Tomas feared he would lose the city.

And this was only the first hour of conflict.

As night wore on, Tomas had his dead and wounded taken away to the church to prevent the enemy from knowing his mounting casualties. Bishop Balthasar was overseeing the rescue efforts with help from his priests and nuns, preparing the dead for burial, giving last rites to those mortally wounded, offering first aid to the lightly wounded, and offering water and soup to those beleaguered with dehydration and famine.

Near the southern ramparts, Tomas met with several of his top captains to discuss battle strategy.

"Gebhard's first charge failed," one captain commented. "I doubt we'll see much of him for the rest of the night."

An older, gray-haired captain disagreed. "If he realizes his superior numbers, he'll strike again. This time without retreating at the first sign of defeat."

The two men looked at Tomas, who nodded. "I agree with Herr Germaine," he said, referring to the older captain. "While we still have room to move, we must retaliate quickly."

He had a small map of the city in front of him, rocks weighing down various parts against the wind. Different sized rocks also signified the location of Gebhard's and Tomas' armies.

From a few paces back, Lord Alvin looked on. "How do we do that?" he asked. Though not a battle commander, he did hold a significant amount of land in Bedburg, earning him a place at the strategy table.

Tomas moved a pebble beside the large rock that denoted Gebhard's main force.

"We flank them," he said, "by moving two small groups out from the eastern and western gates and circling around Gebhard's lines."

"If they're seen, they'll be surrounded and slaughtered," Germaine said, frowning.

"That's why we send them now, while they still have the cover of night," Tomas replied.

Germaine crossed his arms over his chest. "I don't know if we can afford to send out such troops. That would seriously reduce our forces inside the city walls."

"As long as Gebhard remains oblivious to our numbers, we should be fine," Tomas said.

"And how long do you think he'll remain oblivious?" the young captain asked.

Tomas sighed. "The forces I'm considering sending won't be footsoldiers. They will be cavalry. Skirmishers. It will be a lightning attack. Strike, then retreat—just enough to scare them, give them pause."

Lord Alvin smiled. "I like that. Why didn't you say that to begin with, Tomas? It's a worthy plan."

"I still don't know if it will help us . . . in the long term," Germaine said.

Tomas frowned at his most experienced captain. He didn't want to argue with the man. The quickest way to lose morale was for soldiers to see their superiors bickering. But Tomas pressed on.

"If I die on this battlefield, Captain Germaine, you'll be the one to take my place. And when that happens, you're free to lead the army as you wish. But until then, what I've described is the plan. At the very least, it will buy us time."

"Buy us time for what?" Lord Alvin asked.

"For me to think of our next plan," Tomas said, frowning

again. "Now, who will lead the charge?"

When no one spoke up, Captain Germaine sighed. "To make sure it goes without mishap, I will."

Tomas smiled, resting his hand on Germaine's shoulder. "Your loyalty and fearlessness is unfaltering, captain. I promise you your deeds will be remembered."

Late into the night, Tomas sent his men out the eastern and western gates. The soldiers he chose were specialized for this type of covert operation. Riding into the countryside on steeds with padded hooves and no steel to clank, they moved with stealth and precision.

Germaine led the group from the eastern gate. If all went well, the two groups would move from Bedburg, forming the outline of a heart around Gebhard's army and attack from the rear. Once they'd frightened the Protestant camps and killed a few men, maybe even captured a captain or two, they'd quickly flee into the night and return to Bedburg by dawn.

Tomas wasn't expecting a major victory here, just something to reinvigorate his outnumbered forces and cause the enemy concern.

An hour after the men parted Bedburg, he heard the first cries of battle.

Clenching his teeth, he watched the horizon and saw smoke rising from the sound of guns, and the ringing out of steel-on-steel. But steel-on-steel was *not* what he wanted to hear. That meant swords clashing and the plan had been that his men would not engage in close-quarters combat.

As the next hour passed and the sounds of shouting and battle continued, Tomas grew more nervous. Two hours later, the cavalry returned to Bedburg and a soldier approached Tomas with a battle report.

"Captain Germaine is dead. The western attackers went unnoticed and hit Gebhard's flank hard, but they were waiting for our eastern attack. Germaine was one of the first to fall, and when he did, it demoralized his men. We had to escape before we were massacred, sir."

Tomas cursed under his breath. He'd forgotten that Bedburg was home to numerous Protestant sympathizers and turncoats. Clearly, Gebhard had gotten advance word of his battle plans.

He'd just lost his most experienced commander, and the morning had just begun.

How will I explain that to the men? That I sent Germaine to his death, even though he disagreed with my plan? I'll face deserters, that much is certain . . .

Tomas paced the rampart, close to where he'd stood during Gebhard's first charge. But before he had time to consider his dilemma, cannonfire rang out.

Gebhard's forces were attacking again.

Depleted and exhausted, Tomas' sword felt like an iron weight in his hand. His eyes could barely stay open. Covered in the blood of his enemies, he and his men had been fighting with valor and courage for three hours now.

The sun now fully illuminated the bloody battlefield. Between his nighttime fiasco and the morning's battle, he'd lost nearly three hundred men, either dead or incapacitated. A third of his force. They couldn't go on much longer.

Lord Alvin had recommended Tomas forfeit the city to Gebhard—opining that it was a lost cause. But Tomas had pushed the fat lord aside and gone on to personally lead his troops.

Now he was in the thickest part of the fight, fending for his life, fighting back-to-back with his fellow soldiers. He'd charged the ground troops with twenty men, trying to defend this side of the gate, but was now down to six. They'd fought hard, but as he blinked sweat and blood from his eyes, he glanced over his shoulder and saw another comrade fall, this time from a spear to the neck.

Taking a step back, he almost tripped over a fallen comrade. Instead, he crashed into the city wall, dropping his sword and sinking to his knees in total exhaustion. The scene around him got fuzzy, the sun stifling. He could not go on. He was resigned to his death.

Then came the sound of angels. Or at least something unworldly.

At first he thought he was staring up at the sun, or God. But as the image slipped back into focus, he saw the face of the young captain whose name he'd forgotten, smiling down at him jubilantly. As the young soldier helped Tomas up, he exclaimed, "It's a miracle, my lord! God has sent us his favor!"

Tomas blinked and his mouth opened, but nothing came out, his throat too parched.

Guessing his question, the young captain explained. "Reinforcements have come from Cologne. Archbishop Ernst's nephew, Ferdinand, leads the charge. Bedburg is saved, my lord!"

Tomas coughed and laughed at the same time.

Then his blinking slowed, the face before him blurred out, and he fell backward into blissful unconsciousness.

Upon Ferdinand's arrival, Gebhard Truchsess von Waldburg, former archbishop of Cologne, current bishop of Strasbourg, France, was forced to retreat.

Bedburg's new savior shared the same name as his predecessor, his uncle Ferdinand, who had saved Bedburg from destruction back in 1589 during Count Adolf's attack.

And once again, Gebhard was foiled by his nemesis, Archbishop Ernst, this time for the last time.

Upon realizing that his army was sandwiched between the hearty defenders of Bedburg and the fresh army from Cologne, Gebhard abandoned all promises he'd made to his subordinates—of wealth and land—and fled. In fact, he'd been one of the few to make it away safely from the battle. Most everyone else was butchered or captured.

With his conquest for Cologne foiled yet again, Gebhard disappeared from Germany as quickly as possible—in shame. He returned to France, never to engage in another campaign as his name was high on the list of dangerous Protestants to watch out for.

By the time Ferdinand came to the rescue, Tomas had lost five hundred soldiers, half of Bedburg's entire garrison. Of those still alive, many were put up inside the city's church. Others received accommodations wherever there was room: at Claus' inn, the jailhouse, the tavern, and the houses of other obliging citizens.

It would take many months for the city to recover from Gebhard's vicious assault.

But, much to Archbishop Ernst's satisfaction, Bergheim and Bedburg were safe.

Which meant his bishopric was safe as well.

On the night of that final battle, there was no celebratory feast. Too many people had died, too many were still recovering, and no one was sure if the battle for Bedburg was truly over.

There was, however, one ceremony that night.

A large contingent of peasants arrived in the city at dusk, bringing with them a cart carrying the bodies of three men: Anthony the blacksmith, Cristoff the tavern owner, and Dieter Nicolaus the revolutionary.

The procession was led by none other than Sybil Nicolaus, a woman feared as the Daughter of the Beast, lauded as the Pale Diviner, and loved by the masses for her honesty and never-ending battles against tyranny. In the months since Dieter had been helping the Protestant refugees and sympathizers, her name had become legend in its own right.

Cradling her son Peter in her arms, she marched solemnly through the streets of Bedburg where she faced both frightened and awed gazes. No one tried to stop the ceremony, despite the fact that she was known to have supported the very people that Tomas and Bedburg had just fought.

Until they reached the church.

When they did, and the wounded men surrounding the hill stared at the fiery woman with both fear and admiration in their eyes, Bishop Balthasar came out and stood in front of the church.

Unknown to Sybil, an almost identical scene had occurred in that very spot not long before—when two Protestants had been killed by Heinrich and their burials at the church had been denied.

And once again, Balthasar repeated his last rebuke.

"You cannot enter the church with those blasphemers."

Then he pointed a lumpy finger toward Sybil. "And I won't have a witch entering my holy house! There is a public cemetery just outside the gates of Bedburg. Take your procession there, if you wish."

But this time Balthasar did not have the support of Tomas or his garrison, as the commander was off being treated for his wounds. Also, one of the men in the cart was a much-loved figure to all—no doubt more respected than the bishop himself.

"Dieter Nicolaus was a staunch supporter and citizen of Bedburg," Sybil announced, fighting back tears. "My husband only sought to do what he believed to be right for the city. He fought against tyranny and oppression. He has done more for God than you could ever hope to achieve, bishop."

Balthasar brought his hand to his mouth. "You'd dare disrespect me in front of a house of God? I shan't condone this heresy, especially coming from the lips of a known witch and blasphemer!"

"You forget, bishop, that Dieter was once a man of the cloth belonging to this very congregation. He has a right to be given prayers."

"Before his sacrilegious and impious actions caused him to be excommunicated!"

A few peasants in the group grumbled, but none louder than Georg and Rowaine. Having heard enough, the big man and his daughter stepped forward.

"Heinrich Franz is dead, bishop," Georg said, putting his hands on his hips. "And Tomas is injured."

"You have no one to defend you," Rowaine added. "So step aside."

Then Sybil spoke. "Unless you plan to condemn all of our

souls for eternity," she said, gesturing to all the peasants behind her.

Balthasar's lips twitched. Seemingly on the verge of an outburst, Sybil offered a compromise. "I don't plan to bury him here, beside your revered saints and tomes," she said. "But he deserves to be consecrated, so his journey beyond this place can be blessed . . . so that he may arrive safely to his new home in Norfolk—where he will be buried."

With a show of great reluctance, Bishop Balthasar moved aside, allowing Sybil and her company to enter the church.

Inside, the ceremony was bittersweet. The people who had faced persecution from their lords every day, the people who had lived in the darkness of evil for so long, all prayed and wept and gave thanks for Dieter Nicolaus, their savior and champion. The man thereafter known to all as the Martyr of Bedburg.

EPILOGUE

1595 (Two Years Later)

Awaiting his guests, Prince-Provost Ferdinand of Bavaria sat behind his lavish oak desk, moving papers and signing letters in one of his many decorated conference rooms at Cologne Cathedral.

He'd recently taken over most of his uncle's ecclesiastical and secular affairs, acquiring everything Archbishop Ernst had worked for with the exception of his title. All in all, Ernst's twelve-year reign as one of the Holy Roman Empire's most powerful men had been exceedingly trying. Following the near-loss of the three territories of Bedburg, Bergheim, and Erftstadt, as well as nearly losing Cologne in the surprise attack by the hated reformer Gebhard von Truchsess, the archbishop's blunders had forced him into early retirement.

And now Ferdinand, his eighteen-year-old nephew, was in charge—a situation not particularly endorsed by many of the region's other powerful players. For not only was Ferdinand young and inexperienced, he was also callous and hellbent. While most of the other six electorates of the Empire were striving for peace treaties—and actually offering mercy and forgiveness to many of their opponents—Ferdinand remained on a warpath against all Protestant rebels. He'd already expanded the witch-hunts and overseen many new executions.

And soon, whenever his uncle died, his power and influence would become even greater, covering huge sections of the country—Bonn, Berchtesgaden, Cologne, Hildesheim, Münster, and Liège.

But what was done was done. Ferdinand was Ernst's replacement and there was little to be done about it. He had appropriate family ties and it was now too late for an election. Ernst had seen to that, using his considerable influence to ensure that the power remained in the family. Some suggested that, since the Protestants were so strongly opposed to just this sort of blatant nepotism, Ernst had intentionally acted as he had to thumb his nose at them.

On this day, Bishop Ferdinand had formally invited two couples to his chambers to discuss their obedience to the Church and to make sure he could still trust them.

His usher escorted in the first two, formally announcing them.

"The lord and lady of Bedburg, Your Excellency," the guard proclaimed.

The young man, about Ferdinand's age, entered the room, limping slightly, accompanied by a timid woman with large spectacles. Ferdinand stood and, shuffling out from behind his desk, held his hand out, palm down. The couple bowed, then kissed the young bishop's ring.

A few seconds later, the guard ushered in the second couple.

"Your Excellency, the baron and baroness of Bergheim," he announced, then took a position near Ferdinand's desk.

A fair-haired, thin woman stood beside an elderly man who may have been her grandfather, her arm wrapped around the man's waist. They too approached the bishop and kissed his ring, though the older gentleman had trouble bowing.

Ferdinand motioned for both couples to join him at the table on the other side of the room. "Please," he said, leading the way. He sat at the head and, when everyone was seated, joined his hands together. "Now, please remind me of your names, my lords and ladies. So that my scribe here might not forget who you are."

He well knew their names, having specifically ordered their presence. But in his immature mind, this formality elevated his status as a man too important to remember such trivia.

"I am Hugo Griswold, lord of Bedburg," the younger man said, "and this is my wife, Lady Hedda Griswold." He smiled and turned to the other couple across the table from him. "Though I did not expect to see such . . . *familiar* faces, Your Excellency."

The older man returned the smile, then cleared his scratchy

throat. "And I am Baron Rolf Anders, and this is my wife, Lady Lucille Engel von Erftstadt und Bergheim."

"Superb," Ferdinand said, parting his hands. Wasting no time, he leaned over and read from a parchment in front of him. "It is my understanding that, two years prior, all of you took part in the events surrounding the traitor Gebhard von Truchsess in and around Bedburg and Bergheim. Is that correct?"

The four nodded hesitantly.

"And you each acted on the side of the True faith," he said, smiling. "With the exception of . . ." He looked up and pointed to Lady Lucille. ". . . you."

The blonde heiress inhaled deeply but her elderly husband spoke quickly on her behalf. "Originally, Lucille sought to marry into a Catholic union. With the former lord of Bedburg, Heinrich Franz. In order to expand and solidify the Catholic's reach, Your Excellency," Rolf said, clearly trying to minimize the young bishop's implication.

"But," Ferdinand continued, "when that marriage was"—he tilted his head, searching for the right word—"nullified . . . did you not flee Bedburg and take refuge with the enemy? Gebhard von Truchsess?"

Rolf started to answer, but Ferdinand held up a finger. "I'd like to hear it from the lady, if you will."

Lucille stammered, then took in another breath and composed herself.

"I was taken prisoner before my marriage to Heinrich Franz," she explained. "Locked in his dungeon after he killed my father and my warden. It was only from . . . fortunate circumstances"—she glanced at Hugo—"that I was able to escape. And although I did flee to Bergheim, my home, I had no way of knowing Gebhard's army was entrenched there."

Ferdinand frowned. "As lady of Bergheim . . . I find that hard to believe. How could you not know that Gebhard had taken your city?"

"It's God's truth," Lucille replied. "I was imprisoned—how was I to know? Though once I reached Bergheim and advised Gebhard of my predicament, I will not lie, he offered me sanctuary."

"So you assumed Gebhard would win the city? You wagered against Catholicism? Against God?"

Lucille shook her head. "I was in no position to deny him, Your Excellency. Though I was pleased to learn of his defeat," she lied.

For several seconds, Ferdinand studied her. Then, changing the subject, he asked, "And how long after your 'escape' did you give birth?"

Lucille's face flushed red. She looked down at the tabletop and opened her mouth, but no words came. When Ferdinand's gaze stayed on her, she managed to finally say, "I gave birth to my son eight and a half months after my escape."

Ferdinand scribbled something on the paper. Without looking up, he said, "And your son is Heinrich Franz's charge, of course?"

When Lucille hesitated, Ferdinand looked back up at her. But once again, Rolf intervened.

"The lady and I had a brief dalliance prior to our wedding arrangement, my liege," he explained, his tone contrite. "I am not proud of it and have repented my sin. But we were married and the child was birthed within wedlock. Our boy, Odelus Griswold Anders, was baptized a Catholic Christian! And Lucille has always maintained good Catholic standing." The old man smiled proudly, flashing small, yellow teeth.

When Ferdinand's eyes returned to his paper, Rolf's smile vanished as he glanced over at Hugo.

Ferdinand frowned. "I would have thought it impossible, given your advanced age, to birth such a child. And he is without defects?" he asked.

Rolf nodded. "He is one of God's miracles, in fine health, Your Excellency."

"And you, Lord Hugo."

Taken by surprise, Hugo's gaze quickly turned from Rolf to Ferdinand.

Ferdinand continued. "You were once Heinrich Franz's deputy and emissary. How did you meet your lady?"

Smiling at Hedda, he answered, "Hedda was Lord Ludwig von Bergheim's scribe, Your Excellency. I met her during a visit to Bergheim on behalf of Heinrich. We now have two beautiful children: a boy and girl."

Ferdinand couldn't have cared less about Hugo's offspring. He considered Hugo's last answer. "Let me see . . . *this* woman"—pointing to Hedda—"was under the employment of *this* woman's warden?" he asked, pointing to Lucille.

Hugo nodded.

"My," said the bishop, his smile not pleasant. "How very closely linked it seems your two houses are."

Rolf had had enough, though he continued to use a respectful tone. "To tell the truth, Your Excellency, Heinrich Franz was playing us all for fools. I can assure you, no one here is aggrieved by his death. We are all aware that he nearly brought both our cities to ruin. And more."

"Indeed, old man," Ferdinand sneered, his voice rising. "He nearly brought *much* more than just ruin to your cities. He nearly cost my uncle his electoral seat. Do you know what would have happened had Gebhard taken Cologne? If a *Calvinist* were to have taken that seat again?" He pushed his chair away from the table.

Rolf knew better than to speak. Ferdinand was much too young and volatile.

The young bishop raged on. "We may have had a Protestant majority in the electorate! The papacy would have been doomed! That foolish bastard nearly single-handedly destroyed the very foundation of Catholicism in Germany." He stopped to catch his breath, slowing himself down. "You four do understand that, don't you?"

They all dutifully nodded.

"We are all glad Heinrich Franz is dead, Your Excellency," Hugo said.

Ferdinand's smile was hardly a friendly one. "As the newly-appointed lord of Bedburg and successor to his role . . . I'm sure you are," he told Hugo. He folded his hands in front of him again. "I can trust your houses will continue to stay true to Catholic principles then?"

More dutiful nods.

Ferdinand arched his brow in a feeble attempt at maturity.

"After taking over for my uncle, I need to make sure I can trust my neighboring territories."

The four kept nodding.

"Good," Ferdinand said, standing up. "Then I will have you join together to make reparations for Heinrich's ill-conceived actions. You will further your pursuit of Protestant rebels and expand your investigations of witches in the area." He eyed each of them one-by-one. "Leave no stone unturned, find my enemies, and destroy them. Can I trust you to do that?"

The four of them glanced at one another before again nodding, though less vigorously than before.

And with that, they were dismissed.

As the two couples walked back down the massive hallway, Hugo turned to Rolf and smiled. "Rolf, you old dog," he said quietly, "how *did* you find this beautiful woman? I thought you for dead!"

The old man was suddenly in high spirits. Shuffling along the marble floor, he explained. "When your sister came to Bedburg looking for Dieter, she helped me escape the jailhouse. I fled Bedburg, knowing I couldn't return to House Charmagne—that Heinrich would have my skin. I've since heard that Charmagne is haunted now, replete with apparitions of ghostly hounds. And that the spirit of Heinrich Franz drifts through the halls."

He chuckled for a moment. "So I went to our southern neighbors, managed to escape the battle, and found this lovely woman once Gebhard fled."

Addressing Hugo, Lucille tenderly put her hand on Rolf's shoulder. "Your uncle is a good man. As heiress-apparent of Bergheim following my father and Heinrich's deaths, I refused to settle with any of the suitors that approached me. Rolf is a softer, kinder man."

Hugo reddened slightly. He didn't correct Lucille's statement about Rolf being his uncle, which he most assuredly was *not*. What lies the old man had been telling her! Nevertheless, Hugo was happy Rolf had found joy—the old man had been like a father to him when he'd needed it most.

Rolf raised a finger. "I'm also a fair politician and spokesman, as well, if I do say. Especially given my rather . . .

sorted background."

Hugo grinned. "That much is true, I suppose."

They all chuckled as they reached the end of the hall. Two guards opened the doors and they were ferried into another room, this one leading to the cathedral's front doors.

"Now it's your turn to tell us," Rolf said, turning to Hugo and Hedda. "How you two came to find each other? Is yours an example of this mythical thing called love?"

Hugo laughed, then nodded, smiling warmly at Hedda, whose eyes twinkled.

"Hugo helped me escape Bedburg's jail as well," Hedda said. "Since the entire city knew he'd killed Heinrich, his reputation preceded him and Lord Alvin didn't stand a chance competing with him for the lordship," she said proudly.

Rolf arched his brow at Hugo. "Though I'm happy for you, I am somewhat surprised you could take such a position given your youth." Then he thought more about that and chuckled. "Though I dare say we just witnessed how youth and inexperience can mean nothing when it comes to positions of power."

They all smiled at that.

Hedda then continued. "Anyway, that's where I came in," she said with a sly smile. "Helping this 'young and inexperienced' man navigate his way into his new lordship." She kissed Hugo on the cheek. "I have long understood the ways of politics, given my day-to-day assistance working with Ludwig. So I'd say this young man was most fortunate to have my talents at his disposal." Hugo grinned, grabbing her around waist.

"Ah! Besides being a mother of two, she's also quite humble," Rolf joked.

"With a third on the way," Hedda added, rubbing her stomach.

"Congratulations," Rolf said. "You two *have* been busy!"

Then Hugo faced Rolf, his expression turning serious. "I would like to visit your son some day, Rolf, if that might be possible. Our children could become friends."

Lucille and Rolf both knew there was more to the suggestion than mere friendship. The birth of Lucille's son—exactly eight and one-half months following her escape from Bedburg—certainly raised questions of paternity. Especially when Rolf's advancing age and infirmities made the probability of bedroom follies less likely.

Rolf smiled knowingly. "You need only say the word, young master," he said with full sincerity. "Bergheim's doors are always open to you and your lovely wife."

When they pushed out the cathedral's double-doors, the warm sunshine greeted them with a rush of hope and happiness. As they stood at the top of the church steps, side-by-side, looking out over the vast German countryside, Hedda chuckled to herself.

"What?" Hugo asked.

"I was just thinking of the unexpected surprises life brings," she answered. "Consider this . . . if it weren't for the vilest of the vile, the four of us would never have ended up together with our loved ones here."

"How so?" Lucille asked.

"Well . . . Rolf and I were both rescued from Heinrich's jail, and you and Hugo from Heinrich's House Charmagne."

They all took in the view, pondering the irony of it all.

"So," Rolf finally said, "I suppose in a twisted sort of way, we all owe the Devil his due and a bit of a thank you."

As they headed down the stairs to their new lives, Hugo put his arm around Hedda.

"Though I'll still never toast the bastard," he mumbled.

In a little town in Norfolk called Strangers Shire, Sybil sat in her chair on Claire's patio, fidgeting with her fingers. Though she had her own house now, she preferred spending time here, near her best friend. In the front yard, little Rose and Peter played in the grass as young children do, without a care in the world. They chased bugs, and laughed, and fell over each other and giggled. It gave Sybil such joy to watch them play like that. Her promise long ago to Claire, that her son and Claire's daughter would be best friends, had become a reality.

Seated across from her, Claire also watched the children. Looking over at Sybil and her twitchy hands, she said, "You must calm down, Beele. Your nervousness makes me nervous."

Sybil sighed. "I know, I know. But what do you think she'll be like? Kind, as I've heard? Or mean, because I'm not English?"

Claire snickered, setting her thread and distaff in her lap. "We are called *Strangers* for a reason, dear girl! And besides, weren't you the one who once said, 'I've known enough nobles to know what they're all like' or something to that effect?"

Sybil took a deep breath, which didn't help much, then gazed out at the town she now called home. It certainly looked different from when she'd first seen it. It now had two proper granaries, a smithy, a tavern, a tannery, several tailor shops and textile factories, and of course the church.

Truly a flourishing village.

People milled about, darting from building to building, to and from workshops, sweeping roadways, laying down drapes, doing all the busy things that growing towns do.

Down the roadway, Sybil saw Rowaine and Aellin walking toward them, holding hands. A few minutes later, when the two reached the porch, greetings and kisses were exchanged, then Aellin curtsied and went inside. Rowaine held out a jar of something which she presented to Sybil.

"From my father . . . he says it's the best batch the tavern brews, made just for special occasions like this."

Sybil took the jar and smiled, setting it down by her chair. "Thank Georg for me."

Rowaine rolled her eyes. "I doubt I'll be seeing much of him now that he's got that damn harlot to rummage around the sheets with."

"Row!" Sybil scolded. "You should be happy that your father is happy. After all, *you've* found delight of your own," she added, referring to Aellin inside.

Rowaine nodded. "I know, I know." She turned and, like Sybil and Claire, stared out to where the children played and to the bustling town beyond. After a time, she said, "My, how Daxton would love to see this, how much this place has changed."

Sybil smiled warmly. Not a sad smile—Daxton wasn't dead, just in a different place. Upon his return to Norfolk, he'd relocated with his family to King's Lynn, taking over Georg's job as the Hanseatic League's representative so he could remain close to the sea. He still captained the *Lion's Pride,* though now, instead of a pirate ship, it was officially a trading vessel. And he still sent a portion of his proceeds—a generous amount—back to the shire each month, which had definitely contributed to the town's growth and prosperity.

Sybil said, "Yes, it is quite a sight to see. Dax would indeed enjoy knowing how much he's helped make it what it is."

The three women drifted off into their own thoughts for a while, until Martin and Ava came running around the side of the house, clearly excited. Ava held her new one-year-old child in her arms. The boy already had Martin's curly hair.

"They're here, they're here!" Ava announced with contagious enthusiasm. "The first procession just arrived on the other side of town!"

Sybil clasped her hands and said a silent prayer. Then she asked, "S-Should we go to them?"

"No, no," Martin said, waving his hands. "They're making their way here. Believe it or not, Reeve Bailey is directing their parade to *you*, rather than to his own house. I think even *he* is a bit overwhelmed this time!"

They all laughed, nervously.

Ava saw Peter and Rose playing and, with love in her eyes, shook her head. "I can't wait until little Ezra is old enough to play with Rose and my godson!"

Sybil took Ava by the hand and smiled. Following Dieter's death, she'd asked Ava and Martin to become Peter's godparents. It had filled a hole in their hearts, until of course the birth of their own child, which had raised everyone's spirits.

Sybil finally rose from her chair and began pacing the patio.

"Christ Almighty," Claire told her. "Could you please stop that?" She gestured down the hill to where a man with blue tattoos was sitting next to another young man on a bench, their foreheads almost touching. "We already have one madman in this town. We certainly don't need a mad*woman*." The "madman" she was referring to was of course Salvatore, the *benandanti*, who apparently was performing his "gift" on the bench down the road. As the town's new resident soothsayer, he regularly had twenty or more citizens seeking him out each day to be "healed" or to have their dreams realized.

As for the other members of Sybil's close-knit group, Wilhelm and his mother had settled in the heart of town, where Wilhelm made and sold his dyes to several local textile factories and tailors. He and Mary shared one of the largest estates in the shire, and *both* were constantly harried by suitors seeking a stake in their wealth—though neither had the time nor want for such frivolities, at least now. Mary still grieved for her husband William and Wilhelm was simply too busy for affairs of the heart or flesh.

And Corvin Carradine had gone missing at sea a few months back during a routine supply run to Amsterdam and no one knew if he was dead or alive.

Suddenly, the first line of emblazoned chariots and carriages appeared in the distance. Two lines of impeccably attired soldiers lined both sides of their route. A few minutes later the procession stopped at the foot of the hill. Nearly every citizen had come out to witness the spectacle. Guards now surrounded the main carriage, spears and arquebuses at the ready.

Sybil froze as her heart pounded so hard she could hear her pulse in her ears. Unable to contain herself any longer, she rushed down the porch, out past the front yard to greet her guest.

A royal squire in white gloves hurried out from another of the carriages to open the coach door for the guest of honor, delicately helping her out of the carriage.

Her hair was reddish-gold, the color of the sun at autumn sunset. Her skin was white and immaculate, her lips and nose thin. She was indeed a handsome woman with a regal aura befitting her station. She walked gracefully, confidently, from the carriage steps, escorted by the squire, as the townsfolk caught sight of her and gasped, then kneeled.

Sybil bowed her head in respect, then noticed that everyone

was kneeling but her son Peter. Rushing over, she grabbed his arm and gently pushed him to the grass, then kneeled beside him.

When the guest and her guard were several yards from Sybil, the squire spoke the formal introduction, though of course none was needed.

"May I present to you the monarch of the House of Tudor, and savior to the people. First of her name, Her Majesty The Queen, Elizabeth!"

The Queen of England smiled warmly at Sybil, then wobbled a thin, long finger toward her, urging her to stand. She spoke in a surprisingly jovial tone.

"It's my understanding that this place is named after me," she announced with a slight smirk.

A few patters of nervous laughter sounded from the crowd, as they rose from their knees to better watch the proceedings.

Suddenly realizing the Queen was directing her comment to her, Sybil nodded—a bit too vigorously, since her words weren't coming at the moment. Finally, she found her voice. "Indeed, Your Majesty. This is the home of Elizabeth's Strangers, named such for the remarkable kindness Your Majesty has bestowed upon political and religious refugees of all creeds."

A small smile crept across the Queen's lips. "And with whom do I converse?"

Sybil stuttered. With her mouth open, she pointed dumbly at her own face. Elizabeth chuckled brightly, causing everyone else to do likewise.

"My n-name's Sybil, ma'am. Sybil Griswold."

Elizabeth clapped her gloved hands. "Ah, just the person I was hoping for."

Sybil could only blush.

The Queen whispered to her squire, though loud enough to be heard. "I thought she was a German girl?"

The squire nodded back, speaking something indiscernible.

Elizabeth furrowed her brow at Sybil, who nodded and said, "I am, ma'am, a German refugee. But I sought sanctuary here, with my family"—she nudged her chin toward her son—"and was given shelter thanks to your tolerance and kindness."

"And you speak English! I do say, I had not expected that."

Sybil smiled. "I'm still learning, Your Majesty."

Elizabeth took a step toward Sybil so they were eye to eye. Then, much to her amazement, the Queen took Sybil's arm.

"I've come to give my gratitude to the woman who fought so hard against our enemies in Germany, my dear. And, besides, it's been some time since I've seen the countryside of Norfolk and I was due a visit."

She started to lead Sybil by the arm away from the house. Immediately, a contingent of guards took positions around them, but the Queen waved them off.

As they walked on, Elizabeth said, "I also wish to give my heartfelt sympathy to you at having lost your husband in the battle. It is such a terrible thing, war."

Sybil nodded, literally touching shoulders with the most powerful woman on earth.

"He would have loved to hear you say that, ma'am," Sybil replied softly.

"And now, you must tell me how you came to be known as the Pale Diviner. Oh, what a magnificent title that is! And, please, leave no secrets untold. I want to learn all about you, Sybil Griswold, and how anguished Pope Clement was at the loss of his leading archbishop, and how Ernst must have squealed! And please leave no detail unsaid, my dear girl . . ."

Sybil chuckled lightly. "I'll try, ma'am."

As they strolled along arm-in-arm, enjoying a fine day in the English countryside—two very different symbols of hope and goodness, doing their best in difficult times—only faint parts of their conversation could be heard.

"It all started one day by the church when I was picking apples for the homeless, and Dieter walked into my life . . ."

THE END

Fact Versus Fiction

I took a bit more creative liberties with this novel than with the two previous installments of the trilogy. That said, the story was still inspired by many actual historical events occurring in late 16th century Europe.

The Hanseatic League was a real and powerful organization in Europe, formed to help protect traders and merchants from tyrannical laws and despots, although its influence had greatly diminished by the time this story begins in 1592.

Of course Queen Elizabeth was real, as were the *Strangers*, although I'm not sure if the monarch ever visited the actual refugee community—Elizabeth's Strangers—that was indeed her namesake (though there was never an actual village called *Strangers Shire*).

Amsterdam did become one of Europe's commercial superpowers after the Duke of Parma (Alexander Farnese) sacked Antwerp on behalf of Spain. And when the Protestants fled north after Antwerp's fall, they forced the Catholics to flee en masse to Cologne and other parts of Germany.

By 1595, Ferdinand of Bavaria—Archbishop Ernst's nephew—had taken over all secular duties for his uncle, becoming the de facto Archbishop of Cologne. He also orchestrated one of the largest increases in witch-hunts during his reign.

His uncle, Ernst, retired to Arnsberg, Germany, where he lived until his death in 1612.

England and Germany were definitely not on friendly terms when my story takes place, mostly because of religious differences. As a result, most trading between them occurred on the sly through neutral regions like Amsterdam.

From 1597 through 1794, Bonn, Germany was the capital of the Electorate of Cologne and the residence of the Archbishops and Prince-electors of Cologne. My story displayed only a small glimpse of what Bonn would become.

The novel describes the political unrest prevalent in and around Cologne during this time period, resulting in repeated land-grabs, power struggles, and economic uncertainty.

Historians point to many reasons behind these turbulent times, including unfair taxation, public spending, regulation of business, excessive market supervision, and limits on corporate autonomy, to name a few. Of course, right up there at or near the top is (as always) religion.

Lastly, the *benandanti* were in fact true "spirit wanderers," regularly persecuted as witches and warlocks, although Salvatore himself was my invention.

Once again thank you all for reading my stories and for your tremendous support! I hope you enjoyed the trilogy. And, who knows, I've grown pretty attached to some of these characters, so it's quite possible that someday they'll return. ;)

About the Author

Cory Barclay lives in San Diego, California. He enjoys learning about serial killers, people burning, mass executions, and hopes the FBI doesn't one day look through his Google search history.

When he's not writing stories he's probably playing guitar, composing music, hanging with friends, or researching strange things to write about.

Subscribe to CoryBarclay.com for news on upcoming releases!

87836512R00221

Made in the USA
Lexington, KY
01 May 2018